Cover Painting
Sydney Heads from Watsons Bay/Vaucluse
(where the story ends)
By Joseph Lycett (clipped)
https://www.sl.nsw.gov.au/collection-items/view-heads-entrance-
port-jackson-new-south-wales

Inside the front page.
Jonty Drawing
By Alissia Polonzi
https://www.deviantart.com/alessiapelonzi/art/Gentleman-317012398
alessia.pelonzi@gmail.com
Thanks for giving permission to use this, Alissia!

KEY

~ Time passing in the same locality

Different locality or country

Australian Historical Novels

Unlikely Convict Ladies Trilogy
Dancing to her Own Tune
(co-authored by Sheila Hunter & Sara Powter)
Amelia's Tears
A Lady in Irons

Stand Alone Novels
No More, My Love
The Vine Weaver
Waiting at the Sliprails
Scotch at The Rocks
In Defence of Her Honour
Gentle Annie Soames
Convict Shadows of the Past

Lockleys of Parramatta
Hands Upon the Anvil
Out Where the Brolgas Dance
Diamonds in the Dirt
The Earl's Shadow
Once a Jolly Swagman
Jonty's Journey

Shelia Hunter's Trilogy
Mattie
Ricky
The Heather to the Hawkesbury

Jonty's Journey

Sara Powter

ISBN: 978-0-6451107-7-7
Paperback

Pacific Wanderland Publications
ABN 99 768 734 831
Kincumber NSW 2251

saragpowter@gmail.com
www.sarapowter.com.au

1st edition 2023 printed by Kindle, an Amazon Company;
available on Kindle Unlimited & KDP

<u>*Dedication & Thanks*</u>

To the many hero warriors
who have to cope with living after the horrors of trauma.

To the artists, poets and those who seek peace in their natural surroundings,
and to the many who help the hurting.

May your stories never be forgotten,
Life was tough but for you and others like you,
Our lives would be vastly different.

Horace Arthur Colless
SRN #1301 Boer War,
NSW Imperial Bushman, Boer Was 1899-1902,
Source: Murray, page number - 104
b 1882 in Penrith (Castlereagh)
d 1965 Lane Cove
*(Horace was my father's great uncle and gave him the silver
Natural Trumpet from the Imperial Bushmen,
which is now in the Australian War Memorial)*

Thank you!
To Stephen, my wonderful husband, who is always so supportive.
Thank you will all of my heart.

And to **Roby Aiken**
who patiently corrects all my punctuation errors,
and **Noreen Robertson** and **Linda Upcroft**,
my Beta readers
Thank you too.

NB

The story of **Will English**, *a character from* "**RICKY**"
by Sheila Hunter is revealed in this book.

For **Brodie Stewart**'s *story, watch for*
"**SCOTCH AT THE ROCKS**" *due for release Nov 2023*.

Table of Contents

The grammar and language in this book are
Australian English spelling.

Character list at the back of the book

Chapter 1 Gorgeous Gems

"*G*ood morning, Jonty! Are you ready for another day? I have an order for a large blue sapphire. Do you have any cut already or any that would be suitable?" The jeweller, Richard Lamb, looked over at the young man already at work on the faceting table. Compared to the work the lad produced, the jeweller felt like the novice when cutting and faceting the beautiful gems. Jonty seemed to have the knack and rarely made a mistake. His gems sparkled and were sought after by many other jewellers in Sydney and surrounding areas. Jonty loved working with Mr Lamb, and every day was different.

Jonty greeted his boss with a smile. "Morning, Mr Lamb, I do actually; I finished a beauty last week. About five carats and a lovely pure blue."

"Oh, five carats might be a little large; I was thinking maybe three or four. It's for a brooch." He showed Jonty the sketch of what was required. Mr Lamb was wondering about the size of the stone for the design. They put their heads together and decided that a three-and-a-half to four-carat royal blue round sapphire would work best; Jonty knew he had the perfect stone in the blue's collection. He flicked open a clipped box and carefully picked out the particular stone with some long-nose tweezers.

Mr Lamb gasped, he'd not seen this particular stone, and it shone. "Oh, Jonty, it's perfect!"

Jonty's eyes glinted with appreciation at the praise just given him. He would do anything to help with this man's work. Jonty had just turned fifteen when he approached Mr Lamb for an apprenticeship. Before that, he had worked Saturday mornings helping him in his shop. He'd fallen in love with gemstones when he was tiny. His parents had returned from an adventure with his cousin, Luke Lockley, and Reverend William Clarke just before he was born. One of the stones his parents had found years before, his father had Mr Lamb cut and mounted into a pendant. That stone was a beautiful blue topaz mounted in a double heart.

His father, and a good friend, Luke Lockley, had been asked to accompany Reverend William Clarke to chart mineral deposits up through the New England area of New South Wales and then up into Queensland. The purpose of that journey had been a government mineral survey. Jonty had called both men "Uncle" all his life. Uncle William had used the time to teach Luke about geology and science as he had arranged for Luke to take over his teaching position at The King's School. Jonty's father, John, worked at the Sydney Museum as an entomologist and assistant to Uncle William.

His parents married after a whirlwind romance. The trip for the survey departed weeks later. He was born ten months after their marriage and only weeks after their return.

On that survey trip, Uncle William found diamonds at Bingara. Once they knew what they were looking for and where to seek them, they unearthed more. The sale of the stones collected on that trip over the following years had set up the three families well.

That had been over twenty years ago. Jonty had been born the day of Uncle Luke's wedding; his mother had gone into labour in the middle of the service. Jonty smiled when he thought of the relationship between the two families; there was a very tenuous connection with his cousin's marriage to a Lockley. Jonty waited until he finished his apprenticeship to ask permission to court Lottie, Uncle Luke and Aunt Ellen's youngest daughter. His father and Uncle Luke were firm friends, and Jonty intended to see that they stay close, and he hoped to ask Uncle Luke this coming Saturday. He had not said anything to either his family or Mr Lamb. He was nervous about the forthcoming visit, and his heart was in his mouth.

The men worked together and created another jewellery design masterpiece; the brooch was a bow set with diamonds around the outside and the sapphire as the centrepiece. The work was completed at the end of the week and was a triumph of their skill. The order was ready for completion by noon on Friday. Mr Lamb knew that Jonty was to go to Parramatta for the weekend, as he often did; however, Jonty had been unable to head out there for some weeks. Mr Lamb told him to have the afternoon off. He also realised who was drawing him out there, and it wasn't his Uncle. Jonty thanked him and said farewell. Before Mr Lamb could say much more, Jonty had gone. He heard the chime of the shop doorbell and saw his apprentice disappear up the street. He stood watching the departing figure with a frown on his brow. He was puzzled over what could be concerning the lad. He shook his head and went back to work.

The customer duly arrived and was delighted with the brooch. He purchased a matching pair of ear-bobs Jonty had made while his mentor worked on the brooch. They had ostensibly been made for stock, but Jonty had suggested that for each order placed, they also make matching items not requested and offer them when the customer collected their orders. Sales had increased fourfold.

Richard Lamb smiled at the departing customer. When he collected his order, the customer had paid for the brooch and a pair of patching earbobs. His shop had made enough profit from that one sale to pay the rent for the next three months, let alone Jonty's salary. Richard was about to close the shop early when he saw the postman coming, and he stood in the doorway waiting for him to pass. Jerome Bentley was a friend, and they often stopped for a chat on his mail route around the shops.

This day Jerome had a letter for Mr Lamb. Richard took it without looking and slipped it into his pocket. They stood chatting for some time before Jerome excused himself and departed. Richard turned to go indoors and shut up shop for the afternoon. By the time he had put everything away, he had forgotten the letter, which still sat in his pocket. An hour later, he locked the door and walked home. The letter was still unread.

Jonty, in the meantime, had hot-footed it home, grabbed his bag and headed to Parramatta by rail. He walked the few blocks from the station to Uncle Luke's house, where he planned to stay for the weekend. It would be the last time, as if things went as planned, he would not be allowed to stay there. He arrived and greeted his Aunt Ellen and Lottie, his eyes meeting hers with a shy smile. Her twin brother, Carlo, was up at the family blacksmith's forge, but it was Lottie he had wanted to see. He had to swallow his enthusiasm until he'd spoken to her father.

"Hello, Jonty, you're here early," Ellen greeted the young man.

Charlotte stood silently, watching him. She smiled, then dropped her eyes demurely.

Jonty smiles at her shyness, "Yes, Aunt Ellen, I got an early mark. We've been working on a special order, and I finished it this morning. Mr Lamb gave me a half-day instead of the extra hours I had worked. I can return later if it's not convenient. If I could leave my bag, I'll go up to the forge and see who's up there." Jonty had met Lottie's shy smile with his own, his heart racing.

Ellen laughed. "No, no, Jonty, you're welcome whenever you arrive. You know that. It's always a delight to see you. We were going to have afternoon tea with Mama Sal if you'd care to join us. She's staying at the cottage this week, so it's the usual trail of family visits past her door." That explained why she was answering her own door. They were dressed to leave.

Jonty's face brightened, "I'll come if I may. I'll pop my bag in my room and join you."

The three walked to Sally Lockley's cottage a few blocks down Phillip Street. It was now nine years since Earl Charles had died, and occasionally she moved back to her cottage. She was there for the week, supposedly to have some time to herself. However, the family was dropping in often, and one or other of the grandchildren or even great-grandchildren took it upon themselves to have a sleepover.

They let him pass, and he deposited his bag in his room and joined them in less than a minute.

Soon Jonty had a lady on each arm, and they walked down the side of Phillip Street, away from the passing vehicles. He wished there was a footpath like on some streets in Sydney. It had rained that morning, and the roadway was still muddy.

"Please, Aunt Ellen, let me walk on the roadside. If a carriage passes, you'll get muddy." Jonty dropped Lottie's hand and moved to the roadside just as a speeding gig passed them. He saw the splash coming and was able to turn his back before it hit them. He took most of the mud onto his coat but spared the ladies the worst of the splash.

"Oh, Jonty, your coat, it's ruined!" Lottie exclaimed.

Jonty, rather than be angry, chuckled. "We swapped just in time, Aunt Ellen," he said, grinning. Mud dribbled down his face as well as his coat.

Lottie got the giggles. "Jonty, you have a spot of mud on your cheek in a heart shape." She pulled a fine lawn handkerchief from her bag and wiped it away. There was not much they could do to clean him up there, and as Grandma Sal's cottage on Phillip Street was closer than their house on Church Street, they kept walking.

Jonty thought back to Parramatta when he was a small child. Many years before and well before his birth, Christina Meadows had lived in this cottage, and it was still called "Christina's Cottage." Before she bought it, the cottage was used for various purposes. When some of the cottages were first built, they had been rented privately and years later used to house expectant convict women rather than spend time in gaol. Christina Meadows had purchased the top one and later married Ned Grace, as he was then known. He had proposed the day he discovered he had inherited the title of Duke of Gracemere from his brother. Ned later found that his best friend, Charles Lockley, was not only his third cousin but Earl of Coxheath. Ned and Christina had spent the first four months of their marriage in the top cottage.

Years later, Duke Ned and Earl Charles died the same week, only half a world from each other. The family on both sides of the globe were devastated. It had taken time to recover, but life doesn't stop when a loved one is lost.

To the Lockleys, the Duke and Duchess were known as Uncle Ned and Aunt Christina, and Jonty had not called them anything at all if he could help it. He was in awe of the tall blonde and later white-haired Duke. Jonty had had the honour to meet him many times, as the Ducal couple had stayed with Uncle Luke's brother Ed when they visited. Jonty's great Uncle Thomas was Uncle Ed's partner in the Parramatta Emporium. Ed's son Neddie had married Jonty's cousin Miriam. So they were now all family. Yet he felt inadequate when he realised that many of them had titles and he didn't. He was a nothing, a mere jeweller.

Yes, he had money, as his parents had set up a trust fund for him and his five siblings. His skill at cutting gems had also increased his bank account somewhat as he had also learned to cut diamonds. This skill now brought in funds to his bank account as he was the only one in the colony with that skill and knowledge. When he was little, his parents were asked to show a geologist where they had found the diamonds. They had made a quick trip to Bingara again and, whilst there, had found some more stones. Rather than sell them, his mother, Colleen, divided them into six equal parcels and gave them to each child. Jonty's parcel had a fabulous collection of top-quality stones, as did his siblings, and he decided that he wished to learn to cut them, so he started on his own stones.

When he turned fifteen, he approached Mr Lamb and started an apprenticeship. Now some eight years later, he was at the top of his field in Sydney. Jonty finished his full apprenticeship last month. He had spent over a year in Europe and England, honing his diamond-cutting skills at Tiffany's in Antwerp. Then later, he stayed in Kent with the Duke of Gracemere, Charles, known as Chip, and his cousins. Since his return, life had been hectic with new orders. Now he was enjoying the first long weekend he'd been able to have off for months.

The three arrived at Christina's Cottage door without further mishap. The Dowager Countess of Coxheath greeted her visitors when she opened the door herself. She gasped in horror at Jonty's state of filth, and then she giggled. She gave each a kiss and ushered them into the kitchen. At seventy-nine, Aunt Sal, as she liked to be called, was still fit as a fiddle.

Jonty peeled off his coat, and Sal took it into the bathroom and sponged off most of the mud. Lottie dealt with his face, and Ellen tackled his hair. The look on Jonty's face made Lottie giggle too.

He bit his lips, trying not to laugh. While Lottie worked on his face, he could gaze at hers, but he said little. He hoped that her face would look on his more frequently. He let out his held breath as she turned to rinse the cloth.

Sal joined them in the kitchen. "Well, that was an unusual welcome. Jonty, I'll hang your jacket in here while we have tea. I have sponged off as much mud as possible, but I think you may need a new coat. Would you mind if I gave you one of Charles' jackets for today? I've not thrown his clothes away. Yes, yes; I know I should, but I just can't. Jonty, you're his size, none of the boys is, so if you're happy, you can have some."

Jonty laughed to himself. Her boys were all now over fifty.

"I'd be honoured, Lady Sal." Jonty was stunned. He could never get his tongue around calling her "Aunt."

Sal smiled joyfully. "Good then, Ellen, you put the kettle on and make tea while we go and look at the wardrobe. Lottie, you can come too." Sal led the way into the bedroom. "Jonty, please, do you think you can manage to call me Aunt Sal? I hate the title."

"Are you sure, ma'am?" Jonty asked nervously.

"Yes, lad, I am; it should have happened years ago." Sal swung open the wardrobe door. "Now, let's find you something to wear." She slid her hand down the sleeve of a jacket that had been her husband's favourite. The clothes still smelled of him, and she was reluctant to part with any. However, she knew Charles no longer needed them, and Jonty did. She drew a deep breath and released it as a sigh. "I think this one for today." She drew out a lovely afternoon coat and stroked it lovingly. "I will never part with his old jackets, but Charles never liked dressing up. Try this on, Jonty." She held up the jacket for Jonty and told him to slip it on.

Lottie smoothed it over his shoulders and then wiped away a tear. "I remember this one, Grandma." Another tear escaped.

Jonty thumbed it from her cheek. "We all miss him, Lotts; how could we not?" he said quietly.

She met his eyes and nodded. "It still smells of him, Grandma."

"I give hugs, too," Jonty said with a grin. He opened his arms to her. Lottie walked to him and deeply inhaled her grandfather's scent. Before he knew it, she was sobbing into his shoulder.

Over her head, his eyes met Sal's. They, too, were glassy. "I have to let him go, Jonty, but it's heartbreaking." She took a deep breath and said, "Come, Lottie, we are going to sort out some more for Jonty. I'll keep a few, but the rest can go somewhere useful, especially the good clothes. At least you'll get some use out of them. Go fetch your mother, dear, and tell her to bring the tea tray in here."

They drank their strong tea, then sorted through Charles's clothing for the next hour. Sal insisted on Jonty having the tails jacket and trousers. She explained why it had taken nine years to let them go; once the boys started working at the forge, their arms became so big that Charles' clothing didn't fit them. "I didn't just want to throw them out."

Jonty had never been the total centre of three ladies before, and as he was naturally shy, it took a firm decision for him to try to blow away the sadness of their activity. On each change of clothing, he'd appear doing a different silly walk. The first was the top hat and tails; he strutted out hands behind his back, and the top hat tilted at such an angle that it looked like it would topple off. The three ladies giggled, and he knew that if he could do this each time, it would be fun, not sad.

The afternoon passed with much laughter. By the time Jonty had tried on each outfit, even Sal was happy to see them go to a good home. When he tried the black and gold court attire, he bowed over Sal's hand and kissed it.

"Oh begone, young man! Charles never did that," Sal said with a laugh.

"I bet he did, Aunt Sal," he said a little nervously. It was the first time he'd called her that, "Just not in public."

She nodded. She went and found a bag for him. He now had six suits of clothing, and they had a wonderfully fun afternoon. Sal had given him shirts, cravats and a collapsible opera top hat too. Her boys had taken most of the cufflinks, and she had given Charlie his watch and Eddie his coin fob. Wills and Luke each received items of value. Wills wanted his walking cane, and Luke took his gold desk stationary set that Ned had given him. Sal had only kept four of Charles's favourite jackets, one was almost threadbare, but she would not part with it. She said she wanted to be buried with it. The wardrobe of clothes he had kept at Ed's house had long gone. The closet in the cottage was the last to sort through. Making the afternoon fun helped Sal decide to let them go.

By the time Jonty walked the ladies home, he was carrying armloads of clothing with a bag slung over his shoulder with the suits in it and an armload of extra items. Their arrival at his Uncle's house, Glenmere, in Church Street, coincided with Luke's return from school.

Luke relieved him of some of the clothing. He recognised his father's things and asked, "How on earth did you get her to part with them, Jonty? We've been trying to for years, but she was clinging tightly to them." Luke assisted him in carrying the clothing to his room.

"I was covered in mud, Uncle Luke, and needed to change." Jonty was now really worried. "Next thing I knew, she decided I needed to take the clothes as they fit me. Do you mind?"

"Mind? Why? No way! We're thrilled. Dar will never need them again, and none of us fit them. Put them down and come into my office. I gather you wished to see me over something?" Luke helped lift the bag from his back and then led him back downstairs. Their footsteps were muffled on the new carpet on the staircase. This house contained the latest in everything. It was the first house in the area to have a flushing privy and running water in the bathing room. The house had hot water directly into the bath with an overhead shower.

Jonty was nervous again, his mind had been occupied all afternoon, but now the purpose of his visit had arrived.

"Make yourself comfortable, Jonty. Tea?" Luke walked to the tea tray and poured two big mugs of sweet black tea. "Now, how can I help, lad?" Luke hoped he knew why Jonty had come, but only time would tell.

Jonty took a deep breath and forged forward. "It's Lottie, Uncle Luke; I'd like permission to court her, if I may. I've not said anything to her because I've still been under apprenticeship. I finished last month and have been taking on freelance work. I have been asked to take on more gem cutting for some miners that father met and other jewellers, so my income is good."

Luke smiled. He hoped that this was why Jonty wished to see him.

"I'm delighted, Jonty. I willingly give permission; however, you will no longer be able to stay with us when you come for visits, you know that."

Jonty's heart was beating a tattoo with joy. He felt like punching the air but held his emotions in check. "Really? Oh, and yes, I do realise; thank you so much, Uncle Luke."

Luke smiled, "Yes, I give permission, but she also needs to be asked, Jonty. She's not said anything to me, so I have no idea if she is interested in that way, so I expect that you will be sensitive to her wishes." Luke looked at the young man before him. "Jonty, if she says no, you must accept that as final."

"Uncle Luke, I care too much to push her into something she doesn't want." His joyous heart almost stopped. He'd not thought of rejection. How would he feel if she said no?

Luke saw his anxiety. "Go see her, lad; I think she's in the kitchen. It's a nice evening; go and ask her for a turn around the back garden." Luke watched him leave. His buoyancy was now somewhat deflated. He hoped Lottie would say yes. Luke stayed in his office and shot up a prayer for Jonty. He had no idea what Lottie's decision would be. He knew how tender a young man's heart could be and how sensitive he was to rejection. At the same age, Jonty was now, Luke had heard that Ellen had married someone else. He stayed away from home for four years, fearful of returning if he saw her with her husband. When he eventually came home, he discovered he'd been misinformed; she was still unmarried and waiting for him. It had been her brother who had married. They became engaged that very hour. So he knew the hurts of an uncertain relationship. He heard the back kitchen door close and then heard Ellen enter. He reached out for her, and she snuggled under his loving arm. "Do you think she'll say yes?" he asked Ellen, a little concerned.

"Are you kidding, Lukie? She's head over heels in love with the boy! Of course, she will." Ellen turned to him and lifted her face to look at her wonderful husband. "Lukie, she's been mooning around for a year waiting for him. I hoped he would finally ask her when I heard he was coming this weekend."

Luke looked down at the adorable woman in his arms, gently dropping his head to kiss her waiting lips. He wished it was a little later in the evening so they could retire upstairs, but that would wait.

Chapter 2 Future Promises

*J*onty asked if Lottie wanted to stroll in the garden before the evening meal. His Aunt Moira and Uncle Connor Murphy lived with Uncle Luke and Aunt Ellen and worked as the housekeeper and groundsman for them. It was a strange situation, but Connor was his mother's brother, an actual uncle, whereas Luke and Ellen were not related, yet he was as close to them as his blood relations.

Moira shooed him outside and said she would call them when it was time to eat.

Jonty grinned and mouthed, "Thank you" to his aunt.

Lottie was already out of earshot and walking down the back stairs of the verandah to the moonlit orchard. She felt like skipping but made an effort to walk calmly. She should have waited but didn't.

Jonty followed her down the steps and caught up to her without looking too keen. The uncertainty of his emotions made him feel almost ill. He caught up to her and offered her his arm.

She accepted it and wrapped both small hands around his arm. That surprised him a little; his heart lifted slightly.

They wandered through the backyard without talking for a few minutes. When they reached the back fence, Jonty stopped and turned to her.

Both were nervous about what to say, yet knowing silence would not answer their questions, he said, "Lottie, I wish to ask you something and can think of no way other than directly, so I shall dive in boots and all." He took a deep breath and continued. "Lotts, I have just received your father's permission to court you if it is your wish. I dare not to presume on our friendship, but do so wish...."

Gentle fingers stopped his words on his lips. "Jonty, dear friend, I would be honoured. More than honoured, but delighted too if this is your wish. I have so hoped, but you have never shown signs of partiality to me." She was a little embarrassed even interrupting him, but he was showing his nerves.

He gently removed her hand from his lips and kissed it. "You mean it? Really?" He released his breath. "You have no idea how nervous I've been."

"Oh, trust me, I do." She flicked her eyes up to his. She could see the joy now etched on his face.

"Lottie, I can't kiss you, but I can hug you again. You have no idea how right it felt when you melted into my arms earlier today. I just wanted to keep you there." He gently drew her to him and enfolded her in his arms once more. "Oh, this just feels so nice." He bent and kissed her hair.

She laid her cheek on his chest. "When I heard you had finished your apprenticeship last month, I hoped you would come, but you didn't, and I wondered."

"I couldn't get away, Lotts; I had a pile of orders to complete and needed to work weekends to finish them. I have come as soon as I could." His heartbeat was racing with her so close. "I can't believe it. Can I say I'm over the moon?" He stroked her hair so gently she hardly felt it.

Lottie pulled away slightly. "You can, but I'm sad that you won't be allowed to stay here after this weekend."

Jonty nodded. "I know, society rules and all, but I'll see if I can stay with Uncle Ed; if not, I'll go up to Roseneath and stay with Uncle Brodie and Aunt Shauna." He kissed her hair again. "We had better walk, Lotts, or you might end up being kissed." He took her hand and slid it through his arm, covering it with his. They set off slowly around the backyard.

After a few turns around the extensive back garden, she said, "We had better go back." She threaded her fingers with his.

She dropped his arm as they reached the steps. She turned and planted a quick kiss on his surprised lips. "Shh! I've wanted to do that for some time."

As they were now at eye level, he took a step closer and was about to return the action when his Aunt Moira exited the kitchen. Her hands were on her hips, and such a look on her face that brooked no argument. "Jonathon Evans!" was all she needed to say.

"Coming, Aunty!" he said guiltily.

Moira turned to go indoors, and Jonty quickly gave Lottie a peck on the cheek. "One day, I will give you the sort of kiss I wish to, but until then, your cheek will have to do."

The weekend was over all too soon. Jonty returned to Sydney; his heart was singing. He returned to work early on Monday morning. He had a diamond to cleave and needed the early morning peace to cut the stone.

Soon after Jonty's arrival, Mr Lamb bustled in an hour early. He burst into the door and said in a loud voice. "Jonty, we need to talk. The letter, I have a letter, and you need to read it." He closed the door behind him and locked it. "Jonty… Jonty, did you hear me?"

Jonty sighed and put down the dopping wax. He had already melted the special thick wax and was about to set the uncut gem to then cut it. "I'm in here, Mr Lamb." He knew he would not get the stone started this morning. Jonty put everything down and sat back in his chair, and waited.

Mr Lamb came into the well-lit back room at a pace. He was waving a letter as he entered. "You have to read this, Jonty." He positively shoved the letter at Jonty.

Jonty took the missive and dropped his eyes to the writing. He perused the entire letter before responding to the last line. "Cor, Mr Lamb, why me?" Jonty turned over the page looking for the last one.

"I have it here," he waved the final page in the air. "Mr Field says you are the only one he can trust as he knows that you know your gems. You are still his favourite student. He said that the six months you spent learning to cut diamonds with him in Antwerp proved your worth to him. He wants you to go to Africa on his behalf as you are not part of his firm and, therefore, will be able to negotiate prices better than a representative from Tiffanys."

The £1000 fee was a huge temptation. "But Africa? Where the heck is the Transvaal? And how do I get to…" he looked at the letter again, "… The Kimberley. And oh, crikey, Lottie!" The look on Jonty's face made Mr Lamb shiver.

"Lottie? What's Miss Lockley got to do with things?" Mr Lamb looked at Jonty and gasped. "Did you ask her father this weekend? You've been mooning around after that girl for ages."

Jonty nodded. "Yes, I asked her if she would be interested in courting me, and she said yes, but it's not an engagement, just courting." The smile on his face told Mr Lamb of his happiness.

"Darn! Bad timing then, but do you wish to go?" Mr Lamb asked, knowing the conflicting emotions that the young man would be feeling.

"Yes, I'll go, but I want to see Lottie a few times before I do. I wish to be engaged before I leave, if not married, and take her." Jonty dropped his head onto his folded arms. "Damn, damn, damn!" He uttered.

"Jonty, you don't have to go." Mr Lamb laid a caring hand on his shoulder.

"I do, and you know I do! If Mr Field trusts me and wants me to go, so I must. But the timing could not be worse for me." Jonty released another deep sigh. "Oh well, it does mean we can marry when I return. With what he says he'll pay me, I'll have enough funds to do that without touching my trust from my parents." He thought for a while, "I think I'll go about Easter, if not just before, if that's all right, Mr Lamb, that should give me enough time to see her more than a few times."

Jonty wrote the tidings to Lottie, and although saddened, she fully understood.

~

Five months later, Luke allowed them some supervised time to say a fond goodbye before Jonty left for his African adventure. He was able to kiss her for the first time. Jonty would have been overjoyed had her father not stood in the room listening. He had brought her a beautiful sapphire ring just in case he'd been allowed to propose. However, Luke had refused permission for an engagement, and Jonty felt crushed. Lottie had arrived only moments after her father's refusal.

Rather than feel sad, Lottie kept the mood light. Her laughter brought joy to Jonty's heart. They were all heading to Rick's place at Roseneath for dinner that evening. His old swagman friend, Jack, wanted to have a campfire dinner to celebrate his fifth year since his return to civilisation. He had been with Rick and his wife, Mary Louise, another of Jonty's cousins, for three years, and they had a campfire dinner every now and then. This weekend was one such occasion. Jonty would see his Uncle Brodie before he left and more of his extended family. He wasn't looking forward to the trip because he'd be alone. He was, however, looking forward to seeing the gemstones that the Transvaal was famous for. He had seen some fabulous diamonds in Antwerp. The first stone he cleaved was a Kimberley diamond. To be asked to be a buyer for Tiffany's of Antwerp was extraordinary.

Lottie knew it was an opportunity not to be missed.

Luke's refusal for them to become engaged or even to have an understanding hurt. Luke had felt that it was rushed. He said Lottie had not yet been officially presented, and Luke knew that they would need to go to London to do this sometime soon. As an Earl's granddaughter, this was required. No debutante was allowed to have an "understanding" before her presentation. So although the family knew they were courting, that was it.

At the evening barbecue, Rick noticed his best friend looked a little down and came and offered an ale. Jonty didn't share his problem, but Rick guessed it was "girl problems" as his eyes rarely left Lottie. He broached the issue, and Jonty replied with a nod. There were only ten months between the two men, and they had always been close.

"Lottie, eh? I would never have guessed, Jonty. What did Uncle Luke say?"

Jonty wondered if he should say anything, but he was bursting to tell someone of his sadness, so he did. "Only that we were allowed to court as we have been for five months, but he's refused permission for her hand. I'll be gone for up to a year, and I had hoped to be engaged before I went; however,

Uncle Luke said no. Hence the long face."

"Gone? Where are you going? Did I miss something?" Rick looked at his friend.

"I'm going to Africa to buy diamonds for Tiffany's in Antwerp. It's a long story, but Mr Field himself has asked me. He's too old, and he said he trusts me. Don't tell anyone, Rick. I don't want anyone else to know, so keep it under your hat."

Rick looked stunned. "How come I didn't know about the girl or the trip?"

"Because we've kept it pretty quiet. It's not something you go around broadcasting, is it? Like your father's finds, some things are best left unsaid," Jonty explained softly.

They both knew their parents were rolling in wealth from mineral finds they had found. Gold and gems are two of the most valuable commodities on earth.

Rick said, "Well, I'll say safe travels, Jonty. I hope you come across some corkers while there. I'm sure on your return, she'll be waiting. I'll keep my eye on her while you're away. She and Mary Lou have grown close." Rick listened to his cousin's laughter and added, "She's a great girl, always the heart of a party, but in a really good way."

Jonty nodded; he knew what he meant. He wasn't sure that his quiet nature was what she needed; however, she was just what he needed. His heart hurt, yet he was still allowed to court her, and that was something. Realising time was short, he had not spent more time being morose. He hopped up and told Rick he would not waste a moment with her. Without looking back, Jonty collected two raw doughboy sticks and went to her side. He handed her a raw doughboy, and they stood around the campfire cooking them in the coals. Aunt Shauna had a table of fillings off to the side of the yard, and once the doughboys were cooked, they filled them with butter and cockies joy. This cockies joy or golden syrup dripped from the bottom of Jonty's, and she giggled as he sucked the bottom of the doughboy. She, too, dribbled some on her chin; he gently wiped it off, then kissed his finger and put it to her lips. "I wish I didn't have to leave, but I should be back in six months, possibly a bit longer, a year at the latest."

"I'm not going anywhere, Jonty," she whispered.

He didn't know that she had heard her father refuse his suit for her hand. She had sobbed long and hard that night.

It was not in Jonty's heart to mention it. Uncle Luke's explanation made sense; Jonty didn't like the decision. He would wait. He would come to her the moment he returned.

The extended Lockley family were together again at Eddie's place for an after-church Sunday lunch. There were so many family members now, and Ed's cook, Cara, and her husband, Paddy, were getting on in age, so rather than her cooking, everyone now supplied their own food. It became a "bring your own picnic" in the backyard. At mid-afternoon, Jonty knew his time was drawing to a close. He had told very few people he was leaving, and there was no fanfare as he left to catch the train home. Lottie, Ellen, and Luke went to say goodbye. Luke again allowed them a moment or two of privacy to part.

Lottie managed to speak to Jonty and say she would wait for him and not worry. If he still wanted her, she would be there on his return. This made the parting somewhat easier to accept, but Jonty still hated leaving. Luke had told him he could kiss her. This he did, but her soft and pliable lips only whetted his appetite for more. He pulled from her arms and thumbed her pale cheek as a tear slid down it; he stood memorising her face with his hungry look. After another long hug, he released her and said his farewells.

~

Jonty arrived home shortly before dark. His large bags were packed for his embarkation tomorrow afternoon. He had to head down to the shop to collect some storage boxes, an eyeglass to inspect the stones, and unique light and magnifying glass to check the clarity. There was a container of small tools and other equipment he'd require. Amongst the clothing he packed was Earl Charles' coat that he had on when Lottie cried into his shoulder. Her scent was now on it, and it had become his favourite.

His parents, John and Colleen, siblings Reenie, Blue, Hettie, Finn, and six-year-old Cara, accompanied him to the dock where the clipper ship, *The Rodney*, waited. Mr Field had paid the £35 fare, and his cabin was a two-room saloon suite. Everything was included—top-quality linen and every modern convenience he could wish for. He would be delighted if the rest of the trip were like this. Captain Loutitt introduced himself to each cabin class passenger before he left them to prepare for departure. Usually, they would leave at dawn, but the winds were favourable as they were from the west, and as soon as the passengers were all on board, they would set sail.

His mother was somewhat tearful and didn't want to let him go. His father, John, finally managed to extricate his oldest son from her arms when Jonty had mouthed "help." He kissed each of his siblings and walked onto the deck to wave goodbye. He hoped Lottie had been allowed to come at the last minute, but she was not there.

Just before he had left the house, his family gathered around him. The entire family and the Macdonalds from next door had joined his grandparents for a prayer circle, with him in the middle and everyone laying a hand on him. He had not experienced this before, but their neighbour, Hamish Macdonald, had said that their village in Scotland did this whenever someone travelled. Jonty felt empowered, knowing that his entire family and all the Macdonalds would be upholding him in prayers for safety. He also knew Uncle Luke said their family would also keep him in prayer.

Now his family group was huddled together on the dock. He could see his mother wipe away tears. Mr and Mrs Lamb had arrived to see him off, and just before the gangplank was pulled up, Mr Lamb came up the access way and handed Jonty a bulging letter. "Get what you can for me, lad. There's a letter in there too."

Jonty nodded and stowed the fat envelope in his inside coat pocket. Mr Lamb didn't take very long returning to shore.

The sailors were waiting to cast off when he arrived back on the wharf. Ropes were pulled back on deck, and the ship was pulled away from the quay by the tug boats.

Jonty's heart was in his mouth, but this adventure had begun. It was how Hamish had termed the trip, an adventure! He certainly hoped it would be a profitable one.

~

It took half an hour before the ship was out of sight of the waving family. He waited on deck until the clipper was through the heads and heading south. Unlike most journeys to London via Cape Horn, this one went in the reverse route. Most would go to Wellington in New Zealand before continuing to South America and then to London. This ship was doing the reverse as it was heading to Cape Town before London, though its first port of call was Adelaide, not Melbourne.

He watched as the breeze filled the sails and felt the ship lift as the many sails filled and picked up speed. He knew he had about six weeks on board, so he intended to unpack his bags to be comfortable. Each saloon cabin came with a steward or a maid, and he had met his allocated assistant, Neville Mitchell.

Nev seemed nice. Jonty pumped the man for some information about the ship. Jonty discovered that *The Rodney* was two-hundred and thirty-five feet long and thirty-eight feet wide. She was a steel hull ship, and the three-masted ship weighed nearly fifteen hundred tons. He was impressed that each cabin had a lavatory and basin, with running cold water, a chest of drawers and a wardrobe.

Neville showed Jonty into the main cabin class saloon, and he was stunned to find live plants growing inside. The room was light and airy. It had a well-stocked library, which was free for all the cabin class passengers to borrow. Once Jonty had investigated the ship's layout, he settled himself into his cabin. Nev had gone off duty for a while. He, too, had to settle into his cabin. He said he'd come back half an hour before the evening meal was called.

Jonty found his clothing had already been unpacked and his bag stowed. He flopped back onto his bed. He had no idea what was before him. He had yet to read Mr Lamb's letter, so while on his back, he pulled out the envelope and flicked open the seal. It held over £500 in cash and a letter. "Woah!" Jonty exclaimed.

George Street Jewellery
George Street Sydney
April 10th, 1880

Dear Jonty,

Today is the first day of what I hope becomes a wonderful and profitable adventure.

I have supplied some funds to buy us some stock. I have heard that gems are ridiculously cheap, and I hope this will enable you to have some petty cash. Use some if you need to for unforeseen incidentals. Write when you can, and Jonty, have some fun too.

Stay safe, lad and see you in a few months.
Richard Lamb

Jonty fingered the cash in his hand and decided to split it into various places. He hated carrying much money. Mr Field had wired funds into a bank in Cape Town and had arranged access to it in a town in the Transvaal. He had done the same with his own money. He knew now that it was some six hundred miles north of Cape Town and that he had to find a way to get there. No use worrying about that; he would deal with all that later. He hoped Mr Field had that all sorted too.

He must have dozed off as he woke to a knock on the door. He was still lying on his back on the bed. His hand still held the £500, and he sat up and stuffed it in his pocket. He wondered if the ship also supplied safes in each cabin; Nev should know.

Chapter 3   The Transvaal

*T*he weeks on board slipped by.

A storm had put them behind schedule, and it was early June before they saw the coast of Africa. After leaving Adelaide, they had met a storm in the Great Australian Bight, but the ship had made it safely, despite the occasional wave breaking over the bow and flooding the deck. They needed to do a minor repair in Fremantle and purchase another sail. Thus done, they proceeded to Cape Town without further mishap. Sadly, the wind was a headwind which meant tacking the entire way across the Indian Ocean.

For the final leg, the ship was tugged into Table Bay Harbour and towed into Alfred Basin behind a new-looking break wall. Jonty noticed a ship in a fancy dry dock and others waiting to be slipped. He noticed the difference between the people and was horrified that some were being treated as slaves. The more he watched, the more injustices he saw. He had heard about how the convicts had been treated in Parramatta, but he had never seen it for himself. He didn't like what he saw.

Nev had packed his bags, and Jonty had emptied the safe in his room. He gave Nev a good tip and many thanks. Nev escorted him as he disembarked and led him to the harbour office to see if there was any message for Jonty.

Nev arrived back not only with a message, but porters followed him. "Sir, if you follow this gentleman, he will escort you to your accommodation."

As expected, Mr Field had everything arranged, and soon Jonty had been loaded into a carriage and taken to a luxurious hotel some distance away. Again Jonty said farewell and thanked Nev, tipping him again, and they parted ways.

Jonty was handed an envelope on entry to the hotel, including an itinerary. He discovered to his horror, that there was no railway and that the journey had to be done by both carriage and horseback. He wasn't keen on the horseback transport, as he had heard about wild animals and attacks. Jonty had to be at a specific place at a particular time, and everything was arranged for the next leg of his journey.

Jonty saw that he was only staying one night in the hotel. So at nine the following day, he was in the lobby, ready to be collected. A two-month cross-country trip was before him; no wonder Mr Field couldn't come himself. Thankfully the first few days would be in a carriage. After that, it was going to be hard work.

If Jonty didn't value diamonds before, he knew that this trek would give him a new appreciation of them after this trip. He adored these gems and the rainbows they produced.

~

Jonty discovered that his arrival on the diamond fields was expected by the soldiers at the nearby garrison. His accommodation was in a small farmhouse on the edge of the village as there was no hotel in the town where the mines were. Use of a small cottage had been arranged for him; it was pretty comfortable, and he felt safe. That was a word he would learn to love and a condition he would not feel very often.

For the first weeks, Jonty was escorted by a guard of English soldiers to various areas where diamonds were mined. He was able to purchase a large selection of fine gems and was happy with his purchases. He discovered that after a week, word had spread that he was a buyer and many miners came directly to him with their finds. He learned to barter, and his negotiating skills soon exceeded his expectations. The quality of some of the gems far outweighed what he thought he would be able to purchase.

~

By the time he had been in the area for a month, whispers of unrest were reaching his ears. He observed the English's abominable treatment of the local villagers and Boers.

Jonty kept buying, and he kept an accurate tally of which money was buying what stones. He divided his booty into three draw-string bags he had purchased in Cape Town and itemised each stone. Quite a few of the diamonds he bought were so large they looked like large chunks of hail. The majority were small, but top quality, and some were black. One looked like a chink of rusty ice.

Mr Lamb's money would cover many, many stones, and he would still have some over. Mr Field would get the majority of the gems. The diamonds, however, were on the whole small, and even the large volume he intended to buy would be just a small bag each. Jonty heard of other gems available from different areas and decided to invest in some rough stones for himself and Mr Lamb.

One miner from Letaba brought him some chunks of green crystal that made Jonty question him more. He had rarely seen raw emeralds before, and these caught his eye. The colour was vibrant, and although many were cloudy and some had cracks and crazing, they were still cuttable. As neither Mr Field nor Mr Lamb had instructed him to purchase other gems, Jonty bought all this man had for himself. The man wanted only £5 for the bundle, and Jonty insisted he accepts more for it, but the man wouldn't. Then he produced a huge diamond that Jonty promptly purchased well above the going rate. This he added to Mr Field's stones, although he paid with his money for the emeralds. The diamond was a perfect double-pointer gem specimen. He asked a mere £20 for the rock and, knowing its worth was far more, gave the man £30. However, he did ask him not to spread the word. £30 for this village man was some ten years' wages. On top of the emeralds, this man's life would change. Jonty watched him leave with a big smile on his face.

Jonty had £100 of his own money, and as he didn't have to pay cutting fees, his funds would hopefully be converted into a small fortune. Emeralds were also popular stones and much easier to cut and polish than diamonds. Sapphires were easily sourced from the New England area at home, so he did not need to buy those. Jonty also purchased some lovely deep purple amethyst crystals. These were both popular and easy to cut, so they were added to his own tally. As they were only a few pounds for a full bucket, he decided to send them home by the sea. If they got lost, he would not have lost much. But there were too many to carry with him. He sent a letter with them and sent a parcel to Cape Town with a returning battalion. So the amethysts and emeralds were posted to Mr Lamb.

When he completed his apprenticeship, Mr Lamb arranged that he would be charged only half what he charged other cutters. This benefited them both as he let Jonty use the cutting room at the shop.

Jonty figured that at that price, they would share that beautiful bounty. He had only been in the Transvaal for a few weeks and had already sourced some fabulous gemstones, but he'd also seen some incredibly sad sights. The poverty of the poor black men, slaving away digging stones for the Boers and English, made him recoil in horror.

Jonty decided early on to see if he could purchase some stones from the private miners rather than big businesses. He had talked to some locals digging in river beds. They took many more risks dealing with wild animals, like crocodiles and hippos. Some were digging with nothing more than pointed sticks. The riverbanks were a potential diamond mine for each one. Many a small African child was treated to a boiled lolly as Jonty spoke to the locals. He felt safe amongst them and treated them as equals.

The Dutch and English were more stand-offish and surprised that he intermingled with the local people. His house boy was bilingual, so Jonty took him when buying.

One night Jonty sat looking through the stones he had already purchased; the small fortune in gems would have fitted in the palms of his hands. He planned to spend another three weeks in the area, but as the next day was Friday, he thought he would go and see some of the local mines.

He already had refused to buy directly from the English miners, as he knew the stones were probably illegally taken. They did not own the mines, and he would not be seen encouraging theft. He'd been warned of this before he arrived, and, not wanting to cause trouble; he stuck to the individual local buyer's rules. He knew sellers would not be directed to him if he didn't. Eventually, after seeing so much cruelty from one particular mine, he refused to buy any stones at all from them. It was English owned, and he expected repercussions.

When they came, they were not as he expected.

He came across a miner being beaten, and Jonty stepped in and stopped the belting. He reported the incident to the mine manager, who laughed at him.

"If you don't beat them, they won't work," the manager said.

Jonty was so angry but managed to hold his tongue; he did not buy from them again. His money was cash and it was plentiful. He was known to give fair, if not extremely good prices, and they wanted the sales; they would suffer, not him.

His trip to the various other mines was eye-opening. Some were only minor concerns, with one or two men digging in a hole. Some were massive mines, with thousands of workers labouring under challenging situations in extreme conditions. He was taken down to the mine face. At one spot, he was shown how the stones were found. They were firmly embedded in the bank of the mine.

One gem was unearthed while he was there, and he saw how laborious it was to extract the precious stone. It made him appreciate the efforts even more. In other areas, they were mined like sapphires, being sieved, washed and panned. These were often the smaller stones. The entire process was eye-opening to Jonty.

In many mines, the workers were treated humanely. The gems were as good, and he decided to buy more from those sellers. He now had various people who acted as translators. Most of these were Afrikaans-speaking locals. Jonty started a list, marking these mines as ethical, with good treatment of his fellow man.

Occasionally the local children would bring him a stone to purchase. He would always ask where their sources were, ensuring that they were not used as mules for illegal stones or, even worse; twice he found unscrupulous mines, surreptitiously using a child to get him to buy from them. He dared not turn them away, but he paid them very little, giving them a receipt for often only half the stone's value. This made those mines not bother with the sales to him, but it kept the children safe.

He knew that many children would risk death or danger to help dig gems to provide income for their families. There was little to no regulation of diamond mine practices, boundaries or even land ownership. But he knew that the larger foreign mine companies often ostracised the local villagers. Jonty always bought the local children's stones at way beyond their average price just to help them out. Having said that, he would still make a good profit with them.

Crocodiles, snakes, and hippopotamuses were the cause of many deaths of children in this endeavour. He felt so sorry for them and never turned one child away. One little girl named Nandi stole his heart. She had been the first child to bring him a stone she had found herself. She was about eight and had the most adorable round face, huge dark chocolate eyes, and a dimpled smile. Somehow she had even managed to learn some English words. "You buy?" she had asked, then uncurled her fingers from around a huge diamond.

"I buy," Jonty had replied, nodding; she had hugged him when he paid her.

He had purchased the stone she had brought him for himself, paying £50 for it. He decided to cleave it and make half of it into jewellery for Lottie. It would be worth thousands when cut. Half his money would be worth it in the long run.

On her second visit, she brought him a tiny, injured, spotty lion cub rather than a stone. She gave it to him, along with another big hug. "You heal him?"

The tiny cub could barely walk as it had hurt its paw. Jonty attended to the cut on the cub's foot, treating it with alcohol, then honey and binding it. The spotty cub had three pure white stripes on his head just above his eyes. It looked like God's fingers touched it. It loved cuddling him as he slept, sneaking up to Jonty's chin or snuggling into his back.

Jonty found the local Afrikaans word for lion was *leeu,* as the villagers nearby called him "the *man en leeu,*" but it didn't suit the little cub. Someone told him he'd heard of another name in Swahili was, simba, but the cub ended up being called *Chimbu* from a conversation he'd had with another friend a long time ago.

Soon, Chimbu even came when called. Jonty bought goat's milk and fed it using a leather glove finger with a hole to suck from. Soon it could lap from a bowl. Its paw healed, and the cub was strong enough to follow him where ever he went. Chimbu was now his constant companion. He was even coming with him on the horse when out visiting. As the cub grew, he carried it in a bag slung over his shoulder as he didn't want him running off.

~

On the distant journeys, to and from the mines, Jonty took great pleasure in seeing the many strange animals. On these days, he left the cub at the cottage, knowing that it protected his luggage while he was away.

Jonty had his first view of zebra; he was so excited, but then came elephants, buffalo, giraffes, hyenas, springbok antelope, and monkeys, and then his guide pointed out a cheetah chasing a gazelle. Jonty was unsure if he wished the gazelle to escape or the cheetah to catch it. He knew the circle of life must go on. He saw two different sorts of fat-horned beasts that he later found were rhinoceroses.

On another trip, he saw his first warthog, wildebeest, and a pride of lions. He wondered if Chimbu was part of this pride. He hoped that this was not the pride that had been attacking the locals. The big male was dark-coloured and looked nothing like Chimbu's honey colour coat. Jonty was often on horseback, though he wasn't too keen to be a target and be made into dinner. He knew each journey was dangerous, and he thought he'd much rather be at home with spiders, snakes, and the occasional shark, but he enjoyed seeing the amazing sights around him.

Chimbu was earning his keep while Jonty was away. On his return to the cottage, Jonty found dead snakes, including three sizeable black-mouthed mamba snakes and a few dead giant spiders.

One evening, from his cottage window, if that's what you could call it, as it was just a leaf shutter held up by a stick, he saw a mother baboon with a baby piggybacking as she walked. Unseen was the father and other females from the pack. Jonty chuckled at the red bottom flaunted proudly as it sauntered past the cottage. Jonty laughed loudly, and the surprised beast flashed its huge fangs at him. Stunned at the instant threat it posed, he pulled the pole and shut the window with a bang. Another smash followed it; the baboon had hit the now-closed shutter.

Even Chimbu was frightened and crawled onto Jonty's shoulder, digging in his sharp claws. Jonty knew he'd had a close call. He also knew that had the baboon wished to get to him; it could have shredded that shutter in mere moments. His heart skipped a beat, realising how close a call that was. He had flattened himself against the wall and had broken out in a cold sweat. Chimbu snarled as he got slightly squashed.

They stayed inside in the shuttered room for the next hour, just in case the animal was still around. An hour later, he heard a knock on the door, and his dinner had arrived. The meal included a large raw bone for Chimbu to gnaw on. Jonty realised that it was now safe to venture outside. He pushed up the shutter again and let the airflow inside. Chimbu carefully sniffed before venturing outside and relieving himself.

~

Due to not wishing to leave a small cub, Jonty had extended his stay. Over the next month, Jonty saw many of what he called "social injustices." He was angry at the squalor the miners were forced to live in. Their local village didn't even have a well. He could not voice much to the mine owners as he didn't speak Dutch or even the local Afrikaans dialect. His new English translator would not allow him to interfere, often pulling him back or refusing to translate a phrase for him. His only recourse was to not purchase from those mines at all.

By late October, he had decided that it was time to go. Chimbu was now around six months old. He was too big to cuddle, although he still tried to climb into Jonty's lap. Jonty no longer kept him inside except at night. He allowed the cub free access to the world outside during the day.

When Chimbu started bringing home his own dinner, Jonty realised he could hunt for himself. It was often rats, mice, or the occasional snake. The cub would leave it at the door until Jonty congratulated him, and then he would devour it. He still lapped up the goat's milk with his rasp-like tongue, then tried to curl up on Jonty's lap, but he preferred to lie at his feet and purr. The rumbling sound was strong enough to make ripples in Jonty's mug of tea. When he woke, he would turn and lick Jonty's bare feet. He would lick between his toes and once tried to nip him. Jonty's immediate withdrawal of his feet and verbal chastisement put a stop to that. Chimbu gave Jonty a sombre look, and it made Jonty chuckle. He used to try to reach Jonty's cheek as he slept, but Jonty had put a stop to that, too, as it hurt as he grew older. His tongue was so rough that it almost took the skin off his feet, let alone his cheek.

Jonty knew he still needed to deliver the stones to Antwerp before returning home. He still had a two-month cross-country trip yet to get back to Cape Town. He had stayed much longer than he had planned because of Chimbu. Sadly, he could not tell his family of his plans as there was now no mail leaving the town. Jonty had heard of some local political unrest and thought it was time to go.

After some months in the village, Jonty had let Chimbu out one morning the last week in October, and the lion did not return. Chimbu had now been gone for a week without being sighted. He had returned to the wild. Jonty was sad, but as he knew his time there was at a close, it solved the problem of what to do with the almost tame cub. Jonty was both happy and sad for the young lion, but he now felt vulnerable in the cottage. Chimbu had been a built-in security system.

The villagers knew of the crazy jeweller with a pet lion. They were in awe of him and stayed clear. Chimbu had actually claimed the village as his territory. He had already scared off a leopard from the outskirts. Reports of this had been brought immediately to Jonty. The children got into the habit of leaving bowls of goat's milk for the growing cub.

At the end of the first week of November, he'd spent all the money he could on the gems needed. He still had £100 of the Antwerp money and some £50 of Mr Lamb's.

Even the children were now prevented from selling to him. The stone supply had dried up as he still refused to buy from the big mines.

Finally, when all avenues had been blocked, he walked to the military compound nearby and asked for a security detail to take him back down south.

Jonty had kept his nose out of the stirrings of unrest in the area. He knew things were unsettled between the English, the Boers, and some of the local tribes, but he had no idea what they were about.

On arrival at the barracks, the English Major told him that he would inform him in a few days if a security detail were available.

Jonty sat in his cabin alone, waiting. Food was still provided, but no one was prepared to bring him any gemstones.

Sadly Jonty had left his departure a week too long.

~

On the morning he was to leave the compound, an auction was planned in the town to sell a confiscated cart belonging to one of the locals named Piet Bezuidenhout. He had an outstanding tax account, and the sale of this cart would cover the cost, but it was needed for his work; the tension in the town was tangible as the villagers supported their friend. A security detail had been arranged to escort him out; however, because of the trial, it never happened.

Jonty didn't overthink it when he had heard of the auction. He learned that he had vastly underestimated the situation.

Piet was a Boer and was unhappy with what he considered an unfair tax. His treatment had been the straw on the camels' back for the Boers.

Later that afternoon, an escort of soldiers called for Jonty at his cottage and quickly escorted him into the barracks compound for his protection. Jonty was protesting loudly as this was not what he wanted. He had been expecting to leave, not relocate. Thankfully he was all packed as he had been waiting for word to go, and he was able to store the gemstones on his person. His coat pockets were filled with the small draw-string bags, three of diamonds and another small parcel of emeralds and other assorted gems that had come to him. He was thankful he'd sent the amethysts home soon after he'd bought them. He had received no mail at all.

On his arrival at the compound, the Major said, "Sorry, sir, but we have a small problem, and we will be unable to leave today."

Jonty was shown into a small room at the back of the building and told he could stay there for the night. It was no more than a storeroom. The room contained a narrow mattress, a pillow, an empty bucket, a pitcher of water, and a mug. There was no window or light source of any type. Jonty was horrified and released a small gasp.

The Major was walking out as he spoke. "Leave your things there, lad, then come back and join me in the mess room."

Jonty saw the furrowed brow on the soldier and realised he looked very concerned.

By late that afternoon, the Major's fears were justified. Over one hundred Boer men arrived armed and ready for a fight.

Jonty was sent to stay in a storeroom and told not to move until one of the soldiers called to collect him. It was hot and stuffy, but Jonty stayed put, knowing his life may well depend on his silence. He prayed; it was all he could do in the pitch blackness.

He could hear the fighting ensuing and knew enough to stay quiet. Shouts of pain were followed by feet running and calls for the medic.

With no fighting skills, Jonty knew he was useless, not that he would fight unless he must, so he did as told. He lay down and tried to sleep, but wasn't tired, so he sat crosslegged and prayed for the safety of the soldiers.

It took hours before the noises quietened.

~

When the door finally opened, a soldier said, "It's safe now, sir." The soldier held the door for Jonty to leave.

As Jonty was now busting to use a privy, he exited quickly. He had not wished to use the bucket for its intended purposes. As he wandered through the courtyard, the ravages of the battle were in stark evidence. Pools of blood and injured men were staggering toward the small hospital ward, and soldiers attempted to repair the damaged compound.

For the remainder of the afternoon, the situation settled a little. Shots had been fired, and the emotions of both sides were volatile.

The commanding officers said Jonty must delay his journey until it was safe. Little did Jonty realise this would take months as no one could be spared for a security detail, and even if they did leave, they probably would not get far.

~

Over the next five weeks, Jonty was only allowed to wander inside the fortified army headquarters in the town. The A and F companies of the 94th foot were stationed in the garrison at Lydenburg.

Lieutenant Walter Hillyar Colquhoun Long was in charge of the area. He now demanded that Jonty not step a foot outside the garrison town as he could no longer guarantee his safety. Even wandering through the town was risky.

Jonty finally understood the danger when a major incident happened on the 20th of December when a column of soldiers departed Lydenburg for Pretoria.

The column of soldiers included six of the officers who had

befriended Jonty, along with two-hundred and forty-six-foot soldiers and twelve more from the area service corps. A two-hundred-and-fifty-strong group of Boer rebels attacked them. The battalion of soldiers was caught in the surprise attack, and one hundred and fifty-six of them were killed, and more than a hundred were captured. Only two Boers were killed.

Word of the demise of these brave men filtered back into the town. They had marched out in scarlet coats and white helmets, looking immaculate. Jonty had debated if he should accompany them. He had decided not to join them, as they were heading into Pretoria to the north rather than Cape Town to the south. Lieutenant Colonel Anstruther led the column, and as the soldiers marched, they sang. Some miles into the march, Burgher de Beer had issued an ultimatum to surrender. Within fifteen minutes after the refusal to do so, the fifteen senior officers lay dead; Anstruther was mortally injured, surrounded by dead and dying men.

Jonty was stranded.

~

The weeks of December passed in a blur of stress, blood and horror.

Christmas came and went unnoticed and uncelebrated, and soon it was early January, skirmish after skirmish occurred.

Jonty made and lost friends faster than he could count.

Soldiers he ate a meal with one day, he'd nurse as they died the next. He sponged their heads, held their hands, and prayed with them so they would not die alone. He could not weep; he was too busy keeping himself alive.

De Beer's success with his Boers motivated more skirmishes over the following months. Laing's Nek 28th of January 1881 and Ingogo 8th of February followed; the name of Kruger, Jonty now heard often. He asked who he was and found that Paul Kruger's name was spoken with hate and vehemence. "Down with Kruger and the Boers" was often heard and became a saying at the end of each meal in the mess room.

~

Jonty became an eyewitness to atrocities, including beheadings.

The first of these monstrosities he came across was a dead child. Worse still, he was horrified to see that it was beautiful little Nandi. Her head was nearly severed. Thankfully he had not seen it happen, and as she was still clothed, she had not been violated, but he lost his temper. She had been so adorable and so innocent.

Jonty knelt next to her and closed her staring chocolate eyes for the last time. He covered her face with the only thing he had, a clean handkerchief. The white cloth with his blue embroidered initials was incongruously pristine in the filth of the blood mixed with dirt.

His many tears added to the mud and gore. Jonty wished to pull her into his arms and hold her. To cradle her to his chest in one last hug, but he was pulled away from her by his security detail and forced to leave her lying in the bloodied mud.

His heart broke, and he wept unashamedly.

Jonty stood and let out a roar of anger at the top of his voice, "Why her?" he shouted. "What did she ever do to any of you?" He had no idea who had killed her, but she was dead. She was innocent! He shrugged off the caring hand of the accompanying soldiers. Finally, he was dragged from the gruesome scene and back through the streets of the walled town. He stormed back to camp. He knew he was in shock as he was shaking, but he was also angry. Angry at the evils of war, of greed, and the senseless killing of innocents. Angry that he did not leave when he should have done. His eyes were filled with floods of tears. His gait was unsteady as he had tripped a few times, as his eyes blurred his vision.

Within sight of the fortified gates, Jonty heard two gunshots. The two soldiers were concerned but had already born his wrath. They walked silently behind him. The men, who moments before were comforting him, were shot as they all walked back into the garrison walls.

Jonty didn't run; he hardly moved. He turned and faced the shooters. He stopped and lifted his arms, "Shoot me too! She was as innocent as I." Nothing happened. He shouted again, "Her name was Nandi, remember that, *N A N D I*," he screamed as loud as he could. Without a word, he looked at his dead protective detail, turned on his heel and walked into the compound.

After that, he often saw women and children killed all through town. He refused to stay safely inside the fort. Often he would leave alone, almost hoping he'd be shot too.

The English soldiers did some atrocities, and some by the Boer rebels. Some poor women were even raped within his view, and he tried to pull off the abusers. He was held by other soldiers and pushed aside. One woman was violated while she lay dying. He could do nothing to stop them, and he felt ill knowing how useless he was.

He had neither training nor a weapon. He refused to kill and would go to the aid of anyone injured, regardless of race, colour or creed, disregarding his own safety.

When challenged by the Major, he said, "We are all God's people, and we all bleed red."

Jonty saw English soldiers laughing at a partially naked Boer woman at their feet. He presumed she had just been pack raped, at least her body had, as she was dead. He turned and vomited at the disgusting sight before him.

How his world had changed. He was just a jeweller who had come to buy beautiful gems and was now caught up in the ugliness of war. His innocence was stripped away, and the horrors around him made him fear that he would never get home.

He soon dared not venture far, for every time he did, he saw more atrocities.

Chimbu, he glimpsed only once.

The cub was nearly grown. Jonty had been on the compound walls when he saw the tawny lion crouching in the bushes. He knew it to be him as the three white fingers of fur on his head were easily identifiable. Jonty yelled at him to leave. "Chimbu, go!" With a look over his shoulder, the big lion gave a half roar, walked back into the bushes, and vanished.

Many times Jonty had to help with the wounded. He originally had little knowledge of how to nurse someone; now, he had learned how to stop the bleeding, as this was always the number one thing to do. Gunshot injuries were often fatal. His medical skills were still nil, but at least he could bring water and help hold items for the doctor. February and early March brought more news of the fighting.

Jonty had been waiting for instructions outside the General's office when he overheard the results of the last battle. He fell to his knees and prayed for protection.

At the end of February, Jonty knew over four hundred soldiers were being deployed to Majuba Hill. General Colley led the 58th regiment and 92nd Highlanders and some two hundred other soldiers. The supposedly invincible red-coat soldiers were annihilated, and the General was shot and died. Ninety-two were killed, one hundred and thirty-four wounded, and another fifty-nine captured. The British were defeated, totally and absolutely.

Would he ever get out of here? How could he get home?

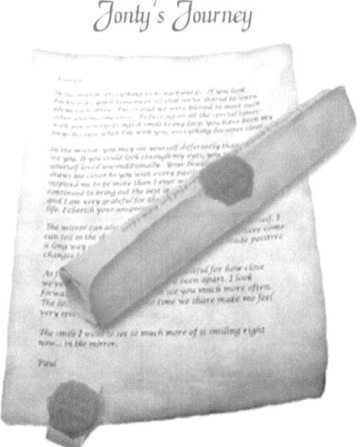

Chapter 4   Treaty and Release

The months stretched on with an ambiguous future for the garrison town.

Leaving to go anywhere was no longer an option. Jonty was known to be impartial and still refused to injure anyone. The Boers had sent messages that he was free to leave and would be assured of safe passage to the coast. But the British officers at the garrison town refused to let him go alone. Unsure of what to do, he stayed put.

March, April, and May passed in a haze of stressful days. Skirmishes had quieted, but everything was tense. June brought news of a probable treaty, and discussions were underway to draft this document. It was due to be signed in August.

In the meantime, in early July, the Boers demanded that Jonty accompany them, or they would storm the garrison. They promised to escort him safely to Pretoria. The General, now under the supervision of the local Boers, had no choice but to release Jonty into their care. He apologised to Jonty for not keeping his promise for his safety. He told him to keep praying. Jonty had not stopped. Every night he faithfully had a prayer time, but his heart was still in turmoil. Every night he closed his eyes, he saw Nandi's gentle smile with her dimples asking for his help. He would often start awake. Knowing that the Boers had won every battle and now surrounded the English forces, the General acquiesced to the demand by Paul Kruger, who was now the leader of the Boers. Jonty was absolutely petrified. He wondered if he would be killed as soon as he left the compound. However, his luggage was loaded into the back of a cart, and he was given a horse. He had now sewn the gem bags into his trouser pockets and hoped the gems would survive the journey. On release, he was taken to meet the leader. He was greeted by name and in English.

Jonty begged for an answer. "Mr Kruger, why me, sir?" He had no confidence that he would survive this journey and needed to know why he was the chosen scapegoat.

The man looked at Jonty and smiled reassuringly. "Why? Because you are the only one who showed impartiality. You showed you cared by dealing justly with the poorer miners and the locals but not favouring the big English companies over the poor local diggers; you proved your worth. It's as simple as that. We trust you, and you deserve release. Jonty Evans, not all the Boers are my men; many rebels are amongst them. They do not always fight fair. No man does." Paul placed his hand on Jonty's shoulder, trying to comfort him. "This is the only way I can assure your survival. If my men had the choice, everyone in there would now be dead. If the treaty fails, that may yet happen. Hence, I wanted to get you out. You grieved for the little girl. I saw that myself. The two soldiers with you deserved to die for what they did to her. So I saw to that for her sake." He spoke in a thick Dutch accent, but his English was good. Mr Field's accent was much the same. The smile he bestowed on Jonty instilled some confidence. The man rode off and instructed Jonty to be kept safe at all costs.

Stunned, Jonty knew he would probably survive if this man had any say over his life. Jonty silently praised God. He closed his eyes, saw Lottie's face in his mind's-eye and prayed for her. Her blue eyes and fair hair haunted his dreams. She had no idea where he was or even if he was alive. He was six months overdue already, but it would still be months before he could get home. Pretoria was in the opposite direction to where he had planned to go. It was landlocked and well away from an English port. How would he get to any ship from there? The closest port was Lourenço Marques in Mozambique, and later, he was informed it was where he had to go to catch a vessel.

At the end of the first week on the road, a sound sent chills through the hearts of the escort, and Jonty wondered if it was Chimbu. A golden lion had been seen shadowing the convoy, and all the soldiers were well-armed. One evening Jonty was relieving himself when he was aware he was being watched. He turned, and an initial chill went through him, then chuckled; the giant lion was purring, and as he stood, the lion came and licked Jonty. "Hello, boy; I was wondering if it was you." The lion sat next to him and leaned against him. Purring so loudly that the soldier guarding him heard a sound. He let out a shriek and lifted his gun to shoot. "Stop!" shouted Jonty, knowing the man could not understand him; he stood scratching the lion's nose. "This is my pet. He won't hurt anyone." Jonty lifted his hand and stood between the soldier and the lion. He was still stroking the lion's head with his other hand.

The soldier lowered his rifle. "Sir?" His mouth opened wide in amazement. Jonty wouldn't move until the gun had been shouldered. He waved for him to do so. He then waved the soldier aside. "Stand back as I'm heading to camp." Jonty placed his hand on the tawny mane and walked back to camp. The lion went passively and walked closely beside Jonty. He was constantly purring. As they drew closer, Jonty called a warning to Paul, knowing he was the only one who understood English.

Jonty heard the order bellowed and saw the rifles lowered. He waited until Paul gave him an "all clear."

Paul called to Jonty and said it was safe for him to come. Paul stood and watched their progress towards camp. The nearly fully grown beast and his carer were observed by every one of the soldiers. All remained silent and in awe. Paul knew of the cub; he had seen it soon after it had arrived and was surprised to see how much he had grown. He was one of the most enormous lions he'd ever seen. Paul had told the men to stand down. Yet they all held their guns in readiness.

Jonty progressed to the fire near his tent with the lion in tow. In the firelight, Chimbu's three white stripes on his head were visible, and he sat beside Jonty while the others stood watching in awe. Chimbu spent the night in the tent with Jonty, snuggled up to his side as he had as a cub.

In the early morning light, the golden beast woke Jonty with a lick to his face. He then turned and stood at the flap of the tent. Chimbu had given Jonty time to pull on his boots; Chimbu looked back at him, waiting, then slowly walked out of camp with Jonty now on his heels. As they reached the outskirts of the tents, Chimbu turned, rose on his hind legs, gave Jonty a velveted claw hug, then dropped back onto all four pads and walked silently into the scrub without a backward glance. Jonty was sad to see him leave but knew he was free. He had no scars on him, so he was surviving well. He was healthy.

Almost a month was spent on horseback, and it toughened him. They arrived in Pretoria in time for the prearranged meeting with the English. The Boers were wonderfully kind to him; however, Jonty knew that one wrong move and he could end up like any of the soldiers he had assisted in the small hospital at Lydenburg. Yet they made sure that everything possible was done for his comfort. He still did not speak their language, and none spoke English but Kruger, and he did not approach Jonty again. So, any conversation was non-existent, and communication was by hand signals. However, the Boer rebels were so impressed that such a young man had stood against the English's instructions and taken the poor's side that they could not do enough for him. They all knew that he had many gems hidden, either on his person or in his luggage, but they kept him safe and protected his bags.

~

August saw Jonty witness the signing of a treaty between the Boers and the English.

After all the official duties were done, Jonty was surprised that the Boers told the English that they must now form an escort and take Jonty to the coast. The double protective detail would guard him on the last leg of his journey. The soldiers were half English and half Boer. Once there, the English and Jonty would be loaded onto a European-bound ship.

Jonty was placed on the back of a half-starved English horse and surrounded by a ribbon of English soldiers and officers. The Boers then followed the column of now unarmed tattered red-coated soldiers. The trip was slow as most were on foot, and many were injured. After a month of walking, Lourenço Marques came in sight, and the column was marched straight to the waterfront and onto a waiting ship. His luggage was also intact, and the gems were still safely in his pockets. His mind flashed back to Chimbu, and he wondered if he was still alive. He had not seen him again since that night. He had heard a lion in the distance but had no idea whether it was Chimbu. Some English soldiers had heard stories of a golden lion who had protected some villagers from a dark lion. Another story told that the great golden lion had saved a child from an elephant.

Over a year after Jonty arrived in Africa, he was standing on board a British ship in the harbour in Mozambique. The harbour was under Portuguese control and had become the main shipping port. Jonty knew the boat they were on was heading for the Suez Canal and then to London. Standing on the deck as the ship departed, Jonty wiped away a tear or two of relief. As the ship was tugged from the wharf, he saw a line of small gum trees along the foreshore. He smiled, thinking of home. Home! How he looked forward to being there. Lottie would hopefully still be waiting as she promised.

In Sydney, Jonty's father and grandfather, John and Douglas Evans, were pouring over every newspaper that arrived. One had been delivered in April, and both were horrified at what they were reading. Neither had heard from Jonty since Mr Lamb told them a large box of amethysts and emeralds had arrived with a letter saying he was in the Transvaal, so they knew that he was somewhere in the area but not exactly where. They had not heard anything since his arrival in Cape Town months before. Both were extremely worried. Jonty should have been home by now, and they had not been able to find out anything.

Mr Lamb had also been worried, as he had heard nothing except the wire from Mr Field in Antwerp to ask Jonty's expected arrival time, as he was overdue. This did not bode well as Mr Lamb knew how the journey had been arranged. If Mr Field knew nothing, then Jonty must be in trouble. Something was seriously wrong. Eventually, he confided his fears to Jonty's grandfather, Douglas Evans.

The Transvaal wars were discussed and dissected by every paper, and still, no word was heard from Jonty. Every London paper brought more bad news. None gave any hint of Jonty. John pleaded with Luke and Eddie

Lockley to ask the governor if he had heard anything. That, too, drew a blank.

By May, John was almost panicking. Colleen was beside herself. Her eldest son was now considered missing in Africa.

They waited… and waited.

After months of silence, word had finally arrived that the Boers had taken Jonty from the English compound. Then silence again. At least they knew he had been alive in May. Lottie and her family had been to London and back in the time that Jonty was gone. He had not even known of their journey. Lottie had a letter waiting for her return saying he'd arrived safely in Cape Town, but then there was silence.

Rick's old friend, Jack, died soon after Jonty had left. Jack left Rick a surprise in the form of a massive estate in England. Rick had packed up his family, and they had gone to England with Luke, Ellen, Carlo, and Lottie. Luke insisted that his children needed to be presented. They took their cousins, Jem, Margaret, and Molly Saunders, from Bathurst. After nearly a year away, they returned home last December. Lottie was beside herself that she had not heard from Jonty. Nothing, no telegram, no letter and no mention in his parent's mail, just silence.

Luke and Ellen often found her curled up on the settee in their sitting room, just watching out the window. She had no tears, but she was sad. She had even lost her appetite and had consequently lost weight. This was not the Lottie they knew and loved. She was not the bouncing, bubbly girl of old. She was usually the life and soul of any gathering. Now she was almost maudlin. Ellen tried everything to comfort her and to distract her, she was taken to visit her nephew and nieces, but nothing cheered her. If only Jonty would write, but there was silence.

Lottie wished for her own children with Jonty. Where was he? Why had he not written to her?

By the last week of August, Colleen was in tears daily. Her son was still missing.

Finally, news had come through from Pretoria. Word arrived that a Peace deal had been signed in Pretoria, and the troops had been despatched from various ports. The official party had been sent to the port in Mozambique and then to England via Suez. A photo showed Jonty at the signing of the Peace Treaty, and the article said the English contingent had been escorted to the coast. Yet there was still no word from Jonty himself, although the Governor had officially told them that he was still alive. But was he well? No one knew.

A telegram finally came in September that the English were out of the country, and Jonty was with them. He was alive and uninjured. The information came in the form of a longish telegram to the Governor. Then soon after the post office opened the first Monday in September, another telegram was delivered to the Evans' household. Then Douglas arrived at their door waving a letter he had just collected from the postman. Jonty was alive, and he was safe.

The English official party had arrived back in London with the soldiers who had been with Jonty in Pretoria, and they sent word through to the Governor. The second telegram received was that Jonty was safe, well, and now on route to Antwerp. With so few wire depots and Jonty not knowing how to use them as he could not speak Arabic, he asked the officers to send information to his family about his safety. He had posted various letters from Port Said, but they would take weeks to arrive.

On receipt of the news that her son was alive and well, Colleen promptly fainted for the second time in her life. Her firstborn son was alive and well. The only other time she had fainted was when she was expecting him. John was by her side in an instant. When she roused, she turned to John and wept with relief. "He's alive, Jonny, he's alive." She then dissolved into happy tears in his arms.

"Colly, we must give the good Lord praise and thanks." John gave his wife a loving kiss. Now they could relax and wait.

It took three more weeks for Jonty's long letter to arrive from Port Said. He had written it while on the ship. In it, he poured out much of the saga to his parents. He'd left out the atrocities he had seen, what had happened to Nandi, and the trauma and deaths of his friends. They did not need to know what he'd seen happen to the local women. No, he did not wish to distress them. He told them what he termed his kidnapping by the Boers. This brought gasps to his family, and Mr Lamb had been invited around to hear his news. Another letter arrived in Parramatta, as it was hand-delivered; it had been slid under the door at Luke's house; sadly, it slipped under the heavy doormat and had not been found, and there it still lay.

On receipt of their letter, John Evans sent a message to Luke Lockley in Parramatta that Jonty was alive and they had received a long screed.

Word filtered through to the rest of the family. Few had known where he was, only that he was travelling for work. Luke had already told his brother, Wills, what Jonty had told him about the purpose of the journey. Those who found out where he was guessed he'd gone to buy diamonds. Then they heard that he was in the Transvaal, and they fell silent. News from that area was terrible.

It was on receipt of this news that Lottie finally wept in relief. Her father had let on to her some time ago of his refusal to Jonty for her hand. She admitted she already knew as she'd overheard their conversation. Now hearing of the troubles in the Transvaal, Luke was glad he had refused to allow them to marry before he went; she would have wanted to go and would have been caught up in the strife with Jonty.

Sadly this news made her cry harder. "Papa, he's the only man I shall ever love and the only one I will marry. Papa, it's Jonty or no one; I don't want a 'la de dah' titled toff; I just want Jonty."

Luke realised how deeply she felt for the young man whom he'd loved since before his entry into the world on his own wedding day. Like his parents John and Colleen, Jonty was a delight to be with. He often spent weekends at many of the family homes, and over the years, they had come to love him dearly. When Jonty had asked to court Lottie, Luke was delighted, but they kept the news in the family. He hated refusing his request for her hand, but Luke knew that she must be unattached when she was presented to the Queen. He hoped that Jonty would ask again on his return.

October saw Jonty arrive in Antwerp. Mr Field greeted him with great joy. He had recently heard the extent of "the troubles," as he termed them and knew precisely where Jonty was supposed to be and was worried. Jonty was happy to produce the diamonds he had purchased for the old man, which delighted him. Instead of the dozen or so gems he'd hoped for, there were some four hundred and eighty stones. The bag had filled one pocket. Most were top quality, and Jonty included an itemised list of the individual cost of each stone. On the itemised list, Mr Field noted that Jonty had ticks next to them, and some others had crosses. Jonty explained the ticks marked ones he had purchased from the villagers and the crosses from the mines.

Most of the gems were 'A' grade cutters, and as Mr Field sorted through them, his bushy eyebrows wiggled up and down as he focused through his viewing apparatus. He frequently muttered as he checked each stone. "Excellent choice," or "Jonty, this one is perfect," "Chipped but good value," or "I can cut around that."

Jonty's itemised list included what he had paid for each stone, estimated cutting cost, and a resale estimate. This made costing simple; he also said how much was left in the account. He had spent over £900 of the £1000 he had been allocated.

After Nandi's death, he didn't feel the risk was worth it. They were just stones. He explained this to Mr Field and also explained that the children's ones were a little more expensive, as not only were they not from a mine, but the money went totally to their families.

Mr Field was content, as the cost was minimal compared to what he would eventually sell them for. One large one, cut and mounted, would cover the entire cost of the expedition. He had no idea that some mines exploited the workers and decided not to buy from them if possible. Jonty had listed the worst ones. He spent two weeks with his teacher.

Some years before, Jonty had lived with him for six months while learning to cut diamonds. Jonty then stayed with some Lockley cousins in Kent for an extended holiday. Mr Field was so impressed with him that he had allowed him to cleave some very valuable stones. He had not made a single error. Typically, apprenticeships for diamond cutting took years, but Jonty had already had experience before arrival and needed his skill honed. Those six months had done that.

Mr Field also trusted Jonty's eye when it came to selecting stones. He'd seen Jonty view and grade a tray of uncut stones in less than half an hour. He had graded them by eye; no eye loop had been required. On rechecking them, each grading was perfect. Mr Field knew Jonty was the ideal person to send on the buying trip. Neither knew the troubles occurring in the area. Arrangements had been made without a problem. When Jonty arrived many months late but with a bag full of superb gems and related to the conditions he saw, Mr Field was horrified. He was so apologetic to Jonty that he gave him a small bag of sapphires in compensation and the promised £1000 fee. He said to Jonty that he was told that they were from Madagascar and Ceylon.

Jonty quickly tipped them into his hand and gasped. They were the prettiest pink and sky blue gems he'd ever seen. "I can't take these, Mr Field, they are superb, and the colours, I've never seen sapphires of this hue." He fingered through the stones. "I had no idea that sapphires came from Madagascar."

Mr Field had taken a quick look, but he wasn't that interested in sapphires. "I'm not so sure they do, I need an accurate provenance, but that's what the man who sold them to me said. I've not heard of more. I'm not prepared to sell them as such; hence you can have them." He saw that maybe he was a little too hasty to dispose of them before checking them correctly, but he had given them away now and would not take any back. He shrugged and smiled. "You will use them, Jonty; send me two cut ones, and we'll call it square," The bushy, wrinkly old man gave him a toothy grin.

Jonty closed his fist around the superb gems. "I will thank you, Mr Field, but this is quite unnecessary." Jonty spent the last week in Antwerp getting his eye back in and cutting some of the new diamonds. He wanted to see if the quality of the gems was as he expected. He chose a small one with a chip from his own bag to see if hardness was as tough as the Australian Bingara diamonds. He had learned his skill using them and figured that he wished to compare them as he knew the source of these ones. The stone he chose he planned to leave with Mr Field as a swap for the sapphires. Mr Field could sell it immediately to offset costs.

Chapter 5   The Nightmares Begin

At the end of the second week, Mr Field booked his passage home on an Orient Line ship called the *Steam Ship Abergeldie*. It was going through the Suez Canal. It should be in Sydney by late December and was to leave London on October 29th. Jonty had to get to England to catch the ship. It was a short crossing, but the vessel was sure to be crowded with immigrants. His passage across the English Channel to London was calm, and his transit in London onto the *SS Abergeldie* went smoothly. His shared cabin was less luxurious than the passage from Sydney, but the trip was fast. The booking office said it was now only a six-week trip on this luxurious steamship. His expected arrival in Sydney was to be mid to late December. He so hoped Lottie would have waited for him. He needed her so much. Thoughts of her had kept him going.

Jonty made the connection and settled into the cabin, but a few days into the journey, Jonty had his first nightmare. He woke his cabin-mate at some unearthly hour in the morning, dreaming that the Boers were attacking them. Thankfully his cabin mate was a retired soldier. He stood beside Jonty, quietly speaking until Jonty woke. He was shouting in his sleep and in a cold sweat. Paul Murray was just the person Jonty needed. He was kind, caring, and considerate. Jonty had never experienced such horror, and it was only now that the aftermath was hitting him. Jonty would wake sobbing or shouting. Paul would be beside him, talking in a comforting tone. During the days, Paul would take him up on deck, find a quiet spot, and get Jonty to talk through what had occurred. Jonty talked and talked and cried and talked more. He sobbed hard when he related the story of finding Nandi's body. He was still so angry that her innocent life had been stolen from her. Paul listened and let Jonty drink in silence when he didn't feel like vocalising his sorrow. They also prayed together. Jonty had almost forgotten how to do that on his long months on horseback. Prayer alone had been virtually impossible. Paul, too, had seen the horrors of death on a violent platform and experienced gruesome deaths and nightmares. He had had a friend who did what Paul was now doing, encouraging Jonty to tell his story. He knew this would take a long time, but the young man would get through it. For the first few nights, the nightmares were frequent. Paul would be beside him each time he woke. He never got flustered or upset; he would sit and talk to Jonty until he felt he could sleep again.

~

By the time they reached Fremantle at the end of November, the dreams had become less frequent, but still, he woke every few nights seeing the same thing, skeletons killing people. Strange, as, of course, skeletons can't fight! The ship restocked and departed the next day. They should be in Sydney before Christmas, hopefully around mid-December.

Jonty was so excited about getting back home and seeing Lottie. He wondered if these nightmares would continue once at home. Maybe it was just his nerves. He sent a telegraph from Fremantle informing his family of his imminent return.

Passage across the Great Australian Bight was calm this time; no storms and, therefore, no damage to the ship. Melbourne was only a day or so away; from there, he could telegraph his family again. The SS *Abergeldie* fired up the boilers and headed north as she rounded Cape Otway. She slowed and negotiated the shallows with a pilot through the dangerous entrance into Port Philip Bay to Melbourne. Here the vessel would unload most of her immigrant passengers and then proceed to Sydney. Paul was also departing, and Jonty knew he would miss him. The ship was to spend three days in Melbourne, and Jonty thought he might as well look around town while there. As he had the cabin to himself, he didn't wish to be alone. So as Paul left, Jonty followed him down the gangplank. He had been there a couple of times before, and Paul had not, so he showed him where things were. Jonty directed Paul to an excellent place to stay and referred him to Swanston Street, where they waved farewell. He gave Paul his work directions just in case he came to Sydney.

Jonty bought a counter lunch at an inn and purchased some fruit. He had been craving a fresh, crisp apple for ages and was quite surprised that they were as good as they looked. For the next few days, Jonty would be alone. He slept on board at night, where he would have time to gather his thoughts and pray as he'd never prayed before. He prayed for peace.

Finally, they departed Melbourne; Cape Howe passed by in the early morning light. Captain Cromby had all the sails hoisted, and she was now going full steam ahead. He, too, was keen to get to Sydney.

Jonty had woken pre-dawn with a nightmare; rather than go back to bed, he got up and dressed. He stood watching the headland as it faded into the distance.

Captain Cromby came and stood next to him. For a few minutes, they stood in silence. The Captain broke the moment with a strange comment. "It gets easier the more you talk about it. Don't bottle things up, lad; talk it out." Jonty did not realise that he'd been rocking back and forth as he leaned on the railing. Captain Cromby had been a Captain for a long time and had seen war service himself. He had also seen the atrocities of war and knew their lasting effects on dreams. "Jonty, Paul spoke to me after I heard you shouting one night. My cabin is not far from yours. Paul didn't want to say anything, but he knew I had the same experiences. Jonty, Paul is my nephew, or he would not have told me. When you go home, these won't stop. What you have to do is find a way to cope. Find some way to release the emotions. If not, you will start displaying anger; you have a big problem when that occurs. Try to sort it before it gets that far." Captain Cromby laid a caring hand on his shoulder. "Never fear asking for assistance, Jonty. Many have experienced similar to what you have had, but they bottled it up and ended up falling to pieces."

Jonty's haunted expression met the captain's kind face. Jonty's eyes were swimming, the captain's smile visible through his well-trimmed, multicoloured beard. "Thanks, sir; I've never had any trauma in my life before, and I can't deal with it. I can't stop seeing things, even when I'm awake. There was nothing I could do to help anyone. They were dying, and I was useless. In the end, I stopped making new friends because every time I did, they got killed." Jonty filled him in on a little of the situation and things he'd seen. "When the Boers took me from the compound, I thought I was the walking dead, but unbeknownst to me, they'd been watching me since my arrival." He paused, then exploded, "I'm a blooming jeweller! What the hell do I know of war and killing? I knew nothing of the seamier side of life, and I didn't want to learn! When I saw how the children were treated, I chose to buy stones from them over the big companies. I chose to help the poor in the villages. For some reason, those choices saved my life."

The captain squeezed his shoulder in a comforting gesture and asked Jonty to follow him to the wheelhouse to continue their talk. Over the remaining few days, they often talked, hopefully arriving at the point where Jonty thought he was beginning to come to terms with everything. His nights since had been peaceful, and he was looking less haunted. At least the dark circles under his eyes had faded. The *SS Abergeldie* sailed past many familiar landmarks; the Captain tried to interest Jonty in where they were. He gazed at them with glassed eyes, taking in none of the information. He just wanted his old life back; he needed to hug Lottie and hold her close; he ached to tell her he loved her, and above all, he wanted to sleep peacefully again. Long dreamless nights as he used to do. He wanted a hug from his mother like when he was a child and even weep into her shoulder. He wanted his mother to be able to kiss away his pains. Her arms used to comfort him when he hurt as a child. At twenty-four, he was too old even for that. He ached where he had never hurt before.

On the last morning, Jonty was packed and was ready to disembark. He had also sent Lottie word of his return from Melbourne, hoping she would be there to welcome him. He still found it hard to believe he had been gone for over eighteen months. His original plans were for six months maximum.

~

In Sydney, Colleen and John had received notification that the ship should dock late that afternoon. From their house, they could see the tops of the masts in the bay; after luncheon, Colleen stood to watch. At three o'clock, she saw what she was waiting for, ships masts.

She shouted to John, "He's here." The top of the three-masted ship was coming around the point at Mrs Macquarie's Chair. She knew that by the time they reached the wharf, the ship would be still on the tugs, but she grabbed her hat and barely waited long enough for John to accompany her. Others in the house heard her hasty departure and soon followed.

They had sent word to Luke as soon as Jonty's message had arrived, and John hoped that Lottie would be interested enough to come and greet him. He'd not heard back, so he had no idea if they would be there. In a way, he hoped that they could meet more privately. As they were not engaged, any public display of affection could cause problems.

"Colly love, slow down, you'll slip and then where would you be? In hospital instead of in his arms." John took his wife's arm and slowed her pace to a quick walk rather than almost a jog. It was downhill all the way and was an easy journey. John had caught up with Colleen before she was at the end of the block. They saw the ship being turned and pushed to the quayside as they arrived.

"Hurry, Jonny. Hurry! Look, there he is!" She started waving as they walked.

Jonty was at the railings and saw their arrival; his heart leapt with happiness. His eyes searched the small group of others waiting on the quayside, but there were no other familiar faces. She wasn't there. His heart sank. Jonty experienced a flash of sadness but was so glad to be home that he would not think about that now. He would go to Parramatta and meet her there.

As soon as the gangplank was lowered onto the wharf, Jonty ran down in long strides. He gathered his parents into his arms, and tears, of course, flowed from them all. He pulled away from his mother and cupped her face. Then bent and kissed her cheek. Her long black hair was now streaked with grey that had not been there on his departure. Looking at both her and his father, then the other siblings who had finally arrived, he said, "I missed you all so very much."

In reply, they gathered around him and gave him a group hug. He didn't try to hide his tears. He could not have done so anyway. Over the next half hour, his luggage was unloaded and now stood beside him. He owned just two small bags and his hat. The gems still weighed down his pockets. The remaining immigrant passengers were also disembarking, and the cacophony of noise emanating from them was immense. They were about to start the slow walk up the hill when he heard his name shouted by a familiar voice, one he loved so well.

"Joonnnty!" She had come! Typical Lottie, not the quiet, sedate lady-like greeting. No, she was running along the wharf and catapulted into his arms. They were open and ready for her. The smile on his face told the world he was happy to see her. Clinging together in front of everyone, he buried his head into her neck and breathed in her familiar violet scent.

"Oh gosh, Lotts, sorry! I shouldn't hold you like that; we are not engaged or anything." He gently pushed her away.

"You can fix that with one question, Jonty. I think you know the answer; I have already told Father," Although she wept with happiness, her face shone with joy.

A tear ran down her cheek, and he bent and gently kissed it away, then fell to one knee in front of everyone. "Charlotte Elizabeth Lockley, will you make me the happiest man on earth and consent to be my wife?"

"Yes, yes, of course, I will; now kiss me, you wonderful man." She was pulling him up and again stepped into his arms.

Jonty did. A cheer went up from the watching crowd, and then they broke into applause. The kiss was no quick peck on the lips but a deep, passionate, emotion-stirring embrace. This was the kiss that Jonty had been dreaming about for many months.

When Jonty could finally control his raging emotions, he merely said, "I love you so much, I only survived with thoughts of how to get back to you. They kept me sane." He finally noticed a tall man standing next to her with his arms folded and a single raised eyebrow. He saw Luke was smiling, though.

Luke said, "As you actually proposed in front of all these people and kissed her, you have totally compromised her, so I suppose I now have to allow you to marry her." Luke's tone should have sounded angry, but the smile on his face and the glint in his eyes belied his words.

"Oh, Uncle Luke, I'm so sorry." He hastily let Lottie go. "I know you said 'no' when I asked before, and I know your reasons. My emotions got the better of me. I will abide by your wishes if you insist."

Luke chuckled, "Well, I'm not going to; she's been to London, done the right things and rejected every suitor we thrust in her way. She is overly obsessed with some jeweller she knows. Congratulations to you both; now let us go where we can have some privacy, eh? I'll give you two some much-needed time together." He turned to John and Colleen. "John, can we gate-crash? We have just arrived on the ferry, and it was late. It was much easier when they came into the wharf next to this one."

John's grinning face assured Luke they were happy. "Absolutely, Luke, we'd be delighted." Luke and John each took one of Jonty's bags. They walked to a waiting carriage. No passengers had required transport to the King's Arms Hotel, so Luke asked the driver if he'd drop off the suitcases at the Evans household in Pitt Street before returning to the hotel. The Lockley family had a standing arrangement with the King's Arms to use the carriage. "It's sometimes handy having an Earl as a brother," Luke laughed as the carriage drove off.

Jonty hooked Lottie's arm through his and set off with the family group to the Pitt Street house.

Lottie was skipping with excitement. Her glorious blonde curls bounced with every step, and her sky-blue eyes were dancing and bright with happiness. Her rosebud lips spread wide with a joyous smile. Her joy was contagious, and soon everyone was laughing. Her dark moods of the past months were well and truly gone.

No one spoke of Africa or the trip that would come later. Now was the time to celebrate.

On the walk up to the house, Jonty discovered that Rick's swagman friend Jack had died shortly after his own departure and that the family had been to London and back in the intervening time. He was able to catch that Jack had been a titled Baron and bequeathed his estate to Rick. He, in turn, had transferred it to his cousin Teddy, as Viscount Edward Lockley, and the new estate would become the Earl of Coxheath's new principal Seat.

The group had returned a year ago, and Lottie had been frantic as she'd not heard from Jonty since his safe arrival in Cape Town. She had not known of Jonty's danger in South Africa until her return, and then all there was, was silence; she had been beside herself with worry. Then early in December, the wire arrived from Fremantle and another from Melbourne. The message told her of his imminent arrival, which made her put her foot down to her father. "I'm going to see him, and I'm going to marry him, Father," she had said when she received the first wire.

Luke explained to Jonty while laughing, "She forced my hand, you know, lad. She said she was coming even if she had to come alone." He saw Jonty's surprised look.

"Lotts, that's not the done thing, love," Jonty gently chastised her but really didn't mind; his heart was singing.

"I wasn't going to miss today for anything, Jonty. I missed you so much." She beamed at her true love. "I behaved in London; I did all the official stuff they wanted me to do. I strutted in front of the Queen, made my curtsy, walked backwards in a satin train without tripping, and rejected every stuffed, frilly-shirted, frocked-coated man and title they threw at me. None stood a chance next to you." She glanced at her father, who was smiling at her words. "I just wanted my jeweller."

Luke's eyes twinkled with mischief, "It's true, Jonty, she rejected how many proposals, love? Nine?" Luke asked.

"No, it was twelve, Papa. I didn't tell you about the three gentlemen over sixty who proposed, sorry Papa, but I just laughed in their faces and walked off. Rude, I know, but I'm no pretty wife to be left in a castle and breed children." She had the courtesy to look a little guilty. "Grandfather's speech is still causing ripples, and everyone thinks they can weasel in on my good side because they have a title. Stuff that! Sorry, Father, Aunty Colleen, Uncle John, but I can't be bought," she grinned. "I'd already given my heart; Father knew that. But Jonty, I had to go and do the official stuff. Well, it's done, and I'm back." She gave a skip of happiness. "And, Jonty love, now I'm taken too, all yours, warts and all."

Jonty was over the moon. His heart was still pounding. With all the bad things that had happened, now this. With her beside him, he could cope with almost anything. He knew he would have to tell her what happened, but not yet. Today was one of joy and happiness. He was home, and she was his, well, almost.

On arrival, the family had piled into the Evans' sitting room; John remembered another return many years before, that of his father. This room witnessed that and many more joyful events over the years. His father had also gone missing for eighteen months and returned to them after being shipwrecked, imprisoned in Japan, and stuck in China. His father's return home had signalled his last voyage as a sea captain.

John stood looking at his children; they had greeted their brother like he had welcomed his missing father. They all had tears of joy and listened to Jonty's re-telling of some of his stories. Of course, he edited it for the younger one's ears. Little Cara was now seven and had claimed his lap. She just wanted to hug him. "Don't go away again, Jonty; I don't like you leaving me."

"That goes for all of us, son," his mother added. She could not tear her eyes from his smiling face. He was home and safe.

Once tea had been served and the hubbub of excitement had died down, Jonty asked Luke if he could take Lottie into his father's study for a private welcome home.

Luke nodded. "Respect her, son."

Jonty replied, "Of course," and escorted her out.

The office door was barely closed behind them before she was in his arms. She had thrown herself at him, and he caught her. She was giggling. He had lifted her into his arms and swung her around. "I can't believe I am allowed to kiss you and hold you like this. I've dreamed about doing this for so very long." He lowered his head and kissed her, intending to hold her and sit on the settee talking.

She wrapped her arms around his neck and very immodestly jumped and wrapped her legs around him while he held her. He was holding her behind in his hands and was blushing. "Lotts, love... this is... so not proper," he murmured while returning her many kisses. His body's reaction to her was immediately apparent to them both.

She didn't move as he expected; she shuffled closer. "I missed you... so much... Jon Jon," she whispered between kisses. Her ardent response was unexpected. Her enthusiastic reaction to him blew him away.

He had never kissed this way before. When she opened her mouth to his, and her tongue slipped between his lips and slid over his teeth, he almost lost all control. He groaned; Uncle Luke's instruction 'respect' ran through his mind as he overbalanced and sank onto the settee with her still clinging to him. Lottie's legs were still wrapped around him when he fell; he again pulled her closer. She was now sitting, straddling him and returning kiss for kiss.

Barely taking time to breathe, she murmured, "I should move Jon Jon, but I'm so comfortable." She giggled, then wiggled closer, her cleavage now just at his eye level. "I can't believe that Father is allowing us to marry."

Her kisses sent pulses of desire shooting through him, his blood pumping into his nether regions to the point that his trousers were now uncomfortably tight. She hoisted her skirts as they were tight around her legs and settled herself on his lap in a very unladylike manner.

What Jonty wanted to do and what he knew he should do, were vastly different things. As she moved her skirts, her breasts bobbled in her gown. He groaned with desire. He should move her from his lap, but she was right; he could hold her close and kiss her. They were engaged, and Uncle Luke had permitted for him to be with her. He loved her so much, and her passionate response to him did not disappoint. She was everything his dreams of her had promised. He couldn't resist; he bent and kissed the top of her breasts.

Lottie was never one to be backward in voicing her desires. She was the ringleader of fun in the family; Carlo was often not far behind her. But what occurred next stunned him. She was as keen to touch him as he was to fondle her tantalising breasts. He caressed them through her gown, and she leaned back a little so he could enjoy her.

Her hands fell to his waist. She felt the swelling in his trousers. Before he realised, she had released the top button on his trouser flap and pulled the cord from the confining fabric of his drawers too. As that was all that was holding him in, he was now fully exposed. Still, neither realised the complete danger of what they were doing. Both were innocent of the intimacies between a man and a woman. Neither realised how strong the desires of the body were. He pulled her to him and lifted her to kiss her breasts. She pulled herself up and moved a little closer; she leaned forward and once again kissed him, long, deep, passionate kisses almost sucking the life from each other's lips.

His angle, too, had changed, and before he realised their danger, she settled back on his lap. Jonty did not know that she wore split undergarments; many ladies no longer followed this fashion, and he thought she would have full bloomers and had not stopped when he had felt resistance.

The next moments irrevocably changed their lives. Their actions progressed far too quickly, and only moments later, Jonty begged his forgiveness. "Oh, Lottie, darling one, I had not intended that to occur. I'm so sorry." Jonty buried his face in her neck, almost weeping with anger at himself.

She was still clinging to him.

He lifted her off his lap, and they both readjusted their clothing. Neither had experienced such intimacies before. Noticing a smear of blood, he asked, "Lotts, is this from your monthly flow?" praying it would be.

"No, Jonty, that was two weeks ago," she explained softly.

He groaned. Long ago, his father had told him how a woman's monthly flow worked. Having a father who worked at the museum meant his knowledge of science was vast. Jonty realised she was mid-cycle.

"Jon Jon, we've just preempted our vows. I love you and had the choice to stop; I instigated it, but I didn't intend it to happen. I just wanted to touch you." She apologised, as did he. "I don't want to wait long to get married anyway." She had thoroughly enjoyed the amazing feeling they had just experienced. "Can we marry by Special Licence? I don't want any big hoo-har sort of wedding. I want to be married to you."

Because he loved her deeply, Jonty was gutted. "Of course, Lottie, my darling one. I'm so truly sorry about this. I don't even have anywhere we can live; I have not even had time to think of those things. I haven't even been up to my room yet, but I'll get on to it this week. I need to sort accommodation for us at least, but if anything comes of, well, this, I mean, us together today, you know what I mean if you miss your flow, you know, a child." He stumbled over his words. "Tell me soon, love. Let me know, either way, my sweet." He was flustered. "We'll get married as soon as I can arrange it anyway, I promise. I'll try to get a Special Licence this week if I can, but no matter what happens, we'll call the Banns and marry as soon as possible; I don't want to wait either, even if this had not occurred. I need to be with you; I find that being alone is not, well… I'm finding it difficult; however, I'll tell you about that later. We may have to stay here with my parents and grandparents for a while, though."

"I really, truly don't care where we live, Jonty," she leaned over and kissed him again. She passionately kissed him and evoked a guttural groan. "Cor Lottie, give me a chance. If you do that, I'll take you again, and I don't want to, at least not until we're married." Jonty was fighting to get control again. His usual self-control had fled along with his quiet equilibrium.

She attempted to look hurt. "Sorry, Jon Jon... well, no, I'm not really, it felt nice. So nice that I can't wait for it to happen again. So get everything arranged quickly." She had already pulled down her skirts, carefully ensuring she didn't get any blood on her frock. She had not intended for things to go so far. She had planned to touch him. She had never seen that part of a man before. She had noticed that sometimes in London, some of her partners would find their trousers became tight when she was with them. She understood a little of why this occurred to them. Therefore, Lottie had thought his crushed bulge must hurt, cramped as it was in his trousers and her sitting on him. With her split drawers, the next step had just happened by accident. Even the initial moment of pain wasn't too bad. She knew she should feel guilty for what had just happened, but she didn't.

A Marquess had kissed her at a ball in London. The fifty-year-old man, whom she considered elderly, had asked her into the garden. She had refused to *step* anywhere with him. He made her feel so uncomfortable. He continued to haunt her every move. Lottie thought that the only way to make him leave her alone was to give in to him partially. She had agreed to go onto the balcony but stay within sight of the door, thinking she would be safe enough there. No sooner were they outside than he drew her into his arms and kissed her. He thrust his tongue into her mouth so far she thought she had swallowed it. She pushed him away from her and vomited down his front. She had been disgusted, and he tasted vile. He had to retire for the evening; however, he never bothered her again.

However, at a later ball, a younger handsome beau had been far more gentle and showed her how enjoyable a kiss could be. She knew she should not have allowed him such freedom, but it, too, had been unexpected and had only occurred once. The slap she gave him made sure of that.

When she heard her father refuse Jonty, she was angry. Allowing a man to kiss her in London had been her form of rebellion, but it had gone no further. She and Jonty should have been wed for eighteen months by now. She was now looking forward to marrying him even more now than before. She loved him so very much. She just hoped it wouldn't take long.

They realised they had been in the office for only about ten minutes. So much had happened. They now sat beside each other, discussing their forthcoming nuptials, and Jonty asked if Lottie was serious about a Special Licence.

"Yes, Jon Jon, absolutely! I don't want to wait. Even if nothing occurs from today." Her pleading reinforced his determination.

Somewhat relieved, Jonty said, "Fine, I'll get things sorted as soon as possible, I promise. I can hardly keep my hands off you anyway." He leaned over and kissed her again. "I need you so much, Lotts. I have much to tell you, but we have no time now. I dare not stay here longer, sweetheart; the consequences are dire enough as is."

Guilt about what they had just done consumed Jonty; they eventually returned to the family. They walked with their hands entwined. Just before they entered the room, Jonty drew her into his arms, kissed her again, and said, "I'll sort things as soon as I can, I promise."

"Jon, I should know in two weeks if I miss my courses; I'm normally spot on time," she whispered. She reached up and kissed his cheek. "I do love you, Jon Jon."

"I love you too, my sweet darling." Jonty quickly kissed the tip of her nose. He opened the door and ushered her into the rest of the family.

Only his parents, grandparents, and Uncle Luke remained.

"Ready to leave, poppet?" Luke asked his daughter.

"Yes, Papa, we were just talking about weddings." She looked at Jonty and smiled, "Do I have to have the whole hoo-har of a fancy wedding? Can't we marry by Special Licence? You know me, I'm not into that sort of thing."

Luke grinned. "You, my darling girl, are a dream daughter, you can have what you wish, but you must let Jonty settle first. He has not been back a full day yet." He met Jonty's look and wondered. It almost looked like guilt. She, however, looked like the cat who got the cream. Although they were grown up and now officially engaged, Luke knew that they were also young, and he knew the temptations of youthful passion. He hoped nothing had occurred, but he would get them married as soon as possible if it had. He thought mayhap a Special Licence would be good for this couple. "Jonty, your father told me that one of Andrew Lenehan's cottages is vacant. His own cottage, actually, as he has moved back in with his brother Michael."

Jonty spun around to his father. "Truly, Father, can we live there? That is splendid!" Delight flooded his face.

John smiled. He had hardly been able to say a word to his son since his arrival. "Yes, son, Andrew has gone, and the end cottage is vacant. It's even furnished and ready for occupation."

"Love? Interested in seeing it? It's on the way down to the ferry," Jonty asked his fiancé.

Joy showed on her face. "Yes, absolutely, Jon Jon, it sounds perfect, but then a tent would be too. I will love it no matter what it looks like, as long as you are there too." Her hooded eyes gave away the desire she was feeling for him. Her father saw her look, and he glanced at Jonty.

It mirrored her own. Jonty wished they were already married. Yes, they had already preempted their vows, but they were committed to each other. He just hoped there would not be a baby from their actions. He swallowed his surging desire and said, "Good, then let's go and see it on the way down to the ferry." He just wanted to carry her up to his room.

The group departed and strolled down to the row of semi-detached cottages. Each had three bedrooms and a large backyard. Jonty's parents had bought the entire row of attached cottages from Andrew Lenehan soon after Jonty was born. Andrew had been declared bankrupt after various clients had refused to pay their accounts. As they were friends, John had given one of the cottages for him to use for life. Andrew had stayed there for over twenty years. John unlocked the door and stood aside while everyone entered. He pulled a cord, and the lights in the corridor flicked on. They spent half an hour wandering through the cottage and found that Andrew had left most of his furniture there. The garden was overgrown, and John said he would send someone down to clean it up. They only needed household linen, food, and tools; nearly everything else was in situ. Colleen and Jonty's grandmother, Caro, who had come with them, said they had many things the young couple could have.

By the time the group locked the door and walked down to the wharf, Jonty was content that they now had somewhere to live. Lottie was excited. Clinging tightly to his arm the entire way down to the jetty, she chatted happily about their forthcoming future.

Luke invited Jonty to join them for Christmas, and with a somewhat nervous glance at his parents, who both nodded, he accepted.

The following week Jonty had much to arrange.

Chapter 6   Interesting Conditions

$\mathcal{I}$t took Jonty a week before he could get an appointment to see the Bishop for a Special Licence. Once he had it, he tried to find a suitable date for them to marry. As it was the week before Christmas, and all the clergy were franticly busy with Christmas services, no one was available. Frustrated, Jonty left a day early to talk to Uncle Luke in Parramatta about the wedding. But more than anything, he wanted to be with Lottie as soon as possible. No, he needed to be with Lottie and the entire Lockley family. It would be her last Christmas at home for a while. It was getting on for two weeks since their afternoon interlude, and she had not yet let him know if she had her monthly flow. Maybe she was expecting already. His heart was racing as the ferry pulled into the wharf. She was standing, waiting and waving to him. Some of her first words confirmed his supposition.

"Hello, darling fiancé." She glanced around to see how close her father was. "Jonty, I should have had my monthly flow three days ago; they didn't come," she whispered as she stepped into his arms. "I'm so sorry." She looked up at him to see what his reaction was. She whispered, "But I love you so much, Jon Jon."

He nodded, smiled, kissed her cheek and said, "I love you too, Lotts. Never mind, I have the Licence and just need a Minister to do the deed." He patted his pocket as he pulled away from her.

"Can I come to Sydney during the week and get it done secretly? I could tell Mama I needed some fabric. I could bring your Aunt Shauna with me," she whispered. With their hands clasped, they still had their heads together, talking privately and not seeing the look her father gave them.

Luke pursed his lips and watched their body language. They were a little too touchy-feely for a couple recently engaged. From how they stood, he presumed things went too far on the day Jonty arrived home. Eventually, they turned and walked towards Luke.

Jonty saw him. "Hello, Uncle Luke." A look of guilt on his face answered Luke's fears.

Luke groaned but said, "Hello to you too, young sir. Come, both of you, we need to talk. Lottie, behave, and please, stop pawing him in public, will you." Luke didn't wait for an answer from either of them. He strode off to his house further up the road. He was not happy. He held the door on arrival and said, "Office, now, both of you!"

They both realised he had probably worked out what had happened. They looked at each other with raised eyebrows and mouthed 'sorry'. They went in meekly.

Luke got straight to the point. "Sit down, both of you." He turned to the window, and he stood looking outside. He was seething and trying hard to control his anger. Eventually, he turned. "I'm guessing that, um, the situation of your welcome got somewhat carried away? Am I right, Jonty?" Neither answered, but the looks they gave each other spoke volumes. "I thought so! Has this happened before?" Luke took a deep breath. "Are you with child, Lottie? Is that what you were telling Jonty?"

She nodded, then said, "No, Papa, it hasn't happened before. It really was an accident, and yes, I think I may be expecting, but it's very early. I'm a few days late, and I'm not usually. Jonty has a Special Licence, and we want to be married anyway. We wanted to before, but you wouldn't let us."

"Lotts, careful, that's not polite," Jonty knew she was right but thought she was being rude to her father. They were in the wrong, not Uncle Luke. "I'm so sorry, sir, I've let you both down." Jonty felt he'd let them all down.

"Don't blame Jonty, Father; I started it," Lottie jumped in; she would defend him to the hilt.

Somehow Luke didn't doubt that she had; she was so different from her mild-mannered sisters. "I'm not exactly blaming either of you, these things do happen, but we have to deal with this quickly. It's only two weeks, and that can be explained away. If I came with you now, we could speak to Reverend Gunther; he might do the deed now. Do you have the Licence on you, son?"

Jonty nodded, pulled it out and handed it to Luke.

Luke perused the document. "You'll need two witnesses, so I'll go and get Ellen. If we are your witnesses, no one will say anything. I'm not exactly disappointed with you, but... damn it, yes, I am, at both of you." He groaned, barely suppressing his rage. "Jonty, the last words I said to you as you left the room were 'respect her,' and now this has happened. It's just as well that she's a 'no-frills' sort of girl. Yes, I should have let you marry her when you asked me before you left, but she needed to be presented. Lottie, I know you will not be innocent in this either, young lady; I know you too well." Luke dared not look at either of them. He took the document and said, "Stay here and keep your hands off each other for a while if you can." He left and closed the door after him. His face was unreadable, and his anger had settled somewhat. His footsteps faded as he walked down the hall.

"I'm sorry, Jonty. I feel now I've pressured you into this." She let a tear spill from her now glassy eyes.

"Oh, Lotts, my darling love, don't! I want you any which way I can. If you are in an interesting condition, then we'll have to prepare a little quicker than we'd planned." He gathered her into his arms for a belated welcome kiss. They were unable to keep their hands off each other after all. She only pulled out of his arms as she heard footsteps returning down the timber floor of the corridor. They were standing apart innocently as Luke ushered Ellen into the room.

Her mother opened her arms to her daughter expecting tears. "Lottie, dear one, are you sure?" Her concern was met with a beaming smile, no guilt or guile at all, just a look of adoration towards Jonty.

"No, I don't know, Mama, but I'm normally on time, and I'm three days late. Yes, yes, I know we shouldn't have, but we did, and we want to get married as soon as we can anyway. That stands, even if I'm not with child. You know me, act first, think later. Silly, I know, but I love Jonty; I always have and want to be with him. I don't care how." She glanced at Jonty. "And seriously, Mama, it wasn't an intentional act, by the way, and no, it's never happened before."

Luke stood just inside the closed door and leaned on it. "I thought if we saw Reverend Gunther now, he might marry them immediately. We would be witnesses, Ellen."

Ellen met Luke's sad look. She could see the disappointment written all over it. "I think that would be best, don't you, my love?"

Lottie looked at Jonty. "Jon Jon?"

"I'd be honoured, Uncle Luke." He was slightly upset his parents would not be there, but this was the bed he'd made, and now he'd face the consequences. If the only drawback were his lack of parents at his wedding, he'd cope with that. House, work, and money were all sorted. He could be a father in about September, if not late August unless Lottie had twins. "Cor, Lotts, I've just realised you're a twin, and they run in the family; what if you have them, and they come really early?"

Ellen jumped in. "We'll cross that bridge later. Let's get you two married first." Ellen said. Her triplets were born only eight months after they married. But as Luke had not been around prior to that, as he, along with Jonty's parents and Reverend William Clarke, had been on an expedition together, there had been no breath of scandal. Thankfully this situation was similar. All the family also knew they had been courting before his departure.

They had made no secret of the relationship.

Before they left for the church, Jonty remembered the rings. He drew out a small velvet bag from his pocket and tipped the contents on his palm. He slid one ring back into the bag and pocketed it again. He took Lottie's hand and slipped on the engagement ring. "You said you loved sapphires, sweetheart, so I made this for you." As he slid the five-stoned ring into place, he kissed her hand.

"Oh, Jon Jon, it's perfect. What are those stones, though?" She asked.

Jonty explained. "The central blue stone is a sapphire I found in Bingara last holiday we went on. The diamonds on either side are from Africa from my trip, and the lighter blue ones are sapphires from Ceylon. They are much lighter than ours."

It was now two days before Christmas, which would be on a Monday this year. Jonty had arrived early, hoping to get things sorted, even possibly married, before the rest of the family were due to come from everywhere the next day.

The three Lockleys and Jonty casually walked up to St John's Church and sought out Reverend Gunther.

Luke didn't explain more than that they wished to marry without the usual family palaver. Knowing what a Lockley family wedding commonly involved, the days of cooking required, and some two hundred guests, Luke meant it. That part of their marriage he was thrilled about. Lottie had always said she didn't want all the fuss.

Being very well-read, Reverend Gunther knew of the wars in the Transvaal. Luke had also confided in him about Jonty being missing over there. If the experiences he had heard about in Africa involved Jonty, it was enough reason to be willing to do the service then and there. So he did.

By the time the four of them walked home less than an hour later, Jonty and Lottie were married. Jonathon Evans and Charlotte Lockley were entered in the marriage register as wed. They signed where directed. Jonty had brought the wedding ring with him, just in case. He had made both for her. The engagement ring fitted her perfectly. He produced a wedding band from his fob pocket at the right time in the service. He was now pleased he had come prepared. He gave her a chaste kiss when they were pronounced man and wife and smiled at her disappointment. "Later," was all he whispered.

Her fingers clenched tightly in his. He was her husband. She looked up at him adoringly. "I love you."

"I know! I love you too." Jonty smiled down at his new wife. He adored her. He just kissed the tip of her nose.

Reverend Gunther didn't give a sermon or say any other words of enlightenment. He knew he would see them in church both tomorrow and at Christmas. He encouraged them to pray daily and that he was available if they needed to talk about anything. Once the register was signed, he gave them a hastily written marriage certificate; the four were congratulated. They thanked him and walked out.

Luke and Ellen followed the newly married couple back home. It was only three blocks away. The conversations between each couple were the same.

Jonty had his hand firmly sitting on Lottie's, which was resting on his arm. They were talking about the possibility of becoming parents. They decided not to say anything to any of the family for at least three months, as even if she was expecting now, she could still lose it. Everything had been such a rush. He still had no time to say anything about his time in The Transvaal. He knew that he would have too soon, and as the rest of the family would arrive later, tonight would be a good time to do so. Luke had said Ellen's elderly parents were to go to Charlie's for dinner. Carlo was out, and it would just be the four of them tonight. He would wait until his Aunt Shauna had taken their meal back to their quarters. He asked Lottie to walk a little slower. "I need to ask your parents about something, sweetie." He spoke as they caught up to them. "Uncle Luke, Aunt Ellen, I wish to say I am sorry and thank you for allowing us to marry so quickly. I have not had a chance to tell any of you what happened in Africa, and I need to. It will explain, well, not this, but much. I was wondering if after dinner I could tell you all at once. I need to get it aired." He turned to Lottie. "I also need to warn you so that you know I have been waking with nightmares."

"Oh, Jon Jon, why didn't you say anything?" She said with such compassion, "Tell us how we can help, my love."

"I don't really know myself. That's part of my problem. I haven't had time to work things through, Lotts," Jonty said quietly. "I came early to tell you all, but this is even better. I just needed to be with you, Lotts; I can't be alone at the moment. Nights are the worst."

Luke looked at Jonty with a new understanding. He had obviously had a terrible time over there. "We'll have tea in the sitting room after dinner and have a talk then, Jonty," Luke said. He did love the lad like another son. Luke had since he saw him moving in his mother's stomach. But the disappointment he felt was profound, both with Lottie and Jonty. That bed was well and truly made; they were now married. They both knew that it was their behaviour he disapproved of, not them. He loved them both dearly.

The dinner passed with a peaceful conversation about Jonty's gems. He spoke of the amethysts and emeralds, but not diamonds, other than to say the trip was successful for Mr Field. He also spoke about his visit to Antwerp afterwards. His Aunt Shauna departed for the evening to her family, and the four retired to the sitting room.

A feeling of amazement settled on Luke. Yet nothing at all was said about the situation in Africa at all. That in itself spoke volumes; Jonty had already admitted to nightmares. From what Luke read in the newspapers about the atrocities, he knew that Jonty must have been exposed to some traumatic horrors. He hoped he didn't share too much about the horrific things he'd seen.

Ellen brought in a pot of tea and set it on the table. She poured and handed round mugs of the traditionally sweet solid brew. Jonty smiled; Earl's family or not, there were no delicate tiny porcelain cups in this house. He took the large mug and cupped it in his hands, looking hard into the sweet dark fluid.

Once everyone had their tea and was settled, Jonty started with the saga of his journey. He briefly outlined the voyage, his views of Cape Town and the journey north to The Transvaal. "You should have heard about that in my first letter." He skimmed over the early part of the trip until he reached the gift of Chimbu. That story brought a smile to all their faces. Then he got to November the year before; he stood and walked to the window, taking a breather before continuing.

The story unfolded as though Jonty was almost telling it as it had occurred to another person. Looking into the blackness outside, he said, "I was supposed to have already left there in October. I delayed my departure because of Chimbu, and the soldiers couldn't be spared as an escort. So then I found I was stuck. By November, I was almost frantic to get out as the troubles worsened. When a platoon or battalion or whatever they call them eventually did leave, it took only a few days before a few survivors straggled back, bloodied and gory, telling of the absolute massacre and those who didn't die were attacked by the Boers. I would have died if I had gone with them. This was merely one of the various skirmishes. I couldn't and wouldn't fight; therefore, I had nowhere to go, so I decided to work in the clinic for the wounded. I had no medical skills but took the water and held things for the doctors. As the soldiers died, I held their hands, praying with them. Even my faith was tested." He coughed, trying not to weep at the faces and memories. He recounted the next few months, keeping the gruesome details to a minimum, and that he had been sleeping in a windowless storeroom for safety's sake.

Luke was pleased he skipped over the macabre events he witnessed; he presumed there was far more.

As Luke discovered later, there was. However, Jonty only filled them in about the poor starving children and the abuse of the villagers. Jonty took a deep breath and continued. "I was stuck in the compound for months; Chimbu was gone by now. For exercise, I would walk around the outside perimeter of the garrison; one by one, the escorts attending me were being shot. I never was and was an easy target, but I realised I could no longer walk anywhere without endangering others. Someone always died, and I was responsible. So, I now have their deaths on my conscience, too." He sobbed, and his tears fell unheeded.

Lottie wanted to go to him, she started to rise, but he motioned for her to stay where she was. "There were now few soldiers left I could call a friend, as, for a good reason, none were prepared to befriend me, let alone be seen in conversation with me in public; admittedly, they were swamped preparing for whatever fight was next. Weeks, then months passed in much the same way; by June, the English had lost every battle they had been in, and they had almost surrendered by then. And me…?" Jonty sniffed. "The English soldiers saw me as a burden. Eventually, I was a liability, and I was handed over to the Boers." He went and knelt before Lottie. "Darling Lotts, I was so scared. They had massacred so many soldiers and every one of my friends." He looked her in the face, desperate for her to understand. A single tear slid down his cheek.

She placed a hand on his face and wiped it away but didn't interrupt. Looking her in the eyes but speaking loud enough for Luke and Ellen to hear, he said, "I could not believe it; the English just handed me over; I felt like I was thrown away like rubbish. The enemy leader, a Boer named Paul Kruger, was the only one who could speak reasonable English, or at least, the only one who admitted he could. After the initial instructions, he only spoke to me once. Kruger had pointed to me and told me to follow him. I was too darned, scared not to do as he said. He explained why they took me. It was because I had shown kindness to the children and locals. After that brief conversation, I spoke to no one for the next months. All communication was now through hand signs. I learned three Afrikaans words, yes was *ja*; no was *geen*, and food was *kos*. Water is the same in both languages. I was put on a horse and told to follow them. By now, we were well outside the compound. I knew a dark-coloured lion had been seen shadowing us the day before, so running was not an option. We were heading north into the wild country with vicious animals all around me: lions, cheetahs, elephants, giraffes, wildebeest and, well, many other man-eating beasts, and don't mention the snakes; over there, more died from their bites than even here. They have one called a Black Mamba. It's a cross between a brown snake and a black one, only the inside of its mouth is black. They are as deadly as a brown," he shuddered. His head dropped as he thought back to that trek.

"A week into the trip, I heard a lion attack the back of the column, but thankfully I didn't see anything, but I heard a shot. Was I scared? Oh, you bet!" He moved and sat on the settee next to Lottie, gathering her into his arms. He lifted her chin and stroked her cheek. He was looking directly into her face again. "Every morning I woke, Lotts, I praised God I had lived through another night. Sweetheart, it was my thoughts of you that kept me going. I was so worried that you did not know where I was." Jonty paused, gathering his thoughts. He gently kissed her, forgetting her parents were watching.

Again none interrupted.

Ellen softly wept as she listened. Luke drew her to him to give comfort. He, too, was becoming emotional. Under his breath, he whispered, "Oh, Jonty!" Ellen heard him and squeezed his hand.

Jonty took a deep breath and continued. He released Lottie, giving her a brief kiss, and got up and paced around the room again, continuing to speak as he walked. "When we arrived in Pretoria, I was dragged in at gunpoint to witness the official signing of the Peace Treaty. I have no idea why they thought they needed a gun or six; maybe it was just for show for the English. Once it was done, I was handed back to the British again, not that they wanted me. Well, sort of, as we were all told we had to march for another month to the coast as Pretoria is landlocked. Again I was given a horse, a sick-looking beast this time, and the unarmed English soldiers surrounded me; the officers were mounted too, and we were surrounded by walking troops who, in turn, were surrounded by armed Boers. I didn't mind that so much, as that meant there were many bodies between the lions and me riding in the middle. At night the English soldiers told me of more gruesome attacks on their march to Pretoria. Again, more of them died from snake bites and others from hunger. The stories of the animals' attacks were graphic. I freely acknowledge that by then, I was so scared of being eaten alive, I was happy to be in the centre of everyone." He shivered. "Lottie, my darling, knowing I was heading home to you gave me strength. I would have collapsed in fear and hunger otherwise. Sometimes when I was stuck in the compound, I was almost paralysed with fear, thinking that I would never see you again."

Again, he paused, thinking back to the march to freedom. The silence stretched for a minute or so, but the listeners knew not to interrupt.

He shook his head to scare away those thoughts. His eyes fixed on Lottie's, and he smiled. "My horse went lame halfway to the coast, and from then on, I said to myself, every step I took was one step closer to you. That march was demanding as there was not enough food, and we could not obtain much *en route*. By the time we arrived, we had lost a few more to starvation, exhaustion, and five to the attack of animals like a snake bite. We were marched straight down to the waterfront at Lourenço Marques in Mozambique and loaded onto a Portuguese ship." He took a deep breath and, still addressing Lottie, said, "I stood at the railing as we sailed out of the harbour. Trust me, Lotts, I shed more than a tear or two. Some nights I wept like a baby on that ship. The relief was overwhelming. Somehow I had escaped." He had returned to sit next to Lottie. "From there, we went up the Suez Canal and to Port Said. I had the captain send telegrams to Father and Mr Lamb, and I posted my letters home reporting my survival. That was the long one I sent you, my lovely one." He saw a puzzled look on Lottie's face.

Lottie said softly, "I didn't get a letter, Jon Jon. At least, not since the one you sent me on your arrival in Cape Town. It came just after we left. So I didn't get that until I returned home." She looked to her father, who shook his head.

A perplexed look crossed Jonty's face. He knew his parents' letter had arrived. That was a mystery that needed further investigation. He shook his head and shrugged. "I don't know how much had been reported in the papers, but I can guarantee that none of the atrocities ever made it into print, they were too gruesome to write about, but I won't go into that. Trust me; you don't want to know. From there, I went to Antwerp and handed Mr Field his stones. If I had not been nearly there, I would have turned tail and returned home as soon as possible. I had sewn the gems into the pockets of my trousers at the English compound. I didn't trust anyone with my bags, as they ended up out of sight for most of the journey. I'm still amazed they didn't get lost. Mr Field was pleased with what I had bought him and arranged my passage home. When I was safe aboard the homebound ship, the nightmares started in earnest."

Ellen and Lottie gasped again.

Luke said, "Jonty, Wills probably forgot to put the letter in with my mail when we returned. I shall ask him if it came." He silently thanked him for not telling the horrific details of his experiences. Then he realised the letter would have been sent well after they had arrived home. "Jonty, I want you to know we will all be here for you should you need us. What you have been through is frightful, but be assured you are not alone." He knew there would be much more to the story than what he had just shared. He would ask for some details tomorrow after church, but he did not doubt that Lottie would hear much more tonight. She would need to know nearly everything; he would be here for them both. His anger had now entirely evaporated, although his disappointment remained. Luke now realised the benefits of their quick marriage.

Jonty was going to need help from them all. "Jonty, having told us, I need you to know that you can come to me whenever you need to talk. Lottie will need more information to assist you through the emotional shock of what you have experienced. You know you need to voice your anxieties." He saw Jonty nod. "Jonty, the memories can't be erased, but you will need to be able to learn to cope with them." Luke could tell that Jonty was choked up.

"Thanks, Uncle Luke; on the ship out here, my roommate, Paul Murray, and Captain Cromby were great. I later found out that Paul was the Captain's nephew, and I had a feeling he was placed with me intentionally, but I'm not sure by whom." He gave a half-laugh and said, "Another God incident. When I had the first nightmare, Paul spoke to me quietly and listened as I talked. He, in turn, spoke to his uncle. After talking through things, the bad dreams went from up to twice a night to a few times a week. They are occasional, although I still wake in a cold sweat most nights. My mind just won't let them go."

Lottie was sitting rubbing his hand. She now had to care for this remarkable man, and she had listened and understood her father's wise words. Listen and comfort; she could do that. She also knew they could both speak to her parents. She would do everything she could to help him through this.

"Uncle Luke, Aunt Ellen, Lotts, I wanted you all to know this, as I know Lottie will wish to confide in you both. She will need your support, as I will need hers." With this, he pulled her into his arms and hid his face in her neck. "I'm so sorry, Lotts," he mumbled. "I should have said something before, but there hasn't been time. I need you with me so very much. I find being alone is, well, not good."

Luke knew his anger had melted away soon after Jonty started this story. The best thing for his recovery was to have Lottie beside him. Of course, he was disappointed with how things had begun, but he would stand by the pair of them. Luke took his wife's hand and thumbed a caress on the back of it. "Ellen, we will need to be available often, especially over the next few months. Jonty, your cottage has three bedrooms, so please prepare a room for us, and we will stay when you wish, that is, if you wish. As I know your father well, he'll not cope with this knowledge as well as your mother will."

Jonty's sad face nodded in agreement. "I wish you both to come, Uncle Luke, and often. We'd love for you to feel at home there. Father doesn't ever see the seedy side of life; he seems to live life on a different plane of existence to us mere mortals." He gave a half-laugh. "Mother, on the other hand, knows it all too well. She already knows I have bad nights; she's heard me a few times, but not to the full extent. I don't wish to burden her further."

Luke said, "I agree, Jonty. Don't tell her more than she needs to know. Your absence really disturbed her."

"I know; I could tell from her new grey hair." Jonty was surprised as she always seemed ageless.

The evening conversation turned to the purchase of the stones Jonty had made, the amethysts, emeralds and diamonds, and then to the gift of the Madagascan and Ceylonese sapphires. Luke's haul of gemstones from the original Mineral Survey had netted them a considerable amount, but it was cast into the shadows compared to Jonty's gems. With the cutting and sale of these unparalleled stones, their wealth would last their lifetime. He estimated that once cut, the gems would bring in over £100,000, if not more, and he still had Nandi's diamond.

Lottie hid a yawn; the day had been exciting and exhausting. She had been tired for the last couple of days. She was sleepy but wished to go to bed, though not to sleep. Tonight was their wedding night, and she was to share her room and oversized single feather bed with Jonty for the first time.

Ellen told them to head up to their room, and they would wait up for her parent's return. "I need to explain Jonty's presence and why he is sharing your room, poppet."

While Jonty and Luke were talking, she had taken a moment to ask her mother if it was safe for them to be intimate again if she were expecting. Ellen gave her daughter a quick, if somewhat belated, mother's talk. She warned Lottie to tell Jonty not to wash with soap in his private area as it would burn her.

Lottie was astounded by the depth of information her mother gave her now, as before, she had never even mentioned a man's differences. There would be time for a deeper conversation over the next few days.

Lottie apologised again to her mother, saying, "I truly am sorry, Mama, but it, well, it just happened," Lottie kissed her and said good night.

"At least you are now married, poppet. Enjoy yourself; make it fun, sweetie; it can be wonderful if you do." Ellen kissed her daughter's astounded face. And gave her an almost wicked smile. "They are called the joys of marriage for a reason; make them so," she whispered.

Lottie stood and held her hand out to her husband. Once standing, she turned to her parents. "Thank you both so very much. We are sorry. We didn't mean it to happen." She kissed them both goodnight and turned to lead her new husband to their room. Lottie took Jonty upstairs and left him there as she went back downstairs to the bathroom. She then returned to her new husband for their wedding night.

As Jonty left to use the bathroom, Lottie mentioned the soap. She was surprised that he also knew about the burning. As he walked out, he kissed her quickly. "I'll remember, no soap."

On his return to their room some fifteen minutes later, he knocked gently before entering. She opened the door rather than call for him to come in. She had changed into a lacy lawn nightgown as it was hot.

He entered and quietly shut the door behind him. He was nervous. He had shaved in cold water, missing various bits of his growth, and had a nick on his chin. They may have already been intimate, but they had been fully clothed. It had all happened so fast that neither had time to be embarrassed or nervous. Now they were alone; both were hesitant.

Lottie broke the tension by handing him a handkerchief for his chin, taking his towel, and telling him where he could leave his clothes. She had made room in her wardrobe for his things while he was gone. He had four days before he was supposed to return, so she thought she would start being a good wife by unpacking for him.

Jonty divested himself of his outer clothing, undid his shirt, and then turned down the lamp. He took her hands and looked down into her lovely face. "Lotts, we've done things a bit around the wrong way, and yes, we were both responsible for that. But we're married now, and I want to start the right way with the marriage. I will have a hard enough time forgetting the last two years, and I will need your help. Before we go to bed, can we give ourselves into God's hands? I can't do this without either of you." They stood with foreheads together, holding hands and praying. After they said *Amen*, he picked her up and carried her to their bed. He gently laid her down and traced his fingers around her neckline, slowly undoing the front ribbons of her nightgown. Unbeknownst to her, her figure had been silhouetted in the lamplight through the fine lawn, and he could not wait to see her without it.

She reached up and pushed off his unbuttoned shirt. His drawers followed, and as she threw them on the floor, he returned and lifted her nightgown over her head. Her body looked almost gold in the soft lamplight. She held her arms to him, and he fell into them, cradling her. He kissed her neck, then raising himself on one elbow, he looked down, gently putting his fingers on her lips, saying, "Lotts, I'm sorry that things happened the way they have, but I'm not sorry that we married so fast. I'll never be sorry for that. I wanted to take you with me to Africa, but I'm now so glad that your father would not let us marry back then. You apparently heard all that?" She nodded, and he dropped a kiss on her waiting lips but then continued to talk. "Lotts, I saw horrible things, things no human should do to another; I won't mention what they did now, but it's why my nights are full of torment, and I only tell you now as you will be with me, and you have to know. When they occur, I need to be touched and comforted. Possibly even woken gently, and I'll probably need to talk or sometimes even get up and go for a walk. I need you to know this now as I don't want you to think it's anything you have done. I wish I could rewind the last two years and start over. I can't, but this will be the next best thing." He was looking down at her beautiful face. "Will you help me? Will you teach me to laugh again, to find peace again?"

"Yes, Jon Jon, I will. Remember that the vows we took were *in sickness and in health*. I'll be here, but thank you for telling me. Now I know how to help you too. We have at least eight months before any children arrive, hopefully, longer. We'll use that time to seek help." She lovingly stroked his still prickly cheek, then grinned cheekily, "Now, husband, I'm lying here stark naked, and you have not even looked at me. One would think you're not that interested," she said saucily with a mischievous smirk.

"Oh, I'm interested; I just needed you to know what might occur." As he spoke, he ran his hand over her smooth skin. He turned to look. "Trust me; I'm very interested." He set about showing his interest in the sight that he beheld.

Soon they dozed in each other's arms. Lottie stirred when she felt a hand wandering over her body. With a gasp and a grin, she hopped out of bed and turned off the lamp. "Ready again?" she asked. "Mama said a bit last night about 'the joys of marriage'; now I know what she means, I'm happy to oblige." She came back to bed but did not lie down. Their first union had been on a settee, and she realised that he could enjoy her more this way. A soft moonlight entered the window, and their eyes had tuned to the dull light. Her silhouette against the window was enchanting. He wasn't sure who was enjoying it more this time; they fell asleep in a twist of tangled limbs.

About midnight, Jonty started softly moaning in his sleep. His cry of "No, don't die, not you too…" woke Lottie to realise he was beginning to have a nightmare. She feared waking him but knew she must try something. She stroked his cheek, but that didn't work; she placed an arm over his chest and kissed him; he struggled against being held. She decided that as he was getting a little violent and twisting himself in the sheet, she pulled the sheet completely off him. As the cool night air hit his naked body, he settled down quickly and fell asleep. She decided not to wake him but cuddled up next to him again, entwining their arms, and listened to him until his breathing was once again peaceful. She now knew what to expect and one way to stir him. She hoped that his nightmares would only ever be like this; she could cope with that.

Morning came without further incidents. He woke to a delicious warmth creeping through his body. Their arms were still entwined but next to him was the sleeping form of his naked wife. She had moved from fully snuggling against him and was on her back. Her face relaxed, and she breathed evenly; a smile hovered around her luscious lips. He was never going to get sick of waking up to this sight. Her riot of blonde curls framed her angelic heart-shaped face. He had never even dreamt of her like this. He knew he'd had a bad dream again last night; he remembered some of it. It was of his friend Cody being shot while they were exercising. He hoped he had not woken her.

She moved, and the sheet pulled down, exposing her breasts.

His soft gasp of adoration stirred her to wakefulness.

She smiled a warm welcome. "Good morning, husband mine," she reached up for him to say good morning properly.

"Good morning, wife." He felt like ravishing her again, but after the second time last night, he wondered if she also enjoyed their nocturnal activities. He didn't wonder for long as she reached under the sheet. Another gasp ensued, and soon his morning got better.

She giggled. "Mama wasn't wrong; it is fun," she said, emphasising the word "is." He rolled her over, and they again lay entwined for some time. Their legs entangled, and they were both content with their current position.

Eventually, she said, "You had a bad dream last night." She spoke gently. "I tried a few things but didn't wish to wake you. So I pulled off the sheet, and it worked. You relaxed and went back to sleep."

A look of sadness swept across his face. "I'm sorry, love, I thought I did. Was I violent? This is my greatest fear. I don't want to hurt you for anything."

Her concern shook him. "No, you weren't. I understand, Jon Jon, but I wish I could do something. Do you know of anyone you can open up to? Tell them everything?"

"No, but when we get to Sydney, we might hunt for help. I'm sure there would be someone or some group I could talk to. Someone in the family might even know."

It being Sunday, they were up and ready for church. They joined the family at the breakfast table. Jonty's Aunt Shauna welcomed him with a bear hug and a congratulatory kiss. There had obviously been conversations before they appeared, and no one asked any questions.

Luke walked in and laid a gentle hand on his shoulder. "How did you go last night? Did you have a nightmare?"

Jonty nodded. "Yes, but not too bad. Uncle Luke, is there someone you know who might help me?"

"I'll put my thinking cap on, son," He liked calling Jonty that. Luke wondered who may have gone through anything similar and could only think of Harry and Jim. He would see them tomorrow as they would be arriving later that afternoon for Christmas festivities. He decided not to say anything to Jonty yet, but he might also have a word with Wills. He already had to ask him about the missing letter when he called in from Roseneath this morning. Wills and Cathy were heading to Eddie's for breakfast.

As they were leaving for church on Sunday morning, Jonty wasn't watching where he was walking and tripped as he walked out the door; the thick inside door-mat moved and showed something underneath. It was the corner of the long-lost letter. He bent and pushed the mat aside, revealing the missing letter. Everyone else had been used to the thick mat and stepped over it. The missing letter had lain there for weeks.

Lottie picked up the fat envelope and giggled. She tucked it into her reticule to read later.

Chapter 7   New Old Friends

$\mathcal{M}$onday was Christmas Day, and in Parramatta, the family descended from all over. All met in the backyard of Eddie's house, which had now expanded by adding the next-door yards owned by Edward and Bette Styles and Rick and Mary Louise Lockleys backyards meant more room for the ever-growing clan. Mary Lou greeted her cousin Jonty with a kiss and then noticed the rings on Lottie's fingers. "You're married? When?"

Jonty smiled. "Two days ago, Mary Lou, we snuck away and got married at St John's with Lottie's parents as witnesses."

Rick and his twin, Bette, joined them, admiring Lottie's ring. Many other family members soon surrounded them. Some had heard of the union after church the day before, but the family had not made any announcement.

Many of the family found it hard to believe that Lottie and Jonty had snuck away and been married. When they discovered Luke and Ellen had been witnesses, any questions of propriety were put to rest. Lottie had always voiced her plan not to have a big wedding. All had known they were courting before they had each gone off travelling. However, only a few knew Jonty had been caught up in the Transvaal war until Christmas luncheon. Soon stories of his travels circulated through the family.

Eddie, Wills, and Luke were off to the side from the majority of the group sitting on bags of stock food used for seats. Luke told them that Jonty had been kidnapped and traumatised after the conditions in Africa; he'd brushed over more details they didn't need to know about. Ed turned and sought out Jonty in the crowd. He saw the haunted look on his face;

something wasn't right with him. "There's more, isn't there, Luke?"

Luke smiled at his brother. "Jenna's wrong, you know; you don't miss things; you see the more important things in life. Yes, there's more. Their welcome in Sydney became a little more romantic than it should have been. Having said that, they were already engaged. He had dropped to one knee in front of everyone on the docks. She, of course, said, 'yes'. He'd approached me before he left and had asked for her hand. I only refused as I wanted her to be presented first. Had I approved, she would have been with him in Africa, so in all, I'm glad I said 'no'. We don't know if anything will come of their reunion, but as that was only two weeks ago, it won't matter."

"Oh, I'm not one to throw stones; it nearly happened to us but didn't. Do you remember my black stallion, James? He saved us, interrupting at the right time." Ed looked at the worry etched on Luke's face and said, "But there's still more isn't there?" Ed's eyes flicked quickly to Wills, then back to Luke.

Again Luke nodded. "Ed, he had a bad time over there, a frightful time. He saw things no one should see. I know soldiers have nightmares about such things, and he's having them now too. I pumped him for full details yesterday afternoon after the Sunday luncheon, and he gave them all in full graphic detail. I almost wish he hadn't!" Luke paused and looked at his brothers. His handkerchief was swept across his damp brown. He had also had bad dreams after listening to Jonty's story. "Jon had made friends with about a dozen red-coat soldiers, each one was either killed in front of him, or he nursed them while they died. He then found a child he knew had been all but beheaded. Another day he was horrified when he came across a group of soldiers raping a woman; some others were doing the same to a corpse. There was more, but you get the gist of his turmoil. Thankfully he didn't tell the girls about that, but Lottie has her hands full. He has had nightmares both nights he has been with us, and I don't know how to help him. Ed, I'm traumatised just having listened to his tale. He told me of other gruesome things, which he couldn't stop; every time the lad went for a walk, his escort was shot as they walked. This happened five times before he ended up staying in the compound for three months. There is more to his story, but that's enough for me to tell you. And then there is his lion. He can tell you about Chimbu. That's one story worth hearing about!"

Ed didn't know how to answer. "Cor, poor lad! I presume he went there to buy diamonds?"

"Yes, for Mr Field in Antwerp, he's the one you met with Ned," Luke explained the outline of the trip.

Wills sat listening but was deep in his own thoughts.

Eddie nodded. "Strange man, but a nice chap, though."

Luke continued, "We kept it quiet, not the sort of thing you advertise. Jonty was supposed to be back last December or soon after, but he stayed too long because of a lion cub he named Chimbu, and so Jonty was caught up in the troubles. Then he was, in essence, kidnapped by the Boers, marched across the country, forced to watch the treaty at gunpoint, transported on foot and then shipped out."

Luke looked over at Jonty; his arm was slung lovingly around Lottie's shoulders, and her arm was around his waist. He noticed Wills was not listening, so he only addressed Eddie. "Ed, it was only two weeks after he sailed that Jack died. We set off for England with Rick and Mary Louise, and well, you know that side of the story. We heard some news while over in England but didn't realise it was where Jonty was. He was literally in the thick of it. He was supposed to have been home by then, so I didn't worry until we arrived home and he wasn't back. I didn't tell Lottie, but she must have heard anyway. She sat pining for him."

Charlie came and joined them. "You all look cosy. Everything okay?"

"No, Charlie, far from it," Ed quickly filled him in about Lottie, Jonty and the haste of the wedding and the African trip.

Charlie said with sadness, "Damn! I wish I'd known he was there. I could have tried to get him out."

His brothers looked at him in surprise. Wills had sat drinking in the story but had remained silent. Charlie said, "I knew what was going on, Viceroy stuff and all, I got despatches, but I didn't think we knew anyone over there. The reports I read were horrifying. If he lived through half of what was in those reports, heck, we're all going to have to pack around the lad. Of all the family, he and John are least likely to have seen the horrors of life. He's a jeweller, and he is so like his father in nature, he would not hurt a fly." Charlie turned to look at Jonty. "He's going to need us all there for him. Harry has been through something similar, Jim too, with his hold-ups. Maybe they can help him." Charlie looked unwell, but only Ed knew his troubles. He soldiered on bravely.

Luke said quietly, "Charlie, he's already having nightmares. He has told Lottie what to do. It's good he's got her now, but she'll need support too. Especially when they have children," Luke said to his eldest brother.

Amongst the family were some from Emu Plains. Jim Leslie had married a distant cousin, and Harry Harlow married Wills and Ed's sister-in-law, Vicky. Charlie beckoned both men to them, and they now walked to join the brothers. Harry had been a soldier in India and had witnessed similar horrors as Jonty. If anyone knew how to help the lad, it would be them. All knew how vital these two men had both been in assisting Charlie to get over his traumatic youth, Jim in particular. Over the years, Jim sat and talked for hours with Charlie, and it was to Jim and Harry that Charlie opened up, and the healing began. The men now put their heads together. They could only help Jonty if he allowed them to, but they would all watch out for him from now on.

During the afternoon, Harry subtly took both Lottie and Jonty aside and suggested they come and stay for a few days before Jonty returned to work. Harry had volunteered to approach him first as he was the only one who knew what he was dealing with. Harry explained his own background and said he had also gone through nightmares. "Wills knows about my nightmares, as he had travelled with the five of us sleeping in the front of John and my wagon, and he saw and heard each of us as we battled our demons and the stresses. Jonty, you will need to talk about what you have seen, but not just that, you need to voice your feelings and go through every other possible scenario of what you think you could have done differently."

"Uncle Harry, I'll do anything to get us through this. I've had nightmares both nights we've been married. I need help and don't know where to turn." Jonty was at least honest with what he was battling.

Lottie answered, "We'll come, Uncle Harry, as long as you don't mind."

"Bring a stack of blank journals or reams of paper, Jonty, because I'll get you writing about everything. Trust me, this really helps. I laughed when Wills got us to record our feelings and emotions, but it was fabulous and cathartic. I still occasionally go back and skim over them. Not to refresh but to release. It also means that when you're ready, others can read them. This will be a strange honeymoon, but hopefully will help in the long run." Harry sounded confident.

"I'm prepared to do anything, Uncle Harry. I can't go on like this, especially now that we're married. I need this fixed." Jonty's stress was clearly visible. His brow was furrowed and the perspiration beaded before trickling down his face.

The day was not overly hot, and Harry knew it was from stress. Harry said, "Jonty, it's not a matter of fixing it; it's a matter of learning to live with it, control it and cope long term. Trust me; I want nothing more than to wipe away my memories. They still hurt and will continue to hurt until I die, but I have learned to cope. It's what you have to do too."

Jonty looked shocked. "You mean I'll never get rid of them? Captain Cromby said the same, but I really didn't believe him. Uncle Harry, I don't know if I will cope." He gulped back unshed tears.

Lottie grasped his hand and stepped close to him.

The plaintive cry from Jonty tore at Harry's heart. "Sadly, I can't wipe your mind, Jonty. Trust me; I wish I could." He placed his hand lovingly on the young man's shoulder. "Come tomorrow when we leave. The sooner we start, the better. We have room in the carriage as the others are staying for a few days. There will only be Jim and Conny with us, and he has had his share of hold-ups, so we'll ask him how he copes."

The afternoon passed, with everyone having a wonderful time catching up. Jonty and Lottie needed to get home and pack for a few days at

Emu Plains before returning to Sydney. They were keen to go with the possibility of Jonty finding some help.

They were packed and ready to leave first thing the following day. Harry collected them on the way out of town and suggested that the three men sit up on the driver's seat while the ladies chatted inside.

Jonty was sitting between the two older men. He had known them all his life and considered them 'uncles.' He also knew their stories but did not realise they might help him. He found it hard to believe Uncle Harry had just turned seventy; he certainly didn't look it. Jim was forty-six and was in his element working with Uncle Harry, training his draught horses and rebuilding carriages. Once they were out of town, Jonty said, "I wish I could turn back time. I would have left in October when I had originally planned. Although because of the wild animals there, you can't travel unattended."

Harry replied, "That's one of the things I'll get you to write. I call them the 'What if's.' You have to get the entire story right in your head. Then you have to ask yourself, 'Why not?' Then see if anything you had done would have made a difference. If so, to whom and why then why not," Harry looked at the puzzled look on his face.

Jim sat listening with his arms folded, his face unreadable. Harry had spent years living next to Jim and had gone over the same things with him after bushrangers had held him up. It wasn't until he retired that he started having the occasional nightmare. These surprised him as he was usually the one in control of his emotions, the one to whom people turned.

After some hours of helpful discussion, they stopped for a change of horses. While they enjoyed a mug of tea, they joined the ladies at the outdoor inn table. Jim's soft voice interrupted Jonty's thoughts. "Jonty, whatever you do, don't bottle it up. I did for years, and it came home to bite me, didn't it possum?" He addressed his wife. "I was fine while working, but it all came to the surface once I retired and started working with Harry. While I lived with Harry and Vicky, I worked through things while building our house next door. I found it certainly helped. It won't help immediately, but over time things will ease." Jim paused, "My nightmares were also over our Stella dying. Trust me; I know that pain of being completely useless. So does Conny, so Lottie, talk to her." Jim smiled at the young man. "Jonty, I want you to come back and talk to me again. I have a few more steps for you to do after you've seen Harry and before you can find complete peace."

Jonty nodded, "I will, thanks, Uncle Jim."

"Me too, Lottie; we went through it when we lost our first child," Vicky said to Lottie. Conny was only ten years older than Jonty, Jim ten and a bit years older again. Harry, at seventy, was the same age Lord Charles was when he'd had a heart attack and died. Harry had been in the Colony for forty years, but many years before, those two men had been unofficially adopted by Lord Charles, Earl of Coxheath, as what he termed "extra sons." They both had very tenuous connections to the family, but as their real families were both in England, they loved the welcome they received.

By mid-afternoon, they arrived in Emu Plains and unloaded. Once the luggage was unpacked, Harry took Jonty straight into his office, and they set to work. Conny took Lottie and Vicky to their house next door, and they sat in her kitchen having a cup of tea. The three ladies were friends of long standing.

Harry got to work with Jonty as he knew time was precious. Both ladies worked with Lottie on ways to assist. The first thing that Harry got Jonty to go through was the entire saga, with no details spared. Only then could he begin to understand where to start. Harry took notes as he listened.

Jonty retold everything and then was told to put pen to paper, and dot points, leaving space between each line. It was hard re-telling Harry all the gory details, but he left nothing out. Even to closing Nandi's eyes. That single act haunted him. He was hurting at the traumatic things, often weeping at his inability to assist. It was even harder writing it all down. This, too, took time. Nandi's episode was the hardest to bear. He thankfully had not seen her die but knew that he was the one who had found and identified her body. He paid for her burial; he had not told anyone that.

Over the next two days, they worked hard, and situation by situation, they worked through other possible scenarios. Incident by incident, they discussed if Jonty could have done anything different that would have changed the outcome of each possibility. Other than leaving early, Jonty realised that there was not one thing he *would* have done differently. He *could* have bought more gems from the English miners, but then he probably would have been treated as the English were and may even have been shot while exercising, as were his friends. He knew the shooters to have been Boers, and the English were the enemy. On his trek with the Boers, he discovered that the English soldiers had killed Nandi. He had noted that the men had no bayonets, as the Boers in the area didn't have bayonets or swords. Maybe he *should* have left earlier, but then Chimbu would probably have died.

By the end of the two days, Jonty realised there was little, if anything, that he would have changed, even if he'd been able to. He finally acknowledged that it was not his fault that any of them died, and there was nothing he could have done to save even one of them. With that revelation, he sat and wept healing tears, but he was despondent. At one stage, Harry called Lottie to comfort Jonty as he was curled in a ball in the corner of the room, sobbing.

She realised that he was well but dealing with the haunting memories. She just sat with him silently with a hand comforting him. Harry gently told her how to calm him, that he would sometimes push her away and that it was not her he would be rejecting, but sometimes he just needed some space to think. He needed to be lovingly touched and reassured, especially after a nightmare. A gentle caring touch could do much healing, like a hand sitting on his arm or a cup of tea and silent companionship.

Harry turned to Jonty. "Lad, this is only a start. But you've taken the first step, and it's one of the biggest. You will need to find others who will sit and listen. And it would be best if you found some outlet. When you go home, I want you to sit and read through all this again, read the changes you make, and write more if you need to. Don't ever throw these out, as you'll find that you need to re-read them repeatedly. Not to refresh your mind of them, but to reassure yourself that you could not change them. Jonty, aim for just one day at a time; concentrate on that."

The night before they departed, Harry told Jonty about two medicines that may help him relax at bedtime and sometimes they helped with the dreams. The first was Valerian, and the other was Passionflower. Both were available in Sydney, and he recommended them, but only for the short term. He must not become dependent on medications as that would defeat the purpose. "Try them occasionally if you have a series of bad nights."

The two days were intensive and emotionally heavy. Jim had joined them for the final afternoon session, and then, with Lottie included, they all prayed together, laying hands on Jonty. He felt more settled and knew Lottie would be there for him. On their last night at Harry's, Jonty slept through. He woke relaxed, as did Lottie. It was the first quiet night he'd had since he'd returned, and he was thrilled. Jonty woke to Lottie snuggling up to him. He stroked her cheek, and she opened her eyes to his with a big smile.

"You didn't have a dream last night, did you?" She leaned over and kissed him.

"No, I didn't. Good, eh? Sad we must return today, but we can always come back." He greeted her with a long morning kiss.

Two hours later, Harry dropped them at the Emu Plains railway siding to catch the train back to Parramatta. From there, they would spend the night, pack Lottie's clothes and head to Sydney in one of Luke's carriages.

Jonty had sent a message to his parents and another to Mr Lamb, telling him of the change in his marital situation and that he would delay returning to the shop until after New Year. They now had three days to settle into their new home before Jonty was to head back to work on January 2nd. It was a funny honeymoon, but it had been a strange wedding. The train puffed into the stop, and they climbed on board.

The night in Parramatta was also peaceful, and they were now well-rested. In the end, the newly married couple caught the ferry to Sydney. Luke had loaded up one of his Logistics wagons, all of Lottie's clothes and some extra items for their new home. He had added spare bedding and linen, and Ellen gave them a beautiful tablecloth as a housewarming gift. It would all go to town tomorrow, and they could spend the day settling into their new home.

Luke, Ellen and Lottie's twin, Carlo, escorted them to the wharf. The trip was joyous, with Lottie keeping Jonty laughing much of the way. Her new life was about to start, and her excitement was infectious.

That night the young couple moved into their new semi-detached cottage. They had a set of sheets and two towels from Jonty's parents that had been delivered in their absence. Colleen and John had made up their bed and added some fresh food for the young couple, but little else was in the kitchen. Yet, they were content. They had each other. Although there was electricity in the new cottage, they loved the soft light of an oil lamp for their bedroom.

Andrew Lenehan had left all his exquisite handmade furniture from western red cedar, swamp mahogany and she-oak, amongst other timbers. Each mirror-finished piece was superb. He had even left some of the household items he no longer wanted. When Jonty's father had said it was ready to move into, he was correct. Even some stores of dry foods were still in the pantry. Flour, sugar, salt, and some cooking utensils were still there. They had just gone into the kitchen to see what they could tussle up to eat for their first night, and they heard a knock on the door. A middle-aged couple stood on the doorstep with a small casserole.

Jonty grinned, "Will, Dimity, welcome, come inside."

Will ushered his wife in first and limped in behind her. "I wondered if you knew who your neighbours were?"

"Err, no, why Will?" Jonty said, somewhat puzzled.

"It's us, Jon!" Dimity said excitedly. "We're just back from Melbourne and have moved in here. Douglas arranged it all with your father; isn't this wonderful?"

Will and Dimity English were long-time friends of Uncle Ed and Jonty's family. They had first met when Jonty was a child. Will was the same age as his father, and over the years, Jonty's grandfather, Douglas, had been working with Will's adopted brother Ricky with the street orphans in Sydney. Will had always been the only one to call him Jonathon; he often shorted it to Jon. Jonty loved it.

Until recently, the cottages had been used as training and accommodation for orphan boys under Ricky's care. Most of the children were now placed, and thus the cottages were vacant. Before Will and Dimity had moved to Melbourne a few years before, they had shared Ricky's big house down the street. On their return, Will had asked John about renting a cottage. They no longer needed a vast space as all the children had married or left home. Will wanted a well-lit room to paint in, and the cottage was perfect. When they had moved in some months before, they had wondered who their new neighbours would be. Will was delighted that it was someone they knew so well. He was an extraordinary artist, and Jonty had always admired his work. As a child, he had spent many hours sitting quietly, just watching him place the colours on the gigantic canvases he worked on. Now in his late fifties, he had been teaching in Melbourne.

Jonty gave him a wide grin, "Hey Will, interested in a private student?" Jonty waited for the surprise to hit, but it didn't. His only reaction was a raised eyebrow. "Will, it's a long story, but I think God has just provided me with my 'outlet'." Jonty turned to Lottie and gave a short laugh, "Sweetheart, what do you think?"

Lottie giggled excitedly, "Who am I to question God's wisdom, love?" She gave a small jump of joy. "I think it's fabulous! Dimity, I'm so pleased we know our neighbours already. This is perfect." She clapped her hands with glee. Will and Dimity stayed and had a cup of tea before returning next door for their dinner. As he was leaving, Will had said to Jonty, "I'm game if you are, but we'll come over tomorrow, and you can tell me all, for I feel there is something behind this."

The next day Lottie's clothes and various other items arrived on the wagon; they spent the morning unpacking and settling into their new abode. Around noon, Dimity arrived with a large basket and suggested they stop and have a picnic in the back garden with them.

As they had just finished unpacking, they invited her in. Will arrived a few minutes later and hobbled in, and Lottie giggled as he had a smear of blue paint on his nose. When she explained why and handed him a cloth, he said, "Hazards of being an artist, Charlotte dear." He returned her smile. "Now, where is this delicious food that I have had to stop painting to enjoy?"

They sat on the newly scythed grass in the backyard, and Jonty and Will had their heads together. "Jon, were you serious about painting?" Will asked as he munched into a hard-boiled egg.

"Yes, Will." He talked a bit about the African journey and the stresses he returned with. "Uncle Harry suggested that I find an outlet, and I was thinking about really learning to paint properly, with oils as you do. I find the watercolours are too wishy-washy for me. I like the depth of the colours with oils, but I know there's much more to just dabbing on a bit of paint. I can't catch the light as I want to with watercolours either or make the water look wet."

Jonty's mention of *catching the light* caught Will's attention. "How about we give it a try? I know you have the skills already, as I remember your father showing me some of your work as a lad, not that you're much older now. I can teach you canvas preparations and how to mix the oils; from there, it's up to you. There are certain techniques needed with oils that are not required for watercolours. Also, oils take a long time to dry, which means they are somewhat forgiving."

Jonty looked across at Lottie, and their eyes met. Hers returning his smile, she said, "I need some art for the walls, Jon Jon; I could imagine nothing better than yours."

As there was little else to do for the afternoon, they went next door into Will's studio once they had eaten. As they entered, they saw his current work. It was not in an easel as it was another colossal work and again in three panels. The first painting any of them had seen of his was at John Landon's house. Tad and Amabel Falconer-Meade lived there now, but the painting was still in the office. Tad still wrote under his pen name of Tad English, but when his grandfather died, his last request was that Tad use his birth name as his legal name. Reluctantly the couple changed their name.

John and Sadie Landon had died some years before, and Jonty's elderly grandfather, Douglas, missed John dearly. The story of how John and Sadie came to know the family and Ricky English was a long and somewhat twisted tale. Amabel had been kidnapped and then rescued by ten-year-old Ricky English. John sponsored Ricky and assisted him where he could. Ricky, in turn, adopted two other orphaned boys, Tad and Will; the three orphans considered themselves brothers. Tad's real grandfather came looking for him and took him back to England a few years later. He stayed for a few years but didn't like it and returned to Ricky and Will. At least here, he could be helpful. Tad worked as a journalist and used the name English for his writing.

The three assisted with other street children, and as Ricky grew, more boys were helped, and then he started what, in essence, became an orphanage, but in reality, the children lived with the three boys. Over the years, the project grew into a babies' home, both a girls' and a boys' house. Then, as the children aged, John and Colleen bought the row of cottages, and they were used as independent group homes for the older children. There they learned to housekeep, then were trained and placed in good jobs. The older children lived in the row of cottages and learned the skills required to cope in life. They were safe and had a roof over their head. They each worked to assist in feeding themselves, and each became a valuable community member. Jonty's family had a lot to do with them as they grew. His father and uncles had attended the same school as the three boys had, although they only sat in the classroom doorways and learned to read using the free slates provided. Lottie's uncles, Ed and Tim, had also been at the same school, as they had been living with Jon's grandparents for some years. It was how they had all met. Ed's son had married this cousin, so now they were related.

Ten-year-old Ed first befriended and then encouraged Will to learn to read and write, hence the fantastic work of art that Will did. It was his first significant work; Will depicted Ed as a teenage blacksmith making a horseshoe. The painting was not small but a wall covered in three huge panels. The blacksmith was life-size, and it was as though you were walk-in into the hot blacksmith forge. To see the fantastic painting made you stop in your tracks, and it had been viewed often over the decades. One man was so impressed that he'd sent Will to Paris to learn from the masters over there. When Will returned, He was a changed man. They travelled for the last ten years, and Will taught at various Art Schools. His works were selling well, but his teaching required more and more time. Dimity nearly always travelled with him.

Lottie and Dimity sat watching the men while Will showed Jonty a blank paint canvas and what had to be done to prepare a new canvas before painting a picture. They had their heads together while the ladies sat on a settee watching them on the far side of the room. This was Dimity's joy. She'd sit there reading while Will painted. She so adored watching him. She learned to stay quiet but was close if he wished to chat.

As Will was not actually painting, the ladies sat chatting. "It's so nice to be home again." Dimity said, "We've lived in many places in hotel rooms and guest rooms. The last one was a six-month stay while Will was teaching at Her Majesty's School of Arts in Kensington, and before that, we were in Ballarat. Lottie, to have friends next door is wonderful. I'm going to so love living here."

Lottie, too, was excited that they had friends close. Knowing that Dimity would become a confidant for her, she dropped her voice and filled Dimity in on Jonty's bad nights. She knew she would also need assistance with their children when they came along. Dimity and Will had four grown children and six grandchildren, so she was well-versed in handling young ones.

~

Within three months, Lottie and Jonty were preparing for the arrival of their first child. Lottie had realised that she indeed was with child by the end of their first week married when her month's flow had not arrived. By six weeks, she was ill in the morning and would weep at the most minor things. Jonty's nightmares were intermittent, but when they did happen, they were terrible. Stripping the sheets from him only worked sometimes, but he was never violent. Lottie's sleep suffered, though. She would often have to have a nap while he was at work. As her condition progressed, so did her morning sickness.

Will needed a quick trip to Melbourne and invited Jonty to travel with him. They would be gone for only two weeks. Lottie told him to go as she would go home for a couple of weeks, and Dimity could stay with her.

Will had to visit one of his students and his friends at the National Gallery School in Melbourne. "Jonty, I think I'll get you to come and meet some of my friends at the Gallery School; Fred McCubbin captures the light as you want to do. Another student, and he's the same age as you, Jonty is a lad named Tom Roberts; his work is amazing. Sadly he went to London just before I left, but he'll be back in a few years. He was offered a place at the Royal Academy of Arts, but you can see some of his works. It's a three-year course, but if, or when, he comes back, he's someone whom you should meet. Arthur Streeton is another who captures the light beautifully. You could step into his work; it's so lifelike. Oh, Jonty, they are so skilled, all of them. I look forward to seeing some of the finished work they were working on when I left."

"Oh, to be able to paint like that." Jonty had thrown himself back into his work. It was satisfying that he could create beautiful things from rough stones. Having exquisite gems at the end of his work was satisfying... but it wasn't painting. There was something in daubing a blank canvas with colour and creating a picture that took his breath away. He also found that he was dreaming of those pictures, too, pleasant dreams. This was something that he wished to pursue. As long as he could have a stock of gems for the orders and for sale, he freed up time to paint more. During the last three months, under Will's instruction, he had learned to not only prepare a canvas but how to mix the paints and various methods to apply the colour. He watched as Will used a palette knife, brushes and even his fingers to get complex textures in the medium. Even the techniques he used with paintbrushes were terrific. He didn't just gently brush the colour on the canvas, but some brushes were stumpy stubs with most bristles cut off and used to stab the canvas with short bristles to daub on colour. Others were cut down to one or two remaining hairs; with these, Will could paint a fine line and add intricate detail.

The day after Will asked Jonty if he'd join him in Melbourne, Jonty saw the advertisement for an auction in Brunswick Street, Fitzroy. He wondered if Fitzroy was near where Will was going and if he could get to the auction while there.

Will laughed and said, "For you, about a five-minute walk, if that, and for me, about half an hour hobble. The darned leg is causing more trouble the older I get. What bugs me is that I have no idea what happened to me when I was little. Being a foundling, I have no memory of my mother or when this occurred. For my first memory, I would have been about five or six, I suppose, I was surrounded by lots more boys, and I hated it. All I know is that I always limped. Ah well, no use crying over something I can't fix, so I get on with my life. It doesn't affect my painting, so I focus on my ability, not my disability. Dimmy says she's never really noticed it." Will paused for a bit, thinking. "Jonathon, a good woman is priceless. When we married, I had nothing to offer her; she stood her ground with her parents and refused to see anyone else but me. Her father finally relented."

"Wow, Will, I've never been game to ask, but I often wondered. Have you ever had a doctor look at your leg?" Jonty asked bravely.

"Actually, you know Jonty; I haven't. I've never thought there was much anyone could do, and there probably isn't. Do you think I should?" Will sounded surprised that he'd never thought of it before. "You know, Jonty, I might do something. It's becoming painful to walk at all." He busied himself in the studio. "Now, to answer your question. Yes, we can get to Brunswick Street easily. We'll take a cab and do a bit of a tour while we're there. What's on offer?"

Jonty grinned. "It's a jewellery sale, of course; it sounds like some of the things in the catalogue are pretty good. I would like to go and have a look. Sometimes it's cheaper to buy things at auction and recycle precious metals. This one seems to be interesting. If I'm there, I may as well make it worth my while. It's my version of art, Will."

"Good; what date is it?" Will hoped it would be soon.

"March 12th for that one, but they are on often, so we can head along on whatever Saturday we are down there." The excited look on Jonty's face made Will laugh.

"We'll work something out, even if you have to go along yourself. But I'd be keen to see what the auctions have on offer." He put his finger on his lips. "I have pre-sold this one so that I might get Dimmy something."

The two men plotted the rest of their trip, and the ladies did the same. Dimity had never had a holiday without Will or her parents, and to say she was excited was an understatement. Will wished Jonty to travel with him to have time to take him out of his comfort zone and have some long deep chats. He also wanted to talk about deep prayer or meditation. It was something he had learned about when he was troubled. While Jonty was at work, Will had worded the ladies up so neither would volunteer to accompany them.

~

They departed a week later on the *Baraboo*. They would travel a few days before arrival in Melbourne and two days before the auction. Will wished to spend that time praying with Jonty. It was the one thing that Jonty had not done yet. Yes, he'd prayed, but he'd not done what Will called *deep prayer*.

As a young man, Will had noticed that some friends seemed more at peace than others, and Eddie was one of them. A long time ago, Eddie had told Will about the power of this sort of prayer. He'd tried it, and his previous anxieties had easily been able to be released. As they left the heads at Sydney Harbour, Will revealed his plan to Jonty. "Jonty, I must now reveal an ulterior motive to asking you along. We're going to do what I have practised many times. It's called meditation, but Eddie calls it deep prayer. The reason is, I do not think that you have fully released your anxieties to God." Will turned and waited for an answer from the young man.

"But I pray, Will, I do honestly!" Jonty was a little offended that Will thought he wasn't praying.

Will frowned but explained, "Jon, it's not ordinary prayer; it's why Eddie calls it 'deep prayer'. We needed uninterrupted time alone and hence the trip. Do you want to try?"

"I have nothing to lose, Will, so let's give it a go." Jonty had been feeling more at peace of late, but sometimes the nights still ate at him. Day times he was now coping well. With the arrival of their child in a few months and as Lottie's confinement progressed, they would both need uninterrupted sleep if possible. So Jonty said, "I'm in, Will; what do we do next?"

"We will settle into our cabin. We're sharing for a reason. It's so we can be quiet." Will turned and hobbled towards their cabin. They unpacked their bags and made themselves comfortable. As the sea was calm, they ordered a tea tray and then settled down to start Will's plan. He explained, "First, you have to be comfortable. It's no use shuffling or sitting in an awkward position. So settle on the bed or an armchair; even standing at the rails will work. The first few times, it will take time to get to the state where you feel the peace. I call it getting in the zone. However, the more you do this, the easier it will become. You will be able to do it if you arrive somewhere early or wait in a queue. Jonty, this is a skill we should all learn."

"Sounds good. Can we start?" Jonty had finished his tea and was ready.

Will gave a laugh. "Yes, we can. But use the privy, and we'll get settled."

They each got comfortable, Will sat in an armchair, and Jonty lay face-up on the floor. He had discovered that he could lay still for hours in this position.

"Now I want you to try to shut out every sound, the sounds of the rigging, the sea sloshing, and the distant voices as they pass; let them all go; just listen to my voice. I want you to breathe deeply, concentrating on relaxing. Relax your body, limb by limb. Then listen to see if you can hear your blood pumping. The swoosh of your heart is a reassuring sound. Relax! Breathe, in… and out…, in… and out…." Will fell silent for a few minutes and saw that Jonty's body had fully relaxed. The stress lines were gone from the young man's face.

As Will watched, he noticed micro frowns cross Jonty's face. He said, "If thoughts come into your mind, treat them like butterflies, don't let them land. Release them to fly away. Once you are at peace, now listen to God. He will speak to you and bring you comfort." A few minutes more passed before Will spoke again. "Jonty, I want you to petition God in your own words to take the dreams from you. You must release them to Him and know He can do what man can't. He can take these thoughts from your mind and cast them away. You know you have done your part; now let God do His." Again, Will watched as Jonty's face frowned, and then after some time, a smile flickered across his mouth. His face was fully relaxed as he shed the past years and handed them to the Lord. Will continued, "Once done, open yourself to being filled with His peace. It can be an overwhelming experience, I wept like a baby, but I felt so clean; you must do this. Jonty, I will leave you for a time; I don't want you to move. Stay there until you need to get up, even sleep. Stay relaxed. I'll come back in a while."

Without saying more, Will got up and left Jonty lying on the floor. He wandered down to the dining room to see if he could get some more tea. Will thought he would sit in the reading cabin and give Jonty some time. As he drank his tea, he prayed too. He was asking for wisdom as to how to help him best. He was sitting back with his eyes closed and the thought of what he termed the prayer release. He had done this himself when he had fallen victim to alcohol when he lived in Paris. He had been so absolutely alone and didn't speak the language. Stupidly he had turned to alcohol to get him through. It had been one of the worst decisions he'd made and had taken a lot of time to master. Even now, he stayed off it most of the time, and if he did have any, he limited it to one drink. Dimity didn't like to drink anyway, so mostly they stuck to homemade ginger beer if they were celebrating anything or apple cider. He knew the battles of the inner beast. As he sat waiting for Jonty, a smile spread across his face. He knew what to do next, and they were in the perfect place.

After an hour, Will returned to their cabin. Jonty was sound asleep on the floor. He was so relaxed and smiling in his sleep. He didn't even stir as Will sat down again. Will watched over him as he slept. A smile hovered on his face. A thought settled; he needed to see a doctor while in Melbourne. If he visited one in Sydney, the word could get back to Dimity or Ricky. Yes, he would do it.

In Parramatta, Luke and Ellen arranged to meet Dimity and Lottie at the wharf. Although the trip was much quicker by train, it was more pleasant to go on the little steam ferry. Lottie was looking forward to some 'girl talk' with her mother and Dimity. Lottie had much to learn about babies. She was admittedly a little concerned; as she was well over three months, she was still experiencing morning sickness. As a twin herself, her older siblings were triplets; she knew there was a considerable possibility of her carrying more than one child. She eventually told Dimity what had occurred as she would wonder if the child or children would be born very early, especially if they were twins. Lottie was impatient for the little boat to arrive. Her parents had come for a visit a few times, but they had not been able to have a private chat. She also noticed that although she fitted into her gowns, one or two of them were getting a little tight. She wondered....

Dimity was looking forward to a holiday. She, too, was looking forward to some girly time. She and Will had spent so much time with other artists, who, on the whole, they were male, she rarely had time to converse with other ladies. Jane Sutherland was one of the few ladies she had become friends with, and another young lady was Clara Southern, but they had to leave just before she started officially at the Art School. Dimity had liked both of their work; however, being artists, the conversation was always about their art, not family. With Jane, the discussion was about suffrage for women. She knew that certain elections allowed women to vote in both South Australia and Victoria. Dimity certainly had her own views and did wish that sometimes more women listened too, but she also was content not to buck against the traces of society. She was happy living a comfortable life with a wonderful loving husband, and she could ask no more. As a mother of four grown children who had each moved away from Sydney, she missed her family. So, for Dimity, this time of frivolous girl talk would be an absolute delight. Babies would be the main topic, and this was wonderful too.

Two daughters and their husbands were in London; their oldest son, Richard John, with his wife, Dominique, and children were in Paris, and their second son, Theodore William, lived in Melbourne. They had stayed with them while at the art school. It was where Will and Jonty would stay this trip. Dimity smiled at the thought of the two sharing a room. Will was untidy, and Jonty wasn't. She had discovered that on the day they met. As soon they had finished eating, Jonty cleared the dirty dishes, and before they had gone inside, he'd already done the dishes while making tea for them all. She wondered if it was part of the problem. Jonty needed everything in the right place all the time, and the mind didn't always work that way. She was sure Will would point that out to him.

As the ferry rounded the final bend, Lottie saw her parents waiting for her. They were sitting on the bench seat under the tree near the wharf. She started waving as soon as she saw them and continued until the ferry docked.

Chapter 8   A Fresh Perspective

*J*onty finally awoke to find Will sitting, watching him with a smile. "Afternoon, sleepyhead; you've been out for over an hour."

"You're kidding?" Jonty mumbled as he sat up. "Will, I can't believe it, but I feel at peace."

His words were met with a smile. "You look it too, Jon. We will do this each day, and you'll get more used to getting in the zone. Eventually, you'll be able to close your eyes at work and find a few minutes just to let things go. We'll have one more session tonight when it's dark, and you'll find out why later, but for now, dinner is served, my boy, so get along and change."

~

Three hours later, the two were sitting on the deck with a big mug of tea. They watched the sun sink over the land as the ship sloshed through the waves.

Will explained the next stage of his *treatment*. "Jon, what we will do soon is what I call *unpacking the baggage*. You told me you've worked through things with Harry and Jim, and that's great. I've seen your notes, and I would have got you to do the same thing. Harry has obviously been through something similar. Jon, this is what I do with all of the students at the Art School. Many of them are carrying some sort of emotional turmoil, and I teach this method of relaxation."

Jonty turned to him quickly. "Why didn't you say, Will?" Jonty said in surprise.

"Why? Well, firstly, I didn't know you had a problem. You certainly didn't when you were younger. It was only the trip that threw you, Jon, and hopefully, you can get back to how you were. No, you will never forget, but there is a way, and we're going to do it tonight. It's why we're sitting out here."

Jonty looked at Will with new eyes. "How? I'd do anything, Will, anything!"

"Good! Well, I shall tell you I have found two ways that both work; I think we'll try the second one. The first is writing it down and then burning it, but that works better in other situations. In this one, you need to metaphorically pull those memories out of your body and literally hand them to God. It's what we are going to do tonight. No one will see, and I will stay here."

"How?" Jonty simply asked.

Wills spent the next half an hour explaining. "In essence, Jon, you are going to stand at the ship's bow in prayer and take those memories out of your body and then with your hands raised and palms upwards, you will hand them over to God's care forever."

Harry could see Jonty's amazed look.

Jonty could not help but ask, "But will it work?"

"Ahh, yes, well, that depends on you and if you are serious." Will's eyes twinkled. "You see, you can go through all the emotions and actions, but if you don't mean it, well, no, it won't work. It's not magic, it's not science, it's what the 'deep prayer' is, or some call it 'power prayer.' If you truly mean it and have handed it over to God, then He will. There is absolutely nothing we can do to remove memories, absolutely nothing... but God can."

"I'll do it, Will! But why has none of the family mentioned this before?" Jonty was surprised that neither Harry nor Jim had mentioned this. Harry had said there was more and that Jonty needed to go back out there, but he hadn't had time. Jim also said that he wished to talk to Jonty again. Jonty sighed; he needed to be more committed to this.

Will continued, "Jon, this is not a magic trick or gobble-de-gook like that. You won't magically forget, but if you let God work in you, He will... well, do His stuff."

They sat in silence, waiting for the darkness to descend. There was the gentle slough of the waves as they hit the bow. Soon they stood and walked to the railing. In the twilight, they stood watching the dolphins play in the foam. They could see the animals playing leapfrog and laughed at their antics. Darkness finally fell, and with no one else on deck, they walked to the bow, and Jonty took up the front position.

Will spoke softly. "Jon, what you do now is act out, pulling these memories from your head and heart, and literally lift them to God. Stand with your arms outstretched and your palms facing upwards, releasing these memories into God's care forever. Let Him fill your spirit and just let things go." Will had done this himself. He also had much to release, and he knew he could not do it alone. Ricky and Tad were good friends, but they didn't understand. John Landon was the one who had set him on this tack, and it had worked. Only in his case, it was through the use of his art. He did all the above things and then left them with God. He turned his prayers into murals and threw himself into the passion of painting. A few years ago in Melbourne, others had noticed his unique aura of peace, and now he would go back there and help others cope with their emotions. Many thought he was teaching just painting, which he did as well, but he was needed for this reason. Each opportunity gave him a chance to share his faith. He had not tried this at sea but couldn't see why it would not work well, if not better.

Jonty and Will bowed in prayer while Jonty stood holding the ropes at the very nose of the bow. He felt Will place his hand on his shoulder, give it a gentle squeeze, and then he was alone with God. He stood in the blackness and, leaning into the ropes, put his hands over his face and, with tears streaming down his cheeks, slowly lifted his arms and clenched hands to God, releasing all his burdens. There was no moon, and it was completely dark. No one but God saw his tears, his grief, or his release. As his arms reached full extension and twisted his hands, he unfurled them. His flattened palms were now outstretched to God. He stifled a sob as he finally released his burdens and accepted God's grace; an incredible feeling of peace swept over him. He had no idea how long he stood with his arms outstretched in prayer. He knew that he did mean what he prayed, totally and absolutely.

In the darkness, his eyes caught a flash of something in the water. He looked down into the murky depths and saw the brilliant sparkles of what looked like starbursts. As the ship sloughed through the gentle seas, the waves from the bow erupted in a myriad of minute lights like fireworks. Jonty stood and smiled; then his smile turned into a chortle, then a laugh. He turned to see if Will was still close by but was unable to peer into the darkness. He called out. "Will?"

Will's gentle voice replied, "I'm here, Jon." He carefully walked to join Jonty, and together they stood looking at the astounding light show. It seemed that an eon passed them by. A dolphin joined in the spectacular light show, and as it slid through the waves, it triggered more explosions of light. It soon was joined by more of its friends, and the two men relished the aquatic beasts playing in the bow waves. Then they were gone as fast as they had arrived. After what seemed like ages, the cold had seeped through the men's coats, and they decided to return indoors. Hardly a word had been said, but the magic of the evening penetrated deep into their souls. They returned to their cabin and retired to their bunks. The conversation could wait until tomorrow.

The only words spoken were from Jonty. "Thank you, Will!"

The ship sailed on while the two men slept dreamlessly.

~

Awaking on the morrow, Jonty turned in his narrow bunk and

stretched. A smile of contentment crossed his face. He heard Will up and about and turned to face him. "Good morning, Will!" Jonty's face broke into a broad grin.

"Sleep well? I can see you did; pity there's no mirror here. You look so relaxed." Will's gentle reply just reinforced what Jonty already knew.

"I slept like a babe, Will. I remember no dreams, and the sheets weren't twisted or thrown off either." He rose and walked to the basin to wash his prickly face. Sloshing the cold water over him, he was now refreshed. "I'm never going to be able to thank you enough, Will."

Will's gentleness was in itself a delight. "It's not me you have to thank; it's God and daily. All this is between you and Him and no one else. If you didn't mean it, it would not work. It's up to you to continue doing this; I recommend you do the same thing each night before retiring. Release the day's worries to Him and retire knowing He is watching over your rest."

The following two nights were peaceful for Jonty even though the sea wasn't. A swell had arrived, and the ship bounced up and down the waves. However, their arrival in Melbourne was accomplished without drama. The vessel needed to be escorted through the channel rather than the pilot board. It was just too rough. On arrival at the dock, Will could see his son waiting. His wave was returned. Theo and Jonty were old friends as their fathers had worked with Will's brother, Ricky, at the boys' home.

Jonty, too, gave a welcoming wave to his friend. They had not seen each other since Theo married. His work took him away soon after.

It took an hour before they were unloaded and on the way to Theo's house. The family lived in a three-story tenement house in Fitzroy, similar to their own place but larger. The house had four bedrooms and a large backyard; Will was on the second floor, and Jonty was on the top floor overlooking the garden. Jonty smiled; yes, he would be able to do his now nightly ritual of surrendering all to God before he turned to his bed. He'd not had a nightmare since that night at sea. His spirit was more at peace, and he was calm.

They had little planned for the next ten days, and Jonty learned that Will rarely ever did plan anything. When questioned, Will replied, "I 'let go and let God,' Jon. He has a much better plan than I for what needs doing. I'm merely an instrument for Him."

They attended St Paul's Cathedral for the church for the early morning service. Jonty had been in the building before but never to a service. A feeling of peace descended upon him as he took Communion, to the point he teared up. He surreptitiously wiped away a stray tear that had escaped and returned to his seat. He bowed in prayer in his pew and let the rest flow. He released a deep sigh and subtly wiped their last traces away with his handkerchief. Not usually an emotional person, Jonty was surprised at his tears.

After the service, they wandered back to Theo's house in Gertrude Street for luncheon. Even for Will, the walk was easy. Jonty was deep in thought. He fell behind a little and prayed as he walked, thanking God for the relief he had already received.

The luncheon was over, and they discussed the next ten-day itinerary. Theo had to return to work, so the two men said they would meander to the Art Academy. Saturday would be the jewellery auction a few streets away. Strangely, Jonty was now more excited to spend his days with Will at the Academy than he was about the auction.

Monday morning came without a nightmare. Again Jonty awoke with a smile and a prayer of thanks. The two departed at eight after a well-cooked breakfast of grilled ham and eggs on toast. Theo dropped them on St Kilda Road, and they walked into the Gallery Art School.

Will introduced him to some of his friends.

"Fred, this is Jonathon Evans, Jon, this is Frederick McCubbin; he's the senior teacher here." Will shook his friend's hand. "Jon, I want to show you some of Fred's work as he's one that captures the light as you wish to do. If you watch while he paints, that's if you don't mind, Fred, you might learn a trick or two."

The artist replied, "As long as you don't chatter, feel free to watch. I'm just hanging the watercolours from last night's class. I think we'll have to keep an eye on this young fellow. Goes by the name of Streeton, Arthur Streeton. Look!" As he spoke, he showed them the most phenomenal landscape in watercolour.

Both gasped

Wills spoke first. "How did he get the depth of colour in watercolour? Jon, look at the way he captured the sky and the trees. Oh, Fred, I say they are brilliant, aren't they?"

"He's one of a few to watch, Will. Some others I've seen at other schools are Tom Roberts, of course. Will, you brought his work to my attention. He's still in London, of course. There's a lady too, Jane Sutherland. I believe you've met her as well?"

Will nodded.

"She said she came across another girl, a Clara something."

"Southern," Will said softly.

"I have not seen much of her work yet." Fred listed off a few other names, "Charles Condor, David Davies and, of course, George Folingsby. He's a teacher here too."

Again Will nodded.

Jonty glanced around the well-lit room, and his untrained eye loved what he saw.

Fred saw his glance. "It'll be a while yet, so go and have a look around. The paint on mine is wet, so don't touch it." He pointed to a large painting, about ninety inches by about one hundred and twenty inches.

Jonty gasped as he caught sight of the artwork. It magnetically drew both Will and Jonty to it.

"Oh, golly-gosh, Fred, this is good!" Will scrutinised the work. "Fred, is this the little girl from Puckapunyal that went missing while I was here?"

"Yes, Will, I could not believe that a two-year-old could survive in the bush alone for five days. For her to survive by herself and not be afraid is a miracle, don't you think? I thought the moment deserved to be preserved for posterity. A goodwill story if you like." The three stood looking at the painting, the man gently lifting the little girl and safely taking her home.

Jonty turned and walked to the other side of the room without a word, then viewed the artwork. From a distance, he could drink in the skill of the artist. The old man kneeled in the bush, his shirt sleeves rolled up and a beaten-up hat on his head. The care and compassion on the man's face made a lump form in Jonty's throat. Then he looked deeper into the work. His eyes were drawn past the characters along the track and into the misty bushland. The light Mr McCubbin had captured made Jonty feel he was sitting there with him, almost like an observer. Jonty stood rooted to the spot and was totally unaware that his mouth had dropped open, and he was now observed by others who had arrived.

"Blooming heck, Fred, it's brilliant! Why have you been keeping this hidden from us?" one voice enquired.

Another said, "Hey, Frederick, is that the Arthur child? The postmaster's daughter from Puckapunyal?"

As Frederick had returned to what he was doing before their arrival, his simple answer of "Yes," was all the reply he gave.

"It's finished, isn't it? That's why you've unveiled it?" Will said.

Frederick just nodded. The anxious look on his face spoke volumes. His soft question to Will showed his anxiety. "So you like it?"

"Oh yes, Fred, I like it very much." Will, too stood gazing at the work. He flicked his eyes to Jonty, who had not moved since moving across the room. Emotions flicked across Jonty's face; Will watched as his eyes moved from the foreground to the misty light of the trees and the path receding into the distance. He moved to stand beside him and admire the work from afar.

"Will, his perspective is brilliant; everything is… well, it's just right. The morning light, the trees, the child, the entire composition of it, well, it's just perfect. I can imagine my grandfather Douglas doing this. Only he was a sea captain, so he had longer whiskers. Grandfather Finn would have had a grin planted on his face. I never knew him without a laugh on his lips." Jonty fell silent again.

"I was wondering if you could see Douglas in him; I certainly do." Will saw what Jonty meant. You felt you could walk into the bush behind the rescuer from a distance. "Hey, Fred, what's this one called? Miss Arthur? Or what?"

"No, Will." Fred had finished what he'd been doing and now joined them. "It's just called 'Lost'. Sometimes a simple word speaks volumes."

"Did you know the family, Mr McCubbin?" Jonty asked.

"Call me Fred, please, lad. We're about the same age; I'm just an artist. No, I didn't, but the story spoke to me. This one, thankfully, had a happy ending. She was found alive after five days and four nights wandering in the bush. No hat or shoes. No one knows how she survived, but she did. I heard that she was no worse for wear after a month." The three stood looking at the work; the others had moved from blocking their view of the painting. He shrugged. "The story just got to me."

Fred was about to start a new canvas, and Jonty saw that he'd already prepared it for painting. Will had taught him how to do that already. Without a word, he shadowed Fred as he started preparing his painting space. The canvas was soon smothered with background colours. The only noises in the room were the shuffling of papers, the scratching of brushes on the canvasses, or the sounds of paints being mixed. All conversation ceased as the artists became involved in their various works.

Will had disappeared but had said he would return at noon. Jonty wasn't concerned as he knew he had come to do some work. He had not said what it was.

Fred started talking to Jonty out of the blue. "You mentioned perspective, lad, so you know something of art. I love Turner's work, but see if you can find some illustrations to look at and see what I mean. But I was taught by Eugene von Guerard, who's returned to London with Tom Roberts. He's that student I was talking to Will about. Oh, Jonty, that boy has skills. I see his work going far. He's about our age too, so when he returns, invite him up for a visit. I might come with him." Fred fell silent for a while. "He's got more skill in his little finger than some will ever have if they study all their life. Young Streeton is another to watch. He's the boy who did those watercolours. Come and see some of his other works." He didn't wait for Jonty to answer but walked to a large portfolio folder on the darker side of the room. "Have a flick through this, lad," Jonty thought it funny that Fred called him lad, Will had told him there was only a year difference between him and Jonty. But he felt much younger. Fred flopped open the huge art folder and flicked through to a bundle of watercolour paintings already dry and flattening in the squashed folder. There was a sheet of tissue paper between each one.

Jonty saw the first small one and was spellbound. There must have been fifty small watercolour paintings in this section. Each was more beautiful than the last; his skill was developing with each one. Only Jonty didn't stop looking when he had seen all of Arthur's work. The next name in the folder was surprising; it was some work by an obviously young artist; even more surprising was that it was a girl. While there were not many of them, Jonty could see they were good. She had caught the purple mist of the morning light. There was something about her work that drew you to look deeper. The next artist was another lady, Jane Sutherland. He noticed she liked painting other young women, children, and distant landscapes.

He shut the folder, then opened it at the front, slowly working through every artist on file. He had no idea how long he'd been occupied, but it must have been over an hour as Will was soon beside him asking, "Ready for luncheon?"

Jonty nodded. "Oh Will, I'm in awe with this work, so much so I forgot to go and watch Fred paint. Have you seen Simon Marshall's work? It's astounding. He's only a schoolboy, but his perspective is incredible, as is his artistic skill."

"No, I haven't, but I'll look later. Come and eat; I brought a platter of sandwiches for everyone." Will led the way to the bathroom at the back of the studio. They washed up and rejoined the others to eat their noon repast. There was a pile of filled buns. Jonty chose a ham and pickle, and as he ate, the artists around him spoke of mediums and pigments.

Will listened for a while, then when they brought the conversation around to an excursion, he put his hand in his pocket and pulled out some small tins with screw-on lids. "I saw these in the shop next to the bakery where I bought the food." He held up his bun. "I thought they might work as paint pots for outside trips."

The group sat discussing the mixing of paints and how long they would remain usable. They decided to try the idea. After they had eaten, about eight artists went with Will to the shop down the road.

They returned in about half an hour, all burbling with excitement. They set about preparing for an outing the following day and would try them out in the great outdoors.

Chapter 9   En Plein-Air
(Painting Outdoors)

*T*he following day Will and Jonty arrived armed with baskets and assorted

other items. They carried a flagon of ginger beer, and a basket full of utensils, foodstuffs, and fruit. Each wore wide-brimmed hats and old clothing. They were excited to join the art school and soon arrived at the school building. Fred was there with a wagon, and stacked on that was a pile of easels, boxes of palettes and paints, a bundle of cloths and rags, numerous blank canvasses, and folding chairs. The vast volume of equipment needed made Jonty's eyes pop.

Jonty leaned over to Will and whispered, "All this to paint outside?"

Will nodded. "Yes, Jon, thus the need for organisation. Some twenty of us are heading out today, which makes carrying all the equipment easier. It's why artists normally only draw outdoors and then head back to the studios to paint. It's not worth the effort."

They finished loading the wagon, and various gigs, horses, and carriages soon appeared from the park across the road. All were on time.

After much discussion, Fred decided just to paint the Yarra River today and see how they went. The spot he'd chosen was one of his favourite places, and there was room for everyone to set up without having to go far from the wagon.

It took until mid-morning before they were set up enough to start painting. Each had brought their own food and intended to continue work to eat.

The base coats and preparations were done weeks before *en masse*. All they had to do was to collect a pile of pre-prepared canvasses and go. All these were of reasonably small size, about forty-eight inches square, and fitted in the easels.

Throughout the day, Jonty heard the grunts and groans from various artists as the light changed. They knew it was time to pack up when one artist yelled, "Ahh, I've had enough, the light keeps moving, and I can't get the shadows right!"

~

The next day they spent finishing their *en plein-air* works at the studio. It was a lot less stressful, but the subject could no longer be accessed for reference; having said that, the bugs didn't get stuck in the paint, and the sun didn't burn them. All the works produced were delightful.

Frederick viewed Jonty's own efforts. He stood looking at the painting with his head twisting from side to side. A frown over one eye made Jonty think he'd failed. His heart sank. Frederick finally spoke. "Is this truly your first time using oils?"

Jonty nodded, not trusting his voice, unsure if an unkind critique or a compliment would follow the comment.

"Well, I wouldn't have known. Jonty, you do have skills. Your perspective is good, as is your composition, the use of the colour is well-balanced, and the application technique is, hmm… well, easy. When it's dried a little, tackle the water, it needs to be a bit murkier, or it won't look like the Yarra. Considering you've never touched this medium before, it's good."

Jonty was stunned. Coming from the artist who painted that magnificent painting, Jonty was struck dumb. What an accolade!

A voice behind him spoke in glowing terms, too. "I told you he had talent, Fred. I've been only teaching him the preparation of canvasses. He has been too busy to do much painting, but his watercolours…."

"I've invited myself up, Will; when Tom comes back in a few years, we'll both come for a visit." Fred grinned at his friend. "A few of us may well come during the holidays, so think where we can stay, Will."

~

The week passed in a slather of turpentine, paint, linseed oil, and many clothes. Twice Jonty had somehow worn a palette of paint that he'd forgotten sat on his seat. Thankfully he had a dedicated pair of painting trousers which he donned once he arrived at the studio. Will had initially just chuckled the first time Jon sat in the paint. When he did it again, Will doubled up laughing as the palette stuck to his derriere.

Jonty had finished his first painting by Thursday, and Fred gave him another smaller canvas to work on. "This time, I want you to paint, from memory, something you love."

A slow smile spread across Jonty's face. "I'll try." He knew what he would paint, and he knew how he's set the composition. They each went off to their own easels, and Jonty set up his own so no one could see it. If he didn't finish it today, he still had a couple of days before they were due to leave.

In Eddie's backyard was the family's favourite October occupation; an enormous mulberry tree that was laden with fruit each spring. As children, many used to climb it and pick and eat the purple fruit. It was up this tree he first kissed Lottie. He was about nineteen, and she was fifteen. Before that, she had just been a pretty distant cousin. He had done it as a dare from her cousin Rick; however, from that day onwards, he was just waiting for her to grow up. When she turned eighteen, he stole another kiss behind the same tree. She had stuck her head around the tree, and quick as a flash, he had given her a peck on the lips. It was a memory he had never forgotten. He set to work.

Ellen woke hearing tears. She snuck out of bed and stood outside Lottie's room before knocking softly. On receiving no reply, she opened the door a little.

Lottie was sobbing into her pillow.

"Oh darling," Ellie said as she went inside and shut the door.

"Oh, Mama, I miss him so much, and he's only been gone for a week. I want him back, but I want to be here too." She sounded so miserable.

Her plaintive cry was met with a giggle by her mother.

Ellen was relieved. She could easily cope with this; she was fearful that there was something wrong with the marriage. "Oh, sweetheart, welcome to motherhood. Your emotions are all over the place; everything will be 'all wrong' no matter what happens. If he were here, nothing he did would be right, and if he weren't here, that wouldn't help either." Ellen sat on the side of the bed and drew her daughter to her.

Lottie's blue eyes were swimming with the unshed tears. "Mama, I'm so scared. You said I should be just feeling movement, but if it feels like butterflies in your tummy, then I've been feeling it for a week or more. I didn't tell Jon Jon before he left, but I'm pretty sure we're having more than one… and I'm so frightened… and he's not here… and I want him home…." She sobbed in her mother's arms.

Ellen lay back on the bed head with her weeping daughter cradled against her. She stroked her hair back from her wet face. "That's a bridge we will cross when we get to it. Two is not really worse than one, not that I've ever had just one. We'll come for the first few weeks, and then Dimmy will be next to you, and she will be a wonderful help. You can always get paid help in too. Don't try to do it all yourself. But oh, you two were such a delight, my sweet." Ellen stayed with her for some time, discussing the joys of parenthood. When Lottie cheered enough, Ellen kissed her and returned to their room.

By the time they were all up and having breakfast, it was as though the incident had never happened. Lottie was bright and bubbly and giggling. Halfway through breakfast, Lottie said, "Mama, I have made a decision; I have always been an 'accept what comes' sort of girl, and if this is two or three little cherubs, then I'll accept what God sends us."

Dimity and Luke had no idea what she was talking about. She saw the puzzled look on their faces. "I think I may be carrying twins," she said, rubbing a gentle bump. "I should not be showing at all, and I am. This morning is the first one I've not been ill, but the day is not over yet." She chuckled. "So instead of tears, as Mama can attest, I am going to change my attitude to trust rather than fear." She folded her arms in a stubborn manner that her parents had seen often.

Her father laughed. "That's my girl; I'm so proud of you I hope you know that."

Jonty was totally oblivious to everything that was going on around him. He was so deeply involved in his painting that he had not noticed the fading light or the absence of noise around him. He lifted his head only when it became too dark to see his canvas. "Damn!" he muttered.

He heard a burst of laughter. "I was wondering when you'd notice it was nearly dark." Will had been sitting quietly behind him, watching the intensity of his passion. He could see the scene develop and thought he knew that tree well. It was under that same tree that he had met Luke and then all the Lockley family. He and Ricky had been invited to Luke's wedding, and it was the day Jonty had been born. Will had been sitting watching him for over half an hour. The intensity of Jon's face while he was painting was one Will knew.

Will was intrigued that Jonty could get the paint onto the canvas with a minimum of time. He had hardly taken a break in the ten hours since he'd set up the blank canvas. The mulberry tree was laden with deep purple fruit, and he could see the beginnings of a figure hiding behind the trunk.

"Can we come back tomorrow after the auction? I want to finish it before I leave. I want Lottie to know I missed her." He had not looked at Will since he first noticed him behind, watching.

"We can only come if we leave now." Will started putting the lids on Jonty's paints and began to tidy up the area.

Fifteen minutes later, the two were ready to leave. Jonty had left his wet painty trousers in the studio, and Will had locked up, and they caught a cab to Theo's house. Tomorrow was the auction then they would return to the studio for a few hours. Will had a few strokes to add to his own composition then it too would be complete.

~

They were waiting at the door of the auction house at nine the next morning in Brunswick Street. Will chuckled when he showed Jonty where the auction house was. It was the corner of the next street. Getting there required no transport. The doors were to open two hours before the auction started.

Will smiled; it was as though Jonty had switched off the artistic side and switched on the jeweller again. He was intrigued that he had this ability.

Row after row of jewellery was laid out, each with a number: number description and an estimated value. Jonty had a journal and was jotting notes in this book. Others in the crowd were doing the same.

Will had not been to a jewellery auction and watched on with interest. He'd asked Jonty to keep his eyes open for something Dimity would like. Row after row, Jonty took notes until he paused at one item. He lifted his head and caught sight of Will standing off to the side. Jonty beckoned him over. In front of him was an exquisite brooch. It was made of blue and white topaz set in gold, designed as a spray of flowers. There were matching screw-on earbobs.

Will took a look at the pieces before him. "Oh, Jon, these are perfect, but how much will it go for?"

Jonty checked the catalogue. "Will, they are not reserved, so I'd say you will get them for about £10 to £20 plus commission. Retail they would go for around £100."

Jonty saw Will smile. "Good, I have £40, so with the commission, bid what you can, but allow for the commission."

By the time they left at noon, Jonty had the most important items he wanted for himself and Mr Lamb, and Will got his gift for Dimity. They left quietly before the auction finished and returned to the studio after leaving the gems at Theo's house.

~

Will finished his small work and packed up. Jonty was adding the last strokes of his painting. Will again came and sat quietly, watching his skill. The intense look on Jonty's face showed his total involvement in the moment. He had yet to add the face to the character half-hidden behind the tree trunk. Will sat with arms folded, watching; he had a smile hovering, knowing whose face would appear.

Will watched in silence. Jonty even added blurred black dots as the mulberries fell from the tree. He could see a child's face up the tree and another figure at the bottom behind the trunk. He felt he was almost there and able to pick them himself. He could practically taste the fruit. Sure enough, Lottie's face was added last and then Jonty stood back, looking at the final strokes.

"I'm ready now, Will," he said.

Will looked puzzled. "Ready for what, Jon?"

"Ready to go home and become a father. I wasn't ready before. I needed to get my own head straight, and now..." he stood looking at Lottie in the picture. "Now, thanks to you, I think it is. At least it's getting there."

"So, no dreams at all?" Will's quiet concern made Jonty turn to him.

"I've had one dream, but I have discovered that I can now turn them off. I've never been able to do that before. Each night I stand at my window and 'do my release.' My sleep is peaceful, and although the memories have not gone, I know that I can cope." He turned back to his painting. "I'm ready also to go back and be the best husband I can be, Will. We married so fast, and my head wasn't in the right place. I love her, don't get me wrong, but well, we did things the wrong way around. Now she's with child, and things moved so quickly, neither of us really had a chance to prepare mentally; we had to marry when we did; we had no option. Mind you, neither of us wished to have a big lar-de-dar wedding, but it was quick. Lately, she's been so ill most mornings, and meat smells make her sick. It's been hard, but this week has let me get things in the correct perspective. The entire time I was in Africa, all I wanted to do was to get home to her, then when I did… well, I blew it."

Will had not realised that their marriage was necessary, which was why it had been so hasty. Yes, he knew they had married soon after Jonty's return but didn't know the details. "Ahh, yes, the stresses of married life can be a bit of a shock. Dimmy is a strong-willed lady and our first weeks together took some getting used to. That goes with any new relationship, Jon. Marriage is just far more intimate. There is no place to really have your own space."

He saw Jonty nodding. Will said lovingly, "Even in my studio, I have the settee. Don't get me wrong, I love her there watching, but sometimes I need the 'alone time' that is rare in marriage. More often than not, I forget she's there watching. She doesn't chat or anything…." Will smiled to himself. "But I adore her, Jon! She is my life. I would do anything for her." He thought back to just after they were married. He had been more than content to be with her every moment of the day. Then he was sitting talking to her over the breakfast table, and the painting bug hit one morning. He had been admiring her elfin face and her adorable brown eyes and hair. The feeling of adoration almost overwhelmed him. Without realising he was being rude, he stood and took his tea into the studio, picked up a blank canvas, and started painting.

Throughout the morning and into the afternoon, he painted almost wildly. That was the first time Dimity came and watched him at work. The background was done, and a void was left in the middle. As Dimity watched, she emerged onto the canvas. But it was not the brown mouse she saw in the mornings in the mirror. What she beheld was a glowing, lovely, confident woman in a jonquil-coloured gown who reflected love from her eyes. As she watched, she realised the depth of his love for her far more than his words had ever expressed.

Will now smiled at this memory, that painting hung in their bedroom. He'd let no other see it, as it was thought his heart hung framed on the wall.

Jonty continued. "Yes, the same with Lottie, although at least I can go to work. But the funny thing is, when I'm at work, I wish to be at home with her."

Will said, "Now that we live next door to each other, we will encourage the girls to go on jaunts together. Even to assist with the babies at Sadie House. They always need more hands." Will glanced at Jonty. "Jon, when children come, life really starts to get complicated. That's when your time together really becomes precious. Use that time wisely. Please don't waste it. Those years flash by so fast, and then suddenly, there are just the two of you again."

With both paintings now finished, they did the final cleanup, and once everything was tidy and stowed, they set the paintings to dry and went back to Theo's house.

As they walked, they talked more of the children. "Will, how the heck did you name your son Theodore? That's Greek, isn't it?"

Will chuckled. "Yes, well, that takes a bit of explaining. You see, our oldest boy is Richard John, after Ricky and John Landon. I have no knowledge of who my parents were, so I named him after the two most influential men in my life, that was Ricky, of course, and his mentor. Our second son we named Theodore after Tad, as that's his real name. His second name is William, after me. I suppose we should have added a Frederick in somewhere after Dimmy's papa, but well, we decided not to after… well, we decided not to." He gave an embarrassed smile.

Jonty knew the Roger family and how they had initially disliked Will intensely. As Dimity was their only child, they were very protective. He had heard the entire story from his parents years before.

They spoke some more about names, and Jonty laughed at his explanation. "I know you were at the wedding on the day I was born, but explaining to people that Jonty is not actually my name is funny. Jonathon Finn Douglas Evans is a mouthful enough, but Uncle Hamish Macdonald gave me the name on that day. Jonty apparently means 'Little John' in Scotland. Hence my name."

Will remembered that day well. His first meeting with the Lockley family *en masse* was totally unforgettable. Tad and Amabel were on their honeymoon, and only he and Ricky went to the gathering at Jonty's grandfather, Douglas Evans' invitation. They had all drunk too much fermented ginger beer and all woke with headaches. Jonty's mother had gone into labour during the service. He remembered that they had gone home on the ferry with a tremendous amount of leftover food. That weekend had been the start of many visits to Parramatta and then to Emu Plains. Will had finally been able to visit Eddie and his forge. The friendship had grown from when he had first met Ed over fifty years before as children. Eddie had mentored and encouraged him to learn to read and write, and Will was never forgotten.

He owed him much, and so his first significant mural-size painting was of Eddie.

Later that evening, Will, Theo, and Jonty sat talking around the dinner table. Theo's wife had gone to put the children to bed.

The conversation covered many topics, but they fell silent. Will looked at the two faces staring into their tea. "I haven't had a chance to tell either of you something. Jonty, I thought I would do what you said while I was in Melbourne and ask a doctor about my leg." That comment caught their attention. Four eyes were suddenly fixed on him. "Well, one afternoon this week, I went and had a team of doctors prod and poke me. I was bent every which way and jabbed viciously." He chuckled. "And all to no avail. Apparently, I was born like this, or it happened soon after I was born. He thinks my hip was a break, not a birth defect. But even that is good to know. I was wondering if I had been in an accident that caused my parent's demise. I do wish I knew something about my background; alas, nothing. My first memories are of many, many cruel children, and I ran away from them. It was Tad who found me not long afterwards and brought me to Ricky."

"Wow, Dad, had you never asked before?" Theo was stunned that his father had never had a doctor look at his leg before.

"Why should I, Theo? It's never really worried me. It was only because Jon here asked if I had. I happened to be near a hospital, so I went in." He shrugged. "Nothing, anyone, can do, so in the end, pointless."

Jonty looked at him with a twinkle in his eye. "Actually, Will, if this is so, someone may have written something down. Sixty years ago, birth details were recorded in Sydney, so there could well be a record; even possible, that you may have a Baptism record if we can find out about your birth. Would you mind if I had a look when we return home?"

Will and Theo stared at Jonty. "You mean you might be able to find out who I am? Truly?" Will asked, stunned.

"We probably won't, but it's no harm looking. If a child was born in a hospital with a gammy leg, I'm sure it would be recorded. I'm thinking that if that was the case and you don't remember your mother or your early years, then maybe you were put in an orphanage." Jonty had sat through many a dinner with Lottie's Uncle Tim. He and his own uncles, Phil and Steve Evans, had assisted many orphan children in accessing information about their records.

Will found that he had a lump in his throat. After some moments, he finally found his voice. "Jon, if there is any chance, can we look when we go home?"

"Willingly, Will, but remember there may be nothing in the records." Jonty did not wish to sow false hope in either of them.

~

Monday morning, they went to the studio late. They arrived after everyone had started work, well, everyone but Frederick. He was waiting for them. As they entered, they saw that he was standing in front of Jonty's painting, his arms folded, and he was pondering the subject. The more he looked, the more children's faces he found in the tree. At first, he thought they were patches of light but saw they were the blonde heads of children. A smile broke when his eyes reached Lottie's smiling face at the tree's base.

The two new entrants walked to stand on either side of him.

"I found nine!" Fred said.

"Nine, what, Fred?" Will asked while staring at the picture.

"Children, Will. How many are there, Jonty?" Fred queried.

"Sixteen actually; they are some of the young Lockleys." One by one, he pointed out the many fair-haired children. Some were only a splash of yellow, and others had faces visible. "I had many, many happy memories playing in Uncle Ed's mulberry tree." He paused, smiling to himself. "That was the day I first properly kissed Lottie. She stuck her head around the trunk, and I gave her a peck on her lips. We were only really children ourselves, but even then, I knew she was special to me." He blushed as he met the smiles of the two artists. "Well, you told me to paint something I loved. So I did."

Fred laughed. "I' would willingly give this wall space in my home, Jonty. To think you have done it in a few days is amazing. But it's perfect." He stood nodding at the life-like tree that Jonty had captured. "Yes, I like it a lot."

They spent the morning watching others paint.

By five o'clock, it was time to pack up and head home. Will showed Jonty how to wrap his painting so that he could carry it home, hopefully without smudging it.

Their last day was Tuesday before heading down to the jetty and catching their ship back to Sydney. Will spent the entire day with his family, and Jonty left them alone. He wished to catch up with his friend Paul Murray and found he'd moved out of town a bit. He found him just before noon, and they spent a few happy hours catching up. Jonty filled him in on the deep prayer therapy Will had told him about. He saw Paul smile.

"I call it power prayer Jon, and I know it works," Paul told Jonty about his traumas during his time as a soldier. "My uncle walked me through it, you know, the Captain you met. But it wasn't until I did, as you called the release, that I could finally come to terms with everything. I stopped having nightmares after that."

They spent the afternoon talking, and just before they parted, they shared a prayer, and Jonty issued an invitation if he wished to visit Sydney. Jonty mentioned that he had since married, and they were expecting a child in early spring.

Paul said, "I'll come one day." Paul paused before adding, "Jon, you have never asked me why I'm here. I'm on the hunt for any trace of a missing family member. I would have come earlier, but my little sister married and I had to stay home as part of the wedding party. Before that, I'd been serving overseas. Anyway, I doubt if I shall find any trace as it was six decades ago, but I'll try. One set of my grandparents died not knowing what happened to their eldest daughter. My father was the youngest sibling; he barely remembered his sister. Captain Cromby married my aunt, who is the sibling above my father. Aunt Addy came out here to join her husband and sent a letter to say she had arrived safely and met up with her husband. They did not hear from her again. I can't find any trace of them here, so I might have to try Sydney next. They may have gone west farming, but I should be able to find some record somewhere. So once I have exhausted my search here, I'll try up your way."

They parted after Jonty gave him his direction.

Chapter 10 Revelations

*T*he trip back was a little rougher than the southbound journey. The ship's bow ploughed into the oncoming waves, making sitting outdoors uncomfortable. They tried to manage at least an hour outdoors each day, sitting in the fresh air. They would give up when one or other of them got drenched. Chuckling, the two would retire inside, dry off, and sit in the reading room for the remainder of the day.

With objectives now to achieve at home, both were keen to return. A headwind slowed the trip in the steam sailing ship, but every hour brought them closer to their destination.

Jonty had promised he would search for Will's roots, and with his uncles to assist, he hoped he'd be able to find an answer. He didn't hold out much hope as sixty years was a long time for anyone to remember. Any of the old hospital staff would be long dead. Jonty thought it funny that both he and Paul were doing searches from the same decade.

By the time Sydney Heads was reached, both men were keen to disembark. They hoped the girls would have returned home and would be waiting for them. They had sent through the information about when they were returning.

They saw their loves waiting for them as they pulled into the wharf at Circular Quay. The two men looked at each other without saying a word and smiled. Jonty was down the gangplank before the deckhands had even fixed it into place. He swept a giggling Lottie up in his arms into a passionate, loving kiss. Once he put her down, he said, "Hello love, I missed you."

Will, too, strolled hobbling down onto the wharf and gave Dimity a loving kiss. "Hello sweets." He gently caressed her cheek with his knuckles, just adoring her welcome. "Have I told you how much I do so love you?"

"You have my permission to do so often, Willy, my love, but let's get your things and get home." Dimity soon took control of the porters.

Jonty took them to their cabin to collect their things. He went so he could carry his still-wet painting. He would trust it to no one. He intended to hang it in their bedroom. Luke had arranged for a carriage to take them home, not because the distance was far or arduous, but because he didn't wish Lottie to walk far. Will also found the walk uphill hard, not that he ever acknowledged it. He released a deep sigh of contentment. The more he knew of the Lockleys, the more he loved them.

~

Within a week, Jonty had spoken to both his Evans' uncles in Sydney and asked them if there was any way they could access the records at Sydney Hospital and search the files. He then thought no more about it, thinking there was just no possibility of finding anything; he put it out of his mind.

His uncle, Phil, knocked on their door about two weeks after the conversation. Jonty looked stunned when he met his uncle's grin.

Phil just said, "Found him!"

Jonty pulled him into his arms. "Uncle Phil, are you kidding? Can we go straight in and tell Will?"

Phil nodded. "You bet it's quite a story."

Jonty called for Lottie to join them, and they quickly went next door. Jonty knocked, and when Dimity opened the door and met the massive grin on Jonty's face, she clapped her hands and giggled. "Come in, come in! He's just upstairs prepping canvasses." They went into the sitting room and made themselves comfortable. It wasn't long before the two men heard Will's uneven footsteps. The door crashed open as he entered. "Sorry, didn't mean that. Dimmy said you found something." Will looked from Phil to Jonty and back to Phil.

"Sit down, Will; it's a long story, Dimity, you too." Phil sat back in his chair. "Okay, now where to start?" He paused, looking at his friend of long-standing. Thinking back to the scrubby, undernourished child of about eight he had first met at school. "In 1820, a married lady arrived looking for her husband. She arrived with her husband's sister-in-law, Mary, and her young son. Both were planning to meet their husbands and find some farmland. William arrived, and he and his wife, Adelaide, left to find a farm. They planned to meet up back here once they had settled. Time passed, and they found land, and William built a small cottage. They planned to install a manager, or hand management over to the younger brother and then head back to England. The couple lived contentedly for a year. Adelaide wrote to her dear friend and sister-in-law but heard nothing more; she then wrote to the Governor, searching for her, as he was a family acquaintance. It's how we know this much, as the letter was still on the file. As you know, I'm on the Governor's staff. His staff had come across this as he was tidying the archives. Intrigued, he opened the sealed letter only a month ago. It had sat unread for the best part of sixty years." Phil was watching Jonty's stunned face. However, he continued. "Here, we have a gap, but we can surmise that Adelaide was expecting and came to Sydney to deliver her child. Sadly as they entered the town, there was a bad carriage accident, and her husband, William, was killed instantly. She was injured and taken to hospital. Being nearly full-term, they kept the news from her for as long as they could. When she was eventually told, she collapsed. The child, a boy, was born the next day. Unbeknownst to anyone, the child was also injured in the accident, born with a badly twisted leg. Sadly his mother died soon after his birth. The child was alone. The hospital didn't know the whereabouts of the other family who had accompanied them. One young nurse was asked to care for him. She idolised the injured little baby. The poor mite's leg was so painful, but there was little they could do. They later realised that his hip had been injured in the accident. By the time they found the cause, it was too late to do much about it. The young nurse cared for the babe for six months until disease hit the hospital, and they needed the beds. Sadly for everyone, the baby boy was sent to the orphanage. They had named him William Richard after his father."

The four listeners sat spellbound; Jonty was obviously itching to say something but held his counsel.

Phil took a long deep breath, "This is where it gets good, Will. I didn't have to dig far to find out their surname. It was written on the back of the letter. They know the letter was connected to the couple in the carriage accident due to the documentation on the father's body. He had the bank account details and the title to the land on him, which by the way, he had fully paid for and is now yours, Will."

Dimity was watching the tears slide unnoticed down her gentle husband's face. He was slowly shaking his head in disbelief and swallowing as he listened. Phil saw but kept talking. "I'll continue; the years roll by, and the young nurse herself married and moved away. No one visits the little boy anymore, and he's left alone in the orphanage. All the paperwork is kept safely for him when he reaches his majority. However, aged about seven, he runs away, and they never find him."

Will drew out a very painty handkerchief from his pocket and blew his nose. "But Phil, who am I? Do I have a name?"

"Oh, you have a name Will, and you have a family. We all trust God and know He works in amazing ways. William Richard, your real surname is…." He paused and watched his friend's face. "It's… English."

With that, Will choked a sob. "How? How can it be my real name?" He sat digesting the information. "Mary English, Ricky's mother, was my mother's sister-in-law and my aunt? His father, Richard, was my uncle, and Ricky is my cousin?" He watched Phil nod to each question, and he turned to Dimity and wept in her arms. His deep hacking sobs shook his body. They all stayed silent for some time while he digested the information.

Phil was watching Jonty's face; it was incredulous. With a sideways nod, Jonty motioned for Phil to go with him. They silently left the room and walked down the corridor. Jonty was almost bursting to tell his uncle of what he knew. "Uncle Phil, there's more to the story. More jigsaw bits have just fallen into place. You know that when Lottie was presented in 1882, Chip's twins were also presented. Christie announced her engagement to their cousin, Stephen Hunt. We know they were planning to marry last year, well word arrived while we were in Melbourne that they certainly did marry in December last year. But so did CJ, her twin. They had a double service. CJ married Adelaide Murray."

Phil nodded, "Yes, all that I know, but what's the connection?"

"Do you remember I told you about the man who helped with my nightmares on board? His name is Paul Murray; he is out here looking for his lost Aunt Adelaide. He told me the entire story, which parallels what you just told us. The only thing he didn't mention was about her travelling with anyone. They knew about the farm and that fact that she was expecting, then silence. If I'm right, Will is that child and, therefore, Chip's cousin. That also makes him a Lockley cousin."

Phil's response was only, "Cor!"

Jonty asked, "Should we say anything? It might be too much to take in." He looked worried.

Phil smiled and said, "In for a penny, in for a pound Jon. I think you should tell him, but maybe we should make them some tea." The two men entered the kitchen and quickly found the ingredients to make tea for everyone.

Ten minutes later, they returned to the sitting room. Jonty placed the tray down. Dimity poured and handed around the mugs. She pulled a funny face and smiled. "Mugs, really, Jonty?"

"Yep, not enough in those dainty china things, and we haven't finished the story yet. There's more," Jonty said, smiling at Will.

"No, no more, I have a name, and Ricky is my cousin." He grinned. "I have a name, love; William Richard English is my name, my real name."

Phil sat back in his chair, "I'll finish my story before Jonty tells his bit. I'm sure you remember our conversation at Luke's wedding. About you not having a birth certificate and therefore you could not get a government job?"

Will nodded, "Yeah, thanks for fixing that."

"The date I used happened to be August 1st. I guessed about 1823, estimated from the size you were when we first met." Phil saw the slight nod of acknowledgement, so he continued. "The accident occurred in July 1823, and you were born on August 2nd. So I was one day out. Not a bad guess, eh?"

Will's jaw dropped. "You mean I even have a real birth certificate?"

"Yes, and a Baptism Certificate too; what's more, the young nurse is still alive and, although very elderly, is of sound mind. She had this with her all these years. She asked the minister to Baptise you soon after you were born. He did it in the hospital." Phil handed him the old and faded certificate.

"Will, she prayed for you every day of your life." Jonty sat clutching Lottie's hand. He leaned and whispered something to her, and she nodded.

Will was reeling with the overload of information. "Jon, you said you have something; you may as well add to it. It can't be more incredible than what I have just heard."

"Want to bet?" Jonty grinned almost wickedly. He took a deep breath. "Fine, we go back to the ship on my way back from Europe last year. I told you about Paul Murray and his uncle. Will, while you spent your last day in Melbourne with Theo, I went and found Paul. He told me why he was here as I'd never asked him before." Jonty related the story of Paul's search. All sat looking very puzzled. "Well, we have to confirm it's the same family, but the names are right, and I'm pretty sure that it's all the same one. Will, we told you Chip's son had just married in Kent?"

Will and Dimity nodded.

"CJ married Adelaide Murray, and she is General Murray's granddaughter." Jonty grinned as he said these words.

Looking puzzled, Will said, "Yes, but…."

"Well, General Murray had at least two daughters, Adelaide and Catherine, and two sons, Paul and Algernon."

Will was about to interrupt again.

Jonty pulled a sheet of paper from his pocket; he'd been doodling with some designs. "Here, let me draw it for you." He wrote the General on the top line; under it, he added the children's names, Adelaide, Algernon, Paul, and Catherine. "There may be other Murray children, but these four are the important characters. Paul is my friend Paul's father, Catherine is Captain Cromby's wife, Algernon is the name of Chip's son CJ's father-in-law, and Adelaide, the eldest child, married a man named William and came to Australia in 1820." Will went to say something, but Jonty silenced him. "Do you see where I'm heading with this?"

Will shook his head in disbelief, "Not really! But Chip is the Duke, and CJ is the Marquess. This Adelaide is my cousin? So I'm related to the Lockleys too?" Rather than weep, Will started chuckling, then laughing. His deep belly laugh made them join him. This time tears of joy were flowing down his face for some minutes. He finally wiped his cheeks, again smearing paint on them. He didn't care. "Phil, Jon, you two have just answered every question about my background that I've ever wished to know." He gave a big and loud sniff. "This is just so darned good. How can I ever thank you both?" Dimity sat holding his hand.

"I have a way…." Jonty said with a smile. "Please let us be there when you tell both Ricky and Tad?"

Will looked at Dimity, then the others. "That's a given!" His grin lit up his face. Suddenly a thought occurred to him. "Lottie, I'm a distant cousin!" He gave a chuckle and clapped his hands, "This is just so good!"

Jonty sat thinking for a while. "Will, can you telegraph Theo and get him to… no, that won't work, write to Theo and suggest that he goes around to meet Paul, then tell him of the connection."

Will sat nodding. "Yes, yes, that would work; then Paul can come and Phil, can you re-tell him what you have found? In the meantime, I'd like to meet the nurse if she's around."

Phil nodded, "Tomorrow at ten, Will; I have already made an appointment. Dimity, you and your neighbours, are invited as well."

~

The following day, Phil arrived with his wife, Alice; the other four were ready and waiting. Will was almost hopping with glee. He had not slept much due to his excitement.

As she used to be known, Sister Vera Abell was waiting at the door for her visitors. She greeted them all with merely a nod and held the door open for them. She led the way into the sitting room, Will hard on her heels. It was only in the privacy of this room that she turned and held open her arms. "My Will," she said.

Will then had the closest he had ever had to a mother's hug. They stood embracing for a long time. Vera pulled away and looked up at the man before her. "I have prayed for you every day, Will. I married and moved away; whenever I came to Sydney, we would visit you, then one day, when you were about seven, you were gone. We looked everywhere."

Will led her to what was obviously her chair. She sat and revealed more about the accident that took his father's life. "We did not know until you were born that you had been injured. Your mother's stomach was bruised, but there were no cuts or blood. Had we known, there was little we could have done anyway. You were alive, and I had to focus on that. Will, I was only fifteen. I worked as an aide and ran messages, but you were given into my care. I slept in there at the hospital to look after you until you were weaned from the wet nurse. You were about eight weeks old when we realised that your leg didn't work properly. We knew you were in great pain before that, but even so, you cried little. When the doctors looked at it, they found that your hip was probably broken. They had no way to fix it. I found one doctor who at least tried, and it certainly helped. We strapped your legs together and tried to straighten your hips. We thought we had it right until you started crawling. We knew by then it was too late to do more, but although you had a limp, we knew you would walk."

Will returned her apologetic look with, "I can walk, and I dance too, Vera. May I call you that?"

She nodded willingly.

"We don't dance often, but enough to dance at our four children's weddings. We have two boys and two girls." He looked over to Dimity. May I introduce my darling wife? Dimity, this is my …" he paused before looking at the elderly lady. "This is my foster mother, Vera. The only mother I'd known."

Dimity gave her a slight nod and mouthed, "Thank you."

A maid brought tea, and the group had many details filled in for them. The revelations of that morning were a delight, but more was to follow. Before they left home, Will had sent notes to Tad and Ricky to meet at his house at two o'clock.

Phil had returned home for luncheon and returned at two, just as Ricky and Tad arrived together. "Hello, Phil, what's this all about, Will's note gave no hint."

"Ahh," said Phil. "It's not for me to reveal. Come and settle yourselves down."

Jonty arrived moments later and let himself in too.

"Hello, everyone. Isn't it a wonderful day? I think so." Will gave a mischievous chuckle. Then he proceeded to stun Ricky and Tad with his story.

"You're my cousin? We're really blood-related?" Ricky finally uttered.

"Yes, and look, I have my real birth certificate to prove it. We went to see the nurse who looked after me when I was born; she still had it with her and my Baptism certificate too. She had kept it all these years. She and her husband had never been able to have children, and they kept visiting me in the orphanage; she told me that they decided to adopt me and when they came back to get me, I had vanished." He saw the looks on his brothers' faces. "Tad, you found me first, but Ricky, if you had not taken us both in, we would possibly both be dead. I may well be an English cousin as much as you are, Ricky, but I'd choose to be your adopted brother any day, yours too, Tad." His two big brothers returned Will's silly grin.

Jonty and Phil listened in silence; Lottie dug Jonty in his ribs. He dropped his head to listen to her words. "I'm sure he'll get around to it, sweetie."

Will had heard them. "No, I won't; I want you to tell that bit, Jonty."

"Sure?" Jonty asked.

Will nodded. "You'll get the details right."

Jonty sat back, relaxed, and revealed the missing link between Jonty and the greater Lockley family. "Will is not only related to you, Ricky, but also to Lottie. By marriage, but still, we are claiming him as family."

The revelations of the afternoon were much discussed. It would make no change in any of their attitudes to Will, but for Will, it was life-changing. He knew who he was. He knew the answer to his limp, and he knew he was loved. It was that final thing that finally made his face melt. Soon his two brothers were on their knees in front of him. Dimity hugged him while seated, and Jonty and Lottie stood behind him with their hands on his shoulders. His weeping, however, did not last long. Soon the room was filled with chuckles, giggles and chortles. The group relived many of the fun times they had shared.

Phil had sat listening to his friends. He looked at the three debonair men and asked, "How did you three meet? I have never known."

Ricky related his tale in a short time, "As we heard, my mother and I arrived to meet my father, only he didn't turn up. I don't even remember an aunt coming with us. We ended up in a poor boarding house where my mother eventually died. At ten, I was out on the street. I found a safe bolt-hole in a stable and was befriended by an old convict bloke named Tom. I'll cut a long story short. One day I witnessed the kidnapping of a little girl; I followed the scum and rescued her. That was Amabel Landon, who is now Tad's wife. Mr Landon became my mentor, but I wanted to do stuff for myself. He allowed me a small room with a brazier and the basics. Not long after, in the middle of a bad storm, I found Tad sleeping in the doorway. He moved in with me too. Soon after that, Tad found Will. The poor kid could hardly walk and was so skinny we didn't know if he would even live. That's when we three became family." Ricky thought back over the trials and traumas they experienced before finding their life partners. "Soon after Will came, I wanted the boys to learn to read and write, and I knew Mr Cape allowed kids to sit at the classroom door and listen in. That's when we met you, Phil, along with Stevie, John, Ed, and Tim. But Lottie's Uncle Ed made the most difference for Will. He told him to learn to read and write, and his world would open, and people wouldn't notice he couldn't walk properly. Hence that first painting Will did."

Ricky remembered that first time he had seen Will's skill manifest on a canvas. He painted and prayed while Amabel was travailing in labour pains. Will painted what he called his dream, but it was far more than a dream. Will painted as though almost possessed. It was certainly not the first large painting he had done, but Ricky had never watched him work before. Will had painted a vision of Heaven. That was the turning point in their openness to discuss faith and their belief in God. It had changed them all.

Chapter 11 New Arrivals

The first of the new arrivals was Paul Murray. He packed up in Melbourne and caught the next ship after receiving the summons from Theo. He had also left word for his uncle to contact him as soon as he arrived. He had also sent a wire to his English family. It just said, *"Found her son. Letter following."* Paul had not even met Will at that stage. He arrived at the end of the week, unable to believe he could finally answer his family's questions.

Once Jonty introduced them, he left them alone. He needed to go to work anyway but would have dearly loved to be a fly on the wall. As Paul was staying with them, they would catch up in the evening. Ricky was to join them during the afternoon. Although they were not related, they shared a cousin in Will. Tad arrived with Ricky. Paul filled the men in on the English background. The three did not tell Paul initially about Jonty's connection; that revelation would follow later in the evening. As the last of Ricky's orphans had recently moved out of the cottage next door to Will and Dimity, Jonty asked his father if Paul could rent it for a few months.

Paul was in residence by the end of the month. Paul had written the story and sent it to his family in England. Will was astonished that he even had an uncle who was not much older than himself. He had married the youngest of the Murray sisters; there were some twenty years between the siblings. Paul revealed the extent of the Murray family, eleven children, and Adelaide was nineteen years older than the youngest.

Will was still reeling from the many revelations. He found he had cousins, aunts, and uncles and now knew the names of his grandparents too. Sadly some were dead, but just knowing who they were was genuinely fantastic. That first night he had wept when everyone had departed. "Dimmy, I belong; I'm no longer a no-one. I have family and sweetheart; I'm Ricky's blood cousin." As they lay in their bed that night, they did something they rarely did; they chatted once the lights were turned out.

Laying snuggled to her beloved, she softly replied, "Darling Will, I didn't care then, and I don't now. I love you for who you are, and that is a truly wonderful man. Yes, it's nice to know your roots, but it makes no difference to me; you know that."

He continued, "I know Dimmy, but now I know what happened to my leg too. I often wondered. It will now be a symbol of love and care. Both from my parents and Nurse Vera. I'm so glad we got to meet her. Did I tell you I'm taking Paul to meet her tomorrow? I want her to tell him the story, so he'll know I'm not making it up." He kissed the top of her head, "Dimmy, I'd love you to come too. Would you?"

"Of course, sweetie. But if we don't get some sleep, well…" She turned and kissed him goodnight but did not pull away from him. He needed that security that only she could give him.

Over at Jonty and Lottie's house, Lottie was snuggled in her husband's arms. "Amazing how Will's injury was the missing clue to his identity; clever you for thinking of that, Jon."

He was about to answer when Lottie said, "Ooh, feel this." She took his hand and placed it on her growing stomach; he felt a kick. And then she moved his hand, and there was another movement.

"I think that we are in for a fun time with these two. I presume that's what you mean?" Jonty said, trying to sound confident. He was feeling far from that. Being thrown into parenthood even before they were married was hard enough; now, it was frightening to find that they were most probably having twins. There was no way he'd ever admit that to her. With so much going on, he'd not had much chance to tell her of his news. He was about to when he realised she was sound asleep. Her deep, even breathing and her regular breaths on his neck made him smile. "Oh well, there is always tomorrow," he thought. He had not had a chance to do his release prayer at the window tonight. He presumed one night wouldn't hurt.

How wrong he was.

Soon after midnight, Jonty started tossing in his sleep. It had been a month since the last bad nightmare. This time he was being chased by twin skeletons. His weapons were a magnifying headset he used for cutting stones and an artist's paintbrush. He was stabbing them with the brush handle, and as they got closer, he started punching it. Behind him, he was trying to protect Lottie and a bevy of tiny identical babies.

Lottie woke when he tried to push her out of bed with his fist. She stripped off the sheet, but that didn't work. She was so tired; she didn't need this but knew that unless she could settle him, neither of them would get back to sleep. Then he began to get violent and was yelling and punching the pillows. She was worried that he'd wake Dimity and Will. Nothing worked. Whenever she drew close, he would fight her.

She was now cowering on the chair on the other side of the room, sobbing. For some reason, that roused him; soon, Jonty was beside her, both taking comfort in each other's arms.

"I am so sorry, Lotts. I went to bed with too much on my mind." He had gathered her into his arms and held her while she wept.

"I couldn't wake you, and you were getting violent." Her fear was evident. She looked up into his face as she spoke.

Her horrified look made him groan. "I'm so sorry, Lotts."

"I didn't want to leave you asleep, but I didn't know what to do." She wrapped her arms around his neck. "We won't forget your prayers again, Jon Jon."

They went back to bed, and Jonty told her to go back to sleep, which she did while he cuddled her. He waited until she was breathing evenly, then he crept out of bed and stood at the window, worried about the dream. More for the fact that he knew he really was stressed about the birth of twins. He just wasn't ready. He closed his eyes in prayer and went through the ritual of releasing his stress. Eventually, he settled and went back to bed.

The following day the images were still with him. They sat and talked about his nightmare without going into details. He apologised, gave Lottie a quick kiss and went off to work.

Mr Lamb was at work before him, which was unusual. "Good morning, Jonty; oh, you don't look as though you slept very well." Mr Lamb was stating the obvious. He looked terrible.

"Morning, sir, no, I didn't. The first night of bad dreams for ages." Jonty didn't feel chatty. "You're in early, sir."

"Yes, I thought you'd be here. I have a job for you. Do you remember the pendant I made for your mother? It was a topaz heart necklace." Mr Lamb watched his reaction. The look was very rude and very unlike Jonty.

Jonty realised that Mr Lamb had seen the dirty look. "Sorry, sir, I shall change my attitude. You really don't want to be near me today."

"That bad, son?" his boss asked.

Jonty didn't know why but his kindness made him feel worse. He even teared up. Jonty found himself unable to answer, so he just nodded.

"I'll go get tea. You get settled, and then we'll talk." He walked out to their kitchenette at the back of the workroom.

Jonty put his head down on the workbench. Tears cascaded down his cheeks. "What the hell is wrong with me?" He remained like this for a few minutes, then blew his nose and started to prepare for the day.

Unbeknownst to him, Mr Lamb had stuck his head around the door and saw his shoulders shaking. "Get this into you, boy," Mr Lamb said as he handed him a steaming mug of sweet tea. "Now, do you want to talk about it?"

He started to shake his head but found that he was nodding instead. "I nearly hit her last night. She got so frightened that she was cowering on a chair when I awoke. Oh, sir, what am I going to do? I thought I was over these nightmares." He took a sip of his tea and burnt his mouth. Cringing, he said, "I deserve that."

Mr Lamb was worried. "Oh, son, it's not your fault. You didn't hit her; you didn't even realise she was there. You can't be blamed for that." He knew the words were right, but they didn't help much. "I do wish I'd never sent you, lad. It wasn't worth it."

This time Jonty had no hesitation in agreeing. "No amount of gems is worth hurting the woman I love. I'd give them all away if I could never dream again, good or bad," Jonty said mournfully.

They sat talking in the cutting room until opening time. It certainly helped. Jonty praised God that he had an understanding boss. By opening time, Jonty was feeling much more himself. Their first two clients were just in to collect repairs. Once they had gone, Jonty asked what Mr Lamb had initially come in early for.

His friend and mentor was concerned. "Are you sure you wish to talk work?"

Jonty nodded. "Yes, sir, I've shaken the blue devils; sorry, sir."

"Well, I have an order for you. One you will like. Something similar to your mother's necklace, but they also want matching earbobs, brooch and rings. Only they have a caveat...." Mr Lamb's eyebrow raised, wondering how he'd react.

Nonchalantly, Jonty enquired, "What stones? Sapphires, diamonds, rubies or something else?" Jonty loved his mother's pendant. His father had found the blue topaz, and Mr Lamb had cut and set it into a heart.

"They were wondering about some of your diamonds from Africa. That is what the special order was; this order is especially for you, Jonty. After reading about the unfair mine practices in the article Tad wrote, they knew your story and knew you had bought your stones from the local miners. They have particularly requested your diamonds." Mr Lamb saw the grin slowly spread across Jonty's face.

"Seriously? I've been so caught up with everything happening that I've not even thought about them." He released a deep sigh. "Thanks, sir; I really need this today."

Mr Lamb pulled out the design the client had brought in, and Jonty sat gazing at it, his mind hard at work. Without saying a word, he walked out of the room to the safe. Mr Lamb heard him at the lock of the vault and then swung the giant door open. His small bag of gems had sat untouched since his return. There was one stone he would never get rid of, and that was the big diamond the little girl had brought him. He wondered if she was bringing him more when she was killed. He had long ago decided to cut it and give it to Lottie. It would cut to a five-carat stone, and if he cleaved it correctly, he could get another three-carat gem. It would be worth a fortune, but compared to a life, he would throw it away if he could bring Nandi back to life. Shaking off the thoughts, he collected the bag, took it back to the cutting room and tipped it onto a tray. The gems reflected the various lamps in the room. A shaft of sunlight also caught the tray and sent rainbows onto the ceiling. "I love them when they do that," Jonty said, looking up at the ceiling.

"Let me just lust over these again, lad." Mr Lamb smiled as he ran his hands over the tray's hundred or so raw diamonds.

Jonty leaned over and picked up one large stone, holding it to the light. "This is the one the little girl, Nandi, sold me; I will never part with this one. Lotts is going to get it." He had told his boss about the murder of the child earlier that morning. Jonty picked a new small drawstring bag from his drawer and popped in the big stone. From the remaining pebbles, they chose eight to cut. Only five would be needed for the set, but cutting didn't always go to plan.

Once Mr Lamb had approved the quality of the stones, Jonty packed up the rest and put them all back in the safe. The deal was Mr Lamb was a brilliant goldsmith and Jonty was the cutter; they worked together, only this time Jonty would take the price of the cut stones from the £2000 order. The half share was enough for Jonty to purchase the cottage from his father, or he'd ask Lottie if she would prefer a free-standing house. He knew they would need space with twins on the way, but having Will and Dimity next door was a delight. He foresaw much discussion ahead. He smiled, knowing that this would set them up comfortably. His concentration was now focused on the work in front of him, and that was faceting the diamonds.

On arrival home, he was met with silence. The house was empty. He made a cup of tea, expecting Lottie to return from wherever she was soon, but after an hour, she was still not home. He went next door and asked if they had seen her.

He saw the look Will and Dimity gave each other. "She's gone home, Jonty," Dimity finally said.

"What? Why?" The look on his face was one of horror.

"She needed a bit of time, Jon. I gather you had another dream last night?" Will asked.

Jonty nodded. "And I got violent, but not against her. She got scared." As they were still standing at their front door, Will dragged Jonty into their sitting room.

Jonty stumbled into a chair; he was devastated. She'd left him. This is what he was so petrified of occurring. "What do I do, Will? Do I go after her? I so want to."

Will looked at his tear-filled eyes. His heart went out to him. "Jon, she's coming back tomorrow, but she wanted a good night's sleep and needed her mother. I expect Luke and Ellen will return with her."

Jonty nodded. "What do I do, Will? I forgot to pray one night, one blooming night."

Dimity excused herself and left the two men together.

Will waited until she was gone. "Jon, there was more to this dream, wasn't there? Lottie said you were yelling about not coping with two. Are you fearful of the twins' arrival?"

Jonty felt gutted; he'd had no intention of her finding that out. He nodded, affirming Will's suspicion. "Oh no! What did I say?"

"I don't know, Jon, but it was enough to scare her dreadfully. She didn't explain fully, but she caught the morning ferry home."

They spent an hour together in the sitting room before Dimity called them for dinner. The last thing Jonty wanted was to eat. He felt ill. He wanted to go to Lottie and beg forgiveness.

Later that night, he stood praying for a long time at his bedroom window. He shed no tears, they had long dried, but he was heart-sore. Finally, he went to bed. He overslept, and although he was up, he was still not dressed when he heard voices coming in the front door.

Halfway down the hall, he was cannonballed by Lottie, who was in tears. He opened his arms to her; she was clinging to him and begging for forgiveness. He was oblivious to everything, but she was back.

After some time, he realised his parents-in-law were observing them. Luke said, "Go and get changed, lad, then we'll talk. Go with him, Lottie." Luke's compassion for these two was almost overwhelming him. Somehow God would get the glory from this, but he had no idea how.

Ellen went and put the kettle on for tea; by the time the two young people had arrived back downstairs, she had the tea tray in the sitting room. She poured, and they settled down for a lengthy discussion.

No one knew how to start this particular talk. None doubted the affection the two had for each other; it was just how to survive the nights. So Jonty jumped in with his thoughts. Jonty sat holding Lottie's hand. "I stood for hours last night wondering how we are going to cope, and I was wondering if maybe we sleep separately, at least until the babies are born."

Luke gave Jonty a deep penetrating look. "That's not quite the issue, is it, Jon?"

Jonty looked puzzled.

"Are you worried about having twins? Is that what is eating at you?" Ellen asked. "Lottie said something about being chased by twin skeletons, and it made me wonder."

Jonty drew Lottie under his arm and nodded. "I'm sorry, Lotts, I'm blooming petrified. I know I should have said something, but I'm fearful of us not coping with being parents. And I know they often come early and are usually very small." He kissed Lottie's hair. "Darling, I'm terrified."

"As am I, Jon Jon," Lottie murmured softly.

Luke looked at the young couple. "Well, I have a suggestion, It may not be what you had planned, but as you two seem to have done little of that in your relationship, planning that is, I ask that you will let me guide you." He noticed their attention was now focused on him, but neither said anything. "As you know, our business has done very well, and we didn't give you a wedding present. I have discussed this with your mother, and if you were in a larger house, you could employ some staff and even a nanny."

Rather than joy on Jonty's face, he saw a different look. "Uncle Luke, one reason I came home early yesterday was to tell Lotts that I have an order for five of the diamonds I brought back. Well, at least I have to cut them first. But the amount of £1000 I will get will allow us to buy a big house. I could tap into my trust, but this would be money I will get will allow us to buy a big house. I could tap into my trust, but this would be money I have earned myself. I also have the money from Mr Field, but I don't want to use that; I almost feel it is blood money. I just wasn't sure she'd wish to leave Will and Dimity." He glanced down at Lottie. "But, sweetheart, they want to go to England with Paul, so they won't be here either."

He felt her nod against his chest. She said, "They told me yesterday; it's why I went home. It wasn't you, Jon Jon, but I didn't want to stay here alone."

"So we buy a house then?" He felt her nod again.

They left the cottage soon after and called into the jewellery store. Jonty told Mr Lamb that he would not be in today; they were going house hunting while Luke and Ellen were with them. He knew his money from the diamonds would not eventuate until the sale was finalised. On the way to the store, he and Luke had fallen behind the ladies and discussed a loan. If Luke still wished to contribute, they could look at houses a little larger than he had planned. Luke agreed, but the amount remained ambiguous until they looked at what was available. The four spent the morning looking at the properties on the market. An advertisement in the paper showed two houses in Surrey Hills and one on Pitt Street. At £360 each, both were well within budget. They viewed them and found one was next door to Hamish and Effy Macdonald, with Fergus and Katy on the other side. Hamish lived next door to Jonty's parents. When they saw the address, the four stopped and just looked at each other. They all knew the property well.

Sight unseen, Jonty exclaimed, "I think we've found our place, love. We'll have all the help we need and can fit staff too, what do you think? We can build out the back as Hamish has, and…." He stopped speaking because Lottie had thrown herself into his arms and kissed him again.

Lottie was so excited to think they would be living close to family. Eventually, she said, "It's perfect, yes please, Jon Jon. Father, what do you think?"

"I think it's perfect Charlotte, my dear," her mother said.

Lottie clapped her hands with glee.

They were leaving Stephen Glossop's office a little further down the street within an hour. Luke had put down a deposit of £40, and as it was supposed to have gone to auction, he added an extra £10 to the price. Even at £370, the house was in the perfect price and position, which outweighed its size of only four bedrooms. That could always be remedied.

By the end of the week, they were the owners, as Luke had expedited the sale. Many of the family were coming to assist with the move the following weekend. As the new house was unfurnished and as the Lenehan furniture was all handmade and exquisite, Luke arranged for a fleet of flatbed wagons to transport their goods. Lottie was to stay in the new house and direct placement; Ellen oversaw all the men in the family packing up the cottage. The wagons then hauled the boxes to the new home, and Lottie directed the placement of the possessions. The cottage was empty by noon. Ellen insisted that the first items to be taken over were the beds. The new house had an alcove to the side of the main bedroom, and Jonty suggested they set it up with a narrow bed for him.

By the time the new house was arranged to everyone's satisfaction, it was dinner time. Everyone had pitched in and helped unpack the kitchen foodstuffs into the oversized pantry.

Once most of the work was done, Luke finally had time to poke around at some of the doors he'd not looked into. "Jonty, come look at what I've found." Everyone who was within cooee came to the call. Luke stood in the hallway, which was identical to the one in Jonty's parent's house. Luke had looked into the one next to it, which contained shelves, just as in the Evans' house. Once the couple was next to him, he turned and opened the second door. It didn't contain shelves but a staircase leading downwards. "You have a cellar too. Hamish's house doesn't. I know your parent's house has one but not with a hidden entrance like this. Have you been downstairs?"

Jonty was delighted. "Hardly, Uncle Luke; I didn't know it existed," he said excitedly.

"Want to have a look? Do you know where the lamps are?" Luke asked.

Jonty gave a laugh. "Uncle Luke, we're in Sydney, not Emu Plains, remember? Look, there's a cord. Give it a tug." He watched as Luke gently pulled on the hanging cord.

The stairs lit up. "Oh, Jonty, I forgot you have electricity. The cottage doesn't, does it?"

"Yes, it does, but we like the softer lamplight in the bedrooms."

The family group descended into the well-lit cool room. The agent must not have known about this, or if he did, he forgot to mention it.

Once down the stairs, Lottie and Ellen got the giggles. What met their eye was a room lined with shelves full of preserves, for half the room was set up as a cold store pantry. There were also many jars of dried foodstuffs and many large crates of wine placed on their sides. Each was labelled in calligraphy writing with the date and contents. A quick glance showed they were mainly freshly bottled in the last two years.

"Well, you two won't be going hungry. You have enough food here for a blooming army," John Evans exclaimed.

"Oh, Mother will think she has died and gone to heaven with this. She's going to love it," Jonty's mother, Colleen exclaimed, chuckling.

A voice spoke from the other end of the room. "That's not all that's here; there's a full load of coal and a pulley system to get it upstairs. Look." Eddie stood looking at the bucket. Unable to resist, he loaded up a few shovel loads into the empty pail and left it hanging. "I'll go and see if it works." He left them waiting.

After a minute or so, a square of light appeared above, and they heard his voice. "There's a cupboard next to the fireplace in the sitting room. Its rope system seems to go upstairs too." He pulled, and the whole bucket lifted quickly.

"Jonty, this will make life easier. It must go up to your bedroom as well." Luke grinned. "I do love these sorts of gadgets."

They had just finished in the cellar when Effy arrived at the kitchen door. She merely said, "Dinner's on, folks." They walked through the new connecting gate in the dividing fence and went to Hamish and Effy Macdonald's place for dinner.

~

By the end of the month, Will, Dimity, and Paul were on their way to London. They had delayed going as they wished to travel back with Captain Cromby on the *SS Abergeldie*. He had arrived in March and had a month turnaround in Sydney. He was thrilled that Paul's quest had been successful.

All had been a little surprised when they first met him as neither Jonty nor Paul had mentioned he was Scottish, hailing from Aberdeen. The night before they left, Jonty visited them, and the four friends, Will, Paul, the Captain, and Jonty, prayed, laying hands upon Jonty and asking for mind healing; then, they prayed for a safe trip to England for the family.

~

May, June, and July arrived and went.

Jonty's nightmares were once again under control. He'd not actually had one. His five diamonds were cut, and the order was ready for collection. By mid-July, Jonty paid his father-in-law back £300 for the house. It was the figure agreed upon when they saw the building. This would leave Jonty and

Lottie with ample funds to extend should they wish. Jonty still had many more stones. He had, however, cut four of the exceptional sapphires that Mr Field had given him, two pink and two blue ones. Each was a carat and cut into a heart shape.

Lottie was almost rolling as she walked. Ellen and Luke arrived at the end of July and said they would stay for a month until the babies were born.

Early in the morning of August 17th, Lottie woke with backache. "Jon," she pushed her sleeping husband in the back. "Jonty, wake up. It's time."

A sleepy Jonty replied, "Time for what, love?"

"Time for us to be parents, sweetheart," her mother had told her that often the first sign of the imminent arrival was a backache. She had tried to ignore it last night, but the pain was so bad this morning that she couldn't.

"Oh," Jonty mumbled. Then it hit him. "Oh, cripes, Lotts, I'll get dressed, love, and we'll get you to the hospital." He threw on his dressing gown and went and knocked on the other bedroom door.

A dressing-gowned-clad Ellen followed him back into their room. "Have the pains started yet, or just the backache?"

Lottie, who had not yet stood up, said, "No pains yet, but you said that the backache comes first." She stood up and immediately doubled over. "Check that! Cor Mother, that hurt."

Ellen chuckled. "Yes, and they get worse. You and Carlo gave me a good run. For the triplets, I went into labour in church on Easter Day."

"You're supposed to be encouraging me, Mother," Lottie replied with a half-smile that was quickly followed by another groan of pain.

Ellen rubbed her back while Jonty went and changed.

Chapter 12 More Arrivals

*A*n hour later, they were at the maternity ward. Luke had hailed a passing carriage from the hotel, and it dropped them at the hospital.

By three o'clock that afternoon, Jonty and Lottie were proud parents of twins Samuel Nicholas and Patricia Marie. Their parents had spent many hours choosing names no one in the family had. The children were to be known as Sammo and Patty.

Luke had insisted that Jonty be present at the birth and had worded the doctor up well before the event. Ellen, too, was beside her daughter. Luke waited outside. Lottie agreed to stay overnight instead of returning home. The babies were small but healthy. Sammo was five and a half pounds and needed a smack to breathe. Patty came out fist-first and screaming.

The following day, when Jonty went to collect her, he pulled a small bag from his pocket. It contained a heart-shaped pendant he'd made with two heart-shaped sapphires, one blue and one pink. "I made this for you ages ago, Lotts; I just needed to know what the twins were. Boys, girls or one of each, as I had four stones cut ready. These are some of the stones Mr Field gave me in Antwerp."

Lottie loved it.

~

Life in Pitt Street for the family was a delight. And they had received word that Will and Dimity had arrived safely in London. Before they left, they asked if Jonty could keep an eye on their house. Will had decided to stay in England for a while and get to know the family. He could paint there as well as in Sydney, so although they eventually did plan to come home, they had no return date.

Jonty's dreams occasionally bothered him, but the extreme ones rarely visited him as before. Life was busy but enjoyable.

Ellen and Luke were regular visitors, as were some of the cousins. One, in particular, was Lottie's younger cousin, Allie Lockley.

~

Four years passed, and Will and Dimity were still away.

Jonty and Lottie were sitting on the back verandah of their home. Lottie had just come back from having their third child, Paul. He was currently asleep upstairs, which was unusual, and Sammo and Patty were running around in their backyard.

Their nanny was a teenage girl named Julia Green, whom Ricky English had found for them. She was only fourteen and had no family. She lived with them in a small room just off the kitchen. They also had a cook cum housekeeper who came in daily. Her children had grown, and her husband was away at sea. She was a lovely lady and loved helping with the children. Mary Henderson was perfect for them. Their agreement was that when her husband was home, she would stay with him, but he was usually only home for a month every year; the situation worked well. Julia was an orphan, and this was her first job. She had worked with Mrs Yates at Ricky's Sadie House for orphan babies. So she had lots of experience with small children. At four, the little ones were undoubtedly lively.

Rather than sitting in the comfortable cane chairs on the back porch, Jonty was sitting with Lottie on the steps leading to the backyard. "Can you believe we've been married for over five years? The twins are nearly five, and now we have Paul," Jonty said as they were playing with the children. He had entered into parenthood with great trepidation. Lottie, too, had been fearful; but having many hands close by and the fact that her mother had stayed for most of the first month after the twins' birth had really helped.

Her father had to return home a few times for work commitments, but most things he had managed from their new house. Hamish and Effy were next door, and his brother Fergus and Katy were on the other side of them; they always had someone to call on for assistance. Luke was still in the logistics business with both men, so the three used the time to have extended meetings about the future of their Logistics company. It turned out to be a blessing as the added time allowed for the pooling of many new ideas.

Now, Luke and Ellen were frequent visitors, as having a permanent and convenient base in Sydney certainly was beneficial. Jonty had sold more of his diamonds and extended the back of the house, so his in-laws had their own suite with its own bathroom and office. There was still a guest room at the front. The twins shared a room, but Patty would get her own room when Paul was old enough, and the boys would share.

Ellen never needed to sit through another meeting as she was perfectly content playing grandmother to the three adorable imps. They had only just returned home after the birth of Paul, so Jonty had taken the day off to spend with his wife.

Julia brought out two mugs of tea for them and handed Jonty the mail, which had just arrived.

Jonty flipped over the letter, but there was no sender on it. Intrigued, he flicked open the seal. "Oh, Lotts, it's from Fred McCubbin; he's asked if he can come and visit for a bit. He wants to bring a couple of friends to have a look around town. He asked if I knew of some accommodation they could stay in." He looked down and kept reading. "Lotts, are any of Father's cottages vacant?"

"Yes, the top one next to Will's is empty. And it's furnished too. It's the one Paul was in. Did they say how long they are coming for?" she asked.

"Not really, but they can't stay long, so I'm guessing only for a few weeks." Jonty smiled as he tucked the letter in his pocket. He looked forward to seeing his Melbourne friend again; he hoped young Simon Marshall would come. He'd not met him, but his works stayed in Jonty's mind. Fred had mentioned he was a schoolboy back then but didn't actually say how old.

~

On a cold, somewhat blustery but sunny Saturday morning in September, Jonty heard a knock. Julia answered it to a group of well-dressed gentlemen. They inquired if this was the Jonty Evans household and, on being told it, asked if he was at home.

Jonty had heard Frederick's voice and hot-footed it downstairs, away from the pandemonium upstairs. "Fred, welcome; come inside, gentlemen; please take a seat; we'll be but a minute. The children have just had a mud fight; I'll return in a moment; Lottie is trying to sort them out. Julia, leave that and go assist Mrs Evans, please."

Leaving the guests in the sitting room, Jonty ran upstairs, knowing the twins were a filthy mess.

It took some fifteen minutes before Jonty returned, still wiping his hands. He had a swipe of mud on his jacket, "Sorry, friends, the joys of parenthood." He gave a half chuckle. "This is a delight, Fred; now you have my full attention."

Frederick McCubbin introduced his two friends, "Thomas Roberts and Arthur Streeton; may I introduce Jonathon Evans? Tom, Smike, this is Jonty."

Jonty smiled at the informal introduction. He greeted the two with a bow. "Smike? How did you get that moniker?"

"He's a Dickens character from Nicholas Nickleby. Tall and skinny like me," Arthur said with a cheesy toothy grin.

"I saw some of your watercolours in Melbourne, Arthur, they are good, and Tom, I believe you've been in London?"

Arthur smiled in acknowledgement, and Tom nodded.

"Talkative chaps, aren't they Fred?" Jonty chuckled.

"Give them time, Jon; you'll not be able to shut them up." Fred lay back and relaxed in the armchair. "We have a favour to ask Jon. We were wondering if you could show us around a bit if it's not too much trouble." He saw Jonty's eyebrows flick up with interest.

"Are you thinking of moving up?" Jon caught the twist of a smile in Tom's eyes.

"Possibly, it's why we wish to have a look around. Do you know of any good spots to paint? We're thinking *en plein-air,* of course."

"Actually, your timing is perfect. Feel like a picnic after you've dumped your bags? I have sorted a cottage for you, and we'll go via there if you wish. Or we will do the picnic, then visit the cottage, your call." He waited for the three to confer, and they decided to go afterwards.

"So, where are we going?" Arthur asked.

"We're going across the bay and over the headland to Balmoral to the beach. It's a good spot for the children to play, and the beach is reasonably safe for them to paddle and has no mud. It's also out of this wind." He gave a mock groan. "There's a ferry that will take us partway; then we catch a carriage to the beach. We're actually planning to go to Balmoral Gardens Pleasure Park and spend the day out in the fresh air having a wonderful time. Did you know that Balmoral means *the magnificent place* in Gaelic, literally *Baile Morail,* so Balmoral was aptly named? Hamish, my next-door neighbour, told us. You'll meet him if you come. It's stunning; wait until you see it." Jonty told them to leave their bags in the sitting room and grab what they wished to bring, saying, "If you have swimwear, dig it out."

Fred's reaction was laughable. "Jon, it's September; we'll freeze."

Jonty smiled, "Fred, this is Sydney; the shallow water will be quite warm. Trust me."

~

Two hours later, the group, accompanied by the entire Evans entourage, Hamish and Effy Macdonald, their daughter Elspeth, son-in-law Liam Wallace, and their baby Calum were heading to the ferry. Jonty's siblings were amongst them, his parents and even his elderly grandparents. Both had trouble walking, but they loved to come as it was either by ferry or cab. Many other families were enjoying the beach and park.

Their arrival at noon showed the bay in full sunshine. It looked truly magnificent and took the breath away from the three Melbourne artists.

"Smike, I have to paint this," Fred said in awe.

"You're not the only one, Prof," Arthur said with a smirk.

Jonty leaned over to Tom. "Prof? Another nickname?"

"Yes, we call him 'The Prof' as he's always philosophising, especially when we're painting like this. You'll get a name too, if you hang around us long enough," Tom chortled. "But then again, you already have one, don't you, Jonty?"

Jonty laughed. "I certainly do, Tom." Knowing his real name was Jonathon.

The three artists asked if anyone would like to join them for a meander along the beach.

Twenty-four-year-old Maureen and her husband of six months, Andrew Rivers, joined the rest of Jonty's siblings, Blue, Hettie, Finn and Cara. Jonty and Lottie stayed with the picnic and the older generation.

Fourteen-year-old Cara was running, in a very unladylike way, after her young nephew, Sammo. They were both barefoot and enjoying the freedom that the beach could bring. The joyous laughter of the children was a delight. Meanwhile, Lottie was building a sandcastle with Patty. Jonty had Paul asleep in his arms. He was one of those whinging babies that always wanted to be held. The family group had finished their picnic when two more familiar faces were seen and welcomed. Luke and Ellen had arrived by ferry and joined the party.

Ellen noticed Jonty gently bouncing the sleeping baby. He was lying on his tummy as he slept. As soon as Jonty stopped, the baby would awake, usually crying. She leaned across to Colleen, and they were discussing their mutual grandchild when the infant awoke properly. She reached for the baby. The cries of the child were not of hunger but of pain. He was four months old and should have been sitting up; each time Ellen sat him between her legs and tried to get him to sit up, he'd bellow. "Colleen, look at this. Each time I straighten his leg, he screams. Do you remember what Grandmother Sal says? Check their backs when they are born. I wonder if they have with him?"

Ellen called to Jonty; he was currently stretched out on the grass. "Jonty, would you mind if we stripped him and checked his back and hips? He's yelling like he's in pain."

"I'll go get Lottie, and she can watch." He walked down to the sand and swapped places with her.

"Mother, do you think you can help? He cries all the time." An exhausted Lottie knelt next to them. "I'm so tired. He's not slept through a single night."

With the child undressed, he was lying face down on a towel on Ellen's lap. "If this doesn't work, come out to Parramatta and let Mama Sal have a look. She's brilliant at it." She proceeded to run her thumbs gently down his spine. "Yes," she rubbed her thumbs along his backbone in the middle of his spine. "Here, feel this."

Lottie reached over; she did the same with her thumbs. "There's a lump," she said with a gasp.

"Yes, and watch. He relaxes when I stretch his back, and when his legs stretch out, he cringes." She straightened Paul's legs, and he let out a bellow.

"Poor munchkin, no wonder he's crying. I'll massage his back and see if that works. I'm not game enough to do more; Mama Sal can." Ellen gently massaged his back while he was stretched out between her legs. His arms were splayed over her knees, and his little feet were sitting on her tummy.

Lottie held his arms and stretched his back. Ellen just rubbed gently. "Mother, he's gone to sleep. He must like it, so keep going."

Ellen dropped her knees a little and stretched him further. Lottie lifted his tiny body a little higher on her mother's lap.

They kept up the gentle rubbing; Ellen was now rubbing the area around the lump. Ellen was massaging on either side of the bump when he coughed. The pressure and the cough combined made it go 'click.' Ellen said, "Oh look, it's gone." Sure enough, his back no longer had the bump.

"Oh, thank you, Mother," Lottie's face was alive with joy. "If this works, oh, if this works, I shall be overjoyed."

Ellen finished the massage and redressed the now-sleeping child. He'd not stirred since his cough. "I think we've done it, love. He's out cold. You might get some sleep now."

Little Paul was still asleep when the wanderers returned. He'd not slept for more than an hour in the four months since he was born.

Fred came and spoke to the group. The sleeping baby didn't stir. "Jonty, we're thinking of coming back for a long holiday. We may even camp here." Fred was so animated that Jonty chuckled.

"I thought you might like this place. I have a few other spectacular sites to show you. Most are around here in Sydney, but some are a little inland. I have to head to Emu Plains this week, and I was wondering if you'd all like to come?" Jonty was sitting on the grass, looking up at his new friends. "There's also someone out there I want you to meet. His name is Jim. Tom, I saw a sketch or two of yours, and for some reason, I just feel you two should meet."

After another hour, the group returned to the ferry and then back to Pitt Street. Baby Paul was still asleep. He'd not stirred. Jonty had now wrapped him in a blanket, and he was snuggled to Jonty's neck.

Tom looked at Jonty. "You look totally content, Jon. That babe has not moved for hours."

Jonty smiled. "Tom, you have no idea how wonderful this is. He's four months old and has not slept this long ever. My only worry now is that he won't sleep again tonight. One of us has been up with him for half the night." Jonty didn't even have to bounce him. He was just dead to the world. "Poor little mite, he's been in pain, and we didn't even know."

The trip home was accomplished with ease. With so many hands helping, they arrived back at the three houses in a short time as the tram dropped them off near their home. As there were so many of them, the stop took a while. Paul still didn't stir.

~

While Jonty helped Lottie in the kitchen, Julia settled Paul into his room; the three artists waited in the large garden in the back with the two older children.

One thing an artist always has at hand is a sketch pad. Tom kicked the ball with Sammo while Fred and Arthur sat drawing Patty. She was playing with a branch of gum nuts she had found at Balmoral. Her brown curls were adorable.

They had yet to see their accommodation and unpack. As they sketched, they discussed the beach they had just seen. Fred had also caught sight of a bay near the ferry and liked the views from there. They added that bay to the list of possible venues to paint. Each had spent some time drawing the scenes they saw earlier in the afternoon. Their sketches were marked with notes of colours and light directions. Each would attempt to paint what they had seen.

~

Jonty joined them after Lottie had fed Paul and put him to bed. "He only stirred when we bathed, changed, and fed him. He went straight back to sleep. I can't believe it. Lottie and Julia are going to put the others to bed. We've got time to take you to the cottage; then we'll come back for dinner. You may as well eat with us while you're here. So grab your things, and we'll go now. We have about an hour until dinnertime. That's if you wish to come back. It is roast beef, so it will keep. But there's enough for us all."

Tom answered for them. "You bet! We're ravenous. But we always are. I'm sure you've heard artists are always starving." He chuckled as he walked inside to collect his luggage.

Fred and Arthur packed up their sketch pads and quickly grabbed their bags.

Jonty took the children to their mother and suggested that she put her feet up once they were in bed. The four men waited just outside with their luggage. They hopped onto a passing tram that took them back down to the quay and then back to the cottages. Jonty used the tram daily, unlike many of the family who preferred carriages. Jonty could hop on and off at many of the shops around town. It was convenient and meant he had no need to keep a stable of animals in the mews at the back of his house. He knew the driver, so he asked for the tram to stop in front of the cottages rather than at the usual stop up the street. He showed the three where to catch it for further exploration on other days. He also showed them where to catch the steam tram to Bondi, explaining that it was another venue he thought they'd love. "From Bondi, make sure you go to the other beaches, especially Coogee. It's one of my favourites, and I'm sure you'll love it too."

Their arrival at the cottages was late, and it was getting close to dusk.

Jonty pulled out the large key ring from his coat pocket. Once the door was unlocked, he flicked on the light switch, and the three followed him inside. He left them to investigate the cottage while he stayed at the front door. He had not checked on Will and Dimity's place for a few days, so he left them to settle in while he went next door and checked it over. Hopefully, they would not be away too much longer. He missed them. Standing in the kitchen in the empty cottage, Jonty released a sigh. The view brought back memories of the first months of their marriage. He had not had a bad dream for a couple of years. Not since the night he'd frightened Lottie. He stood looking out the back kitchen window when he realised it had been five years ago. It was shortly before the twins were born. He shot God a prayer of thanks, then returned to the front door and locked up, then walked back to the small front courtyard of the artist's cottage.

Fred was waiting for him. "We'll unpack later, but this is great, Jon. Thanks for arranging it with your Papa."

"Smike and I tossed for the front room, and he lost; I get the one overlooking the garden," Tom said with a smile. "The top room we're all going to use for a studio. Don't worry; we'll put down a drop cloth."

Jonty chuckled. "You've met Father. Do you really think he'll worry?"

The four heard a tram coming up from the quay. Leaving the front light on, they quickly locked up and hopped on the passing conveyance; all were looking forward to home-cooked roast beef.

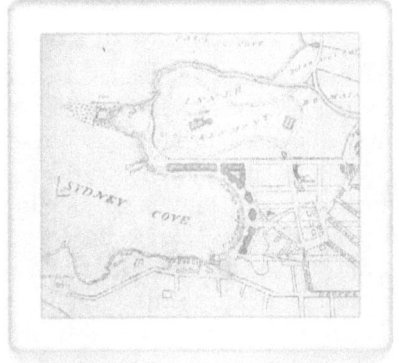

Chapter 13 Exploration

Over the next few days, the three investigated many beaches in and around

Sydney. Coogee, as expected, was a favourite; they made another trip over to Balmoral and leaving there, they explored Little Sirius Cove and some of the area around the ferry wharf. They loved the ferry trip so much that they didn't alight anywhere; they discovered many other beautiful points in and around Sydney. They asked the crew about any areas they liked. Milson's Point was another venue they all agreed upon. Sadly they had no time to capture the views. That would be for another day and possibly another trip. All were enthusiastic about returning for a longer stay.

On Wednesday, they arrived at the Pitt Street house early, as Jonty had planned an early start to their trip to Emu Plains. Again they were travelling by public conveyance. Only this time, it would be on a train to Emu Plains. Jonty and Lottie were taking the children and would stay at Jim and Conny's house. Jonty had not said his reason for the trip, but that was unimportant. They planned to stay for only one night before returning. All Jonty mentioned was that they were heading west, and it was all new to the artists, so he advised them to take some sketch pads. Jonty, however, had started having dreams again, but they were not all bad ones. For some reason, he felt drawn to introduce the artists to Jim Leslie. He had no idea why; he just knew they had to meet.

As the train travelled westward, they sat discussing their visits to the various beaches. Fred waxed lyrical over Coogee Beach, but the early morning visit to Balmoral Beach stole their hearts. The beauty of the foreshore, the lapping water and the sunlight on the sea was so peaceful. On the weekend, it had been too busy to admire the serenity of the bay. The sown seed had already germinated. They would certainly return, and it would be as soon as they could. They sat discussing the possibility of a longer-term artists' camp at a site like this.

An adventure into the unknown was always a delight to the keen eye of an artist. They had all heard about the blueness of the Blue Mountains, but none believed the colour... until they saw them for themselves. Now they were on what they termed a "magical mystery tour" heading west.

By the time the train reached Parramatta, the two oldest children were curled up asleep near their parents. Paul was sleeping in a basket on the floor. He had been such a different child and barely made a noise for four days, and he had even begun sitting up by himself. He would wake up giggling and giving a toothy grin most of the time. Lottie and Jonty were more rested and were once again the happy couple they had been before his birth. For all Jonty's earlier anxiety about the arrival of the twins, they had been dream babies. Colleen was over every day to lend a hand, and Jonty delighted in seeing more of his mother. Lottie adored her, as did Ellen.

Jonty was looking forward to seeing Lottie's Uncle Wills and Aunt Cathy. They lived just a few streets away from Jim. They often visited as his mother and Aunt Cathy had been best friends since they were small. Uncle Wills's business of now over sixty Emporiums kept growing and growing. His three sons were all involved in the firm.

Rick had started a new arm of the business with a mail and wire order branch. It now had a more significant turnover than the actual stores. Jonty had spent many happy days as a lad wandering around one or other of the stores with Rick. His father, Uncle Wills, was someone that just drew people to him. You just could not help but like him. Jonty knew him to be fabulously wealthy, but he stood out from the social set as his wealth did not change his loving care of those who needed help.

The groups' arrival was one of pandemonium. The toddlers both needed to find a privy, Paul needed a feed, and the three artists wanted to look around but knew they needed to assist their friends.

Once safely on the siding, the group gathered their belongings. Jonty led them off the raised landing. He'd seen Jim waiting for them. While they waited, Fred and Arthur had pointed out the colour of the mountains and were astounded that they did indeed look blue from a distance. Jonty let Sammo find a tree to satisfy his needs, and Patty was assisted in her ablutions. As there was no station building, it was the bush or nothing for the young ones.

Tom soon had Sammo sitting upon his neck; the squeals of joy from the young lad made him chuckle.

Jim was leaning against a post with his arms folded. He was smiling while watching the chaotic antics of the children. He saw Sammo lifted onto his elevated position, and calm reigned. Chuckling to himself, he remembered his own lad, JJ, doing the same thing. As the group drew closer, he opened the carriage door for ease of entry.

"Uncle Jimmy, look at me; I'm up high on Uncle Tom's neck," the child greeted him with glee.

Jim laughed as he lifted the child down and hugged him. "Hello, young Samuel; I see you are well, and what about your sister? Have you been looking after her?" He saw him nod, then shake his head.

"I'se trying, but she's a girl and doesn't like doing things I like." The lad looked crestfallen.

"Then, young sir, maybe, just occasionally, you could try to do some things she likes doing? And she might do the same for you later." Jim watched the realisation cross his face.

"I'll try," the young boy chirped happily.

Jim then turned to Patty. "Good morning, young lady; I see you, too, are well?" He bowed over her hand.

She returned his bow with a perfectly executed curtsy, nodded, and then threw herself into his arms. "Hello, Uncle Jimmy; I missed you."

"As I did with you, poppet," Jim placed her directly into the vehicle.

Jonty was admiring the carriage. "Another commission, Uncle Jim?"

"Yes, this one is for Government House, so I thought you'd like to travel in style; I've just finished it." Jim handed in Lottie. "Morning, pet, I see Paulie has settled down." He took her still-sleeping son's basket and placed it on the floor.

Lottie was looking forward to the day ahead, chatting with Conny. "Thankfully, yes, Uncle Jim." She gave him a welcome kiss and got into the carriage.

Jonty introduced the three artists. When Jim heard Fred's name, he looked intently at him but remained silent.

Fred stood looking at the tall coachman. "Sir, did you drive for Rutherford, then Cobb and Co in Melbourne about twenty years ago?" Fred asked, his heart racing with excitement.

"Yes, I did; I was wondering if you were my young tiger from back then." Jim shook Fred's hand and then placed a gentle hand on his shoulder. "You've grown!"

"One tends to, sir; twenty-five years is a lifetime ago, sir." Fred was thrilled that the coachman remembered him.

Jonty puzzled. "You two have met before? Where?"

Jim chuckled. "Patience Jon, all shall be revealed. Up you all get, Conny is waiting for us. Harry and Vicky have both come for tea, so we can't keep them too long. We'll talk then."

Jim pointed for Fred to climb up next to him while the others got into the carriage.

The trip to Jim's house was short. It was only about a mile away. Conny was waiting for them and welcomed Lottie with a huge hug.

Over tea, the story of how Jim and Fred knew each other unfolded. Jim started the story, "I had been in Melbourne for a few years, and one day a small lad appeared in the stables. I feared for his safety as the business was full of comings and goings by then. The boy was fearless of the many horses. On meeting, I called him 'tiger,' so he became my 'tiger.' Which, as you know, is like a junior footman. He knew my schedule better than I, and whenever I was due to arrive with a coach, he would be waiting to hold the horses' heads." Jim smiled at the recollection. "You would have been four, Fred?"

Frederick nodded. "Fearless and silly about horses. You were the only driver who would let me near them."

Jim continued, "Soon, the gentle beasts came to know the lad and nuzzled him when he took the reins. Admittedly I was the same as a lad; I knew and understood the passion that dwells deep with one, and the adoration of horses." Jim's eyes rested on Fred. "I gather they didn't take over your life as my obsession did?"

Fred shook his head. "No sir; I then discovered the ability to capture them and other things in colour. I now paint, but, sir, I have discovered the beauty of the Australian bush. I've painted horses, but the soft hues of the morning mist speak to my heart. The glowing colours of the sunlight filtering through the leaves, the beauty of the weather-beaten faces of the battlers of the bush. These are now my passion." Fred watched the expression of the man he'd known so long ago. He had but vague memories of those days being so young. He did, however, remember Jim. "I would have been about six when you left Melbourne, sir; I was banned from the Cobb and Co stables soon afterwards and had to then go to school."

Tom was intrigued. "You drove for Cobb and Co, sir?"

"I did, Tom, for many years until my hands failed." Jim held up his knobbly hands. They were huge, gnarled and bent; calluses were still visible. "Harry and I breed and train heavy horses for transport. He breeds, and I train. I refurbish vehicles as a sideline. Hence, the Government carriage today is why draught horses were pulling the carriage. I give them cross-training in all conveyances, from pulling a plough to fancy carriages. I train them to be the gentle, placid beasts I know them to be, but they are strong. Many farmers need a beast for plough work, but it benefits the family if it can double as a family horse. They are also trained to work as a team, a pair or alone. This also gives versatility."

Tom nodded. "Sir, may I question you further on the coach driving days a little later? I have a passion for the trades of the bush."

Jim nodded. "After luncheon, lad, we shall sit on the verandah and chat," Jim said, watching the animation on the young man's face.

"May I ask, though, have you been held up, sir? You know, by bushrangers?" Tom asked.

Jim's eyes flew to Conny. She still hated the topic. Jim replied without his gaze leaving his beloved wife's face. "Yes, four times while driving here in New South Wales and another in Queensland. The first time was the worst, yet one of the funniest. I suppose it was because of the surprise that it actually had happened to me."

Arthur prompted for the story, he, too, was interested.

"Conny, do you mind, possum? I won't tell them if it disturbs you," Jim asked sensitively.

Her warm brown gaze met his. "No, Jim, tell them; it was so long ago now I'm okay hearing about them. I'm just glad you no longer endanger yourself."

Jim nodded, and he settled back to tell the story. "I suppose I should start at the beginning. Long ago, before I came to Australia, Lottie's uncle Eddie was attacked and held up on the road when returning from Emu Plains to Parramatta back in 1841. He had a roll of cash on him from a job he'd delivered, which, when he alighted from his wagon, he dropped in the long grass. I'd heard of that story, and it stayed in my mind. It's a long one, so I won't tell you that now; remember that bit, though."

Jonty and Lottie had heard the story of Uncle Eddie's attack and still shivered when hearing about it.

With the collective audience now hanging on his every word, Jim continued. "As Fred said, in early 1862, I left Melbourne and came north with Cobb and Co; we had over one hundred horses and many carriages. We arrived in June and were met in Bathurst by The Earl and Countess of Coxheath, better known as Lottie's grandparents Charles and Sal Lockley." Jim saw the three artists swing around to Lottie in stunned silence. She was an Earl's granddaughter?

She stayed silent, shrugged and smiled in return.

"Lord Charles, as he was officially known, had met me before departure in Liverpool in 1856. There was an incident on the docks, and well, he took me under his wing. I was a lad of nineteen, setting out for adventure and a new life on the other side of the world. I was afraid but tried not to show it. Lord Charles also met my Father that day and talked to him while I checked in. To have someone who knew my family when they were half a world away is a comfort. We stayed in contact, and he was there to meet us on our arrival in Bathurst. I have to explain a bit here. When a new route is set up, the first 'run' is to navigate the road and place grooms along the way for changing the horses. He knew this, as I'd told him in our regular correspondence through the years. He and Sal, sorry, Lady Sarah, were my first passengers on the Parramatta trip and helped with the placement of the grooms. Have you met her yet?"

The three listeners all shook their heads in unison.

"You must; she's an amazing lady. I'm sure you've met some of the Lockleys, but in the six months since I'd first notified them of our imminent, they had built staging posts every ten miles from Bathurst to Parramatta. Most are still there; some have gone with the advent of the railway. One that has long since gone was the Linden one through Ellison's Pinch." He saw everyone was still listening, so he continued. "Ellison's Pinch was called that as Conny's father, Thomas Ellison, had the Linden Toll Gate, and it was the only feasible way to put the train through, but it was resumed and demolished. On that first trip, it was our second last night on the road; I met Conny. She was only sixteen, and…" He smiled at her. "If I start on her, I shall never finish. Suffice to say, I visited as often as I could. On one visit some months later, we were all having dinner after dark, and we heard horses. Conny, her mother and her sister, Betty, disappeared as fast as possible, and their places were cleared from the table. The front door crashes open moments later, and a group of stinking bushrangers burst in. Over the half-hour or so, I hear a few names as they raid the food stores. One is Ben, and another is Frank." Jim looked at Conny, "Are you okay, possum?"

She nodded, so he continued. "Well it was very soon after that, on one of the first runs, that I'm on one of the gold or mail runs. Mr Hazelton would pack the gold in one locked box and the mail in a lead-lined box. The drivers never knew which they had as they weighed the same. We have no idea if he alternated or if it was potluck who got which one. Anyway, we'd just left town one day, and around a corner, I came across a tree blocking the road. Not a huge one, but too big to drive over. This wasn't an unusual occurrence, so I always carried an axe. I was about to hop down to clear it when I saw the tree had been chopped, not fallen naturally. I halted my descent and stayed seated. The tree they had cut was only about a yard off the road. There was a hill to one side and a vale to the other, making turning difficult. All this had flashed through my mind in mere moments. Then five or six horsemen arrived from the shrubs beside the fallen tree. I knew what would be next. Robbery!"

A gasp emanated from the artists.

Jim smiled, "Now I return to the beginning of my story, Eddie; remember he had dropped the roll of notes into the grass when he was held up. One of the passengers, who I later discovered was a jeweller in Parramatta, questioned me about being bailed up. I had told him of Eddie's story, and others had joined in the conversation as we were waiting to leave Forbes. Now back to the hold-up. The passengers were told to get down, and each did, leaving their bags in the coach. Unbeknownst to the robbers and me, the conversation about Eddie had been continued once we were underway. As the jeweller stepped off the coach, he 'tripped' and managed to drop a roll of money into the knee-high grass on the verge. Another dropped a coin fob, and apparently, others followed suit. I was left seated with a rifle pointed at me."

He reached over and took Conny's hand; he knew she hated this bit.

"Possum, are you okay?"

She nodded, so he continued.

Jim released a sigh before saying, "I recognised one from Conny's place the month before. The one called Ben was there. He told me to get down, but I refused as I wanted to keep the horses quiet. They were still fresh as we'd not travelled far. Again he told me to get down. I agreed when someone was sent to hold the horses. One of the ladies on board was travelling with her son, so the lad was sent to hold the reins. As I got down, I, too, dropped a roll and my coin fob behind the coach wheel, hoping they would not see the action. They didn't, as by now, they had the heavy box on the ground. They shot off the lock and were livid as they had only found the mail. They slit open the letters and found some £100 or so but no gold. After some time, Ben walked back to me and saw I had my silver timepiece still on me. He told me to hand it over, but again I refused. After Frank cast him a dirty look, he gave me a short shift and told him it wasn't worth my life. I unbuttoned it and passed it to him. It is not an expensive fob, but it was the last gift my mother gave me before she died. I also needed it for my work. He was about to walk away when I told him both things. To my utter amazement, he looked down at the fob and handed it back and told me to hide it until they had gone. He kept the few coins I had also given him." Jim chuckled, then added, "Oh, that was something else that Eddie had suggested years before, so I always carried some loose coins and passed them over. They left shortly afterwards." Jim pulled out his fob watch and held it by its chain. It spun around as he smiled. "After they had gone, I collected my hidden belongings, as did the jeweller and other passengers. The bushrangers had missed some £600 or more from that bit of trickery. Over the years, we took more precautions, using many different hiding places. Once a passenger had a roll of £200 tucked in her hair. Another had some in her bodice. They missed it all." Jim's eyes were sparkling with unuttered mirth. "So, Tom, to answer your original question, yes, I was bailed up. It was not a pleasant experience, but eventually, we caught most of them. Ben turned out to be Ben Hall, and Frank was Frank Gardiner, but he later escaped to America, I believe. The majority of the gang was hung, shot or gaoled. They were John O'Meally, Johnny Gilbert, Henry Manns, Alexander Fordyce, John Bow and Dan Charters. Nowadays, the roadways are reasonably safe." Jim could see that Tom's interest was piqued. He wound up the story. "Only days later, they stopped the gold coach and struck it lucky, getting over one hundred and fifty pounds of gold and cash."

"Oh, sir, that is most unfortunate for you; you say there were three more hold-ups?" Tom's gaze was fixed on Jim.

Jim's glance flicked over to his wife. "Yes, Tom, but let's adjourn outdoors and discuss them." Jim looked at Connie and waited for her nod; then, he and Tom excused themselves and went into the garden under the shade of a large tree. The next hour was spent discussing the hold-ups away from the ears of the ladies. Jim revealed many more details to Tom that he had never told anyone else. Jim had never even told Harry, so he had never heard much of what Jim disclosed to Tom. It was not because he had anything to hide, but he realised Harry would tell Vicky, who in turn may accidentally mention it to Conny. "Tom, Conny was so frightened that over the years, I stopped telling her of the incidents. The one in Gympie in 1868 was in the papers, and she was so frightened I'd be killed that we came back. I gave up driving after that. So I try not to discuss the incidents in front of her. She knows all about the first one, as all the details were in the papers. I never told her much about the one in Gympie in Queensland or the others in western New South Wales, but she knows there were more."

Tom plied Jim with more questions. Tom was also asking about the set out of horses, as he'd heard they often changed the arrangement.

Jim was intrigued and asked him why the interest. Jim said, "Tom, I've driven everything from teams of nine in three rows of three to the usual two-by-three team. I use a whip but never hit the horses, only the shaft."

Tom had more questions. "Have you ever had any accidents? I can't imagine that you've escaped without any."

Jim nodded. "The worst was coming down one of the passes on the Bathurst Road. I didn't have an accident, but it was close. Back then, many carriages had no brakes. An accident that happened only days after my incident changed all that. One pass is really steep, and we often have to get the passengers out of the carriage and walk. The horses can then normally cope with the tare weight of the carriage and luggage, but once I had an, um, shall I say oversized, passenger onboard. His girth was so wide that it made entry into the carriage difficult. When he refused to walk down the hill, he wouldn't get out with the other people; the extra weight made the carriage hard to hold. I had the horses just at a slow walk, but it nearly got away from me towards the bottom of the hill. Later that week, there was another incident; when asked to alight, the passengers did, and then one refused. The others re-entered the carriage and insisted that the driver move on. Remember, there was no brake, and you can imagine what happened, the horses could not hold the extra weight, and it took off. It overturned before the bottom of the pass. A few were injured, but two were killed, including the obstinate passenger. The accident did, however, change the carriage design. Brakes were added, and the safety improved drastically."

Tom gasped and said, "No brakes? Who'd make anyone drive a vehicle without a brake? Why that is madness!"

Jim agreed. "It wasn't by choice, Tom. It was partially the reason my hands were so bad. In the end, I didn't have the power in them to hold the horses back."

"But, Jim, that's dangerous," Tom said quietly, knowing their voices carried.

"Yes, things got much better after the brakes were added, but accidents still happened." Jim blew out his cheeks, releasing a long sigh. "The early days were rough, Tom, carriages were virtually unsprung, and the roads were horrific. If it had been raining, we'd often have to stop and rebuild a road. If rivers were up, we'd have to swim the carriage across. When the builders in Bathurst added the leather green hide suspension to the carriages, the trip became much better. The roads also had improved, so their travel was relatively comfortable."

They heard footsteps approaching. "Luncheon is ready, Jim." Jonty so wished he'd been able to sit and listen to Jim. He loved his stories.

They returned inside for lunch.

In the early afternoon, the men and older children decided to walk along the Nepean River's embankment. The sky was clear, and the sun shone, making the colours vibrant. Arthur gushed enthusiastically about the afternoon colours, the blues and greens related to the river's blueness. At one stage, he stopped still and gazed at the magnificent waterway before him. Arthur said, "Fred, I have to come back here. I need to capture this in the purple noon-day glory."

Tom was equally loquacious. "I want to speak more to Jim about the Cobb and Co travels. Oh, Smike, his stories stir the blood. He told me about the hold-ups in detail. Do you know that the original coaches didn't even have brakes?" Tom had not stopped thinking about his earlier conversation.

Fred was walking with Jonty, Jim, and Harry. The four were talking about snakes. Jim related a story of the day Conny taught him how to use a wire coil to flick and kill them. "I only ever tried it the once, and that was on a dead one. I had nearly walked on it before Conny despatched it with cool efficiency. Conny had this wire contraption in her hand on our second walk as a courting couple. I thought it a very odd accoutrement to accompany us on a romantic stroll. I asked her what the odd thing was, and before she could answer, she flicks it and killed a huge snake at my feet. I had nearly walked on the darned thing."

"Oh, sir! It didn't spring at you?" Fred was astounded at his calmness.

"No, thankfully, it was too cold; they need to warm up before becoming active. Even though it was summer, the night before had been cool. We were in Bathurst, and it can get really cold there. Had it been a few hours later, I doubt if I would be here telling the story. We chopped it up and fed it to the birds."

"I presume it was a brown one, Jim?" Harry was astounded. He had not heard this story, and he had lived next to them for over twenty years.

"Yes, a king brown at that and about eight-foot-long, a very nasty beast." Jim thought back to that morning and shook his head as if to dispel the memories.

Fred gazed at his feet. "Are they here too, sir? I'm not that keen on snakes. They move just too fast for me." Fred knew that if he sat in the bush painting, he'd come across more than one.

"We have the Eastern Browns here, Fred," Jonty said. "If you come across one, stomp on the ground as hard as possible. Do not get close, but they don't like the vibrations and will often slither off. If you do get too close, freeze, and I mean it, don't move a muscle, not a flinch. They only strike at movement. If you watch animals when they freeze, the snake finds it hard to find them, but when they move, they are dead meat."

They kept their walk to the shortened grass pathway on the top of the river bank. Although it was September and the nights still cool, the snakes were beginning to be active during the day. They walked upriver for about half a mile before turning and heading back. Both children were now tired and asked for up-up rides. Tom and Jonty lifted them, Sammo on Tom's neck and Patty on her father's neck. On their return, they worked out who would sleep where and what they would do the next day. Arthur was keen to head towards Windsor, and as Harry had a delivery to do, he offered to take all the men on the excursion.

Lottie was content to stay with Conny. Milly, Jim and Conny's youngest daughter, was fifteen and loved having little children to entertain. Her older siblings were all now married, and she was the last one living at home. Lottie was still relishing that she could feed Paul, and he'd sleep when put down. He was such a different baby now; he was out of pain. He had two teeth and had nipped her a few times. Conny told her to pull him off the breast and gently tap his cheek with one finger. He opened his big blue eyes to hers, his little face screwed up to cry, then grinned instead. Lottie put him back on the breast. He went to nip again, and she repeated removing him. The next time she put him on the breast for the third time, he didn't do it again. He was asleep once more before he'd fully finished his feed. Lottie put him straight into his basket.

Early in the dawn light, Harry's wagon arrived at the front door with the three artists on board. Jonty and Jim hopped up with a basket of food Conny had supplied for them.

"Where are we heading, Uncle Harry?" Jonty enquired.

"Do you remember Mrs Walker's farm? After she remarried, her son Oliver took it over, and now his son, Joel, is working it. They have increased the production of honey. So I'm bringing some empty honey barrels back for refilling, and I have to collect a load of small new casks. He makes the casks himself too. They are each about a foot high. Do you know they started off with a lady cooper? She made them from silver wattle. I can't stock enough of them as people reuse them for all sorts of things. I commissioned a hundred of them, hence the large wagon. More than half will be sent to Parramatta for the mail order catalogue business that Rick started."

Jonty nodded. "Yes, Uncle Harry, Rick told me before I went to Africa. His swagman friend Jack was working with him, learning Morse Code. They tried to teach me…" he shrugged, then fell silent, leaving his words unfinished.

Fred chuckled, "Not your forté, eh?"

Jonty shook his head. "Nah, I'd rather cut diamonds and sapphires. At least I have something to show at the end of the day."

Fred had meant to ask Jonty about a comment from earlier. "Tell me about that, Jonty; you said something earlier about Africa. Did you go there?"

With a raised eyebrow, Jim caught Jonty's eye and enquired if it was something Jonty wanted to discuss. With a subtle nod, Jonty started on his reply. "Fred, I went to get diamonds for a firm in Antwerp. Father had worked with this man before, as had my boss. Buying the gems was eye-opening in itself. Do you know how they are exploiting the locals? It's disgusting. Don't get me started on that, though. I refused to buy from the big mines and only bought from the local villagers and small, locally owned mines. I gave them above award price too." Jonty flicked his eyes to Jim. The compassion in his eyes almost hurt. Jonty continued, "Fred, one little girl brought me a beautiful gem. I paid almost double for it, knowing her family needed the money desperately. I can still see her adorable face. Her huge chocolate eyes, velvety cheeks, and two huge dimples, just like some of our family but dark-skinned. What amazed me was that she even spoke some English. I had hoped that she would be able to bring me more. I only saw her once more. Fred, the English rogues, had decapitated her because I purchased from her." Jonty had a catch in his voice.

"Don't say any more, Jon; I can tell it hurts too much…" Fred was in the middle of speaking.

Jonty shook his head. "I need to tell you, Fred, because out of the beauty of these gems, there is greed, lust, hate, and intolerance. What I saw over there was nearly enough to crush me. Even now, I have nightmares if I go to bed without releasing my cares to God. Yes, it was years ago, but the memories still haunt me."

"Oh gosh, Jon, that's horrible," Tom gasped.

Jonty continued. "The story doesn't finish there, Tom. Because of me not purchasing from the English mines, the Boers saw me as impartial. It was that fact that saved my life." Jonty explained to his listeners more of what had occurred. Jim and Harry had heard his story, but the three artists had not. In the years since the retelling, facts had changed little, but Jonty's attitude to the details was vastly different. As he retold the incidents, he related them with maturity and the wisdom of hindsight. Yes, it still hurt. There was still nothing different he could or would have done that would have changed anything. But for the first time, he could relate his feelings without tears, physical or emotional.

Fred nearly exploded. "Blooming heck, Jon, that's horrible, all right. Tell us about those mines. What do you mean the owners aren't fair?" Fred asked.

"It's the conditions of the mines. Yes, they employ occasional locals as their contracts say, but they pay them a pittance, the English workers are paid more, and the Boers and villagers are not even considered. And then they try to make rules that only the big mines can dig for gems. That will cut out the little mines and the family concerns. It's unfair. No, it's just not fair, and there is not one damn thing that I could have done to make a difference." Jonty fell silent, looking but not seeing the beauty surrounding him. His mind was back in Africa. A gasp from Arthur broke his reverie.

The wagon had just turned a bend, and the view down the river was breathtaking. The sunlight was sparkling on the water, the trees overhanging the riverbanks, and the entire scene was so inviting that Arthur just wished he had time to paint it. An exclamation of awe sprang to his lips. "Darn Harry, why did you have to show us this? I'm going to be haunted until I return and paint this scene." Arthur pulled out a small sketch pad and etched the outline. "I'll call it *The purple noon's transparent might.*" He dropped his head to concentrate on his sketch.

Jonty noticed that the three artists called both Jim and Harry just by their Christian names. He smiled at the informality. He had a feeling that they would meet again after the trip.

Chapter 14 Returning Wanderers

*T*he artist's trip lasted another week before they had to head home. They had made two more journeys across in the ferry to Balmoral Beach. The seed of a return one day had more than germinated, it had grown into an entire forest, and they even worked out which of their artistic friends may be interested in joining them. Young Simon was one whom they had decided to ask. He was an only child and needed to see more of the world.

Life settled back to normal for Jonty and Lottie once their friends departed. Will and Dimity were still in England, and having been gone for many years, they missed them. Since retelling that trip, Jonty found that even his dreams had been virtually non-existent. Occasionally he would wake in a cold sweat, but he never had another violent one.

By Easter 1888, Lottie was expecting their fourth child. At one-year-old, little Paul was now up and running everywhere. Paul never looked back after that trip to Balmoral. He had slept through every night since.

The Friday after Easter, the postman delivered a long-awaited letter. Will and Dimmy were coming home. They had waited until his elderly aunt died. The letter announced that they had booked a suite on the *SS Abergeldie* and would arrive in May. Jonty was astounded. He knew tickets on this particular vessel were costly as he had travelled on it himself. Mr Field had purchased his ticket and said he was worth the luxury of the tourist class ticket. Jonty knew the fare for a tourist class cabin on this ship would be over £35, and a first-class suite would be about £50 or more. Will wasn't that wealthy, and although they had travelled cabin class on the way over, they had sailed out on a brig.

Time would explain much.

Will and Dimity had a wonderful time meeting the Murray, English and Lockley families. Although Will had gone to meet the Murray family, it was the revelations of the English family that shocked him. Unbeknownst to him, his position in society had changed somewhat from what he expected. He spent valuable time with his paternal grandparents before their death. Paul had neglected to tell him that his paternal grandfather was a Baron. Therefore, because of his father's demise, when Will was born, he would have been able to use the title of 'The Honourable', and he had never known. Now that his grandfather was dead, Will had inherited the title; he was Baron William Summerland. His eldest son was now The Honourable Richard, and his family now lived in England at Summerland Hall. One of the things Will had to sort out after his grandfather's funeral was setting Richard up to run the family. From having no relations at all, Will found he was now head of a large one; it was a rude shock. Will wished Ricky was here to both meet the family and help him. Thankfully, his son Richard had his head screwed on and coped with the transition well. As The Honourable Richard English, his life was different as he had been an art teacher in Paris. His grandfather had been able to give instructions on what was expected, and both men learned all they could from his wisdom. There were advisors and lawyers to assist him.

Soon after the new family had been met, Will and Dimity said they would have to visit more relations. This time, the Lockleys at Gracemere Castle. Will had brought letters and parcels from home and promised to deliver them personally. One, in particular, was to reconnect with Teddy, Charlie's oldest son. He had met him nearly twenty years before, but he also had to catch up with the Duke and the Castle family. Will initially wondered why his cousin had been allowed to marry into a Duke's family but figured it was a love match. Now he found it certainly was, but of social equals. He was looking forward to returning and telling Ricky everything he'd learned. But that would be some time in the future.

Although Will was Ricky's younger cousin, his father had been the elder of the two brothers. He confirmed that his father had come to find some farms with his younger brother and then intended to stay and run them while William returned to England. Both brothers had died, albeit Ricky's father did return injured, having lived with an aboriginal tribe for some ten years. He had died soon after his return. Will remembered him and had no idea that he was his uncle, his death leaving Ricky bereft. Will's grandparents had no one else to send; they thought they would never know what had occurred. His grandparents had been childhood sweethearts and married young. As Will was sixty when he left for England, he was surprised to find his grandparents alive but in their late nineties. It was one of the main reasons Will extended his trip. His grandmother died the year after his arrival, and his grandfather two years later. He was weeks away from turning one hundred when he didn't call his valet one morning. He had fallen asleep for the last time.

Will had been thrilled to spend every moment possible. Because of his friendship with Eddie and the Lockley family in Parramatta, Will was keen to meet the extended Lockley family in England. He decided to visit Teddy Lockley at Coxheath, but on arrival at Bramblemere House, found the building being refurbished after a fire. The builders gave him the direction to Gracemere Castle, and as it was only a few extra miles, he thought they would call in to see if that was where they were. They were welcomed with open arms on arrival by the Duke. It was almost overwhelming. Chip remembered him from a few of the later visits to Eddie's house. Will had not realised that Eddie's daughter married the young Duke. They were invited to stay for a few days.

Will had also not realised that Lottie's cousin, Rick Lockley, had handed over the gigantic estate he had inherited from his swagman friend to his cousin Teddy, heir to Charlie, Earl of Coxheath. Will and Dimity had a delightful time. The Dowager Duchess Christina remembered him. At eighty-three, she was still of sound mind, and although her body was feeling her age, she was still mobile. Will and Dimity had met her a few times in Sydney and Parramatta. Having spent many years in the colony herself, she welcomed them both with a big hug, anxious for news of her other home.

Dimity was somewhat overwhelmed at the reception. The extraordinary lady was a Duchess, and Dimity was just an Australian mouse of a girl. Her own parents were long since gone, as they were much older when she was born. Catching up with this family was a delight. The current Duchess, Ed's daughter Tina, and the Dowager sat with Dimity and pumped her for every bit of information about Australia she could think of. Her news that Lottie and Jonty were having twins was a big surprise for them. Dimity told them of their hasty marriage but not the reason why. She then told them about Jonty's experience in Africa. Both were horrified.

Dowager Duchess Christina said, "But Jonty is such a gentle boy; how did he cope? He's just a jeweller."

Dimity explained. "He had awful nightmares for a long time; my Will, Harry Harlow, and Jim Leslie all helped him. By the time we left, he seemed to be coping well." One by one, they went through what all the family members were up to.

Will was having a similar conversation with Chip and his brother-in-law, Kit. Will had not realised that another of Eddie's children, Kit, had married Chip's sister, Charlotte, called Charl. He knew Kit was ordained but not that he was now the Rector at Maidstone. They lived in the Dower House and had seven children. The youngest, Thea, was only three. Will had heard that Charl and Kit had quadruplets. It seemed not long ago that he had heard about their birth. Therefore, he was surprised to find out they were about to celebrate their seventeenth birthday. It had been so hard to keep track of all the children of someone else's family. Now they were his relations too; he knew he had to take more note of who each was.

Chip filled them in about Princhester Court. "It's blooming big! Even my eyes popped when I first saw it. Will, I believe that your place here is nearly as big." Chip had been to visit Baron Summerland sometime before. He had no idea of any family connection back then. Although it was tenuous, there was a link. CJ's wife, Addie, was related by marriage to the English's; she was the first cousin to Will, heir to the Barony. Chip chuckled; he'd seen God's strings being pulled so often over the years that he thought nothing surprised him. But to find the orphan, Will, was now Baron Summerland and his daughter-in-law's cousin; this tickled his funny bone.

Will and Dimity stayed for a week before leaving to meet Teddy. Chip had sent a wire to him and asked if it were convenient for Will and Dimity to come for a visit. Ted replied within the hour. "Tell them to come; they are welcome." They had to go to Aylesford to see Teddy and find Princhester Court. Chip sent them with his coachman in the Ducal carriage. After many farewells, they set off in luxury. The journey only took about fifteen minutes. The hired chaise that had brought them to the castle had been sent back to London soon after their arrival. They were now travelling in absolute opulence. Their chatter in the coach stopped dead as they turned in through the gates. They turned into an immaculately kept driveway. They passed enormous oak trees. The driveway was wide enough for four coaches to pass easily.

Dimity's mouth fell open when they saw the first glimpses of Princhester Court. "Oh, Will, who was this Swagman Jack who left Rick Lockley all this? Did Chip tell you?" Dimity had not heard the full story of the old swagman who lived with Rick Lockley. She knew that he had died and left Rick a billy can. She knew that its contents meant that they had to come to England.

"Sir John, or Jack as we knew him, was actually Baron Princhester. He had married Elouise Wickham after David died," Will explained.

"No, seriously, you mean the same woman who threw over Chip's father, whom we knew as Major Ned Grace, then married his brother? The shrew woman?" Dimity was aghast.

"Yes, one and the same; she tricked Jack too." Will knew the whole story from Chip. He was horrified when he heard she had cheated on Sir John on their honeymoon. Will could not voice such deception, not even to his beloved Dimmy. "Chip said Jack left soon after their marriage and ended up half a world away. Eventually, Sir John, whom we knew as Jack, met Rick, and while they were here two years ago, Teddy's house caught fire, and it gave Rick the excuse to sign over the place to the Earldom. His Uncle Charlie, the Earl, had already okayed it, so Teddy just had to move in. I didn't get a chance to catch up with Rick on his return, so I didn't know about the end of the story."

By now, they were driving past a huge lake with a pavilion in the middle of it. The expanse of the vast house was not yet entirely in view; the couple sat in stunned silence. The magnificence of the building was slowly being revealed. "Cor," was all Will could say.

The carriage pulled up to the front door, and the door was thrown open by Teddy. "Will, Dimity, this is an absolute delight. Welcome!" He handed down Dimity and then Will. He ushered them into the front door and introduced them to Basil and Hazel Hawthorn, the butler and housekeeper.

Will had first met Teddy when he was only a lad of fourteen. A year later, he'd left home and moved to England with Duke Ned. They had kept in contact; Teddy probably didn't realise how like his Uncle Ed he was. The first big triple painting Will produced was one of Eddie, and when he met Teddy, it was like the painting had come to life. The nineteen years between them mattered little; they had struck up a friendship that bridged the miles and years. Although now forty-one, Teddy was still recognisable as the young lad Will had known. They looked forward to the week ahead.

~

Now years later, Will had come to say farewell before returning to Australia. They were doing the rounds of the family before their departure. Their visits had become frequent over the years. Chip had also become good friends with Richard and his French wife, Dominique. They had moved from Paris when Will discovered his grandparents were still alive. They had moved in with him when he realised he would one day become the Baron. He now picked up the reins of the position.

It was time for Will and Dimity to say farewell to their son, daughters, and grandchildren. Although they were sad, they were looking forward to going home.

The last months flew by; soon, they were all loading themselves into carriages at Summerland House in London and heading to the dockland. Chip, Tina, Teddy, and Bella had all come to London for the farewell. Richard escorted his mother up the gangplank, Will hard on their heels, and their daughters followed. Soon all clinging to each other in tears. Then, in their suite's privacy, the three siblings hugged them both. The act of parting was hard.

Dimity managed to hold her weeping until the ship had sailed from sight of all the family. Will felt as though his heart was breaking. Returning home was turning out much harder than he had expected. Theo was still in Melbourne; if it weren't for Ricky and Tad, he would think twice about going back at all. He would try to come back again soon. With the Suez Canal open, the trip was not long. The *SS Abergeldie* sailed on with a belch of smoke billowing from the smokestacks.

A few days into the trip, the Captain, Master Levie, had notified Will about a slight change of plan. "Lord William, we have to stop in Cairo and collect some cargo. I knew about this before sailing, but not the volume of beasts." The Captain paused, swallowing. "Sir, we have to load over two hundred camels.

Will was speechless. He was still not used to the change in his status. He certainly didn't expect special treatment on board. Yes, they had booked the master suite, but it was because their cabin over had been almost claustrophobic. It had not occurred to either of them that their titles would change their lives so much. This apology from the Captain foretold of many adjustments ahead.

Sure enough, two weeks later, the ship docked in Cairo. Dimity and Will leaned on the railing from the upstairs deck, unable to believe what they saw. Over two hundred camels were being loaded on board. Neither had ever seen a camel before and thought them bizarre beasts. Many had droopy lips, and one was a cantankerous beast that obviously did not wish to set sail. Will presumed it was a male as it was much larger than some of the others. He certainly gave his handlers a rough time. An assortment of long-robe-clad men accompanied them, and after they were stowed, the arrival of two fully veiled ladies caused a slight stir.

"I thought that camels had two humps, Will?" Dimity said. The captain, who was standing nearby, heard her question.

"Lady Summerland, these are dromedary camels, not Asian ones, which have the two humps. These ones are heading to be pack animals in the central parts of Australia. We're one of the few ships that can carry them." The three stood watching the vast quantity of the incredible animals' board. "I just didn't think there would be this many. When they first booked my hold for 'camels,' I thought there may be some twenty, not two hundred and twenty of them."

"Where are we taking them, Captain?" Will asked.

"Thankfully, only to Adelaide, but I'll be going full steam for the next three weeks. I have no idea how they will travel. If we run into a storm, we may be in trouble. I just hope they are not noisy." He gave a long sigh and said, "My Lord, My Lady, I really should go and see the final loading of these specimens." He doffed his captain's hat and walked off.

Once aboard, the ship's crew had to settle the beasts and head down the Suez Canal. The Captain was given priority and didn't have to wait in the long queue of vessels. Their journey down the canal was much quicker than on a standard sailing ship. It steamed down the passage and quickly on the way south. Thankfully they didn't hit a storm. Fremantle was the first stop, then the Queen's Wharf in Adelaide. Will was pleased they could not hear the camels inside their cabin, but the noise and stench were noticeable once on deck. He was delighted that he had now booked the more expensive suite. He felt sorry for the lower class passengers, who were much closer to the odoriferous animals; the stench would be unbearable.

It was a supposition that the Captain confirmed as they were leaving Fremantle harbour. "Oh, I cannot wait to unload these ungainly creatures. I shall have to get the hold hosed out. I suggest you take a day trip while we are in Adelaide, my lord. There is much to see in the town if you have not looked around."

"Thanks for the warning, Captain; we shall." Will watched him head back to the bridge.

The few days to Adelaide were traversed quickly. The Captain disembarked the passengers before allowing the camels to be unloaded. The skipper had been down into the hold. He knew what would happen as soon as the doors were opened. Thankfully with the calm weather, they had been able to keep the hatches open to allow sunshine and air to circulate, but there was no way to flush the animals' floor, so the stench was vile. Only when he saw the last carriage depart the dockland did he allow the discharging of the cargo. He asked for the city fire tankers to be brought to the docks to flush the hold once the beasts were unloaded. He knew three had died on the journey, and they had been thrown overboard. But five had been born. He had never seen a baby that was not what he'd consider cute until he saw a baby camel. They were just miniature versions of the parents, only with no characteristic hump. Just a stripe of black fluff along the backs. Thankfully all the babies survived.

It took all day for the ship to be cleansed. By late afternoon the passengers were back on board. The harbour waters absorbed the effluent, and the vessel was to get underway at dawn the following day. Hopefully, it would only be ten days until they reached Sydney.

Home! They couldn't wait.

Word had arrived that the SS *Abergeldie* would come through the heads mid to late morning. Jonty knew it would take until noon, at least, before the passengers could disembark. He asked Mr Lamb about taking the afternoon off to assist with transporting Will and Dimity's luggage. At eleven, Mr Lamb poked his head around Jonty's workroom door and said, "It's quiet this morning; why don't you head down early and welcome them at the quay?"

Jonty nodded and thanked him, finishing up the gem he was setting and then packing everything away. It was nearly noon when he caught the tram home and collected Lottie and the children. They walked quickly down the hill, hoping the walk would burn off some of the children's energy. They could see smoke belching past Mrs Macquarie's Chair and were in time to see the ship dock. All three little ones were in harnesses to save them from running on the road and being injured. The welcome home was all Will wished. Ricky and Jenny, Tad and Amabel, and Jonty and Lottie with their small children were waiting on the wharf. Will had not told any of them about his title. He wasn't looking forward to that either and wasn't sure how to even bring the subject up.

He need not have worried.

The Captain let that cat out of the bag during his farewell. "Lord Summerland, Lady Summerland, it has been my honour to have you sail with us. I do hope our humped passengers did not upset your crossing too much." He bowed to them as he handed them from the bottom of the gangplank.

The family around them stood with their mouths agape. As soon as the Captain had gone from earshot, Will was bombarded with questions. "What's this Lord and Lady bit, Will?" Ricky asked.

"Summerland? Why the name change?" asked Tad.

"Not here," Will said grumpily and hobbled off.

Jonty and Lottie stood back with Jenny and Amabel. "I think Will has not been letting on what he's discovered," Jonty said quietly.

"I think luncheon is going to be very interesting, Jonty, I do hope you will join us. I have caterers coming to Will's house in about an hour," Jenny English replied.

Jonty arranged for the luggage to be collected and taken to Will's cottage. Then they walked the short distance up the hill.

Will had left Ricky and Tad's question unanswered, other than to say, "I'll tell you all at once when we're alone."

Their destination was reached, and Jenny, Lottie, and Amabel busied themselves in the kitchen while Will and Dimity settled back in. Ricky, Jonty and Tad looked after the small children in the backyard.

"Have you got any idea about what the story is, Jon?" Ricky asked.

"Nope, I'm as blindsided as you are, Ricky." Jonty went and stopped the twins from having a brawl over a ball. Tad was sitting on the top step when he heard the kitchen door open. Will joined him.

"What gives, Will?" Ricky was full of questions but knew Will would reveal all in his own good time.

Will didn't answer but held open the door. "Come inside, and I'll tell you all at once."

Tad called for Jonty to follow them.

Once seated and the tea poured, the story unfolded to the amazement of the listeners. "You're a Baron? Lord William, eh?"

Amabel got the giggles. "Dimmy, do you remember your Papa's objections to you marrying Will? What would he say now?"

"I know! It was when I put my foot down that he listened. I had to throw a full tantrum, you know. It was your Papa who finally talked him around. You were allowed to marry Tad before you knew who he was."

Dimity reached out and held her friend's hand. "Thank you for supporting us all these years. You all know it makes no difference to me, but we've found a change of attitude to us is already, it's, well, problematic."

"In what way, Dimmy?" Lottie questioned.

"We were happy being invisible, and now we aren't. Lord this, or Lady that, suddenly we're indispensable to whatever function is on. We just want to go back to what we were. We couldn't do that in England." Will sounded disconsolate. "Richard has moved back from Paris with Dominique and the children. He's taken over running the estate. The children will have to learn to speak English properly now. Etienne will one day inherit the title of Baron. Thankfully, Grandfather English had a few years teaching Richard before he passed on. Our Jenny and Addie have settled with their families and are reasonably close to Richard. We spent a lot of time with them all. It was so hard returning here where we only have Theo."

Ricky thought back to when he had taken both small lads under his wing, and they had become family. Both had connections back in England, and although he and Will were cousins, his ties to England were tenuous. Tad and Amabel travelled back every few years to see his cousin Joshua and the family. However, Ricky and Jenny had never left and had never intended to either. Their own children were running the orphanages and the English Emporium. He felt that maybe it was time for them to travel back to England for a long holiday.

The afternoon was spent discussing the various family members; Will started explaining Princhester Court and its vast size. His ability to describe it did not do it justice. He said, "Hang on." He got up and went to his artist's bag, which was never far from him. It was still in the hallway, having not been taken up the three flights of stairs to his studio. He flicked open the buckles and drew out a drawing pad. Carrying it back into the sitting room, he turned to a drawing he'd done of the front facade. He didn't elaborate, merely passed the sketchbook around. Gasps of admiration emanated from each one. "It's blooming huge, Will," Jonty said in awe. "Rick said it was big but gave us no hint of its splendour."

Will continued. "Oh, the front is nothing compared to the inside, and the glasshouse is incredible. Lottie, do you remember hearing of your grandfather sending over pineapple tops to Teddy? Well, they grew well, and he now has over one thousand plants growing. I'd never seen a pine fruit and didn't know they grew on spikes from the top of the crown. This place had a Roman hypocaust under the floor, and Sir John, or 'Jack' as we knew him, connected that to the kitchen chimney flues. It's heated all year round. I now understand that scholarship that Rick started in memory of Jack. Teddy told me the story."

Lottie knew the history too. Having been to the house, she also knew that the drawing was accurate. She merely said, "It's a fitting home for an Earl, isn't it?"

Dimity nodded. "The first time we saw it was only months after you had all left, Lottie; I can't believe that Rick just turned over a building like that to his cousin. It's worth thousands of pounds."

"Probably more Dimity, but Rick's got enough. He's very like Uncle Wills; he doesn't flash his wealth around." Much had happened in the years since they returned from that trip. Lottie remembered the desolation of finding Jonty was not back. When he finally did return, she had to cope with his nightmares and then the arrival of the twins. Her cousins were far off in her worries.

Will was itching to get back to painting. He had many ideas running around his mind, and although he had used Richard's new studio, he painted very little while at Summerland Hall; he now wanted to throw himself back into his old life. He smiled when one of the first things Richard had asked his great-grandfather was if he could set up a studio. The old gentleman smiled and told Richard to tug the bell pull. The aged butler entered and was asked to have his grandson and great-grandson escorted to his private sanctum. The butler showed great surprise but escorted the two men to a sun-filled, airy room full of the most wonderful array of art supplies one could imagine. Around the walls of the home, both had noticed some beautiful landscapes that neither recognised. Neither realised that art apparently ran in the family. Will was the first to discover the correlation between the easel's part-finished works and those hanging in the corridors. He couldn't get to his grandfather's side fast enough. "Why didn't you tell me you painted too, Grandfather? You're 'W. English' too?"

The old man chuckled and nodded. "It runs in the blood, son. It's how I knew you to be who you said you were. Your father had the talent, but my Richard didn't. He was the adventurer. He was always looking for new schemes and ways to make money. But he adored animals and strays in particular. He brought home so many over the years I lost count." Will smiled, thinking that Ricky had inherited that trait from his father; only Ricky adopted children, Tad and Will being the first ones, then hundreds of them followed over the years. Will was alive today because he had been one of the first Ricky adopted.

Chapter 15 Balmoral Obsession

Will and Dimity settled back into life in Sydney. He soon produced two large murals and several smaller saleable pieces. His work was still in demand, most pre-sold before he even finished them. Not that he had any need to sell his works now, as Richard and he had arranged a regular allowance from the estate in England. It had taken the stress and pressure from his shoulders. Each painting sold still brought him joy, knowing others appreciated his skill. He had been successful enough in his work to support a family and four children. Dimity's father had left them comfortable, but he tried not to tap into that income. However, he would never leave his family short; over the years, they occasionally needed to use some of those funds. Now it lay untouched.

~

One morning about a year after their return, Will asked Dimity to accompany him for a walk. His destination was the bank. He was signing the entire contents of her father's legacy over to her for personal use. He would not ask how or why she would use it. It was to be her money exclusively. Dimity signed where instructed and without question. If he wished for her to access these funds, she'd not refuse. She smiled at the bank manager but was somewhat overwhelmed. She squeezed Will's hand but remained silent. However, once out of the bank, she said, "But Will, Papa gave this to you. By the time he died, you know he had apologised for how he had treated you initially. Your care of them in their final years was far beyond what they expected."

He replied softly, "And we used it, love, but now it's yours. Our Richard ensures that the estate is giving us far more than we have ever had before, and of course, I have my father's money and his land here, although I'm giving that to Theo. He can sell it or keep it, but I'll give it to him. I found out it's over a thousand farmable acres south of Camden. So use your Papa's money as you wish, my sweet. Even if you wish to give it away, it's for you to decide." His darling mouse of a girl he'd fallen in love with so many years ago had stood beside him through thick and thin. Now she stood beside him through the turmoil of their new titles. Will said, "My darling Dimmy, I am going to withdraw my father's money from the bank here and buy some rental properties and a small farm for produce for the poor around Emu Plains. I had a dream that we would need food in the not-too-distant future, and I thought I'd do something useful."

She smiled at him and said, "Will, can I get you to use this money too? I think the idea of a produce farm would be excellent. If what I read in yesterday's paper is a sign of what is to happen, then I think we'll need it." She fell deep into thought and didn't hear Will speak to her.

"Dimmy, did you hear what I said?" Will asked.

"Err, sorry, no love; I thought that maybe we should also buy or build a boarding house for adults with nowhere to live. Ricky and Jenny look after the children, but there are still so many homeless people that I'd like to help them." She was taken aback as Will laughed at her comment.

Smiling down at her, he repeated his words. "Love, I asked if you would mind if we bought the row of cottages from John Evans. He wishes to sell them, as he feels Ricky no longer needs them."

Her face lit up. "Oh, Will, could we? They would be perfect. We could even oversee them ourselves."

"Yes, my darling little mouse, we can. I have already spoken to the bank manager, and now it's just a matter of getting John to fix the price." The smile that lit up her face made Will chuckle. "It's how I knew you had not heard what I had said."

She did a skip of happiness. "And we won't even have to move."

Wheels were set in motion, and soon they were the owner of not only the row of cottages now in Dimity's name but also of a fifty-acre farm in Castlereagh on the Nepean River. Will hired a man recommended by Harry Harlow. He'd worked on his property as a labourer and had since married. His wife was now expecting their first child. Andrew Rohan was a hard worker, and Harry had no problem recommending him as both overseer and manager of Will's latest project. Harry offered to also oversee things for him as his citrus trees and horses needed little daily oversight.

In Melbourne, things were not good. First, one bank, then another, closed its doors. Shops shut down, and businesses went broke. Fred, Tom, and Arthur sat in the now virtually empty studio discussing the downturn in sales. Only a senior schoolboy, named Simon, was at work. None of them had sold anything for over three months. Others had stopped painting altogether.

Simon's parents were wealthy and could afford to keep him at Art School in Melbourne. They knew his skill, and it was this pittance that the other artists lived on. He had arrived at their door, a lad of only ten. They had added some of his works to the college portfolio, and it was these that Jonty had seen years before. Fred remembered him showing them to Will after their luncheon. Since then, Simon's work had improved beyond even their skill.

Three of their artist friends had come to the studio and told them about their decision to leave. "We need to feed our families, and our painting is not doing that, so sadly, we have each decided that any work is good work, and so we are packing our brushes and paints and taking work on the docks."

Their departure made Fred turn to his friends. "I think it's time we put our own dreams into action. Smike, you have been on at me to go back to the Hawkesbury, Tom; you said you wanted to see Jim again; well, he's not getting any younger. I suggest we pack up and head to Sydney. I hear things are not so bad there, and if we all lose our accommodation, at least we can sleep in my tent on the beach." He looked at them and raised both his eyebrows in an unvoiced question, wondering what their reaction would be.

Tom was first to say, "I'm in. Smike, you coming?"

"You bet! I'm in too!" Arthur said, his eyes twinkling with joy.

Simon Mitchell stood back, looking at his easel. The painting was now finished; the seventeen-year-old put down his brush and walked over to his three teachers. "Sirs, it was hard not to overhear what you said; I was wondering if I may accompany you too? My parents have just left for two years in London, and my lease runs out in three weeks. I am supposed to move to Sydney with my aunt, but I'd much rather stay with you." The schoolboy looked anxiously at his mentor.

Fred looked at his two friends; one nodded, and the other shrugged and said, "In for a penny, in for a pound. He's a darned good artist, and I'd love to see how far he can go with his art. Heck, why not?" Tom smiled at his young protégé. "You can earn your keep by cooking for us."

The smile that spread over Simon's face delighted them all. For some reason, the young man had learned to cook and did it well. He'd often bring them a cake he'd made or a tin of homemade biscuits. "You mean it? I can really come?"

"Yes, Simon, we mean it, but I also mean you will have to earn your keep. You cook better than us, but you won't have to do it all alone. We'll help. And we will all have to get odd jobs to keep food in our bellies. As you heard, 'Any honest work is good work.' We'll eat what we can catch and grow some vegetables. The climate is better, but we'll be roughing it."

~

Six months later, the Artist's camp on Balmoral Beach in Sydney was in itself a tourist drawcard. Visitors would be welcome and encouraged to watch the artists at work, but they had to put a penny in the hat for the privilege. Will had put up the four men upon arrival until they had the permission required to set up camp. They had cleaned out the studio in Melbourne, packed all their blank canvases into crates, and shipped them to Sydney. They were in storage until they were needed. Will had arranged with Lottie's father, Luke, to store their possessions in his warehouse in Sydney. A group of them had introduced themselves to Simon's aunt, Miss May Beamish. When they discovered her to be both elderly and forgetful, the decision to keep Simon with them was a foregone conclusion. The old lady had forgotten he was coming to her. The group only took a week before they chose the site on Balmoral to set up camp. Once the permissions were through, they set about making the large canvas tent home for an indeterminate period. As Simon arrived to find his aunt could no longer house him, now guilt-free, he accepted the offer to stay with the three friends.

Weeks passed, and word of the artists' camp was spreading. Weekends were the busiest. Many other budding artists were encouraged to set up easels near them, and, for a penny, a lesson was instructed on technique. Simon also set up a fire and would sell mugs of tea and golden syrup biscuits. As many would picnic there, this was a good source of income. Simon also devised an idea to host private showings of the finished works. They would pack their bedding on a Saturday morning and turn the tent into a gallery. Visitors would have to pay to view them, and all works were for sale. Sadly few sold. Many people spent the halfpenny to see a picture, but money became tight as the financial crash spread.

One by one, the blank canvasses they had brought from Melbourne were used. Only one crate remained, and Fred had forgotten that this large crate also contained works he had completed. He groaned when he opened it. One was the painting that he'd merely named 'Lost.' It was of the little postmaster's daughter. No one had bought it. No one had been interested in it except a photographer who had taken its photo for a catalogue. Even though he'd reduced the price to half, it hadn't sold. He knew it would be sad to see it go, but it would be painted over. After a delightful stay at Balmoral, they decided to join another artist's camp in a more protected spot. They had now moved across the headland to Curlew Camp over near the Mosman Ferry wharf. New canvasses arrived soon after they moved.

Arthur had befriended Reuben Brasch, and he offered accommodation in a more secluded bay. The place had more room and even shacks that were more comfortable. It wasn't long before the others joined him. Simon was still with them, but others had joined them too. Even Will and Jonty occasionally painted with them, as did other artists from the area. Julien Ashton was one of the local residents who frequently joined them for the *en plain air* sessions. Over time the camp grew. More buildings were added. One had a piano and a dance floor; another was a dining tent. Many were sleeping quarters, one for storage and another for a studio of sorts.

~

Three years passed in a flash. They found that they could all live on 12/6 a week; however, even making that small amount was sometimes tricky. Tom was the only one who refused to let his dress code relax and was always neat and tidy. He'd often be invited to places and even to Government House. He adored portraiture and captured the ruggedness in the faces of those he chose to paint. Fred caught him often drawing Smike. Fred loved the mistiness of the bushland and often went to stay with his friends in Emu Plains. He would often drag Arthur along, and they'd sit and paint to their heart's content.

They found a small room in Sydney where they set up an art school. For a penny, they advertised art classes, and although this took them away from their outdoor love of painting, it put food on their tables.

Simon was doggedly persistent in his artwork. His paintings were like colour photographs, yet he had not sold a single one. Other artists came admiring the young man's works, but as the other's work sold, his didn't. He had met many of the now well-known artists, all admiring his skill. Julien Ashton brought many friends to visit, often staying for a period. David Davies, John Llewellyn Jones, and Leon Pole were all introduced to the camp. Even ladies were welcomed, and Jane Sutherland, Clara Southern, Ina Gregory, and Jane Price were invited to paint with the colony. Some came, and some didn't.

~

Four years after their arrival in Sydney, Tom disappeared. He had told Fred he was going west and then just packed and left. Fred knew he had taken a few blank canvases with him. He wondered if Tom would head out to Jim Leslie's place again. He knew Jim's last child had left home, and he had invited Tom to come and stay for a while. Tom had continued to pump Jim for more intricate details about his first hold-up. He would read any article he could, but there was nothing like first-hand knowledge. One thing Tom had not taken though was his small sketch pad; in it, Fred had found some forty pencil and charcoal sketches of the Cobb and Co coach hold up. Jim had told him about his hold-up by Ben Hall in 1862. Fred knew the story had taken hold of Tom's imagination. He was sure he would get around to painting something with that as a subject. It was only after two months that he discovered both Jonty and Lottie had travelled with him, and it was not to Jim's place but further north to the New England area.

With the downturn in the financial situation, Mr Lamb, who was now getting on in years, suggested that Jonty take an extended holiday because he'd be running the business by himself when he returned. He was finally going to retire. He wanted to take his long-suffering wife on holiday back to England. As the journey only took six weeks on the steamers, it was now a quick trip. The news had stunned Jonty, and he wondered where they would go; when he discussed this at the family dinner that Sunday, he noticed the looks between his parents. "Son, it must be the season for retirements. I handed in my resignation at the Museum on Friday. Your mother and I have decided to return to the country for a break. With this bit of news, mayhap you wish to join us?"

The excited look on Lottie's face gave Jonty the answer quickly. "By the joyous look on my wife's face, I'd say that's a yes. So when do we leave?"

The trip took a month to plan. Tom had visited shortly before their departure; he'd been out to Jim's and was flushed with enthusiasm, so he invited himself along for the ride. As the children all adored him, he was welcomed. They had hired two outfitted covered wagons and had an extra canvas to string between the two vehicles. Tom had taken his camping gear and swag from the artist's camp and had a folding easel and a portable box with his painting goods inside.

Nearly forty years before, Jonty's parents had gone on a Mineral Survey with Reverend William Clarke. West of Inverell, they discovered many beautiful sapphires, especially in Bingara. Colleen had only just told John that she was expecting a baby. That child was Jonty. It became a special place for them, and over the years, they had returned a few times to the beautiful camping spot on the river bend. It was to this place that they planned to head. It was safe for the children and somewhere to pan for more gems. With Jonty now turning these river pebbles into stunning jewellery, it would hopefully be a worthwhile trip. The twins were now twelve, Paul was eight, and Carol was seven. The two wagons had set off. They planned at least two months away, possibly more.

In the years since the artists first arrived, Jonty had lost both his grandparents. His grandfather, Douglas, had died not long after Paul was born in 1887, and his grandmother, Caroline, passed away the day after Carol was born. She had cradled the baby girl and cried when they told her she was to be named Caroline. Caro Evans died in her sleep the next night. Jonty and Lottie named their new daughter Charlotte Caroline, after her mother and great-grandmother. It was hard to believe seven years had passed. With the children old enough to be almost independent, this was a much anticipated holiday.

The ageing Hamish was left to look after both houses. His brother, Fergus, had also retired and was on hand on the other side of Jonty's house. It was hard to believe the two Scotsmen were now both over eighty. Both were still active and assisting anyone they thought was in need. Laughter was often heard emanating from one or the other homes.

The trip to Bingara took two weeks; they could have travelled faster, but they were on holiday, and John said, "Jonty, no matter how fast you travel through life, there is always someone who will pass you, drive safely and arrive in one piece. That's what is important."

On arrival, they set up camp in much the same spot as they had nearly forty years before. It was October and hot. The camp area had changed a little, as floods had come and gone over the years, but the river's path was vastly different. Each flood brought change to the river bend. The big rocks and sand island were no longer there, and there was now an embankment along the side of the river. One thing that worried Jonty was the amount of long grass. They decided to burn off the front of the campsite to make sure there were no snakes in the vicinity. Tom, John, and Jonty set the grass alight, and Colleen and Lottie stood guarding the camp with wire coils. Hopefully, no snakes would come near them. They lit the grass fire near the camp, and it burned towards the river edge. Three snakes were seen slithering across the water.

"Wow, I'm glad we did that; they were all browns," John said.

Tom said, "Cor, and I'm supposed to be sleeping on the ground. Hmm, I might rethink that. I'm, um, not on first-name terms with snakes." The artist swallowed nervously; he hated them if the truth were known.

Colleen stood looking at the river. "It all looks so different from when we were here, John. I would not have recognised the campgrounds if you had brought me here blindfolded."

Back then, Colleen had walked across to a sand and gravel island in the middle of the shallow river. There were large boulders visible back then; they were now gone, as was the island.

John knew what she was thinking. "Colly, we knew there was a flood here in January, but it never occurred to us how the river would change." John smiled at her knowing she had her heart set on finding some more gems. "Sweetheart, it may have changed, so we just have to look at where they are now, not where they were."

She nodded and smiled. "I'll find them, John; if they are here, I'll find them," she said as they walked back to the campsite.

While Lottie and Colleen set up the camp with the children, the men and Sammo walked down the river to find some river rocks to place around the fire. When they returned, the utensils, pots and pans were unpacked and ready to fill with water. Before the men had walked off, they set fishing lines and tied the strings to overhanging branches. Hopefully, there would be some fish for tea.

An hour later, the campfire was going, a big pot of water was boiling, and seven fish were filleted and ready to cook. The set lines had caught a giant freshwater catfish, two cod and four sizeable perch. All were big enough to fillet, but the skeletons were kept to make fish soup.

The next afternoon, while John, Colleen, and Lottie were gem hunting in the river gravels, Jonty, Tom and Sammo drove the mile or so into town. Remnants of the January floods were still visible along the track. As they got closer to town, there were foundations of two houses obviously recently washed away.

They bought some groceries from the store, and as the day was hot, they were directed to a public bar for a cool drink. The two men had ales, and Sammo was given a ginger beer. Tom got talking to some of the local men. He was hoping to see some sheep shearing. He found out that most of the shearing in the area was already completed, but one shed near Inverell still needed to finish their shearing. It still had many sheep to shear. Tom's eyes lit up, knowing that his sleeping quarters were literally feet to the fire, he would forgo that luxury to sleep in a shearing shed. Tom leaned over to Jonty and brought him into the conversation with the farmers.

"Jon, I'd like to go if you don't mind. They will be travelling back to Inverell via Copeton Road. I may stay with them for a while as I'm itching to see a shearing shed in action up here, Jon." The farmers chatted together, so Tom turned back to Jonty. "It's one of the reasons I wished to come. I wish to see the workmen of the bush as they labour. I wish to paint these skills for all to admire. I want to paint in vivid colour and action as if it were a coloured photograph. Simon has that sort of skill, even though he is a young lad. The faces of these bush warriors capture my heart and soul, and I want to reproduce them for all time."

Jonty knew Tom well enough now to see that this was something he knew he needed to do. "Oh, Tom, you're a free agent. It's been lovely travelling with you the last two weeks, but we'll see you back in Sydney sometime, won't we?"

"Oh heck yes, I'll stay at Newstead farm near Inverell for a while, maybe even a few months, then I'll come back. It took me over two years to paint the *Shearing of the Rams*, but I promise I won't take that long."

The look Jonty gave him made him laugh. "I'm serious! I have things to do back in Sydney, I've also made a start on another one in the studio there, but I want to do a bigger version of it."

Jonty raised one eyebrow and said, "Let me guess the Jim-inspired painting?"

Tom nodded. "Yes, I have done so many drawings of what I want to do, but it's a matter of finding the time and the canvas size to capture what's in my mind."

They finished their drinks, and after asking the farmers to stop and collect him on the way back to Inverell, they left without further delay. They made their way back to camp, where Tom quickly packed up his belongings and waited for the farmers on the upper track. He didn't have long to wait as he heard the trap coming down the small hill and around the corner. Just as the vehicle came into view, Tom called back to the family group, "Hey, Jonty, thanks for letting me come. See you all back in Sydney."

Once Tom had left, the family settled into searching for some gemstones. Although the flood had washed down much of the mine tailings from further up the river, they managed to find a section with the gravel they were looking for. Their gem searching was successful.

The days were hot, and the children were all encouraged to join in the fun of gem hunting. Carol complained about being hot and so fully dressed, she plonked herself into the water. She sat and looked in the river pebbles for shiny gemstones. She held out her hand with a dark blue rock in it. "Mummy, look, is this what you're looking for?"

"Show Grandmother, sweetie," Lottie said.

Carol turned to Colleen and held out her hand. "Grandma, is this one?"

Colleen pried open the child's fingers, "Oh, poppet, yes, it certainly is one, and a beauty it is too. Take it to Grandfather, and he'll put it away carefully."

Over the following weeks, they found many more sapphires and a few smaller diamonds. There were no big ones like the one Colleen had found on their first visit, but certainly enough to make the trip worthwhile. As Jonty cut the gems himself, there would be no overhead costs. The finds were placed in an empty flour bag as they did forty years ago. Jonty also had another bag for jasper, and assorted other pretty rocks, as Carol called them. Amongst them was a chunk of quartz with veins of gold in it. When Jonty was sorting the rocks around the fire, it wasn't until that night that he realised what it was. "Cor, look at this," he held up the specimen to the firelight.

"I found that pretty one, Papa," Patty said. "It was over there with a lot more of the white rocks. I'll show you tomorrow."

Her grandfather, John, gave his son a look of pure amazement. "Jonty, you did say for them to collect pretty rocks. It seems we may have to change our focus a little tomorrow. Reverend William never told us there could be gold in this area. It's a pity he'll never know."

They woke at dawn as usual and soon followed Patty to her treasure trove of white rocks. She led them to a pile of white quartz that had intentionally been dumped into the river. They sat in one large pile. They had obviously been there for some time as some were green with algae. Sammo was sent back for a hessian bag or two, and the pile of quartz was collected. John knew that if gold was found in some rocks, others possibly had fine traces. Once pounded and smelted, the gold would be released.

Sammo had to return to get another two hessian bags so they could be carried. Finally, the entire rock pile was collected and transported to the wagons. John estimated that there would be some one-hundred and fifty pounds of rock. Some of the pure white quartz Jonty intended to cabochon; any that showed veins of colour at all would be crushed and smelted. They also found jasper, which would be used to make intaglio heartstone seals and wax stamps. Jonty enjoyed carving the raised cameo-like designs rather than inset ones.

At the end of the month, they packed up and returned home. Tom had sent word via the farmers on another supply run that he was staying on for some time. They sent word back to Tom to let them know when he wished to return. He only had to ask Lockleys Logistics in Inverell if he needed a lift back.

~

Fourteen months after they returned, Tom finally came back. One of Luke's wagons brought Tom and a substantial flat crate and delivered it to the artists' studio. Tom only stayed long enough to help unload it. After standing puzzling at the crate, he locked the door and arrived at Pitt Street. He knocked on Jonty's door late that afternoon. "Hey, Jon, I'm back. Will and Dimity are not at home, so I came here."

Jonty ushered their visitor indoors. "They are out at Castlereagh on their farm. Come in. Do you want a bed for the night?"

Tom's grin meant yes. "Oh, a hot shower would be a delight. We only have a bath at the studio." Tom looked as neat as he usually did, vastly different from most camp artists. He had his sleeping roll at his feet and his artist's bag in his hands. Jonty showed him into the guest room. As Tom said thanks, he heard running feet approaching.

"Is he back? Was that Tom's voice?" Paul bounced up and down beside his father as Tom put his things on the bed.

"Yes, young sir, I'm back." He held his hand out to the lad to shake. Paul ignored it and flung himself into his arms.

"I missed you, Mr Tom. Are you staying this time?" Paul pleaded.

"Only for the night; I came to show your Papa something, but you all may come if you like, but I need your Papa's assistance." Tom looked at Jonty. "I brought something to show you, but they are a little too large to carry." His smile belied his excitement; it was hardly visible.

"You've done it, haven't you?" Jonty asked.

Tom nodded. "Yes, I do hope I have it right, but I want you to have a look at it and tell me what you think. I heard of another one while I was up there, but the stories were almost the same, only it wasn't Ben Hall but Thunderbolt. Will you come?"

Paul was tugging at his father's arm. "Can we go? Please, Papa."

Jonty passively said, "Let's go and ask Mama."

Deflated, the young child nodded. "Okay." Then he took off downstairs to "word her up." Lottie was in the backyard with the other three children. They were in the garden kicking a ball, and she was sitting on the low deck, sipping her tea.

The entire family was on the way to the artists' studio within fifteen minutes. Jonty was carrying a claw hammer.

Tom unlocked the door and pulled the light cord. The crate was leaning against the wall in the corridor. "Do you think we can take it upstairs before we open it? I couldn't move it by myself."

Jonty, Sammo, and Tom shuffled the crate along the hall and manoeuvred it upstairs. Lottie carried the hammer, almost bouncing with excitement, as were the children. Plank by plank, the crate was pried open. Tom insisted on doing it himself just in case the hammer slipped. The last timber plank was finally removed, and the paintings inside were freed. They were wrapped in linen bindings and were indeed not small.

"Cor, Tom, no wonder you needed assistance," Jonty was in awe at the colossal size of the works, and he'd not even seen them yet.

"I had to bring these on a stretcher as they were not totally dry. I couldn't risk rolling these. Those are a bundle of rolled ones too. I hope they have not smudged." Tom stood nervously, looking at the wrapped paintings. "I'm shaking, Jon."

"Do you need a hand, or will we wait outside?" Lottie asked, knowing that he may wish to look at them alone first.

Tom just nodded. "Do you mind? I'll unwrap them, then call you back." He'd not taken his eyes from the rolled bundle. They left him alone and were surprised when only twenty minutes later were called back. The door was now closed. "There are two big ones, and I'll bring Jim in to show him before I let the public see it, but, Jon, I need to get an unbiased opinion." With that, he threw open the door. Sitting on two chairs was an enormous rendition of a Cobb and Co coach being bailed up by bushrangers.

Lottie had known of the story all her life, having heard it told many times. She walked up to the image in front of her. She gasped. "Tom, it's exactly as I remember Uncle Jim telling me."

The red of the carriage and the golden hues of the dry bushland brought the reality of the incident to life.

Sammo, too, stood gazing. "Where's the little boy holding the horses, Uncle Tom?"

"This is before he was called Sammo. See, the driver is still up on the seat." Tom gently pointed out various points of interest. He showed the men sitting in the grass on the far side of the carriage. He showed Carol the lady still seated in the coach.

Patty pointed out the calligraphy on the carriage door. She read the letters "VR." She stood looking puzzled. "That's not what is written on the coach doors now. They have 'Royal Mail' on them."

"Ahh, very observant young lady, but when your Uncle Jim arrived from Melbourne, they didn't. I presume it is something like 'Victoria Regina' or possibly even 'Victorian Roads'. I don't know, but your Uncle Jim told me that's what was on them when he arrived. The ones I saw up in Inverell mostly had 'Royal Mail' on them, but occasionally I saw an old one, and it also had the VR. I met another man up there with a similar story to Jim's."

"So it is Uncle Jim on the seat?" Sammo asked.

"Is it? Possibly, possibly not! Whoever it is, he's terribly brave, standing firm against the wills of such violent offenders. But yes, I have referred to Jim's story. I'll ask him to come and look at it sometime soon." Tom smiled at their reactions. "Now, have you seen the other one?"

Unable to tear their eyes from the painting before them, the others had not looked around. Carol had and said, "Uncle Tom, did you see sheeps having a haircut?"

"Yes, miss, only lots of sheep are still called sheep, not sheeps." The others gathered around him as he pointed out the characters and personalities of the figures in the painting. I once saw sheep being shorn down in Victoria, and I painted that scene, but I felt I needed more; I wanted to visit another shed. When I arrived at Newstead farm, they were still shearing. I got to sit and watch. They were so quick. The clicking shears are razor-sharp, wielding them with such precision that it's impressive. The fleeces come off as smooth as velvet. You can see that in the front right one. The tar boy was hardly needed in that shed. The clipped offcuts were swept up, and the shearing shed was always clean. The open windows allowed a nice airflow as the heat was almost overwhelming. They had been shearing all morning, and the sun was just about to hit the side windows. That's why that man is dropping the drapes. That one is the fleece grader, and that man is the overseer." He pointed out each gnarled character in his work.

"I can almost smell the lanolin, Tom." Jonty rubbed his nose.

"Who's the old man?" asked Lottie, pointing to the older bearded man.

"He's the ringer, but the bloke in the front is giving him a run for his money." Tom gave a half-laugh. "They almost came to blows over the title. The man in the front eventually won the title at the end of the shed as he kept choosing the bare-bellied ones. That's what they say when the shearing is done; they say the shed is finished." Tom waited. "So you like it, Jon?"

"No, I don't!" Jonty waited for a reaction. He got one, but from his children.

"But Papa, it's brilliant," gasped Sammo.

"You're right, Sam, except so am I. I don't like it, because I love it! Tom, I can't decide which I like, no love, most. They are both incredible." Jonty felt Lottie's hand slide into his.

They had not realised they had been there so long until Carol said, "Papa, do you know your way home in the dark?" She said, looking out the window.

"Oh, sorry, folks, I didn't realise it was that late," Tom said apologetically. He quickly unrolled the other works and laid them flat on the floor. "I'll fix the rest tomorrow." Once he'd sorted them, the group took one last look at the two masterpieces, turned out the lights and left.

~

The reaction the next morning was interesting. Simon was the first to arrive in the room. He opened the studio door and froze. "Tom's back," Simon said almost breathlessly.

Arthur cannonballed into him, followed by others. The room was soon filled with teachers and students, all standing around the room gazing at the two monumental paintings.

A voice behind them said, "Yes, Tom's back, and I've been busy." A murmur of voices started congratulating him. Tom had left the Lockley's house early, hoping he could sort the other paintings before the others saw them. He chuckled. "I had a painting spurt," he shrugged as he spoke. They hadn't yet seen the pile of canvasses on the floor. He slowly walked to the flattened paintings. He squatted down and took off the plank of timber that kept them from curling up again.

Arthur shouldered Simon aside and asked, "Blooming heck Tom, how many did you get done?"

Tom smiled. "Um, more than I expected." Tom grinned mischievously.

Simon stayed silent. He'd missed his mentor. Far more than he let on. His aunt had died when Tom was absent, and Simon had just been notified that morning that his parent's ship had been lost on the return trip home. With his aunt now dead he was alone. He had gone to tell someone at the studio, hoping one of his friends would be a shoulder to cry on.

Tom stood and walked back to Simon. He quietly asked, "Hey, Si, are you okay?" Tom picked up his melancholy.

Simon nodded, then shook his head. Horrified, he felt his eyes water. Tom shook off the accolades of his peers and said, "Come help me make tea, Si." He gently moved him towards the door.

Arthur offered to assist, but Tom shook his head. Tom had his hands full, comforting his grieving student. He knew he had his job cut out for him; he really wished that Jim or Harry were here to help talk to the lad. Simon was an absolute mess.

Simon had not put brush to canvas in the weeks since his aunt had died. She had been his only remaining relative in the country. For him to have lost her, then the news of the probable loss of his parents crushed the poor young man. Tom was gone, and he had felt deserted. Simon was so distraught he could hardly breathe. They had been gone so long that Arthur came looking for him. Just out of sight, he stood listening to the conversation. Simon turned and stood at the window, looking out.

Arthur stuck his head around the door and was about to speak. Tom silenced him with a hand up, mouthed for Arthur to go and get Jonty, and waved him away. Arthur went as fast as he could. Thankfully the shop was not far away.

Jonty arrived breathlessly fifteen minutes later. He'd had to lock up before he left. As it had been before opening time, he put a sign on the door saying, "Sorry, closed due to unforeseen circumstances."

Arthur had dragged Jonty from work and briefly outlined what he'd overheard. Arthur went back to the students upstairs and started classes. Jonty and Tom sat with Simon for some time. The upshot of the conversation was that Jonty said he'd take Simon home and let him make a life with them. They had a single spare room; if Simon was happy, he could have that permanently.

Jonty had no hesitation in making the offer as he knew Simon already loved being around the children. When the floor falls from under your feet at twenty-one, knowing you are wanted is half the battle.

Sammo already looked up to him as a big brother. With only nine years between the boys, he would fit in well. Simon moved in with Jonty and became one of the family.

~

By the end of the week, Conny and Jim had been invited to see Tom's paintings. Especially the one of the bail-up. Tom had covered it again and not allowed it to be shown to anyone else until Jim had seen it and given his approval. Tom still needed a frame, and he knew what he wanted. Over the following weeks, Tom made a unique frame for the big coach painting. He moulded the plaster ornaments, tiny florets of decoration in each corner, swirls, and more mountings in the centre on each side. All were set on the handmade timber frame. The corners he decided needed even more enhancement. It fitted the painting beautifully, but he wasn't satisfied until he gilded the frame. Only then would he allow the public to see it. He repeated the frame style for the Golden Fleece painting, as he named it. The gold frame made it glow. Once that was done, he stood back and smiled, content with the finished product.

After some six months of working at the jewellery shop with Jonty, Simon asked if he could learn the skill of faceting. As Mr Lamb had now left for England, Jonty agreed. His artistic eye for design was even better than Jonty's. Jonty started him learning to facet quartz. He had many clear crystals collected over the years, and these would often be cut and set in children's jewellery. They looked spectacular as they were big and shiny. But because the quartz was softer than the sapphire, it was more straightforward to cut but also easier to scratch. Simon's ability to set the stones in unique settings made Jonty smile. Jonty remembered the difficulty of learning the fine skills of welding the minute bits of metal together. Simon was a natural. His welds of the tiny slivers of gold were so intricate that Jonty had to use an eyeglass to see them.

Times were changing, as were the faces at the artist's camp, and works of art were still produced.

Life in the colony was evolving faster than any of them liked.

Chapter 16 Unspoken Call

A year passed, then two. Simon's skill was as great as his passion. He was brilliant, but he rarely painted anymore. Jonty set up a second faceting table, and Simon sat down to cut many more saleable stones. Tom had returned to England, and many artists were in different places. Simon settled in well. His favourite thing was to go to Parramatta with the family and join the Lockley Sunday luncheons. Even though he missed his parents, he felt so welcome with this family, and even more important, he was at peace, and after a few hints from Allie, the desire to paint made him dig out his oils again. The artworks being produced by the Curlew Camp at Mosman were incredible. Simon had once again started going down and joining them on Saturdays. Jonty and Will joined him when they could and always enjoyed the day of fellowship, oil paints, turpentine and linseed oil, but it wasn't a huge passion for Jonty, just fun.

Jonty stood behind Simon one day and watched the young man at work. "Simon, I'm releasing you one day a week to come back here and paint again. Your skill is just too great to waste."

Simon jumped. "I didn't hear you, sir." He had not taken his eyes off the painting in front of him. "Sir, am I being banished?"

Jonty chuckled. "No, Si, it's just that you are so talented. Please keep up your skills with this too." He watched as the young man added a few tiny strokes to a head on one character. "I'm not going to let you abandon this. I will even put some on the shop wall to sell."

Stunned, Simon turned and looked at his boss. "Really, sir, um, Jon?

You'd do that for me?"

Jonty actually liked his spur-of-the-moment suggestion. "Yes, why not? We might even add a few of the smaller ones for other artists too. If we can become an outlet for them, why not? We can do our bit to help." He knew that money was tight for the artists. So much so that they were painting on cigar box lids and framing them. Strangely they were quite popular. They were cheap enough for people to buy and enjoy.

~

By early 1898, Jonty's gemstones from his African trip had been cut and sold. He needed more diamonds, and his usual supply of gems in south Africa had dried up. Sourcing sapphires was not a problem; even opals could now be sourced from White Cliffs. They were primarily white stones but also some crystal opal. Occasionally someone would come in with some spectacular opal on a black base. All seemed to be sourced from the same vague area up north in New South Wales, but they would refuse to say where it came from.

One man brought some in a few times. Jonty told the cattle farmer that he would buy the lot if he found more of these fantastic flame stones. All he knew was that it came from the northwest of the state. He'd not heard of any official finds from this area. He knew Queensland was producing some stones that he called boulder opals, but these vivid rainbow opals on a black base had stolen his heart. He loved cutting this soft stone and could achieve the most incredible lustre on the rock. He also discovered that it didn't always have to be cut as a cabochon, but for some of the ones he called black opal, he gently just removed all the imperfections, leaving a unique stone precisely as God had let it form. He called these free form, and once set in pendants or brooches, the majestic gem was spectacular, catching the light and sparkling with every move. He loved setting these beautiful gems. He would often put them with diamonds surrounding them or even cross the stone if there was a significant imperfection. Each was unique. Demand for them forced up the price as few were being found.

Jonty's source, where he bought his raw diamonds in Africa, had also completely dried up. His Agent Jurgen's letter had been returned with "Address unknown" written across the front. He was happy to leave Simon in charge of the shop to make a quick trip to Cape Town and see if he could buy some more stones from a new dealer. He refused to travel up to the mines but figured there would surely be stones for sale in the city. Reluctantly he went home to discuss it with Lottie. He had no desire to go back to Africa ever again, and she knew that. Over dinner that night, they sat talking about the proposed trip. The children had been dismissed and taken to bed.

Simon sat silently for some time. "Jonty, can I go instead? I'd love to have a look around another country. I think I know enough about stones to get some good ones." Simon watched amazement cross Jonty's face.

"You would go, Si?" Jonty heaved a sigh of relief.

At twenty-five, Simon had become an excellent jeweller. His skill in his painting had overflown into his jewellery design.

"I'd love to go, Jon, if you'd trust me to buy for you," Simon said, but the look of delight on his face showed Jonty that he was serious.

Within a week, Simon was booked onto *The Aberdeen*, heading to Cape Town. It was due to depart on March 4th. He was instructed how to access the funds in Cape Town and that Jonty could transfer more if Simon needed more. As they saw him into his cabin, Simon turned to Jonty and said, "Sir, um, Jon, would you mind if I had a look around while I am over there? I want to go to Madagascar and see where my parents' ship went down. It's not far in the scheme of things and may answer some of my questions about their loss. I can't settle. It's been three years, and I just can't let it go."

Jonty was not surprised. "Take what time you need, Si; if you can find answers, follow whatever leads you can. I can manage the store, and with the children now grown, Lottie can come in too."

Lottie had wanted to do something useful for some time and was stunned when she heard Jonty's conversation. She was thrilled and clapped her hands with glee. Their youngest child, Carol, was now ten and fully occupied with lessons at her new school during the day. Lottie had been at a loose end.

Jonty should not have been surprised by Simon's request as he was frustrated that none of his paintings had sold. Other artists' works had been flying off the walls of the shop. Each one sold was another stab to Simon's ego and morale. A change would be good for him, and some extra time away may help answer some questions. He knew the lad was depressed and still flooded with questions about his parents' disappearance. They were still listed as just missing.

The ship Simon's parents had been on went missing somewhere north of Madagascar. Some flotsam and jetsam had washed up, and there were rumours of even some possible survivors, but none had ever returned. Jonty understood that Simon wanted to see that area and ask around for himself. He'd shown no interest in settling down and starting his own family, and Jonty and Lottie were content for him to stay longer.

Jonty also knew their niece, Allie, had shown much interest in the lad. Her frequent stays always ended the same way, with nothing being said. Lottie knew she'd given her heart to Simon; she could tell by her red and puffy eyes that she had even cried herself to sleep more than once. Allie was coming to stay with them to say farewell; however, Simon had shied away from any commitment. His only concession was gently stroking her cheek before turning on his heel and leaving the room.

Both Jonty and Lottie knew he cared for her. Allie's mother, Goldie, was Lottie's cousin. Allie's father was Jonty's cousin Alfred. It was a match that both sides of the family would encourage if Simon showed any interest.

Hopefully, this trip would spur him to think hard.

They stood watching the ship sail away. Allie and her parents had joined them. They waved until it was out of sight, then went home. Allie was quiet and sad that Simon had gone without a word of encouragement. He had kissed the palm of her hand just before he boarded, but that was all. She knew he needed answers, and she told him she would pray for him and that he would find something to help.

Simon stayed at the railing until they were out of sight. He was on a mission to not just buy gems for Jonty but to get some answers. Jonty had told him there was £1000 waiting to purchase gemstones and wire him if he had access to more stones. Simon smiled; that amount was years' wages for him. But he knew that he would not get a salary without the diamonds. Simon loved the family greatly but felt he never entirely fitted in. He was ten years older than Sammo and Patty and more than ten years younger than Jonty and Lottie. Although he was the same age as Allie and he hated leaving her, he needed to make this trip. He felt like a square peg in a round hole. The hardest part about going was not saying anything to Allie. She had not cried, but he had seen her eyes watering. He felt bound to stay silent until he returned from this trip. He had refused to touch his parents' money as they had not yet been declared dead, just missing. The endless waiting, the eternal nothingness of not knowing haunted him. He couldn't move forward until he knew they were dead. It had been years now, years of waking every morning wondering if they'd turn up.

Simon waited until the ship had passed through the heads and was out to sea. He turned to his cabin and went to settle in. The trip would take about six weeks, and he had books to read for the first few and a long letter to write to Jonty. He had decided not to just go to Madagascar, but if he could find no trace of the ship there, he'd follow its pathway up the Suez, calling at every possible port. He had not told Jonty that, only that he wished to visit Madagascar. He planned to send the letter from Fremantle. He would be more than halfway there and too far to call back.

Halfway through April, Jonty received Simon's letter. He sat in the workroom with his head in his hands. Simon had written that he would not come home until he had found something concrete. Jonty was gutted. He was far more than a friend; he was like a son, a business partner and… well, Simon was family. He'd lived with them for the best part of three years. He fitted in well, or so Jonty thought. Simon had at least mentioned that he would take some extra time; it never occurred to him that he would not come home for years, if at all.

Lottie brought in some hot sweet tea. She saw Jonty's stance and immediately knew something was wrong.

Jonty's head lifted and met her gaze. "It's from Simon; he's not coming back until he finds some answers, Lotts." Jonty's voice carried the grief he felt.

Lottie knew the affection her beloved Jon had for their adopted son. This would impact him significantly. She walked to him and was about to stroke his head comfortingly when he pulled her onto his lap and hid his face in her neck. "Did I miss something, Lotts? Did I do something wrong?"

"Darling Jon Jon, the only thing you did wrong is that you, my love, are not his real parent. He needs to do this, sweetheart, and we'll be here for him when he returns." Lottie sat hugging her beloved. "We are still his family, Jon. We shall pray that he finds something concrete. It would be wonderful if he could even find one of them alive, but that's wishing for far too much."

After their shock, life settled back into a normal pace. While Patty was having extra music lessons and Carol and Paul were at school, Lottie was working with Jonty at the shop. By December, Sammo was preparing to sit his final school exams and considering whether he should go to university or work with his father. He decided that he would learn to become a jeweller too. He, too, loved gems and knew much about them. He could already set stones into simple settings well.

Shortly before Christmas, a nun, swathed head to foot in black, arrived at the shop door one day and asked to see Jonty.

Sammo called his father and waited just out of sight but within earshot. Jonty greeted the nun.

"Bonjour, monsieur, I am Sister Marguerite and I have a parcel for you. I met with your son Simon, and he asked me to bring this toy bear gift for you. He said it contained the stars from his eyes, and he looked forward to seeing you soon." The nun gave Jonty a sly smile, raised an eyebrow, and gave Jonty a slight nod and a big knowing grin.

Jonty looked puzzled; then it dawned on him; he used to say that Simon's eyes were like diamonds when he painted. Simon must have filled the bear with diamonds. Jonty graciously accepted the bear and offered the old nun a cup of tea. She politely declined but took a biscuit before she left. They had been so stunned that she was gone before they realised they had not asked her where Simon was.

Jonty sent Sammo to get Lottie, and together the three of them sat in the cutting room and carefully cut the stitching on the heavy bear's back. Inside was a leather pouch, and when Jonty drew it out, there was another; then, he saw a string hanging from the head. He pulled it, and a third bag fell out. By now, the three were chuckling at Simon's ingenuity. He must have trusted and confided in the nun enough to give the stones into her keeping. Jonty looked again and saw it was now empty. The poor bear skin sat collapsed on the desk. One by one, they tipped out the bags. The largest one also contained a letter.

I'm not sure of the exact date, early May 1898
Cape Town

Dear Jon,

I hope this finds you well. I met Sister Marguerite one evening when I was feeling very down. She and her order helped me when I was prepared to give up. Her order had a building on the waterfront, and she saw me late one evening standing on a break wall, ready to jump. Jon, I'm sorry I should have told you how the loss of my parents has been eating away at me from the inside like a worm.

Sister Marguerite and her nuns arranged for me to stay with some priests nearby, and they cared for me for some weeks until I was over my melancholy mood. She was booked to leave for Sydney to start teaching over there, and I have asked her to deliver this bear with our booty. I know she will do this for us as she is a beautiful servant of God.

Jon, I find I do not do well alone in a foreign country, so two of the priests have decided to accompany me to Madagascar, and together, we shall hunt for the ship or any information I can find. They will eventually either go to Rome or head back to Cape Town, but they will stay with me until the end of my quest. Only then will I return home. Ahh, that word again; where is my home? I hope at least to confirm the ship's loss. Then I feel I can let them rest in peace. If I don't find any information at Suez, I will return as I know I will have tried everything possible. For I know the ship had passed through the canal. Pray for me, Jon, for I am in great need. My travelling companions are praying with me daily, and this is giving me incredible peace. I had not prayed since I left you; no wonder I felt empty.

Jon, please keep my room for me; however, I probably will speak to Allie when I return. But until I know if I am entitled to claim my parents' house, I cannot, in all good conscience, ask her to wait for me. I have said nothing, even though it broke my heart to leave her in silence.

I shall not use a second sheet as I will write again from Madagascar.
Your loving foster son
Simon Mitchell

The hundreds of diamonds that Simon sent were astounding. Thankfully he'd not had to travel to the Transvaal. Jonty sighed, saying to Sammo, "Well, at least he's safe. I suppose we just have to wait."

~

So they waited, and Jonty set about cutting some of the new stones. He had a few unfinished items waiting for diamonds to be completed. The weeks flew by with no further word.

In October, the papers carried stories about what Jonty read as potential unrest in South Africa. Paul Kruger was mentioned, as was Cecil Rhodes. Jonty was interested and thankful that Simon was well out of the country. He prayed for the remaining nuns and brothers left there. Jonty had not had nightmares for years, but he had a bad dream that night. Not a nightmare, but enough to wake Lottie. It was about Simon and his fears for him.

A month passed before another letter arrived, this time from Madagascar.

1st November 1898
Toamasina, Madagascar

Dear Jon,

I'm here, and I think I've found something.

I'm writing to you as I'll be going away for a week or two and I hope to have more news when I return. I won't say exactly what I've heard, but I will be happy to return home if my suspicions are correct. Jon, in case I don't return, I have left a letter for you.

This is to say thank you, just in case. My love to you all,
Simon

The letter had been delayed in arriving and was followed the next day by another. They possibly even came on the same ship.

18th November 1898
Toamasina, Madagascar

Dear Jon,

I made it back and found a survivor from the shipwreck. I have travelled up to Antsiranana on the country's northern tip and met someone I am bringing home. I may need to stay with you for a few days on arrival until I can get our house into order.

Jonty, I found Mother!

She must have been injured as she can't speak, but she's alive. Apparently, there was another man who survived, but it wasn't Father. A villager took us to my father's grave, and we prayed together over it. I don't know what's wrong with mother or why she didn't return home. Possibly just a lack of funds, or maybe it was because Father was buried here. I may never know, but now I am at peace. I had a nagging feeling that I had to come here after speaking to Lottie's Aunt Cathy, and she suggested I come. I'm so pleased I did.

Jon, could you let Allie know that I'm coming back? I'm ready to speak to her if she's willing. I just hope I'm not too late. I must away; we are catching the next passenger ship back. This is coming on a cargo freighter. I now can't wait to get home.

Love to you all,
Simon.

On December 14th, the family assembled at the quay as the ship was tugged into the jetty. Simon had sent word from Melbourne, and they knew what day the vessel was expected to dock. Lottie and Jonty were waiting with Luke and Ellen. They all stood ready to assist in any way needed. Will and Dimity were on hand, too and stood beside Luke.

The ship docked at the main quay, ropes were tied off, and they waited… and waited. Allie had not been able to come from Penrith to meet the morning ship but would arrive that afternoon. Her father would not let her travel alone, and her mother was at a meeting. They would meet the family at Jonty's house later.

The group watched as everyone else disembarked, but still no Simon. Finally, Captain Audena came and said they were ready to alight. They had waited until the docks were nearly empty.

Simon appeared at the head of the gangplank, followed by a petite lady clinging tightly to his arm. She was looking around like a startled fawn.

Ellen gasped. "Oh, Lukie, I think we will have our hands full with Mrs Mitchell. We'll need to pack around Simon," Ellen said softly to her husband.

Luke nodded. "I think a stay in Sydney would do us all good, love," Luke squeezed Ellen's hand as the two Mitchells drew closer.

Simon ushered his mother towards Jonty and Lottie. He held a protective arm around her shoulder, and she leaned on him. His eyes had scanned the group and saw that Allie and her parents were not with Jonty. Maybe he'd waited too long. He sighed, then said, "Luke, Jon, ladies, may I introduce my mother, Elise Mitchell? Mother, this is the Honourable Luke and Ellen Lockley, and this is Jonty and Lottie Evans, with whom I've been living for the last few years."

Elise stayed silent for most of the introductions, then put her hand out to Lottie. She grasped Lottie's hand and held it to her cheek. Her eyes were shining with pleasure. "Tha-annk you-uu," she said in a really croaky voice. It was the first words she'd said to anyone but Simon for years. No one had attempted to talk to her in Madagascar. She had been so frightened of all the dark-skinned strangers around her that she had stayed quiet. On board the *Duncow*, Elise was so seasick that she wished she was dead. Every wave movement brought back her fears of this ship sinking too. She had stayed in her bunk with the blankets over her head for most of the trip. Not leaving her cabin for a moment until they docked in Sydney. She had decided never to step foot on any boat again, ever.

Simon had not wished to intrude too much, so he had left her alone, not knowing what to say. He looked at Jonty and mouthed, "Help!" Now he had her home; he had no idea what to do with her. He knew he needed to return to work, but she could not be left alone.

Luke ushered everyone into the large travelling carriage he had waiting. The eight squashed in, and it took off up the hill to their house on Pitt Street.

Elise was fearful of every sound and person she didn't know. She sat holding Simon's arm tightly. Her eyes skittishly flicked around, looking at everything in fear.

Simon noticed. "Mama, these people are my new family. You will be safe with them," Simon tried to comfort her.

Dimity and Ellen glanced at their husbands, and each gave a knowing nod. Elise would need them all, as would Simon.

Simon ushered his mother to the room they had prepared for her. She sat on the bed and watched, wide-eyed, while the young maid unpacked her few clothes. When alone, Elise curled into a ball and wept. She could not voice her fears, traumas, or why she felt how she did; she also wept with relief.

The maid sought out Ellen. "Ma'am, I've finished unpacking the new lady's things. She didn't have much, only one change of clothing, which was not in good condition."

Ellen thanked her, took a deep breath and went to brave Elise. She gently knocked on her door. There was no answer, but Ellen could hear her crying. She carefully opened the door and could see Elise on the bed weeping. Seeing the poor lady in such distress drew Ellen to her side. She tried to make a little noise so Elise would not be startled.

Elise lifted her head and reached out a hand for Ellen. "So scared, so very frightened." Ellen barely caught the whisper. She sat beside her on the bed and rubbed her back. Elise sat up, and Ellen drew her into her arms. The sobbing continued for some time. Eventually, it eased, and she was just hiccupping.

Ellen said, "Elise, I won't leave you, but I feel that staying in Sydney will not be good for you; we live in Parramatta, and it's quiet. Well, it's quieter than here. Please know that you are welcome to make your home with us."

The startled look on Elise's face and the series of nods that followed astounded Ellen.

"You'll come?" Ellen asked to confirm her offer.

Again Elsie nodded.

"Can't go back home. Bad memories! Can't tell Si; he doesn't know what my father did to us." Her words were getting more precise. She started to weep again.

Ellen understood her fears were of returning to her old home, not of the town.

Jonty had filled her in on what he knew of the story. He had met with Simon's aunt soon after Simon had come from Melbourne. He would go with the lad on visits, and they heard about the abuse the sisters received at home. The poor old lady often rambled about her early home life with their father. Simon had been horrified. Thankfully he had never met his grandfather. His home had been in Melbourne, and he knew no one there. Simon had now inherited his aunt's house and intended to move his mother there. This was the home Elise and her sister, May, had grown up in, and she had no wish to return there. It was that that was making Elise fearful.

Ellen realised her life there was not conducive to happiness. "Oh, Elise, you will live with us in Parramatta, and Simon can visit when he wishes." Again the absolute joy on her face was like a light going on. Elise threw her arms around Ellen.

Downstairs, Simon was in deep discussion with both Jonty and Luke. He had come to the same conclusion and had a word with Ellen before she had gone upstairs.

Luke said, "Simon, I suggest your mother lives with us at Parramatta. You can see her when you wish, and she will be in full care, which you cannot give her. We have already discussed it, and Ellen is with her now. We shall wait and see what the answer is. But she's in no state to be allowed to be left alone."

Simon was reeling. "Thank you so much, Uncle Luke; I have no idea how to help her." They didn't have long to wait; Ellen and Elise joined them about fifteen minutes later. Both were smiling.

As they walked in, Ellen said, "We had a little chat, and Elise will make her home with us, Luke. She has no wish to return to her old place; that was her old house, Simon." Ellen expected an outburst, but instead, she heard a sigh of relief.

Simon asked, "You'd be happy there, Mother?" he questioned anxiously.

Her reply was an emphatic nod. "I can't go back there, Si. Can't ever go back there, never ever."

He read fear and panic in her eyes. Simon turned to Lottie's father. "Uncle Luke, are you sure?"

Luke chuckled. "Sure as eggs are eggs, Simon. We have plenty of room as Ellen's parent's suite downstairs is now vacant. We've been using them for visitors, as you know. They are self-contained too, so she can be uninterrupted yet fully cared for, and you can come as often as you wish as there's a spare bedroom in the apartment." Luke caught Jonty's glance at Lottie and then nodded to them both. It was where they used to stay, but there were other rooms.

The morning passed with arrangements being made, and Elise was almost happy when the luncheon was served. She still didn't wish to be far from Simon, but she began to feel more comfortable with the others in the room. She knew more people would be coming that afternoon and felt less fearful. Simon had explained to her that he hoped Allie would have waited for him.

Jonty had managed to tell him that Allie would arrive with her parents at about two o'clock. The grin that Simon gave him warmed his heart.

At the proposed time, Simon was almost bouncing with anticipation. Elise was upstairs asleep, and only Jonty was with him in the sitting room. Carriage wheels were heard, and it pulled up outside; the hackney cab let out the passengers; Alfred, Goldie, and Allie alighted.

Allie met Simon's eyes through the window, and she waved. His heart skipped a beat, and he made a beeline to the front door to let them in. Before he said anything to Allie, he must first ask her father if he could court her. He wished to get Alfred alone as soon as possible, so he asked Jon first to take Goldie and Allie into the sitting room. While he would try to corner Alfred in the hallway. Not ideal, but then he could approach Allie.

Sadly the best-laid plans of mice and men! Alfred ushered the ladies inside, then excused himself, saying, "I'll be back shortly; I have to pop along to the folk's place for a bit, Jon." He was gone before Simon could catch him.

Frustrated, Simon went in to meet his heart's desire. Now that he had found his mother and he knew that his father was dead, he could move forward with his life and hoped Allie could be part of it. Releasing a long sigh, he followed Jonty back inside. Goldie and Allie were seated together on a settee, so he couldn't even sit near her. He stood awkwardly nearby.

Jonty conversed with his cousin, and Allie stole shy glances at Simon. He did the same, and their eyes met, and both blushed.

While Jonty was occupying her mother, he tipped his head to indicate he wanted her to stand and walk to the window. She gave a quick nod and glanced at her mother, who was deep in conversation. She stood and quietly moved to the window.

Simon walked towards her, and there he was, able to chat with her. He had been unable to speak to her father; he thought he would broach his intentions to her to gauge her interest. "Allie, it's so good to see you. I'm sorry I could not speak to your father before I left for Cape Town or today."

Her eyes lifted to his. "Why, Si?"

She didn't pull away from him, which gave him confidence. "Allie, I wished to ask him if I could court you. I know I should speak to him first, but I wished to know if it would be agreeable to you?" His nervousness showed in the waver in his voice. He barely heard her soft reply.

"Yes, Si, I'd like that." Her voice was so low that he would have missed it if he had not been as close.

A look of relief swept across his face. He quickly replied, "Seriously?"

After a swift glance at her mother, she nodded again. "Yes, Simon, seriously," her eyes again checked that her mother was still occupied. "I missed you, Si; I didn't even get to say goodbye properly."

His eyes were fixed on her face. "I couldn't say anything before Allie, as I didn't know if I would even make it back. I had a feeling there was something I needed to do, and I couldn't shake that off; I had to go to Madagascar myself. I'm so glad I did. Allie, Mother, is not well; however, she will live with Uncle Luke and Aunt Ellen in Parramatta. In the years since the shipwreck, she had not spoken to anyone. She was so seasick on the ship here that we had little chance to talk." Simon wanted to tell her more, but at that moment Alfred arrived back from his parents' house.

Allie moved back to her mother's side before he came in.

Simon went to answer the door. Hopefully, this time there, he would have a moment to ask his permission.

Alfred welcomed Simon home, and as they walked down the hall, Simon asked if he could have a word first. Alfred nodded, hoping he would ask the long-awaited question.

Simon opened a door opposite the sitting room; it was Jonty's office. Although nervous, Simon now knew Allie's answer, so he turned to her father as the door closed. "Mr Evans, I wanted to ask if I may court Allie, please?" He knew he should phrase it more officially, but he had been on first-name terms with the family for some years. He usually called him "Uncle Alfred," as did Lottie and Jonty's children.

Alfred turned to look at the nervous young man. "Have you settled now, Simon? I know you had concerns before, but I want you to answer me before I answer you."

"Yes, sir, I hope so. I knew I needed to find some answers. Uncle Alfred, I found mother alive. She's currently upstairs asleep. However, she will be living with Uncle Luke and Aunt Ellen at Parramatta. Now I can settle as I know Father is dead; he drowned trying to save Mother. She does not wish even to visit their old home, so I can move straight in. So we can live at Aunt May's house if things progress as I wish. If Allie doesn't like it, I can sell that house and buy elsewhere; I may even do that so Mother can visit us. Having said that, Uncle Alfred, I'd like to stay here for a bit. I might see if I can find a caretaker couple and install them to clean it up and get it ready for us." Simon waited for the older man's reply.

"You're both in your twenties, so you're starting a relationship later than most couples; having said that, I don't think that's a bad thing. Yes, you have my blessing Ask Allie, lad."

Simon put his hand out to shake, but Alfred hugged him instead. "Thank you, Uncle Alfred." His warm reaction encouraged Simon.

"You've had a rough start, lad, don't keep her waiting long. I'm pretty sure I know what her answer will be." Alfred gave a gentle verbal push for Simon to hasten the relationship.

Simon nodded with a smile as a reply. "Thanks, Uncle Alfred."

They joined the others. Simon now made his way to Allie's side. Without hiding his actions, he put out his hand, and she took it and walked to the window again with him. They had their heads together, quietly talking.

Goldie had fallen silent but glanced at her husband with a raised eyebrow; he gave a nod to her unvoiced question. She smiled back at him.

Simon was beaming; Allie had agreed for him to court her.

Allie shyly said, "As if I'd say no, Si. I've been so keen for you to get back, but I would have waited any amount of time. I hope you know that."

Simon glanced anxiously at her parents. "I really couldn't say anything before Allie; I was fearful you had not waited. I should not have expected you to do so, but I prayed that you would."

Half an hour later, both Ellen and Elise joined them. Simon immediately went to his mother's side protectively. He introduced her to the newcomers and quietly told her he had asked to court Allie. The delight on her face was visible for all to see. Simon beckoned for Allie to come and talk to his mother. They settled on another settee; he stood behind them with his hand on his mother's shoulder, reassuring her of his presence. He wished he could do the same to Allie, but it was too early in their relationship. Occasionally Allie would look up at him and smile. His heart would give a flip.

Simon knew she was staying at Alfred's parents' place for the next two nights. He would have time to at least talk to Allie privately. He had already arranged to see her again as he had asked her for a walk to the Botanical Gardens tomorrow morning before her father said they had stayed long enough.

Alfred rose to leave soon after Elise arrived. Simon realised that it was because he could see his mother was becoming distressed. Ellen now knew that it did not take much to set her off. Ellen looked at her niece and gave a tilt of her head to go. Goldie, with a lift of her chin, gave a slight nod. She, too, realised it was time to take their leave. She suggested that Simon escort them up to Phil and Alice's house just up the street.

Simon jumped at the chance. He ushered them out and left his mother in the care of his foster family.

The next day Simon waited until he saw his mother was settled, then asked her if she would mind if he went and saw Allie. He knew he only had two days before Allie would return to Penrith with her parents.

Elise called him to her side. Having now found her voice she took his hand. As she was now feeling comfortable with the family, Elise said, "Simon, I like her. It's time you moved on with your life. I'll be all right with Ellen. Simon, I shall never go back to that house, but make it your own. Change it as much as you can, though, son. Make it unrecognisable. Ellen told me that May let on some of the things that occurred there. It was the fear of living there that worried me. So, please don't make her wait too long. I would love to see my grandchildren before I die." With that, she patted his hand and shooed him away.

His mother had given her blessing if he wished to propose to Allie, and now she had even told him to go to her. His heart was singing. Still, he wasn't sure how she'd cope. Now the way was clear, he kissed her cheek and left to see Allie.

Ellen and Lottie heard the front door close and went to join Elise. Elise was now comfortable with both ladies and sat chatting with them. She had already said more in the last twenty-four hours than in the past three years. Her voice had returned fully after years of not being used.

Carol had been staying out of the way. She heard voices in the sitting room and gently knocked and said goodbye and that she was heading to school. Without a word, the three ladies waved her farewell.

At ten, Carol would walk to school with the maid and come home with her brother, who had an earlier class. At fifteen, Patty had piano lessons and would not be home until after luncheon. Lottie had told all the children to stay quiet and out of sight for the next few days. At mealtimes, they were instructed to be on their best behaviour. The four typically boisterous children were behaving brilliantly. All were sensitive to the needs of the new lady. The twins took their younger siblings away as soon as the meal was over. Each had homework, and they set to work on that without fuss.

The next forty-eight hours were a delight to the new couple, for they were allowed to wander through the Botanical Gardens virtually unaccompanied. A maid followed at a discreet distance. They talked and opened up about their feelings. Alfred trusted Simon and allowed them a little more freedom than if they had been younger. Simon knew he had to return to work soon but dearly wished Allie could stay a little longer with her grandparents.

On return from their walk, Allie pleaded with her father for her to stay on until next week. Her impassioned plea worked. Alfred allowed her to ask her grandparents. Her stay was almost assured as she had them twisted around her finger.

Simon again met with Alfred, but this time it was Simon who had been summonsed. "Simon, if you're serious about this relationship, propose sooner rather than later and marry quickly. The waiting is hard, and as you already have a house, you will not need to sort that out, but I still wish to be asked before you speak to her."

Simon swallowed. "Then, sir, may I ask now? I'm sure of my feelings, as I'm sure you realise that. Mother has also given her blessing."

Alfred chuckled. "Simon, I was wondering if my comments would stir you. However, two days may be rushing into things. If her grandparents agree, she can stay here for a few weeks, at least until you come for Christmas. Take the time to talk to her. Write a list of things, and describe your feelings on each subject. Use this week to get to know each other because it is hard to break the agreement once you are engaged. Doing so would harm her irrevocably."

Simon grinned. "I will do that, Uncle Alfred, but thank you!" Simon was thrilled. He'd had a lot of time to think on his travels. Allie and his parents had been the only two topics in his thoughts. Now that his mother would be settled with Lottie's parents, that left the door open to pursue his courting of Allie. With her father's words this morning, that, too, could progress faster than he had planned.

Chapter 17 Future Plans

$\mathcal{E}$lise departed with Luke and Ellen three days after their return. She had stayed only long enough to purchase some clothing before heading west. Jonty had already returned to work, and Lottie joined Simon in the jewellery shop after her parents returned to Parramatta. With Elise's fear of the sea, they travelled by road. Even the thought of the ferry was too much for Elise.

Allie went shopping with her grandmother, Alice, and the three joined Jonty's household for dinner. They only lived four doors up, so it was an easy walk. Simon would call and escort them the short distance to Jonty's house. The mood was festive in the younger Evans' household as Christmas was the following week. Simon was positively bouncing. Even the news that they had missed contracting the plague in Madagascar by only weeks brought him joy.

The entire Evans family planned to travel to Parramatta for Christmas, where Simon would again request a meeting with Alfred, as they were coming from Penrith. He was a little concerned about how his mother would cope with all the new faces. At least she could stay in her apartment downstairs.

Jonty told him of the days when Christmas was celebrated in his Uncle Eddie's backyard. Nearly one hundred of the family would descend on their house for the luncheon, each bringing something to contribute. He knew Uncle Luke's house well, as he had stayed there often over the last few years. Jonty's Aunt Moira and Uncle Connor Murphy still worked with Luke and Ellen. It had taken a while to work out the strange relationship, but he realised that they were not servants, but Connor was Jonty's mother's brother, living with family and working for their keep. Luke had built a small cottage for them in the backyard years before. They had never left. Luke and Connor were best friends, and it was a delight having them close by.

Simon was sure his mother would have settled in well. He had not been out to see her in the weeks between their arrival and Christmas, as every waking moment; he had either been at work, arranging the house, or walking out with Allie. He knew it would be better for his mother to settle without the inconvenience of his presence around her. He would be spending a few days with her over Christmas anyway.

Years earlier, Simon knew he had only had one blood relation. That had been his Aunt May, who was now gone. He'd been absorbed lovingly into this wonderful Lockley family. He felt this even more since his return. Before his departure, it was his own reluctance to accept the warm embrace offered to him; now, he was willing to take all they provided. He had been called 'family' from the day he moved in with Jonty and Lottie. He was treated as a son, not a foster son, yet he knew it had been his reluctance to be integrated fully. He knew he was now part of the abundant loving group that he now would claim as family. Soon he would be part of them in reality, at least hopefully. He was pretty sure Allie would answer in the affirmative to his question. He planned to propose over the Christmas break but had not yet worked out how to do it. He had made her a ring with a rare blue diamond he had bought her in Cape Town. Jonty had faceted it, and Simon made it up into an engagement ring for her. Beautiful blue sapphires surrounded it. It was already packed in the bottom of his bag, ready to take with him.

To while away the hours before it was time to meet Allie again, Simon picked up the newspaper. He skimmed through newsworthy stories when he read of more unrest in China. He spent time reading about what was being called the Boxer Rebellion over there. A French Priest had been killed. More unrest occurred in Russia and various other European countries, and a fire occurred in Port Pirie in South Australia.

Simon's eyebrows raised with a chuckle. In Kiama, multiple denominations had met together to pray for rain. It was funny that it took a drought to bring Christian denominations together. He smirked to himself. He prayed hard for rain himself. He didn't really understand farming or the drought, but he knew the wind carried dust and his nose bled when it got too dry. It had done that often of late. Yes, they needed rain. He closed his eyes and added his own prayers for the drought to break.

At the bottom of the column, he read that Anthony Horden's store would stay open until late to purchase late Christmas gifts. Jumping with the realisation of his own forgetfulness, he said to himself, "Cripes, I haven't got Allie a Christmas gift." He ran his hand through his hair and checked his watch. He had an hour until he met them. He would duck down straight away and buy some things from Anthony Hordens'. He would get them sent to

Parramatta tomorrow.

Simon grabbed his wallet, fob and hat, then almost ran down the stairs and sped down Pitt Street to the large department store.

The Anthony Hordens' Christmas display was one of the Christmas sights that Allie loved. Last year, he had stood with her and Jonty's family, watching the display. His eyes had been fixed upon her face instead of the windows.

This afternoon hoards of people were standing outside enjoying the Christmas windows. He squeezed himself through the seething mass of humanity outside and in through the doors. Once inside, he wondered what to buy.

Simon was handed a catalogue by a store clerk who asked if he required assistance.

He breathed a sigh of relief. "Yes, please; any suggestions for a suitable gift for a lady friend? Well, a group of ladies, actually. Something that would not single one from another," Simon asked half-heartedly, not really expecting an answer.

"Fabric, sir? We have a lovely selection of silks, brocades and damasks. Ideal for a gown or an evening wrap."

Simon's eyes lit up, and the store clerk directed him to the correct floor. Upon entering, Simon's eyes fell on the most exquisite brocade silk and another damask. His artistic eye appreciated the display before him; both were draped decoratively over mannequins. He could not decide which of these two to purchase for his beloved, so he purchased both. He bought a dress length of each and added two more yards for extras like reticules. Then he saw one that would suit Lottie and purchased a dress length of the emerald green brocade for her. For Ellen and Goldie, he purchased two different sapphire blue brocades; and added a gold damask one he liked as a spare. They, too, were added to the growing pile. A few extra lengths would not hurt, as his mother also needed new gowns. Will and Dimity were not coming, but he saw an exquisite red and black one that would look lovely on her, so that, too, was added to the collection. Two more lengths for Jenny and Amabel were chosen.

For each fabric bolt picked, he pinned a scrap of paper with a name. He also selected a large variety of other fabrics in gown lengths for his mother. She needed day dresses, morning gowns, tea gowns and even a couple of evening gowns. She needed many more, but ten should keep her occupied for the moment. She could even have some of these made up for her. He had procured some off-the-rack gowns for her the day after they arrived in town. At least he had supplied the money for Lottie and Ellen to buy them and everything else a lady needed. She was so tiny that he had not been able to purchase clothing for her in Madagascar. He knew she could sew well, so this would give her something to do.

The saleswoman tallied up the price, and he gave instructions on where they should each be delivered.

Dimity, Jenny and Amabel's gifts would go to Ricky's house as they were there for Christmas this year. The rest could come by ferry, and he would collect the pre-wrapped parcels from the Jolly Sailor Inn at Parramatta tomorrow. He added six more two-yard lengths for other assorted gifts; he checked that the saleswoman understood what he required and then hurried home. He then quickly went to the men's section and selected a variety of gifts for the various men in the family, including the three who would be staying in Sydney. Twenty more gifts were chosen before he returned home.

The hustle and bustle of the next hour kept his mind off the days ahead.

The family gathered at the ferry wharf now in King Street. Lottie had arranged that all their luggage would be taken by road, and they could enjoy the ferry trip in peace.

Simon was able to stand next to Allie on the trip. He even slipped her arm through his, covering her hand with his own. As he did so, he saw her blush adorably.

With no one around, he bent his head and quietly said, "Allie, I want to see your father when he arrives, but I just want to make sure that you are happy about that?" His heart was beating a tattoo just asking her that much.

"Si, if you want to ask him what I hope you want to ask, then it is certainly in line with my wishes." She chuckled and squeezed his arm slightly. The smile she gave him warmed his heart.

Simon was over the moon. He bit his lip, trying hard not to allow the great joy he felt to overtake him.

The dry heat in Parramatta was overwhelming. The ferry at least brought moisture to their noses. Simon had drawn in deep breaths of the delicious salty air.

Allie pointed out various sights along the sea route and then drew his attention to a thin cloud band on the far horizon. "Look, Si, do you think they could be rain clouds?"

The wispy clouds did not look too much like rain, but he'd learned that December in Sydney often brought violent and torrential thunderstorms. "It would be nice if it were. I don't think anyone would mind a wet Christmas. It would settle the dust if nothing else."

The ferry's arrival was met by a merry throng of assorted family members standing on the wharf. Luke and Ellen were there, with Elise standing close to Ellen. Alongside them were two elderly couples and hordes of younger fair-haired family members. Allie's parents were among them, having arrived earlier by train; they were out to stretch their legs.

Lottie threw herself into her mother's arms as she always did. Simon chuckled to Allie, "I would love to be greeted like that, but Mother would die!"

Allie smiled. "One day, she might surprise you, Si." She gave his arm another squeeze, and she went to greet her family.

Allie did a circle of kissing all her aunts, uncles, and cousins, including her Uncle Rick and Aunt Mary Lou.

They were there with their children.

Uncle Rick's twin sister, Aunt Bette, and Uncle Edward were, of course, never far away from them, nor were their four children.

Allie looked at her cousins and thought that she'd never seen more handsome men other than Simon, of course.

Jax, at seventeen and his twin brothers, Edward and William, at fourteen, were undoubtedly eye-catching. Their cousins, a younger set of twins, Danny and Debbie, had their mother's almost white-blonde hair and curls, with their father, Rick's large blue eyes. Jax had his father Edward's soft wavy brown hair that he wore in a windswept style. Yes, these boys would surely cause many a heart to flutter in the years ahead. Her Uncle Rick's two boys, Jack and Danny, were similar in looks, and although handsome, they seemed a little less groomed than their cousin. Allie adored them all and knew they were all great fun to be around. They had often gathered together in October to pick mulberries in Uncle Ed's backyard. She and her parents were to stay in the next-door house with Aunt Bette and Uncle Edward. Jonty's parents were staying with Great Uncle Eddie and Great Aunt Jenna. The popular couple were in their late seventies and never seemed old. One by one, the family greeted each other and sorted out who was staying with whom. The two Macdonald families were to stay at Roseneath with Uncle Wills and Aunt Cathy.

Allie and Simon said a quick farewell before he left her side and joined his mother.

He hardly recognised her. Simon was stunned when he saw the difference. The shrinking violet was gone, and although still quiet and timid, she did not shy away from the hoard of people. Simon stayed near her as they walked up to Uncle Luke's house in Phillip Street. He beamed at the change in her and said, "Mother, you certainly look different. You are glowing," Simon grinned as they fell slightly behind.

Elise nodded. "I am Si; I love being here. I can hide if I don't feel like people, but there are enough kind ones who sit near me to chat quietly should I desire company. I adore Ed's wife, Jenna, and we seem to... well, we are chalk and cheese, but I just adore her." Elise glanced at her son. "Si, do you mind me living here? I really feel welcome, and it's like I'm coming alive again."

Simon was over the moon. Allie was correct. "Mother, I'm delighted. I can see you are happy. I want you to wish me well as I'm going to ask Uncle Alfred for Allie's hand as soon as I can see him."

His mother's answer was to reach up and kiss his cheek. "Now I'm delighted too!"

By the time the various groups reached the assorted family houses they were staying at, the perspiration was trickling down each of their backs and foreheads. The heat was sapping. The thin wisp of cloud was now a thick bar growing by the minute. By the time they had reached Luke's house up on the corner of Church Street, the cloud had grown even more. The slivers of white had turned into fluffy balls with black linings.

Ellen was the first to say, "I do hope the clouds keep growing into rain clouds. We all so need it." She released a deep sigh.

Moira brought in two jugs of sweet lilli pilli and apple punch. The group made short work of it, emptying both pitchers.

Jonty's Uncle Connor heard a vehicle arrive and left the group to assist with unloading the luggage. Sammo and Paul both assisted in unloading and sorting the various bags. In the short time they had been inside, the clouds were now overhead and turning quite dark.

At dinner time that night, the skies opened. The rain pelted down; the road outside was almost a river.

The family assembled on the back verandah, where they could see the river rising quickly. They realised it must have rained heavily upstream. They stood under cover and in safety in the covered area, watching the forces of nature rage overhead. The wind roared, and the trees bent over so much that they were astounded they remained standing.

Soon, the clouds turned green, and then pea-sized hail fell, covering the back lawn until it looked like snow. For two hours, the deluge continued; the thunder and lightning fought overhead. The wind then rose to such an extent that it forced them all inside as it blew the rain towards them.

Connor and Moira brought out lamps and candles in case they lost power.

Sure enough, a lightning strike occurred close by, followed by a power failure. The children then played hide and seek in the dark and later went to bed by lamplight.

Simon was worried about his mother in the storm but was astounded by finding her giggling joyously.

When he questioned her mirth, she just said, "We can't sink here, Simon. I'm safe, and you're with me." She hugged her son with her arms wrapped around his waist. "It's not the storms I dislike, Si, but the movement of water under my feet. Even the ferry makes me fearful."

Simon was amazed at the change in his mother within such a short time.

While she was wrapped in his arms, she whispered, "And hopefully, by next year, I'll be a grandmother."

Simon chuckled softly. "Her father has to agree first, Mother, though;

I do not doubt her reply." He was not used to being hugged by his mother; he found he liked it.

The following day the rain had all but cleared; however, the streets were awash with mud and debris from the storm, but the air was fresh and even cool.

Simon could not get to Bette and Edward's house fast enough to see if Allie was safe. He was concerned for the family's safety down closer to the river. More than that, he wanted to see Allie, he wished they were engaged already.

As all was well at Uncle Luke's place, he left them to prepare for Christmas festivities while he walked down the road. He also needed to collect his parcel coming on the morning ferry. He would be able to see it coming up the river from Eddie's house.

However, his morning did not go to plan.

On his arrival, a working bee was hard at work cleaning up fallen branches and a large tree that had come down in the yard below Uncle Charlie's house, Willow Grove. The men in the family had saws, axes, and carts, and they all set to work moving the fallen tree. Simon stripped off his coat and pulled up his sleeves. The humidity was already building, so he was not sad to be in just a shirt.

It took less than two hours before the majority of the immense tree was cleared up. The girth of the old tree trunk would take more effort, but the crown had mainly been removed.

Charlie suggested that he hire some men to saw it up and dry the timber rather than just burn it on a bonfire. So they left it alone. It could wait for a few days. It would still be green enough to saw easily. Any longer, and the effort may well blunt the two-handled saws.

As the men pulled the last branches onto the carts, Simon saw the ferry round the river's final bend.

They had been piling the debris at the bottom of the property for a bonfire over the new year. So with the full cart having departed with the final load, Simon followed them down and helped them empty it. As the others unloaded the last of the branches, he hung around to collect his parcel and deliver it to Eddie's house.

He wondered if Uncle Charlie would mind using the cart to carry the parcel up the road. There he could unpack it and leave the various packages at the different homes.

Many youthful hands assisted with the enormous box that had arrived.

Simon did not realise he had chosen so much. It was swiftly loaded onto the empty cart and soon on its way to Eddie's sitting room.

The cart's arrival at Eddie's house signalled morning tea for everyone. Allie made a not-so-subtle move to Simon's side. She whispered a greeting, and then some minutes later, Simon caught her father's eye, who met his glance with a lifted eyebrow.

Jenna was watching the young couple. Simon had caught her eye when Allie crossed the room to stand very close to him. Jenna watched as Simon gave a tilt of his head and motioned for Alfred to walk to the side of the room so he could talk to him.

Simon then bent and said something to Allie.

Jenna watched the three and saw Allie nod, then join her mother. Jenna smiled to herself, wondering if another proposal was in the wind. She hoped that Simon would be brought fully into the family. Jonty needed to know that his parenting skills were exemplary. She knew Jonty was still unsettled after his brush with his mortality decades ago. Luke had confided in Ed, and Ed to her. She had kept her eye on the lad on every trip he made to Parramatta. He had been born in this house many years before. Recently he had been fine, having overcome the debilitating nightmares, but with Simon's return with his mother, Jenna wondered how he was coping. Her eyes sought Jonty out in the room. He had turned up to help with the tree. He was beside Lottie, of course, and they were just leaving.

She had known these two would one day make a match when she first saw them kiss when Lottie was only fourteen. She had watched them with the view to a union since them. Jenna was hoping to have a chat with Lottie later that day. Most of the family were coming for afternoon tea. She would try to extract the information from her then.

Jenna kept watching the activities of the various members of the family. As always, Jenna seemed to see into people's lives and see well below what they wanted her to see. She saw Alfred gently put his hand on Simon's shoulder and pat it. She smiled. Approval has been given; she now expected Simon to go to Allie's side.

While she watched the family's goings-on, Eddie sat watching his wife. He adored her as much now as he did when they married. She had kept him off balance since he had pulled her into the horse trough on the day they met. After fifty-seven years of marriage, he still watched her every chance he got. Their ten children had all flown the coop, and they had grandchildren and great-grandchildren. Ed watched where her eyes wandered; he knew the troubles and activities of many of the younger members, mostly because she told him of them. He saw them fall on Allie, and he watched as she walked to Simon's side. His eyes flicked back to Jenna's, and he was in time to see a smile of delight cross her face. By the time he dragged his eyes from his wife's again, Simon and Allie had vanished.

Alfred had given Simon permission to walk Allie up to Luke's house further up the street. As it was broad daylight, it was considered permissible for them to walk out together in public.

Simon had offered her his arm as they walked down the back steps from the kitchen. In the privacy of the garden, he bent and gave Allie a quick kiss on the cheek. "Soon, my dear, but let's walk up to Uncle Luke's house first. Your father has given permission for you to stay for luncheon."

She gave a little skip. "Really, Si?" She grabbed his arm as they walked across the large backyard.

He smiled at her evident joy. "Yes, but we have to come back with the others for afternoon tea."

Simon had not expected that her father would give him permission to propose that day. He could barely contain his joy, and he could hardly wait, but he wished to have the engagement ring with him when he proposed. Then slide it on when she said yes to his question. Simon still had not worked out how to actually ask her, but he was sure he would think of something. He just knew he wished to marry her. Their conversation was somewhat banal as he was nervous.

However, their arrival at the house occurred with the place in an uproar. They made it inside the door when a blood-curdling scream sounded from below.

Luke, Simon and Jonty had never moved so fast. Luke was downstairs at Elise's door before anyone. Jonty was not far behind him, and everyone else soon followed.

Elise had found a large snake in her bedroom, and her ear-piercing screams brought everyone at a run. Elise stood frozen in the middle of the room; around her ankle was a giant snake. It had slithered out from under her bed as she was brushing her hair. It had twisted around her ankles before she noticed it. When she did, she let out her scream.

Luke saw that it was only a diamond python and sighed in relief. He'd not told her, but they had found a brown snake some twenty years before in the ground floor apartment. His father-in-law, Bill Miller, had despatched it with a brick. The snake had stuck its head out at an inopportune time, and Bill dropped the brick onto it.

In this case, Luke and Jonty carefully unwound the slithery eight-foot beast from her feet and took it outside. As Luke had the head grasped firmly, and he carried it down to the river's edge and released it.

Simon had arrived just as Luke had entered the room.

Once the snake was removed, Elise collapsed.

Simon scooped her off the floor and laid her on the bed. Her long hair spread out like a grey halo around her head. She roused, then she clung to him sobbing.

Ellen was beside her comforting her. "Simon, we'll move her directly to an upstairs room. Would you mind swapping rooms with her? I don't think she'll want to stay in here again."

"Of course, Aunt Ellen, I'll go and pack." He kissed his mother's brow and stood to leave.

Lottie, Allie, and Moira stood watching.

He asked the three ladies, "Can you three start to pack her things, please? I'll go and get started on my room."

Within half an hour, the rooms had been swapped. Ellen did her hair for her, and now dressed with her hair elaborately coiffured, Elise had recovered enough to walk to her new room upstairs.

Through all the drama, Allie sat with Elise and held her hand the whole time.

Ellen now assisted Moira in stripping the upstairs bed and remaking it.

Simon took his sheets downstairs; he would make his bed later. He hoped that no more snakes would find their way into that room, as he was not fond of them either.

By noon the swap had been completed, and Elise's luggage had been unpacked.

Simon was emotionally and physically exhausted. First, the tree, then the snake, and to top it off, he received permission to pay his addresses to Allie. Today so far had not turned out as he'd expected, but he gave a laugh. "What else could go wrong?" he thought.

The luncheon was a retelling of the sagas of the morning by the various family members.

Simon expected his mother to be distressed, but she was giggling by the end of the story, much to everyone's relief. The storm last night had caused a swathe of destruction through the town, but nothing too bad and no injuries.

Luke thought the storm probably flushed the snake out of its home. He'd seen no sign of a snake around; even in the stables, there were no skins. Luke then retold of a storm back when he was a child. In December 1841, a tornado had all but destroyed St John's Church of England Rectory and took off half the roof of the church in town. He remembered collecting slates and stacking them beside the church. They had lain there for over a decade. It had taken that long to repair the damage. However, in that time, All Saints church had been built.

Moira and Ellen had put a hogget roast on to cook while they were at Eddie's house for afternoon tea.

At two o'clock, the family assembled to walk down the street for the family gathering. The children set off first, jumping over mud puddles and laughing all the way down the cobbled and dirt road. All the adults, including Moira and Connor, followed them with Elise and Ellen on Luke's arms. Simon and Allie brought up the rear. He was hoping they could fall a little behind everyone.

They were so deep in conversation that they were unaware of a vehicle coming up behind them until it hit a large puddle and covered them with gluey mud. As Simon was on the street side, he was well doused, but Allie also caught a wave of mud on her face.

Both yelled, and the others turned and saw both young people were now covered with gooey browny-grey sludge the consistency of custard. Allie had been looking at Simon, and so her front caught a full slosh of mud on her face. Simon only got the wave on the back of his head and back. However, his jacket was covered with the gloopy substance. It was the same puddle that had caught Jonty some years before.

Allie got the giggles. Her sprigged muslin gown was ruined, but she didn't care.

Simon stripped off his filthy jacket and placed it around her shoulders. She had no idea her drenched gown was now completely see-through. Very little was left to the imagination until she saw him blush. "Allie, here, take this, quickly. Your gown… um, you need to be covered." Simon left his arm around her shoulders momentarily.

She looked down at her dress. She could see the outline of her corset and the tips of her breasts visible through the wet fabric. "Oh, thank you, Si." She looked up at him blushing. The mud may well be dripping off his jacket and onto her skirt, but she knew better than to take it off.

Soon all the adults were around them and trying to clean them up. As they were nearly at Eddie's house, they decided to press on and wash up later.

The rest of the family had continued into Eddie's house. Standing just inside the back gate, Simon turned to Allie and said, "I'll always look after you, Allie; if you'll allow me to. Will you?" Simon heard the words fall from his lips. The situation was not what he'd hoped, but it would certainly be memorable. He dropped to one knee. "Will you marry me, Allie?"

She nodded. "Yes, Si, I'd love to." Her muddy face was creased with a huge smile. She tugged at his hand to lift him up.

He stood and quickly kissed her. "I'll give you a better one when we're clean."

As the others had already gone indoors, they were alone.

Simon put his hand in his pocket and drew out the engagement ring. "I came prepared, Allie." He took her muddy hand and slid on the ring.

"Oh, Simon, it's beautiful. Is that a topaz?" she asked while gazing at the stunning stone.

"No, sweetheart, it's a blue diamond. I bought it for you in Cape Town. It is surrounded by sapphires from Bingara that we found ourselves. Jon cut them for me, and I made the setting. I thought you would rather have a blue diamond instead of a red one, but I bought you one of those too. They are really rare, but I don't like them as much, hence the blue one. They are the next rarest." Simon spoke with some nerves.

"A diamond, but it's blue?" She was stunned. "I didn't know they came in different colours."

Simon was thrilled. "They do, but they are uncommon. As you are so special, I wanted something different for you." He looked shyly at her. "So you like it?"

"I love it, Si. Absolutely love it." She shivered. Even though it was a hot day, she was still wet. "Let's go and get cleaned up fiancé mine."

They had just arrived at Eddie's back door. As Ellen had wiped most of the mud from her face and they were still hidden from sight, Simon took the opportunity to kiss her. With both still muddy, he just lifted her chin and gently brushed her lips with his. "Allie, I just want you to know how much you mean to me. I love you; I will never be able to tell you just how much, but I'm happy to spend my life trying."

"Oh, goodie, I look forward to that. It sounds so corny, but Simon, I love you too. So much I want to throw my muddy self into your arms. But I'll have to wait as your shirt is still clean, and I am not. Thank you for covering me with your coat. I didn't realise my dress was so, well, see-through." She blushed.

Simon smiled. "I liked what I saw, though. I didn't want anyone else to enjoy the view." He bent and gave her another swift kiss as they heard the back door open.

"Alice dear, did I hear you come in the back gate?" her mother called.

Simon hooked Allie's arm through his. "Yes, Aunt Goldie, we're here, slightly the worse for wear, but we've arrived."

"You both took your time," Goldie quizzed them. "Is everything all right?"

Allie grinned. "Absolutely, wonderfully fine, Mama. Perfectly, absolutely fine!" Allie turned and kissed Simon in front of her mother. "As I said, wonderfully fine, Mother. We're engaged!" She stayed looking at Simon rather than her mother.

"What? When did this happen?" Goldie said. "You weren't when you left this morning."

"No, it just happened after we got covered in mud, but look," she held out her hand and showed her the stunning ring.

"Oh, Simon, is that a topaz? It's spectacular." Goldie was inspecting the ring.

"No, Mother, it's a blue diamond with sapphires. Simon bought the stone for me in Africa. Jon cut it, and Si set it. These will be some of the sapphires that Aunt Colleen told me about from one of their Bingara trips, and I love it."

By now, the three were entering the kitchen. Allie turned to Simon and said, "I'll go and get changed; then you can keep your promise, Simon."

Luke had already spoken to Eddie and had a change of clothing for Simon. He was handed some trousers and used the bathroom to change.

With such a large family and many visitors, Jenna always kept spare clothes. The family would often give excess clothing away. So all the extended family passed on any extra or old clothes to them. Most were taken over the Coxheath Cottage and stored in a large wardrobe for handing out when and where needed. Simon was the recipient of a pair of trousers from this stash. It was so hot outside and only a family function, so he had no need for a coat. He did, however, encourage others to remove their jackets too. Most were relieved to join him in just shirtsleeves. The temperature was nearing ninety degrees. Thankfully the stone house was cool inside.

Allie took some twenty minutes to reappear, but when she did, she was wearing a lemon-sprigged muslin gown that was even more beautiful than the blue one she'd had on earlier. As she entered, all conversation paused.

Simon, who was mid-sentence, walked away from Eddie. "Hello, sweetheart, you look like the sunshine itself." He greeted her with a kiss on her hand. The ring glinted in a shaft of sun and was seen by Jenna.

"What's that you have on, Allie? Is it new?" Jenna said from across the room.

"Yes, Aunt Jenna, very new, like less than an hour old." Smiling, she took Simon's hand and walked over to her Aunt. "It's amazing what a mud shower can trigger."

Simon was beaming like a cat that got the cream but stayed silent.

Alfred came over to kiss his daughter. "Sounds like a story behind this?" He congratulated Simon. "I hope she didn't hesitate?"

"Papa!" She said indignantly.

Simon laughed. "No, sir, not for a moment, but it certainly didn't go as I'd planned. A drenching in mud was certainly uncalled for, but the result was to my benefit, so I'll not complain." Simon glanced at his mother, who was sitting with Lottie.

The rest of the family were now encircling the happy couple.

Simon had still not had a chance to give Allie a proper kiss. One where he could wrap his arms around her and hold her close, but it would come. Soon he would be permitted to give her as many as he wished.

After some of the commotion had died down, Simon drew Allie to sit next to his mother. He was amazed that with all the crowd of Lockleys, his mother was drinking it all in and having a wonderful time. It was the first time they had been able to have a proper conversation. The snake had put paid to any private chat this morning. The festive celebrations would continue tomorrow, but Simon dearly wished to enfold his beloved in his arms.

Two hours after they had arrived, it was time to depart for dinner at Luke's house. Simon hoped he would have a chance to say farewell properly. Eddie gave him one. In the fuss of everyone leaving, Eddie stood at his office door, he opened the door and sent Simon in, and he just said, "Wait here." Simon waited.

Moments later, Allie was ushered in, and Eddie said, "You have one minute, but if you two are like Jenna and me, you will wish to hold her, and you have not had a chance. Don't take long."

Allie went directly to Simon's side; she waited until Eddie closed the door, then looked up at Simon coyly. "I was hoping we'd get a chance to say goodbye properly."

He didn't answer but drew her into his arms. She had a curl come loose, and he gently tucked it behind her ear, then he did what he'd wished to do for a long, long time. He stroked her long neck, slipped his hand behind her head, then slid it down her back, drawing her to him, as his other arm wrapped around her waist and lowered his head to hers.

After what felt like far longer than the prescribed minute, he forced himself to lift his lips from hers. "I'm looking forward to much more of this, my beloved, but now we must leave. I dare not stay longer." Simon offered her his arm and escorted her back to her waiting parents, her lips reddened by their recent activity. As they were about to leave the room, Simon softly said, "I love you, just to make sure you remember." Then gave her a brief kiss before opening the door.

Her eyes were shining.

Eddie was standing guard with his arms folded. At over seventy, he still stood tall and straight. His life as a blacksmith meant his arms were still like iron bars and his hands were enormous. Eddie was still a man to whom one's eyes were immediately drawn. His fair hair was now white; his blue eyes still twinkled with mischief as they always had. Some men aged badly; Eddie had not.

Alfred was leaning against the wall opposite him. Both men looked at the young couple with a smile.

"I told you he would not abuse the situation," Ed said to Simon with a grin, but his comment answered Alfred's question.

Simon nervously met his future father-in-law's face. "I would not hurt her for anything, Uncle Alfred. But I did so wish to hold her once." He reluctantly dropped her hand.

Alfred smiled at his nervousness. "Relax, Simon, we've both been there. We knew you had not had time to have any chance to be alone with her. It's only fair that you now have more freedom as you're engaged. I know you will not take liberties, but you will be given opportunities to be together when possible."

The eyes of the young couple met, and they smiled at each other. "Thank you," Simon murmured as he followed the remainder of Luke's family out the back door.

The next day was Christmas; the festivities overflowed from the church into the various houses in the family. One tradition had only started just two years before. After the Christmas service, the extended family would gather at St John's cemetery. The six Lockley children would stand around their parents' graves and pray, dedicating their now extended family to continuing the work and continuing the faith their parents had started.

Sal Lockley had been ninety-five when she finally joined her beloved Charles two weeks into the new year in 1896. She was six weeks shy of ninety-six and passed away on January 11th. She loved Charles from the day she met him in 1820. Every decision she made since their marriage, she would ask two questions; the first was, "How would Jesus deal with this?" and the second was "What would Charles say?" Both questions guided her until she died. Her husband's leadership was still an inspiration for many. Simon wished he'd met him, but he had died decades before he met the family. Sal had spent nearly twenty-six years waiting to join him. Now she had gone too, and the family missed their matriarch dearly. The Earl and Countess of Coxheath had both arrived as ordinary convicts in chains and served their time. Twenty-two years after arrival, they discovered that Charles had been an Earl for most of his life and never knew. He had found that his title opened doors he had never dreamed about. They had met the Queen on numerous occasions. Charles had spoken in the House of Lords and pushed for the rights of the common man to be allowed to vote. That Bill took time and caused riots, but it passed and changed the Empire, thanks to Charles's speech. Each of their six children followed as closely as possible to their parents' example, which drew Simon. The family called it "living in the Earl's Shadow." The Lockleys had now drawn his mother into their fold, and she too was now at peace.

In the years Simon had lived with Jonty, he had discovered a different side to going to church. Up until he moved in with them, going to church was just something to fill in Sunday mornings. Everyone went. It was just the done thing. Nothing else was open, and it was a time to socialise. He would sit through often lengthy and usually dull sermons. It meant little to him, and the words of the service were said by rote. The words he knew, but the meaning he'd missed. He had the head knowledge, but that's where it had stopped. Bible stories made little sense to him other than good stories, and he had no desire to understand more. Then Jonty and Lottie had shown him a different side, the side of true faith rather than religion. They put the jigsaw of the Bible together.

Explaining that the Bible was not heaps of different stories as he had thought but was one single story told by many, many different people over thousands of years. When Jonty explained the first few chapters of how mankind had sinned, the rest of the Bible showed that obedience to God was a pathway back to Him. Simon knew about the New Testament and figured out that somehow Jesus fitted into the story. Again Jonty had explained that if the Old Testament were like a ladder to Heaven, then Jesus was the key to the door at the top. Only by believing in Him could you get in.

Now he understood he had been amazed by the intense feelings of love and forgiveness he now felt. Their family prayer times had often brought them to tears. Now he knew why. They often beseech the Lord for someone to be healed or for some request to be answered. Simon had never heard of prayer or faith like this before. Now he knew how it worked.

At one family gathering years before, Lottie's Aunt Cathy had told him what a *word of knowledge* was. Suddenly it all made sense; Simon had the final bit of his jigsaw puzzle. He had been feeling disquieted and unsettled; for some reason, he always felt both guilty and inadequate. He had tried to live a good and clean life, but it had not been enough. That year, Jonty had brought the family for a post-Christmas visit, and they all happened to be there when Sal died.

Wills and Cathy had returned to Emu Plains the week before and were not planning on returning for a few weeks. Out of the blue, Cathy had insisted that Wills return that day. They made it back in time to be with Sal as she breathed her last.

Cathy sat with Simon and Jonty as the six children and many of the grandchildren said their goodbyes. Cathy had taken her turn early and left her side to allow others in. It was on that day that she explained the *words of knowledge* she experienced. Every now and then, she felt an immediate compunction about doing something. Sometimes it was to expect someone or occasionally go somewhere or be somewhere in particular. Her mother also had this gift.

Her husband, Wills, had explained it had occurred far too often to be a coincidence. From there, the conversation led to belief, faith, and what being a Christian really was. Going to church didn't make you one, nor did doing good things, nor did being religious. Aunt Cathy had taken the time to lay out for him that only by believing in Jesus, who was and is God's living son that Simon's life could be saved. Even then, Simon needed to follow what Jesus taught in the New Testament, did his understanding of everything he had heard finally make sense. He had never known there was a difference between Religion and Christianity; now, he knew they were vastly different.

It took time to gel fully.

However, this conversation encouraged Simon to act on his feeling that he needed to see the shipwreck site for himself. If God wanted him to go, then he would. He had gone and found his mother three years after the shipwreck; it suddenly was like he understood everything. If he had left it any longer, his mother might not have survived. Now she was nearly back to her old self.

Simon smiled; he was looking forward to the day ahead. No, he was looking forward to his life ahead, a new life, one surrounded by his new family.

Chapter 18   Recalled to Duty

$\mathcal{N}$ot long before Simon moved into his aunt's house, and only weeks before the wedding, Jonty arrived home from work and found Simon throwing all his paintings onto a bonfire in their backyard. Jonty was able to rescue a few small pictures, but the rest of his work was beyond salvage.

Jonty was distraught. "Why Simon? Why destroy such brilliance?" The roaring fire ate the scenes that Jonty adored. Simon had even taken a gifted painting from Jonty's hallway. It was the empty space that Jonty first noticed. Then he smelled acrid smoke emanating from the backyard.

Simon was staring into the flames. "I'm burning my old life, Jon. Do you know I have never sold a single painting, ever? Tom, Fred, and Arthur's works fly off the walls, but no one will touch mine. I know my skill and technique are good, but they lack spirit. Nothing in them draws a person to buy them. They are dead, and it was how I felt when I painted them. Now, Jon, I'm alive, and they do not represent me and who I am. I'll replace the hallway one, it's already finished, but I need to do this, Jon. All my works from the shop are gone too."

Jonty was stunned. "Oh, cor, Simon, but why? Why destroy the evidence of the talent that God gave you?"

Simon replied in a non-descript tone. "I told you why, Jon, they were devoid of spirit. Like a flat photograph if you like, but they had no character." Simon had not taken his eyes from the bonfire. "Jon, I will start completely new with Allie. All this is evidence of a pointless life. I only ever called it dabbling. Oh, don't get me wrong, I will still paint, but I have had what you call an epiphany. The new work I have been doing is different. You'll see when I bring around the replacement painting next week. I'll be moving into the house next week too, Jon. I have three weeks there to settle before bringing Allie home. I want to make sure everything there works well. Mr and Mrs Yates are a delightful couple and are wonderful caretakers. The vegetable garden is full of vegetables and other produce already. Mrs Yates has already started building up some stored fruit as well. Phil is a brilliant worker. He has the yard and house cleaned top to bottom, and I don't even think Mother would recognise it. Ricky English told me he was another one of his... um, finds. Phil and his mother had arrived on their doorstep sick and bedraggled. Phil was apparently only about two. I had heard about that story from Will and Dimity but didn't realise it was the same Phil Yates. Anyway, Aunt May's possessions have now gone or been packed up. Some things, like the china, Allie may wish to keep, she can sort them at her leisure. I may yet sell the house so Mother can come and visit us, if not live with us."

Jonty stood looking at the young man. His determination to change had surprised him. He was undoubtedly not the insecure lad who'd come to their home nearly five years before. He knew that since Simon had really discovered his faith, he had been more in tune with himself. He should not have been surprised that the new Simon had wanted a clean sweep to his life, oh, but to see his magnificent works burned hurt.

Simon was as good as his word and gifted Jonty a new painting for his hallway, which was brilliant. But Jonty thought he was wrong. Technically, they were even better, but this new style was different. They were now a clone of the other artists. Simon's works had been unique. Thankfully Jonty still had a few that he had saved hidden away

~

That Easter break was to be used to celebrate the long-awaited wedding. The weather held fine, and Easter Monday had been chosen. All the family would already be gathered together for services at Parramatta.

It was the one time of the year when the entire Lockley family, along with the Evans, Macdonalds, Harlows, Turners and Leslie families, and all the others termed hanger-oners, gathered. The number grew each year despite the losses of older family members. This celebration would bring in another link. The Mitchells were soon to be grafted in, as were the extended English family, as Will now claimed his connection.

Elise had become integral at Coxheath Cottage, assisting other women who had been abused as she had been and young mothers not coping with their new babies. She was a natural. Jenna, and Charlie's wife, Gracie, had handed over the running of the cottage to the younger family members years before. Both ladies were in their seventies and were tiring. They still attended every Wednesday and taught the skills to the younger ones.

Simon had taken a while to discover that Charlie and Gracie were the Earl and Countess of Coxheath. It was only when their cousins had arrived from England for a holiday a few years before that the reality of whom this family encompassed actually hit him.

Eddie's eldest daughter was the Duchess of Gracemere, and his son Kit was the rector of their parish and lived in the castle's Dower House with his family. Both couples lived in England. Charlie and Gracie's oldest son Teddy, Viscount Lockley, had lived with them for years, but he and his family now lived at Princhester Court, courtesy of Rick Lockley.

When Simon had finally grasped their exalted positions, he stood looking stunned with his mouth open.

Charlie had been up a ladder cleaning gutters on the inn roof. At close to eighty, it was not something he should have been doing.

It was when Eddie growled at him, telling him, "For goodness sake, Charlie, come down, or Teddy will end up as the Earl before his time. We need you around for some time yet. Let John do it." A reluctant Charlie took his younger brother's advice and descended the ladder.

"You're an, an… Earl?" Simon had stuttered.

"Yes, didn't you know?" Charlie acknowledged his status in an off-hand way.

"Um, I knew your parents were, but it never occurred to me that the title was inherited. Oh, sir, I'm so sorry." Simon gave a bow.

Charlie responded to his action with a hearty laugh. "Leave off, Simon, I'm Uncle Charlie, and that's it." He slapped the young man on his shoulder lovingly, and they walked inside with his arm slung around his shoulder.

It had taken some time before it sank in that if Charlie was an Earl, then Eddie, Wills, and Luke were all titled "The Honourable." Even their two sisters, Liza and Anna, had the same title as Wills and Luke. Now the Earl would become his great-uncle. Simon felt very unworthy of being allowed to marry the great-niece of an Earl, but he loved her, oh, how he loved her.

Their Easter wedding at St John's Parramatta was a huge celebration. The church was packed with hardly any standing room. After the service, the extended family and invited guests returned to the courtyard at the Jolly Sailor Inn. This had been the site of many family weddings over the past fifty-nine years. Liza and Bertie Ellis had celebrated the first wedding party in the courtyard in 1841. It had become a tradition that the family continued. Most of the married couples had done the same except Jonty and Lottie. Theirs had been a Special Licence marriage soon after Jonty returned from Africa. The now seventeen-year-old twins, Sammo and Patty, had been born just under nine months after their wedding.

Allie and Simon had a week-long honeymoon in Newcastle. The destination was chosen because neither had been there before. They delighted in long walks along the beach and foreshore and also a walk out to Nobby's Head. They returned to spend another week together at their new home before Simon had to return to work.

Allie had met Mrs Yates before, and they got along well.

Simon was pleased that Allie would not be left alone at the house during the day as Phil Yates worked in the garden. The house sat on a hill in Glebe, a sturdy building made from sandstone. They discovered it had been built from a giant rock from the next-door property. That main stone house was still there and owned by the Garney family in England. Occasionally there were occupants, but more often, it sat tended but empty. The last occupant was a Scottish Baron related to the owner.

Simon had only discovered the house's history when Hamish Macdonald found out where he would live. Simon put more bits of the family puzzle together when he found Hamish's brother Fergus had lived there for some time. "Uncle Hamish, that means your brother is the Baron, then?" Simon said, somewhat stunned.

Hamish cringed. "Eh lad, he is that but has no lands or family left in Scotland. Fergus and Katy came and joined my Effy and me here in Sydney. He never went back." Hamish still had a hint of his Scottish lilt.

"Then you are titled too, Uncle Hamish?" Simon gasped.

"That I am, Simon lad, but I am still me. The same man who lost his leg. The title of 'The Honourable' makes little difference to day-to-day life and less to my missing leg. I still need to earn a living and feed my family. Simon, in this wonderful country, you are who you want to be. Anyone from emancipists to newcomers can make good. Work hard and be fair, and you will probably succeed. I'll not put words into the good Lord's mouth but trust Him, Simon." Hamish pointed heavenward.

By mid-year, Allie told them they were expecting their first child soon after the new year. With Simon's skill growing, his expertise in design brought more custom to the jewellery shop. They had much more competition now, but few others were manufacturing jewellers, everything they sold in the shop they made themselves. Simon was producing unique designs that still were able to be made quickly.

The young couple settled into married life and looked forward to the arrival of their child. They had many visitors, and one of them was a surprise visit from Allie's cousin, Jax Styles. Although brought up in Parramatta, not far from Allie, they thought he was in England. He was welcomed warmly.

At just eighteen, he had confided in Simon that he contemplated matrimony himself; well, more than that, he was engaged, but they had not announced it yet. He had not long returned from some months in England while completing his Theological training, and he had fallen in love. He had been staying at the Dower House at Gracemere Castle in Kent with their cousins Reverend Kit and Charl Lockley, and he'd lost his heart while there.

Their youngest daughter, Thea, still lived with her parents and worked in the parish with them. At nineteen, she had not previously been interested in matrimony.

Jax had been offered a teaching position at Moore College but needed to find accommodation in Sydney. For him to be offered a position at under twenty astounded him. He had gone to England to do some study, and he returned with a totally different career path. His passion for languages had taken him in a vastly different direction from where he had planned. He had hoped to study Classical Greek and Ancient Hebrew further, only to find he knew more than his lecturers. Unbeknownst to him, they had put his name forward as a lecturer at Moore College, where he could also complete his training if he wished. Being under twenty-one, he was not allowed to be ordained, but he wasn't so sure that that was his calling anyway. Teaching and languages were his passion. As a teacher, he had to live off-site, which meant he could also have a wife. The offer had come through by wire while he was in England.

Jax's cousin Edmund, now Earl of Meldon, had offered him Rock Cottage. Edmund had finally decided to get rid of his grandparents' place but would love the building to stay with the extended family.

Jax's parents, Edward and Bette, often used the house as a place to stay when in Sydney. He had been frustrated as there were things he had wished to do to it then, so now, as owner, he could change it at will. He knew it was a suitable residence; ownership would be transferred to Jax when he married. After being interviewed for the position, Jax had come to look at the building. He would then return to England and marry Thea. The trip via the Suez Canal only took some six weeks, so he would get things started, and if Simon and Phil Yates could oversee the building conversion works and gardening, Jax would return and bring back his new wife.

Simon was delighted that Allie would have extended family living next door and asked Jax if he would mind adding a gate in the dividing fence as he was sure it would get used often.

Jax inspected the property and agreed. The building was sound but needed updating and extending. He met both Simon and Phil, and they set tradesmen to work listing the needed repairs and improvements. Nothing had been done for nigh on twenty years. His parents had been content to stay in Parramatta and play their music rather than make improvements to a house they did not own. They had taught their four children the joys of music, and Jax was determined to add a large conservatory out the back of the house using some of the immense market gardens that had originally been there.

Jax had found that Beale Piano's had opened a new store at Annandale and ordered a parlour half grand piano from them. He would have liked a larger one like the concert grand piano at Gracemere Castle but knew that was a bit ostentatious. The house also needed internal bathroom facilities.

He intended to modernise it thoroughly, and all the wiring throughout the house required replacing. Most of all, he wanted a brand new bathroom and had brought back some fancy fittings from London. He had purchased a unique claw foot bath, flushing toilet and matching handbasin. The work thus started, and Jax left for England again. He planned to return before the birth of Simon and Allie's child early next year.

~

Jax and Thea returned in November, arriving with the news that war had broken out in the Transvaal.

Thea and Allie, although related, had only met once before. They became firm friends. Allie was now heavily expectant and recognised that Thea was in a similar condition; however, she was only a few months gone. Allie had guessed Thea had not yet told Jax; she was homesick and felt ill. Allie provided her with a family remedy of a mix of bicarbonate soda and crushed sugar with lemon juice. This certainly helped with her illness, but only time would tell for her homesickness.

Thea had settled in by Christmas and was over the worst of her morning sickness. Jax didn't start his teaching position until the following year, so he could be with her for the first months after their arrival. His musical ability had assisted with his learning languages. He seemed to pick them up very quickly, and thanks to his father, he had mastered French and had a good grasp of Latin by the time he started at The King's School in Parramatta. Edward had started his eldest son on languages when he called out answers in class. He also taught him Latin and basic Greek. Jax absorbed them like a sponge. By the time Jax started at King's, he had become fluent in Spanish and could speak German with tolerable skill. In the years at King's, he studied every language he could. He had seven languages under his belt by the time he left school. Studying in Cambridge had been the next step, but studying there had been fast-tracked, and he had graduated in one year. Having just turned nineteen, he was now to teach students older than he was. He was nervous, but he knew his skill and ability. To have family nearby was terrific.

By the New Year, word of the war in the Transvaal was making headlines in every newspaper. Jonty read every document he could get his hands on. His anger at the Afrikaans' and Boers' treatment by the English made him angrier and angrier.

One day something Jonty had read upset him so much that Simon heard him yell, then throw the dop-stick he had been working on across the room.

"Jonty, what's eating you?" Simon had his own battles. Allie was due any day, and he was on tenterhooks himself.

"Oh, don't mind me, Simon, it's just the damned British in the Transvaal. You didn't get there, but the locals are treated like dirt. I just get so mad. I'm totally useless here but I have no wish to go back. Not that there is anything I could do to help. I won't fight, and I won't kill. I shouldn't let it get to me, but I think of that little girl I knew and saw what those blooming soldiers did to an innocent child. Simon, her name was Nandi. She would have been eight or nine, and they beheaded her. Why? She brought me that diamond I made up for Lottie, and a lion cub." Jonty laid back in his work chair and lifted his headset apparatus. "I nursed Chimbu back to health, then one day he left. Not long after he had grown, he came back for a visit and the soldiers were going to shoot him, but I shooed him away, and he went. I really only saw him once properly after that. He came for a visit *en route* north. I was shipped out not long after that." He released a deep sigh. "All this is over greed Simon, damned greed for gold, diamonds, and land."

Jonty groaned and dropped his head onto his arms. "I feel so damned useless, Si," he muttered.

"Cor, Jon, I had no idea. I was so wrapped up in my own grief that I was unaware of what you have gone through; sorry, Jon." Simon fell silent, feeling guilty that he'd given Jonty the cold shoulder for the years he'd lived with them. He was jealous of Jonty's happy family when his own had disintegrated. Now that he had his own family, he realised how difficult he'd made Jonty's life.

"You had reason, Simon; it's why we gave you space. I'm glad we did, too, as look at your mother now." Jonty stretched again, then retrieved the dop-stick he had thrown in anger; thankfully, the stone had not come off. He put his head down and got back to work.

~

Six months later, Jonty had reason to regret his wishes to do anything about the war in Africa. One afternoon he had his head down, faceting another stone when Lottie came into the workroom at the shop. Jonty looked up.

His eyes were huge in the magnifying headset. He saw men standing behind the familiar blue paisley dress he knew his wife had on. She had been unwell, and he was surprised she was still in the shop. He had made a bit of a fuss about her coming to work this morning. He lifted his headset and saw his father-in-law, his father, and another man in a suit.

"Jon, we need to talk," his father said abruptly.

Jonty turned off the light, his machine and the water tap slowly dripping on the faceting lap. He pulled off the headset and beckoned the three inside.

Luke put his hand out to stop Lottie from leaving. "Lottie needs to stay too, Jon. She needs to be part of this conversation. Simon is watching the shop, but I've asked him to lock the door," Luke added.

Jonty broke out in a cold sweat, "What's happened? Why are you all here? Who's sick? And excuse me, sir, but who are you?"

The stranger answered his question. "I, sir, am the Governor's Aide-de-Camp." He did not give his name.

Jonty stood and gazed anxiously at the three men. Jonty's concern was not appeased. "Father, what's happened? Is Mother all right?" He searched his father's face.

Lottie was now at his side with her arm around him, and she was equally concerned.

His father said, "She's fine, son; this is not about family. This is a Government thing." John looked concerned. "Jon, this is about the Transvaal, and Jon, it's about you. They need you."

Jonty now had his arm around Lottie. He had blanched and was shaking his head; fear etched his face. "No! No, I can't." He flopped back into his work chair.

Lottie stood rubbing his shoulder.

Luke came and squatted beside him. "Jonty, they need a mediator, a liaison if you like, and the local President of the area is someone who trusts you. He has said that negotiations will only be done if you are there. He knows you won't stand for any nonsense. He also knows you won't take sides except that which is right. Jon Jon, this is not negotiable. For the country's sake, for the Empire really, you have to go."

Jonty's gaze left his wife's face, and he turned to the stranger. "Paul Kruger?" Jonty asked.

The aide nodded. "He has specifically asked for you, sir."

Jonty had blanched. His gaze moved this time to Luke, "I can't, Uncle Luke! I can't go back to the atrocities I saw. I won't fight, and I won't kill. I'm a blooming jeweller! What the heck do I know about war, or negotiations, or even being a liaison, Uncle Luke, don't make me go!" Jonty swallowed; he dropped his voice. "You know what I was like when I returned last time. I can't do that to Lottie again. I won't do it!"

Luke's heart went out to his son-in-law. "Jon, it's not a matter of wanting to go, you are going, and this time you will have a full contingency of diplomats and a protective, military detail with you from here." Luke stood. "I don't squat well anymore. Sorry, lad!" Luke rubbed his knees. "If I were younger, I'd come with you, but you know the conditions, and from what you told me before, a month on horseback at seventy-one is not possible for me anymore."

Although seated, Jonty had not let go of Lottie. He pulled her closer; his arms were around her legs as she stood beside him. While she ran her fingers through his hair, brushing his wayward lock from his forehead, she said, "Jon Jon, you have to go. This is not for you, nor for me. This is one way you can help them." Crouching down, she cupped a hand on his cheek. "Jon, do this for Nandi. You can't help her, but you can change the lives of many others like her. Maybe even her family." Her gentle caress relaxed him; his eyes met hers, and she could see the fear on his face.

Unable to break her stare, his white appearance told of his anxiety and emotions. He said, "I have to go, don't I?"

His plea to her broke her heart, but she knew she had to stay strong. "Yes, Jon, you do. You will stay strong for Nandi and for our children and me. You will meet with this President and be the liaison they need. You will keep them honest, and Jon, you will save lives." She again eased the fallen lock of hair from his forehead.

Realising that her words had hit home, the stranger smiled. "Can we find somewhere to talk, sir?" the Aide asked.

"Yes, Simon can lock up, and we'll go to our house," Jonty told Simon that they were all going home. Jonty then suggested to Simon that he shut the shop and go home too. "Have an early day and go to your family. I won't be back today. But first, put the things on my desk away, please, Simon."

They arrived at Jonty's house and ensconced themselves into the sitting room, where the Aide revealed the plans for the trip.

John Evans was not keen for his son to return, but he also realised President Paul Kruger had specifically requested him. John had left his wife in tears at home. After the last trip, Colleen had aged visibly. He didn't look forward to the repercussions of this trip any more than Jonty, but John knew that Kruger would only negotiate if Jonty were there.

The Aide had outlined the situation. He did not understand how Jonathon Evans fitted in as a liaison or why the President of the enemy trusted him. Jonty had to give him a brief outline of their only interaction some eighteen years before. Back then, Paul Kruger had been just a rebel who all but kidnapped him; now, he was the President.

Soon after the departure of the Aide, Luke told Jonty that Uncle Charlie needed to see him as he had more information for him. The Aide had revealed that the Governor, The Right. Honourable William, Earl Beauchamp had made arrangements for Jonty's involvement. Uncle Charlie had spoken up and done some of the official paperwork from his home. Charlie knew that Beauchamp only tolerated him because of his title, but his slur about the birthstain of the convicts ate at him. The Governor assured him that he had taken the comment the wrong way, but he did little to make amends. They tolerated each other, and Charlie avoided him where possible.

John and Colleen had arranged for the children to stay with them while Lottie and Jonty went to Parramatta to see Charlie. At eighty, Charlie could no longer travel, but his wisdom was still much sought. As Viceroy, Charlie was fully aware of the developing situation in the Transvaal.

Lottie stayed with her mother while Luke and Jonty sat listening to Charlie's imparted information.

Jonty was reeling. He had no choice but to leave his family and go.

Once Charlie had been informed this was a possibility, he requested he be kept up to date on the situation. The Governor had acquiesced, as

Charlie had never officially handed in his role of Viceroy. Charlie had his son, John Lockley, as Assistant Viceroy, and he sat in on every meeting where possible. As such, Charlie had been privy to otherwise confidential documents. Kruger had been integral to the trip. Jonty had no idea that his small interaction with the man had been cause to remember him. Apparently, it had made a significant impression on the now President. Even wild beasts trusted him, which made the young man memorable.

Within weeks Jonty was booked on the Africa-bound ship, *The Trevalgan* was heading to Lourenço Marques in Mozambique. He did not wish to leave as Lottie was still feeling ill. He hated parting from her when she was unwell; however, both knew he had little choice.

Luke and Ellen promised to stay with her until she was well again. Reluctantly, in the last week of July, Jonty packed and departed. He knew it would take four to six weeks to cover the distance in the steamship. Although a contingent of diplomats and Australian soldiers accompanied him as guards, he was not looking forward to the time ahead. He had no idea how long he would be away from his family, and he was still angry that his presence had been demanded.

He arrived in Africa in early September 1900. Upon arriving in Mozambique, a large British military contingent met Jonty and his entourage and escorted them to Pretoria.

Once again, Jonty was surrounded by a delegation of soldiers, but they were not only English ones this time. The last time he had made this trip, he was fearful for his life. In a way, this was no different; only he was going into danger rather than leaving it.

They usually would have travelled by rail, but some of the track was out of commission due to the war. Some sections had been sabotaged; others were just deemed unsafe due to lack of maintenance. This trip would again take weeks to complete, but it was safer than the previous time. As they set off from Mozambique, he hoped to be home in three months.

On arrival in Pretoria, Jonty was given officers' quarters in the centre of a military compound. He was given a permanent security detail, and the two men shadowed him everywhere. He didn't let on that the last time this had occurred they had been shot each time.

~

Three months passed in the compound. Jonty was told to sit in on every discussion pertaining to the Boers. He did, but most of which he did not understand, all of which he wished he could avoid. He had run up against some of the English officers, one of whom he decidedly mistrusted. Some were so bigoted that they seemed to dislike everyone who was a different colour to them. Jonty had seen the ugliness of war earlier and had no wish to repeat it. He was already hearing stories of the English soldiers raping the local women. One Captain had even been asked to resign after being reported for such abuse of a local lady. Memories of his last trip resurfaced, and Nandi's face haunted him.

So far, Jonty had been kept so protected that he was frustrated by his uselessness. Surely if he were to liaise, he would need to be contacted by the Boers?

Another couple of months passed before he received a summons to appear in the General's office. He'd had no mail, and although he wrote, he wondered if they would get through. His Australian protective detail escorted him to the office. There Jonty was in for a surprise.

Rather than be needed for another pointless meeting, there were two men he had met in Emu Plains at Jim Lesley's training yard. Bob Lenehan and Harry Morant were friends of the Lockleys. He had met them a few times and knew of their skills with horses. Both could ride like the wind, so much so that Harry had earned the nickname of *The Breaker*. It was how Jonty greeted him.

Jonty's welcome made the men smile. "Harry 'Breaker' Morant and Bob Lenehan! Well, I'll be blown! What are you two doing over here?" Jonty and the two men reminisced for some time. The last time he'd seen Harry was watching Jim Leslie break in a cantankerous stallion he had recently bought. Both men had been at the auction and were keen to see this wild beast mastered. Jim had invited them to watch. What they witnessed stunned them; rather than being beaten into submission as they expected, Jim didn't lay a hand on the animal. Jonty had seen it before, but it never tired him. Breaking in a horse would typically take Jim five days from start to finish. Jim did nothing but stand in the yard with the animal for the first three or four days. On day four, Jim would again stand in the yard, but he would step away from it as the horse approached. It took less than one hour for the horse to be nuzzling Jim, and by that afternoon, he had a cloth on its back. Hardly a word had been spoken until a hessian bag had been placed on the horse's back. Jim stood flicking and then rubbing the bag all over the beast. On the last day, the saddle was brought in and left on the fence. The horse was allowed to sniff and nuzzle it. By that afternoon, the saddle was on the passive horse, and Jim mounted with ease.

Bob and Harry stood in silence. Both had expected whips, blood, and bucking; however, neither was disappointed with what they saw. They had barely heard a word other than the soothing cooing tones as Jim spoke gently to the horse.

Jonty had smiled at the memory, knowing what an almost spiritual experience this was. He had seen this magic often. He would go and watch every opportunity he had.

Remembering the amazing sight, Bob and Harry greeted Jonty, and they sat down to enjoy a few drinks with the other officers. Bob was being sent north, and when Harry heard that Jonty was in the compound, he requested to meet with him before they left. Harry still needed to receive orders.

Jonty sat reminiscing with them about the various activities, "Do you remember how Uncle Harry Harlow used to organise entertainment for the soldiers? He would grease a piglet with dripping and release it into the orchard. He would then send in the men on horseback and tell them to catch it however they could. Uncle Harry laughed as no one had yet managed to catch one. However, the pigs would return to the sty when the dinner tin was rattled."

Harry sat gazing at Jonty with a silly grin plastered on his face. "Jon, I so wish Banjo had not hared off to China. He would have loved listening to your stories. Do you know just how blessed you are to have a loving family as you do? Then for you to marry into the Lockleys, well, I shall admit, I'm somewhat jealous. I count Harry Harlow as one of the Lockleys, of course, and I do with Jim Leslie." A melancholy look passed quickly across Harry's face. He shook it off quickly and soon had his two companions laughing again.

Jonty thought for a moment, "Banjo? Do you mean the poet, Banjo Patterson?"

Harry nodded, "Yeah, he's a mate. He heard about a rebellion in China and has gone there to see if he can catch a story. He's been here as a reporter, but nothing has happened for ages."

The three men sat whiling away the hours over some warm beer that had been unearthed from a dark recess of the store tent.

Peter Handcock came in during the afternoon, and Harry introduced him. He stayed with them for a few hours. None of them knew how the following days and weeks would turn out. They enjoyed the few moments of friendship available. Falling into bed, late Jonty had enjoyed himself. Harry Morant came in at dawn and gently nudged him awake. "Eh, Jon, if you get home before me, can you post this?" Harry handed him a letter addressed to his ex-wife.

Jonty sleepily took it from him. "Sure, Harry!"

~

Eight months after leaving home, in March 1901, Jonty watched the group, now called the Bushveldt Carbineers, move off. They were due in Pietersberg District in April. He watched the column of infantry and artillery pass by; Colonel Plumer commanded them. The Colonel was resplendent in his uniform as Commanding Officer. Major Bob Lenehan saluted Jonty and Harry, then winked. Harry chuckled. They had been to London and back in the intervening months and reformed as their own Australian Battalion.

One of Jonty's security detail told him who the others were. "The others are Captain Edwards, Adjutant; Lieutenant Mortimer, Quartermaster; Lieutenant Peter Handcock; he's a Veterinary Officer; and Lieutenant Baudinet." Jonty waved to Peter as he passed by him. Peter saluted them in return.

They watched for a while before his guard said, "Somehow, I don't expect to see them again. The Boers are attacking, like that bushranger Frank Gardiner is reported to have done. Only they now call it guerrilla tactics." His security detail was neither soldier nor police. They were there to protect him, and although Australian, they came under the authority of the English military whilst there.

Jonty knew of the guerrilla methods. He had seen the aftermath of the original raids some twenty years before.

Harry arrived beside Jonty as the last of the men rode out of sight. Harry had told Jonty that he had proposed to a girl from England and was awaiting her reply. He was hopeful her reply would arrive before he received his orders.

Days later, Harry and his men were sent south on some other order. Jonty was alone again and was still waiting.

~

Harry arrived back a couple of months later, and Jonty was still sitting twiddling his thumbs; Paul Kruger still had not made contact. They caught up again, and Harry waited until Jonty's minders had gone. "Jon, Bob's been having some issues, and I'm heading up with a fresh detachment to Spelonken under the command of Captain Percy Hunt. Bob's been promoted to Colonel too. Percy Hunt is a young chap. We've been dating sisters in England and didn't realise until yesterday when I received my girl's refusal. Anyway, I hope Percy knows what he's doing. I like him so far as he seems to know his stuff. There are four officers of us under him, and he runs a tight ship, and we respect him. He's just getting his orders from Kitchener now. Jon, have you still got my letter for Daisy?"

Jonty nodded; he had read the address on the envelope. He decided to ask Harry what she was doing at Beagle Bay in Broome. "I hope I'll never need to send it, Harry, but it's safe. Um, I notice she's using the name Daisy Bates; I presume she remarried?" Jonty saw him nod.

"Ah, a curly status that!" Harry didn't elaborate.

"What's she doing in Broome? It's in the middle of nowhere. I had to look it up on a map. It's halfway up the coast of the west of Australia."

"Yes, Jonty," chuckled Harry. Then he shrugged, "I was under twenty-one when we married, so it wasn't really legal, I suppose. However, we never divorced, either. Daisy married twice more; neither marriage was very successful. She uses the name Daisy Bates now. I heard from her just before I left on this mission. She works with the Aborigines in Beagle Bay in Broome; at least, that's where she told me to write to her." Harry smiled at Jonty. "She's one hell of a girl, you know, Jonty. Like your Lottie, only Irish. Irish and with a temperament to match. Mind you, I deserved everything she said about me. We were fine until we married, then the wheels fell off," Harry roared with laughter.

Jonty was amazed, "I'll take it home, Harry, and you can collect it when you visit."

Harry was about to leave when he turned back to Jonty and said, "Oh, I meant to tell you, Horace Colless is in my group too. He's now our trumpeter since Bob swiped the official one. He's the one who told me you were here. He hails from Emu Plains' way. I wondered if you know the family?"

"I know the Colless family, but they are at Castlereagh, not Emu Plains. My friend, Will English's farm, is next door. I know they have a son; I think his name is Horace, so then yes, I know the family." Jonty lifted his hand in farewell.

Harry had to go and report in and receive orders. "I hope you won't need to post my letter either, Jon, but I'd rather leave it with you than not. I left Daisy badly; well, she turfed me out. As I said, I probably deserved it, but I still care for her. I'll try to write to you here, Jon; say hello to your folks for me, though." For some reason, he hugged Jonty. "Catch you at the slip rails, mate. And keep up your prayers for me; I feel I'll need them." He then left.

An hour later, Jonty saw Harry again. He said, "Orders are through Jon. Kitchener has said to take no prisoners to Captain Hunt. I'm not sure I like that sound, but orders are orders! I'm not so keen on that side of war. Must fly. Hope to see you at home."

Later that day, they rode out. Harry saluted him as he rode past. Jonty stood watching until the dust was gone.

~

Soon after this, Jonty heard about more skirmishes. He was still in his protected premises for most of his time. He expected to have been summonsed by now for a meeting with Paul Kruger, but he wasn't. Occasionally he was dragged into some discussion and hypothetically consulted. Then everything he said would be totally ignored. He wrote many letters, often repeating the contents and sending them via different routes, hoping at least one would get home. To say he was being driven nearly crazy with boredom was an understatement.

By mid-August, reports of a horrific nature were filtering through. Captain Percy Hunt and Sergeant Eland were dead, and many more were injured, but no word came about Harry, Bob or Horace.

The silence was hard to cope with.

~

It took two months before Jonty heard that a German missionary minister had been killed along with a few of the Boers. What horrified him was that Harry was charged with their murder, along with Peter Handcock and George. Harry had introduced him to all of them. Now they were all under arrest.

After over twelve months of almost total inactivity sitting and waiting for a summons that he was sure would never come, Jonty demanded that he be taken to visit his friends at Fort Edward, where they were now being held. Reluctantly the superiors allowed him an escort, and the journey was planned.

A new security party was assigned, and as the battalion was already heading up that way, Jonty was allowed to accompany them.

One night, when they were some one-hundred miles into the trip, he was woken with a hand over his mouth. Like all the soldiers, he always slept fully dressed while travelling, just removing his boots. He was in a single tent and only had to pull on his shoes.

In complete silence, he was escorted outside and marched through the scrub. He was shown into a railway carriage on a side rail, some half an hour away. Inside was an older man who looked vaguely familiar.

"*Goeienaand,* Jonty Evans. Long time no see." The man's smiling face belied his method of bringing Jonty for the meeting.

"Good evening, President Kruger; I am guessing you wish to talk to me?" Jonty gave a resigned sigh. He hated being a political pawn; he felt like a puppet.

"Call me Paul, Jonty. I want to know if you are still as impartial as you were?" the President enquired.

Jonty relaxed. "I try to be. I will not fight nor kill. I'm on my way to Fort Edward to see my friend Harry Morant, who has been arrested for murder," Jonty explained.

He saw Paul's eyebrows rise, but the man remained silent.

Jonty continued, more out of nervousness than imparting information. "It doesn't make sense. I know Harry. He would have been just following orders. His last words told me that Kitchener had told them to take no prisoners. The reason he told me is that he disagreed with it. I want his side of the story."

The President sat back in his chair. "I was wondering if that was where you were heading. He didn't kill the minister, you know. That was an accident by my men. They still call themselves my men but are getting out of control. Some are rebels, and they don't answer to me. My Boers are being blamed for what these rebels are doing. It's why I have called you in. Jonty, the Captain, Hunt, I think his name was, didn't die straight away. Sadly my men tortured him for information, but he wouldn't tell, only giving his name and rank. He was still alive when they left him. My men knew they would not hear the end of it if they killed someone in cold blood. They certainly didn't gut him nor mutilate his legs." Paul paused and let that information sink in. He called for a tea tray.

After the orderly left, Paul continued. "Jonty, I've seen others with injuries like what was reported. I know the Captain was left alive, and when I heard he had been cut open when found, I knew that was not my men. I think the local witch doctor may have interfered with him and the others. Jonty, I've told all my troops you are to be protected at all costs and your detail. However, I'm only in charge of a section of the Boers now. Quite a few have gone rogue."

Paul noticed Jonty start at that bit of information; he began to speak, "But...."

Paul silenced him. "Jonty Evans, it was that I wish you to report. Not all Boers are loyal to me. I'll do what I can to help your friend Harry and the others, but I'm not sure he'll want to be saved by the enemy. You know that won't look too good for him." Paul's look at Jonty was one of commiseration.

Jonty agreed. "I think you're right, sir; he would rather die. I'm sure he'll stick with his plea of innocence, but I'll thank you on his behalf."

Jonty and the great Paul Kruger sat talking for about half an hour more. Paul handed Jonty a long list of things he wanted the Generals to know, including that he had planned to leave.

Paul said, "I won't tell you how or where I'll go, but just let them know. Please don't even tell them I'm in a railway carriage Jonty Evans. That would make me too easy to find."

Paul had Jonty memorise the list, just in case he lost it. Then gave instructions that he be escorted back to the camp boundary.

As he was leaving, Paul said, "Eh, Jonty, that lion of yours is still around. He's taken it upon himself to protect the local villages up this way too. He keeps the other beasts away. He's a strange one, that one, but the villagers like him near. They even leave out food for him. I just thought you should know. You did a good job with him too. He has sired a few litters of cubs, and they all have your white fingerprints on their heads."

Jonty spun around looking at the President; he started but was grinning. "Chimbu is still alive? That's wonderful! He would be nineteen. I thought he would be dead by now."

Paul chuckled. "Chimbu, eh? Strange name, but apt. It's a Hindi name meaning 'shy.' But I suppose you knew that?" Paul laughed again. "Go to bed, lad, and pass on my messages to the General; we won't meet again, so tell them you can go home now. I'll not summons you as they are not willing to negotiate."

The return trip was completed in complete silence again.

From the edge of the camp, he was left to find his way back into his tent by himself.

Chapter 19 A Golden Angel

*J*onty was taken back to camp as silently as they had left though his absence had been noted at the midnight bed check. As he walked into camp, he was greeted by most of the soldiers up and awaiting him. A note had been left on his bed saying that he would be returned safely. He was pumped for information on his return, but Paul had given him explicit instructions, and he would follow them to the letter.

He now knew he was constantly watched. No amount of probing elicited a response. "Just let me sleep; I'll report in when I get to Fort Edward." He entered his tent, pulled the swag over his head and closed his eyes. The camp settled again, and most soldiers went back to bed, though the guard was now doubled.

Jonty woke in his tent feeling somewhat smothered. A familiar smell greeted his nose. "Hello, boy; I was wondering if you would smell me around." He laughed, imagining the reaction of the escort when they saw his next visitor.

Chimbu had indeed sniffed him out, and as he had done as a cub, he settled at Jonty's side.

"You smell a little worse for wear, though, mate." He stroked the fully grown lion's mane. "You could do with a long bath. I suppose you miss those too, eh?" Jonty slung his arm around the tawny beast and dozed. Chimbu's head still had the three distinctive white stripes on the top of his head, although they were somewhat dirty. It was those stripes Paul called his fingermarks. Jonty woke again about half an hour later. Chimbu was licking his hand. He used to do that when he was hungry. "Okay, boy, I'll see if I can find something to eat. I'm not sure there will be any goat's milk, though. Let's see what's around."

The soldier on guard heard Jonty talking to someone and stuck his head into the tent and yelled. All he saw was the back of a giant tawny lion standing over Jonty. Chimbu was purring until then but bounced sideways at the sound of the call.

"Chimbu, stay!" Jonty said to the lion. He then called out, "It's all right, come here," Jonty had his hand on the giant beast's head.

Jonty heard a flurry of activity outside, then a timid voice of the escorting Lieutenant, "Jonty, are you safe?"

"Yes, I'm fine, this is Chimbu; I hand-reared him. He's tame. Just don't startle him. We're coming out, so stand back." Jonty emerged with his hand on Chimbu's mane.

One by one, the detachment fled.

Jonty went to the food wagon and hunted for some dried meat for his pet. Jonty was smiling. "Let's see what I can find for you to eat, my friend."

One of the villagers nearby had brought them a bucket of goat's milk for the detachment, and Jonty poured out his share for his furry friend. Chimbu's purr was much louder as he lapped his milk. He had obviously not had his delicious tipple for some time and licked the bowl clean instantly.

One brave soldier stood watching. "He can have my share too, sir."

Another called, "Mine as well, sir."

Jonty gave him their share of dried meat and then refilled the bowl three more times. Chimbu drained each one and then turned and licked Jonty's bare feet. His tongue as a cub was rough, but now it literally grazed the soft skin off Jonty's normally shod feet. Knowing that the others had to eat, he grabbed a handful of food for himself and his boots, and they walked to the edge of the encampment so the others could eat. Jonty wondered why his beloved companion had come back that night of all nights. He sat with his arm draped around Chimbu's neck until camp broke. Others had packed up his things. He hugged Chimbu, expecting the majestic animal to return to the bush. But as Jonty pushed him away and walked back to camp, Chimbu followed.

Most of the horses were skittish around the giant golden lion, and only Jonty's steed would allow the lion near it. Jonty's peaceful acceptance of the lion soothed the horse. As he mounted, the Captain instructed Jonty to lead off. The patrol would follow as nothing would dare attack such a huge beast. Chimbu ambled along with a majestic gait beside his beloved master. For three days, this was the routine. On the fourth day, another lion was heard in the distance. The roar set everyone on edge.

Chimbu bounded ahead about a dozen paces and released his own resplendent bellow. His voice was deep and resonated in Jonty's heart. Jonty remembered his first attempts of a roar; it was more of a kitten's squeak.

Now fully grown and at the peak of his vitality, Chimbu would fight for what was his. He may be ageing, but he was still in good health. If this was his territory, he needed to defend it from interlopers. With one backward look at Jonty, Chimbu turned and bounded into the scrub.

Knowing the lion had gone, Jonty fell back into the middle of the group. He heard Chimbu's roar again, then nothing. He knew how memorable this experience had been.

They came to the next village; the chieftain had told the Captain that a dark lion was killing cattle. A child had even been attacked in the last few days. Chimbu had been seen chasing it away. He had apparently done this before, and they would leave out food for the golden lion with the lightning stripes.

Jonty explained that his name was Chimbu and that he had been hand-reared. Somehow, word preceded the patrol that the golden lion's protector was coming, and accommodation and food were offered each night for the last weeks of the trip.

They did not catch sight of Chimbu again. The English soldiers now stood in awe of the young man they guarded. If he could sleep with a fully grown lion at his side, they would do anything to protect him when the beast was not there. They never knew if it would turn up again.

They arrived at Fort Edward, and Jonty requested to see the General. He delivered Paul Kruger's messages, explaining to the General that Kruger intended to leave the country. He gave no details of his whereabouts. Jonty explained that many rebels were no longer under Paul's control and that the President disapproved of their actions. He said Kruger would not seek him out again, so he wished to head home. He asked for a protective detail to head back to Mozambique; from there, he would go home. He had been in the country for more than a year already.

The General sent various messages. Paul's description of what happened to the Dutch minister was brushed aside. Jonty demanded that they listen to him. Eventually, they believed his report about the minister but wondered if they would drop the charges entirely for Harry and Peter. Somehow he doubted that they would. He had learned from others that Kitchener had already denied the 'take-no-prisoners' order. He knew now that Harry and Peter would become the scapegoats for the Empire. Jonty was allowed to spend time with Harry and Peter each day. Although under arrest, they allowed Jonty whatever access he wished.

Harry told Jonty the complete and unadulterated story. "Jon, Percy Hunt disregarded the warnings of the locals. He insisted we go and defend the minister and his mission. Percy went first, and my men and I followed some hours later. By the time we got there, the minister was dead, as was Percy. Just before he had left, Percy reiterated Kitchener's orders of 'take no prisoners,' so that's what we did." Harry was resigned to die. He had sworn to defend his Captain and friend and said, "I did it, Jon; I killed them for what they did to Captain Percy. He was my mate Jonty; you know what that means. Yeah, I killed them, but I didn't murder them. They fought and fought well. It's just as well that I didn't see Percy's body because they'd all be dead if I had. I heard it was mutilated, but I never saw it."

Peter agreed with Harry's story, reiterating everything he said. "It's a cockup, Jon; we're just scapegoats because we're bloody Australians. If we were Pommies too, we'd have been released already," Peter growled. He also gave Jonty private letters to post and verbal messages to pass on. His last words to Jonty were, "We'd be given heroes' medals if we were blooming Poms, Jon."

Jonty stood to leave, but Harry called him back. "I have more letters for my writer friends, Banjo Patterson and Henry Lawson. Don't send them until you hear of my demise, Jonty." As Jonty took the mail, Harry saw the stunned look on Jonty's face.

Jonty gasped, "But they are famous."

"We were all bush poets. I dare say all my works will be destroyed when I die. Tell them to keep writing. I've included a poem of mine. Give it to Banjo, will you? Here, I'll recite it to you." Harry took a breath, then started speaking with his deep, resonant voice.

In prison cell, I sadly sit,
A dead crest-fallen chappie!
And own to you, I feel a bit-
A little bit - unhappy!

It really ain't the place nor time
To reel off rhyming diction -
But yet we'll write a final rhyme
Whilst waiting cru-ci-fixion!

No matter what "end" they decide -
Quick-lime or "b'iling ile," sir?
We'll do our best when crucified
To finish off in style, sir!

But we bequeath a parting tip
For sound advice of such men,
Who come across in transport ship
To polish off the Dutchmen!

If you encounter any Boers
You really must not loot 'em!
And if you wish to leave these shores,
For pity's sake, DON'T SHOOT 'EM!

And if you'd earn a D.S.O.,
Why every British sinner
Should know the proper way to go
Is: "ASK THE BOER TO DINNER!"

Let's toss a bumper down our throat -
Before we pass to Heaven,
And toast: "The trim-set petticoat
We leave behind in Devon."

Harry laughed at his maudlin poem and recited a few more to Jonty before saying, "Pray for me, Jonty Evans. Pray hard, for I feel I shall need it. I don't want to die; I have so much more life to live. If I don't make it promise me, you will enjoy your life and remember me occasionally." Harry shook his hand and said his farewells. His parting words were, "Tell them I was following orders. Make sure Daisy knows that."

Jonty's heart hurt as he said good night. That night he wrote to his Uncle Charlie and asked him to pull whatever strings he could. He outlined the story and his part in it. Jonty had not heard the orders but knew what Harry had told him in Pretoria only moments after receiving them. Harry may have a good-time-boy reputation, but he would never willingly take a life in cold blood. He was sure that Harry would have had his reasons.

~

All pleas were ignored. After a month, the prisoners were dispatched to Pretoria and Jonty to the coast. He said his final farewells to Harry and Peter, doubting he would see them again. He collected more of their mail and said his final goodbyes to the two prisoners. He was heart-sore when he left for the coast on horseback again, once more surrounded by his escort. Jonty hoped that Chimbu would catch up with him again before leaving for the last time.

They were a week out of Fort Edward when they heard the roar of a lion. Having listened to Chimbu's roar, Jonty knew it was not him and told his security detail to be on guard.

The British soldiers carried Martini-Enfield rifles, and his Australian security detachment held their Lee-Enfield rifles. Both groups of soldiers now were on the defence, with spare rounds each in readiness, they all felt safe. Jonty was again riding in the middle of the group when a cry was heard from the rear. A shot followed, and the dark lion limped into the bushes. The soldier was alive but bleeding badly. A single swipe of the lion's claws had shredded his back. He needed urgent attention. He passed out, and as Jonty knew how quickly a scratch could infect, he asked around for some spirits. It seemed he had actually learned something from those months of nursing. A few hip flasks were produced rapidly, and they removed the remnants of the man's shirt. They cleaned the wounds while he was unconscious and liberally doused the gouges with neat alcohol. They knew it would hurt like hell, but it was needed to stop infection. Once done, the veterinarian travelling with them to the coast bound up the wound to stem the bleeding. They needed to get him to help quickly. They were nearly one hundred miles into the five-hundred-mile route. Knowing that they needed to get him assistance, they walked onward. There was a mission in the next town, and they would leave him with them.

The horses were fresh as they had stopped for half an hour, so they moved on quickly. The only place they could put the soldier was on the food wagon. It wouldn't be comfortable, but it was better than trying to hold him upright on a horse. A few of them laid out some swags for him, and he lay face down and was cradled by stores as they travelled. The soldier's bleeding was under control, but he'd not yet regained consciousness.

In the distance, they heard a lion fight followed by a roar, a yelp, and then silence. They rode for a few minutes; then they listened to another closer roar.

Jonty spun around in the saddle. "It's Chimbu, don't shoot." His voice carried over the already quietened patrol. They held their rifles ready but held their fire.

Jonty was off his horse and called him at the top of his voice. "Chimbu, come." He didn't have long to wait. His golden form was seen bounding through the long grass. The tawny lion growled a greeting, stood up to his full height on his back legs, and cuddled Jonty with his velveted paws around his neck. Chimbu's giant tongue licked Jonty's cheek. As Jonty hugged his friend, he realised his hand was wet and sticky. "Down, Chimbu, you're injured." Chimbu dropped and turned sideways, rubbing his giant hairy head against Jonty. Sure enough, he, too, had claw marks slicing his back. They weren't too deep but would be painful. Chimbu had come to the one person who could help him.

Once again, Jonty called for spirits and let Chimbu smell the bottle. He'd used rum before for his cuts and scrapes. He knew it stung and hoped he would remember the smell.

Chimbu dropped his head and tensed.

"You remember, don't you, mate?" Jonty stroked the tawny mane. "Hold still." Jonty knew this would hurt as one claw had cut deep. He motioned for everyone to stand well back, just in case. Jonty poured the strong spirits into the still-bleeding wound. As the spirits hit the raw flesh, Chimbu growled but held still. One swipe of his claw could kill any of them, yet he remained quietly at Jonty's feet. His head dropped when Jonty had finished. "All done, mate," Jonty said as he stroked his massive head, then he covered the wound with a clean rag to keep the flies away. Hopefully, Chimbu would stay with them for a day or so, at least until the wound crusted over.

Chimbu turned and licked Jonty's hand. Then he walked to the front of the troop, turned and waited. He was ready to lead them to safety.

Because of the wound on his back and the noises they had heard, Jonty worked out that Chimbu had probably attacked and killed the other lion. He listened to the talk of the soldiers. They, too, realised that Chimbu had perhaps killed the dark lion. He was their unlikely golden angel, a protector in a dangerous world. While he walked with them, they remained safe.

~

Chimbu stayed with them for ten days. He allowed each soldier to stroke him, allowing Jonty to tend to his needs. He licked and smelled each of the men and absorbed their scent. On the second day, they came across a clear creek. Jonty bathed the dirty lion and cleansed his wounds again. He slept at Jonty's side each night, and Chimbu led the parade with Jonty each day. Every few days, Chimbu killed a gazelle and brought it for them to eat. They took a haunch and gave him the rest. On the eleventh day, Jonty woke just before dawn. He felt Chimbu get up; he turned and licked Jonty's face, then walked out of his tent into the dawn mists. By the time Jonty drew his boots on and stood at the tent door, the lion was gone. He had said his farewells in private this time.

Jonty knew his wound was fine. Chimbu had allowed Jonty to clean it daily, and the injury scabbed quickly. No infection had set in, and Jonty knew he'd be all right. He walked to the night guard. "He's gone. He said goodbye, and now he's gone."

The soldier gently put a hand on Jonty's shoulder. "We've been privileged to get to know him a bit, sir. Thank you."

Their voices carried in the quiet of the morning. Others stirred, and soon the camp was moving.

Word soon spread that Chimbu had gone. More than Jonty had a lump in their throats when they heard the majestic king of the jungle had left them. He had slipped out as quietly as he'd arrived the first time, silently and without fanfare.

~

The last week on the road was traversed without further incident. They heard no more of the golden lion, but each would carry memories of that special time with him.

Their arrival in the capital occurred in early November 1901. Jonty was now ensconced in the town's most luxurious accommodation, all at government cost. Suddenly nothing was too good for him. A freighter was leaving for Melbourne the next week and had room for four passengers; it was basic accommodation, but it was leaving Africa. Jonty was determined to be on it. He had one last request to fulfil for Paul Kruger. Jonty had promised to wait for a final message in the form of a visit from someone.

He insisted on not waiting for the passenger ship due at the end of the month; however, the bulk of the soldiers would catch this. He stood watching the cargo be loaded into the ship's hold and was joined again by some of his protection detail. He wondered if the departure date had been changed and asked the soldier. "It's leaving in three days, sir; you are booked on board."

Jonty knew that already but had wanted to confirm his date of sailing.

The detail had orders not to leave the town until Jonty had left. They divided themselves into four-hour watches and shadowed him everywhere while he wandered around town.

Months ago, towards the end of his nighttime meeting with Paul, he was asked if there was anything Jonty wanted. Jonty had chuckled. "I'm a jeweller, and I'm in the diamond country; I have not even been able to source a single gem." Paul Kruger had given him the name De Beer to ask for diamonds, but Jonty discovered that he was not in town. After two days, a summons was received to meet a mysterious person in the hotel foyer.

Jonty was hoping that this man could access some for him. With only a day left before his departure, he was unlikely to find any. He'd asked for De Beer, but no one knew where he was. He did not have a single gem to take home. No one else was selling uncut gems. When finally, a message arrived for Jonty, he arranged to meet with the mystery man in the hotel's foyer where he was staying. This man was not De Beer, whom he had been hoping to meet but knew the name of Jurgen Van Dyke. He was the buyer he had purchased his gems from in Cape Town. Although they had not met since the first trip, they had often corresponded for over twelve years.

Jurgen greeted him with open arms and a double-cheek kiss.

"*Gooten morgan,* Jurgen," Jonty mumbled. He had no idea if that's how you said it in Afrikaans.

"Ahh, close, Mister Jonty Evans, it is *Goeie more,* but I appreciate your effort, young sir. It is nice to meet you again." Jurgen ushered him to a seat in the foyer but off to the side and out of the thoroughfare.

As they were in a public place and Jonty knew this man, he waved his security detail to stand back and give them some space. Although the soldiers mainly had become friends, this was business. Jonty waved them out of earshot.

Jurgen glanced around at the minders, noting they were standing far enough away; he said in a thick accent, "Our mutual friend PK has sent me with a gift to compensate you for your inconvenience. De Beer is currently away, so it was up to me. He has included a few fancy ones for you, but I have added one special one. These were mostly sourced from places he knew you would be happy to buy from. Although, I feel his men may have stolen some from some English mines." He chuckled. "Jonty Evans, there are many new mines, and they are mines you did not purchase from previously. Some stones are from the local children; one is from Nandi's family; it is a red one. It's the special one. Her brother brought it to me for you. He refused payment for it, but Paul rebuilt their house instead. I am honoured to have you as a business contact, Jonty Evans, and I hope we can continue to be so."

Jonty was thrilled. "Of course, Jurgen, I was sad that we had lost contact. I wrote to your last known address, but my letters were returned," Jonty explained.

"Ahh, yes, I was chased out of town as I undercut the English miner's prices. Sorry, but I have only recently set up my business here. I had intended to write, but then things became unsettled. How long have you been over here, Jonty Evans?"

Jonty had a lot of time to work out how long this almost pointless trip had been. "I find it hard to believe, but it will get on for eighteen months by the time I arrive home. I was only needed for one meeting."

Jurgen smiled. "One is enough. From what I hear, I believe you accomplished more in that one meeting than the English had learned in two years. Trust is something earned, Jonty Evans, and your impartiality has proven to be highly valued in our divided country."

Jurgen and Jonty chatted for quite some time. Knowing they were being watched, nothing changed hands. Jurgen told Jonty his new address. As they stood to part, Jurgen hugged Jonty and slipped a large bag into his pocket out of view of the minders. Jonty felt its weight, but it was done so that his security detail would not have noticed. Jonty walked his friend to the door and took their final farewells. He waited until the man was out of sight before leisurely returning to his room, where he locked his door. Walking to the small table near the window, he pulled out the drawstring bag from his pocket and eased it open. Inside the bag were a series of smaller packs.

One by one, he opened them and inspected the contents. Before him on the table were some three hundred stones. More than half were less than one carat, but all were clear and flawless. There was a bag of fancy colours; the average size was two carats, but a few were more significant. There was one tiny bag he had yet to open. He knew what would be inside; it would be the red diamond from Nandi's brother. Besides the ones Simon had purchased for Allie, he had only ever seen one before, and it was way beyond his funds. There was a bag of twenty coloured diamonds, another bag of emeralds, and one of the exquisite pink sapphires, including a note that said they were from Madagascar. As he had been given some of these from Mr Field, he knew their locality was accurate. He had sold those at an astronomical price; now, he had twenty more.

Once he'd itemised the stones, he repacked them again. Only then did he open the tiny final bag. A red stone rolled out of the inch-wide bag. The sun caught it and cast a prism of vibrant colours across the ceiling. Jonty gasped. He had never seen one like this. Although it was red, it was not the deep red of a garnet, but more a very dark shade of the Madagascan sapphires, but was obviously a diamond. He was almost scared to touch the magnificent double-pointed gem.

"Cor," he said to himself. He carefully raised the stone by the points and held it to the light. "Oh, look at the colour!" He sat gazing at the almost blood-red stone. His mind flicked back to Nandi; her huge brown eyes and dimples came to mind. He smiled to himself; he knew what he would do with this one. He would cut it into two stones and get Simon to set one into a piece of jewellery and auction it. Some would go to the orphanage in Sydney, and most to Adem and Nandi's village. The second smaller stone he would make into a simple cravat pin. It would remind him to pray for their village every day. He would keep the money until the Pretoria area settled and send it to Jurgen for a new well and housing for Nandi's village, perhaps a school and medical centre too. He smiled to himself and repacked the stones. Once again, he sewed the bags of gems into his trousers pocket as he'd done years before. Thankfully the weather had turned a little chilly, so wearing a coat covered his bulky pockets.

With his business settled, the final day ashore passed in a flurry of shopping. His minders escorted him to various stores; mainly, he purchased local fabrics as gifts and some reading material for his trip. Now content, he returned to his accommodation to pack.

His departure was uneventful. As he had done years before, he stood on deck until the port was out of sight. The gum seedlings had grown to nearly full height. He compared the two views in his mind and then smiled at the memories. Only then did he go to his room. On this trip, his heart was joyful to be heading home. He had done what was required. He carried the letters from Harry and Peter. He would only post them once he heard the outcome of the court-martial, but he would not wait in the country for that. There was nothing he could do here to change the situation. He had left his report in writing but doubted it would be used. The attitude of the superior English officers instilled little confidence. His only recourse, besides prayer, was to get home and report to the Government. Maybe there, they could pull some strings.

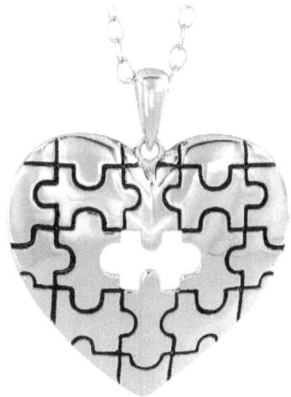

Chapter 20 Assembling the Jigsaw

*H*is cabin was more comfortable than he expected. Jonty would eat with the crew, and he was happy not to have to socialise with fancy dinners of a passenger ship or his security detail. He didn't even need to change for meals. His bunk was not as comfortable as the hotel, but better than on the trip out. As he returned to his bunk, he flopped down and relaxed. He was asleep within minutes. He had not prayed before sleeping other than shooting a prayer of thanks for his safety heavenward. He succumbed to a long deep slumber. He was safe, and he was at peace.

On waking, Jonty lay listening to the sounds of the ship. Much was going through his mind. The sounds reminded him of lying on the floor of a cabin with Will sitting and guarding him. It was the first lesson on deep prayer they had done. He had learned to do this well and discovered that he could pray even on horseback for the many miles they travelled. He could get into the zone quickly now. On this entire trip, he'd been at peace. Admittedly he'd been frustrated, but knowing that he was in God's care, he did not worry.

One of the things that sat on Jonty's mind was how all the people and actions over the past years had an association with the other. Jonty lay on his bunk and thought back over the people brought into his life. It started with his parents; through them, Richard Lamb became his boss, mentor, instructor, and friend. Through them also, he met and fell in love with Lottie. Jonty still found it hard to breathe when he thought of her. A tear slid down his cheek; he smiled as he wiped it away. She stirred emotions in him way beyond any he had ever felt before. He missed her so much. He thanked God for her daily; he relived the years and many fun times with her and their children.

He got up and went along to the galley for some food and to find a book. The crew were all busy, so he sat alone reading most of the day until after the main evening meal. After many hours on deck returned to his cabin, and his mind returned to his previous thoughts.

Soon after they married, they visited Harry Harlow and Jim Leslie. Together they taught Jonty how to deal with the horrific experiences he'd seen. Looking back, he knew it was his youth and his innocence that had caused his anxieties. Harry and Jim taught him to write everything down and list alternate possibilities. Jonty knew there was little he could have done differently. In every scenario, Nandi still died, and so did the villagers. Then later, on a trip to Melbourne, Will English taught him about deep prayer and opening your heart to God. Will had helped him through that next stage of releasing his worries to the Maker, and his life had never been the same. Nearly every night since he'd prayed. He no longer had nightmares, but it was a habit he had no intention of breaking if possible. His mind flicked back to their first night in the cottage when Will and Dimity visited and brought dinner. Then, on their Melbourne trip, Will introduced him to the artist Fred McCubbin. He laughed to think Jim Leslie knew him as a child in Melbourne. It was there that Jonty first saw Simon's skill as an artist. He had never forgotten that a child of just ten had done the works he'd most admired.

On return to Sydney, Jonty's nightmares had become violent; one night, in particular, he had scared Lottie. That was the night she told him she was probably having twins, yet what a blessing they had been. Sammo and Patty would turn nineteen next birthday. He had missed almost two years' worth of birthdays. He had missed so much of everything, but regretting anything was no use. He had had no choice but to go, so it was no use getting angry about any of it. Anger didn't help. He released a long sigh. He prayed for some time for each member of his wonderful family, then fell back to thinking.

Will's friendship had brought Fred, Tom, and Arthur into his life. He had taken them out to Emu Plains to meet Jim. He hadn't known why he felt he needed to take them, but Jim and Fred rekindled an old friendship. Yet it was Tom that benefitted most from that meeting. Jim's story had whetted his appetite to learn more about the Cobb and Co coaches. The artists eventually returned to Melbourne, then returned some three years later for a much longer stay. Out of that meeting with Jim grew Tom's fantastic painting, *Bailed Up*. Although he had painted that in Inverell after meeting another driver, he checked with Jim that the details were also right for his holdup. The painting was a blend of both. Tom also painted other amazing masterpieces on that trip. On the morning of Tom's return from Inverell, Simon discovered his parents were possibly dead, lost in a shipwreck. Life changed again. Jonty took the young man to live with them. He adored having him around; he was such an easy-going lad. He was halfway between son and friend. Simon was also going to be a business partner, but he didn't know that yet. Jonty smiled; he wondered what Simon would say when he heard Jonty's proposition.

Jonty was watching the electric lamp flicker as the ship traversed the waves. He wondered how they worked. He felt the sea growing and was content to stay on his bunk, thinking over the past and also reading. The light would get brighter, then dim again with each big wave. The steamer must have a problem with its alternator.

He lifted his arms and tucked his hands behind his head, and returned to his reverie. Like many other artists, Fred, Tom and Arthur had come and gone. He knew Will kept in contact with them, but he'd been busy. They remained friends but were not vital to his story. They had made many more artistic acquaintances, and Jonty had encouraged Simon to keep painting.

Simon had completed his apprenticeship as a jeweller with Jonty, and his skill as both a designer and craftsman grew. Then came Simon's trip to Cape Town to see if he could find Jurgen. He didn't, although he found other gem dealers and sent back a good supply of diamonds, Simon had then gone to Madagascar and found his mother. His unsettled feelings were correct, or as he now realised, they were a word of knowledge. He brought his mother back with him, and he then married Allie.

Jonty realised that they would be parents by now. He had not even thought of the child she was expecting. He should have been praying for it and for Allie, but his mind had been distracted. He shot them a prayer now. He thought as he had been gone for so long, she may even be expecting another one by now. He gave a half-laugh. Lottie had joked before he left that she was also feeling ill and maybe expecting, but they dismissed that. He chuckled again and thought how unlikely that would be. She would be forty-one now. It would be her birthday soon; he couldn't wait to enfold her in his arms and cradle her to him. With that thought, he decided to try and sleep again. He had a couple of weeks until he reached Fremantle and another couple of weeks until he was home. He spent some more time in prayer, then turned off the light, rolled onto his side, and slept dreamlessly.

~

Two and a half weeks later, they were drawing into the harbour in Fremantle. They were ahead of schedule, and Jonty was thrilled. They would be in Melbourne on Lottie's birthday, and he would wire her from there. He'd be home before Christmas. He sent a wire to the art school in Melbourne, hoping to meet up with Tom Roberts. He sent another to his family in Sydney from Fremantle. He was looking forward to catching up with Tom and hopefully others in Melbourne. Theo was now living in Castlereagh on Will and Dimity's farm. As Theo no longer had to work, he wanted to be closer to his father.

Jonty thought, hopefully, someone would be home to meet him. He chuckled to himself with that thought, knowing that the wharf was usually full of the family when any member returned.

The passage to Melbourne was rough, so meals were basic but filling. Jonty remained in his cabin reading most of the trip due to the waves crashing over the bow. There was not much else to do. Thankfully there was a decent library in the dining room. He had found a copy of the next HG Wells novel, *The War of the Worlds,* when in Fremantle and grabbed it. Sadly he'd finished it. He had loved *The Time Machine* that was in the ship's library and couldn't believe it when he saw another one by the same writer. When he finished it, he added it to the ship's library and started on the fattest book he could find.

Nights were merging into days, and the flickering light was frustrating, but it never died. He was anxious to arrive in Port Philip Bay. He was now reading *War and Peace* and was desperate to finish it before he docked in Melbourne. At least it passed the time.

Days passed, and Jonty read on. A shaft of sunlight slid over the last page of the book. Jonty sighed and slammed the cover shut. He sighed again; he'd finished it. He'd been so engrossed in the book that he had not even noticed that the seas were now calm. He checked his watch and saw it was mid-morning. He had not dressed for two days as a meal tray had been brought to his cabin. Chuckling at his laziness, he roused himself, and an hour later, he emerged from his room to see where they were. He saw they were about to enter the mouth of Port Philip Bay. The pilot boat had just pulled away after delivering the pilot to guide the ship through the shallows. He didn't realise how close they were. He wasn't even packed. He was leaving the vessel and catching the coastal steamer up to Sydney the next day. He knew they would be docking in less than an hour, so he quickly darted downstairs, sorted his things, and packed.

He pulled on the trousers with the gems and packed everything else. He had just clipped up his bags when he realised he had accidentally packed *War and Peace* instead of returning it to the ship's library. He dug into his bag and pulled it out. He looked around the cabin and saw he'd forgotten to pack his Bible next to his bed; he tucked it into the bag. He'd not be sad to leave the small room. After rechecking everything, including under the bunk, he left with the library book under his arm. By the time he made it on deck, they were being tugged into the dock.

Tom Roberts was waiting for him with a lady and a small child by his side. He waved and waited. Jonty was able to disembark quickly. He carried his own bags as there were no porters on board. Tom greeted him.

Jonty noticed some brown paint on his cheek. Tom introduced Jonty to his wife, Lillie, and their son Caleb; then he grabbed a bag from Jonty. Lillie walked in front of them, Jonty waited until she and Caleb were some distance in front of them before saying, "Oh Tom, it's so good to see you, but I didn't know you were married, let alone had a child."

Tom grinned. "Seems the news channels were a little slow. We've been married for four years, Jon. What are you doing on a ship from Africa?

Been buying gems again?"

Jonty shook his head. "Ahh, not exactly, Tom; I'll tell you later." They chattered about the sea trip until they were out of earshot of the crew. Jonty then filled him in a bit about his journey. "I've been gone far too long, and because they kept me under protective guard, I was virtually not only a prisoner but frustrated and useless. It wasn't until I was *en route* to Fort Edward that I was finally contacted and used to pass on a message to an English General." Jonty then spoke about Harry Morant. "Tom, I think you met him out at Jim Leslie's place, didn't you?"

"Yes, he is a fabulous horseman. Harry Harlow sent us chasing some greased piglets through his orchard, stupidly dangerous but great fun. His poet friends Banjo and Henry were with him that trip." Tom smiled knowingly. "None of us caught the darned pigs either." Tom's laugh made Jonty smile; he'd done that activity a few times himself. None of his cousins had caught the piglets either.

On arrival at Tom and Lillie's house, Jonty settled into his room next to Tom's studio. As they passed a door, Tom quietly shut it. "What are you doing, Tom? A secret? It looks huge," Jonty asked.

Tom gave a huge resigned sigh. "It's nearly killing me, Jon; my eyes burn as I paint the fine details. And yes, it's huge, but it's a commission, and I'm being paid to do it, and it will be good, I'm determined to finish it, but I'm finding it hard to see."

Jonty placed his things on the bed and followed Tom into the studio. He had already seen the colossal canvas leaning against the wall.

Tom's sigh had been of frustration. "It's too big for an easel, so I paint it here. It's back-breaking work. It's one-hundred and nineteen inches by two-hundred inches. I'm determined to get every face right and their position on the day."

As they stood looking at the partially finished work, Jonty could see his Uncle Charlie in the group of completed faces. He chuckled. "One face I know well; why did you do him first, Tom?"

"Well, he was there, and I know him. Look, that's your Aunt Gracie too; that was nearly a year ago, Jonty. I hear Charlie is not too well now. I heard that his eldest son, Teddy, has come from England; at least, that's what Will said in his letter last month." Tom filled Jonty in on what he'd heard from Will. "Jon, Harry Harlow is gone. Jim found him; Harry died out in his orchard. A brown snake bit him. He was already dead when they found him. The snake was curled up next to him. Harry was eighty-eight; he refused ever to be old. He was out pruning his beloved orange trees. I went up for his funeral six months ago to support Jim."

Jonty sat catching up with what had occurred in his absence. He was sad that his Uncle was ill, but at eighty-one, he wasn't looking too well when he saw him last. He was surprised he was still alive. Uncle Eddie and Aunt

Jenna seemed ageless, but to know Uncle Harry Harlow was gone was sad. He'd been such an incredible help when he was going through his nightmares after that first trip. Even Uncle Luke looked old when he left.

They talked in the studio for hours. Tom added a few more faces to the ghostly headless bodies. Jonty was intrigued that each person was identifiable as whom they were supposed to be. Tom handed him a journal; it listed everyone in the official party, all two-hundred and fifty of them, what each was wearing and where they were standing. Each had a number next to them. "Are you going to paint every single one of them, Tom?" Jonty was stunned. "It's no wonder your eyes are failing with this."

"Yes, Jon, every one of them, it's a 'me' thing! I was commissioned to record the opening of our first Parliament, so I will make it one they will never forget." Tom stood back and looked at what he'd just painted. "I'm just calling it *The Big Picture*," he smirked. "Appropriate, eh? Well, it is big."

"Yes, Tom, um, you could certainly say that." The immense work before them certainly was huge. "What size did you say it was, sixteen foot by nine?"

"Yes, plus a bit; I would have made it bigger but couldn't get a larger canvas. So this will have to do." Tom started another figure;

Jonty could tell this one would be a judge. The Cardinal had been done, as had the clergy around him. Tom painstakingly turned the long ghost-like blobs into recognisable people.

"I want to go home again, Jon," Tom said out of the blue.

"Isn't this home, Tom?" Jonty asked.

"No, I want to go home again to England. I only stayed to finish this. Lillie is keen too, but don't say anything to anyone yet. I'll let the others know before we leave, but I may not see you again, Jon. At least, not this side of heaven, unless you come to see us in England." Tom sighed and stretched. "It's why I'm hastening to get this finished. Then we'll leave."

Jonty didn't know what to say, so said nothing but, "Oh."

The following morning Jonty said his farewells to Lillie and Caleb.

Tom took him back to the dock, where he boarded the ship, the *Gabo*.

Jonty wanted to catch up with a few other artists, but Tom explained that they were all painting in the country. Tom had wanted to be with them but needed to get stuck into the big picture. Last night, after the light faded, Tom had also shown Jonty his new project, and that was all the moulds for making decorative picture frames. Tom explained the process, "All these are then painted, and then gold-leafed or just gilded. I couldn't afford to buy frames and decided to learn to make them. Since I started, I have been taking commissions. I have already made the one for the big picture. I make more from these than the art. It pays the rent and keeps food on the table for my family." Tom looked almost guilty.

Jonty suggested that Tom return to work rather than wait until the ship sailed.

Tom laughed and said he needed the sunshine on his face. They booked Jonty in, viewed his cabin, found the dining room, and then had a mug of tea in the galley.

Captain Leslie walked through an hour later and gave them a thirty-minute-to-departure notification.

They repeated their farewells, and Tom took his leave.

Jonty waited at the rails until the ship was out of the bay. It should only take a few days until he was home. He was looking forward to changing his trousers as they really needed a wash. However, he dared not take them off as the gems were still sewn into the pockets.

Three days! Then he'd have Lottie in his arms again. He smiled, looking forward to her private welcome. He wished to see his children, but it was Lottie he was pining for.

~

The nautical miles passed quickly.

The sea had calmed, and the steamer almost charged through the waves. Tom said he would send a message for his estimated arrival time. At this rate, they would get in early. The wind and sea were behind them, and they were powering along. As they had cut nearly a day off the expected run, they turned in through Sydney heads a day early, the morning of November 25. He would be home earlier than his wire said and after just a few days after Lottie's birthday.

As they pulled into Circular Quay, the wharf was deserted. No welcoming party, not even Lottie. He shouldn't have been surprised, but normally one of the lighthouses would have wired in the information.

Jonty then noticed all the flags through town at half-mast and wondered which dignitary had died. He collected his bags and thanked Captain Leslie as he walked down the gangplank. He noticed a carriage waiting at the quay, which was unusual considering the ship was early. He was the only passenger, so it wasn't as if it was waiting for a fare. As he walked closer, he noticed it was a Government House one. He was about to walk past when the driver spoke to him.

"Mr Jonathon Evans, I presume?" The livery-clad driver asked. He opened the carriage door for him.

"Um, yes, I'm just heading home." Jonty looked puzzled.

"Yes, sir, I'm here to collect you, then take you to Government House." The driver brooked no argument, so rather than walk up the hill with his bags, Jonty hopped inside. He lay back on the comfortable squab seats.

Arrival at his house was a shock. It was locked up, and the knocker was wrapped in black. The curtains were drawn, as were the houses on either side of his. Their knockers were also covered in black. Someone had undoubtedly died, and it was probably someone in the family; he wondered who. He had no key, so he motioned for the driver to drive on. He may as well get the official duties over first, but he wished he had been able to see Lottie. He presumed Beauchamp was still at Government House. He had not probed Tom for details.

He was greeted by the Government Aide he had met on that day in the jewellery store. It seemed so long ago now. The man welcomed Jonty still without giving his name. He reached in and took his bags. "Good afternoon, sir; your timing is good as we are about to depart. Please come inside; Mister Barton is waiting for you in the red drawing room."

Jonty was ushered into the foyer. The aide placed his bags just inside the front door. Jonty thought this was a little strange but remained silent.

A debonair but unknown gentleman welcomed Jonty. He was slightly taller than he was, with wavy hair and a kindly face that he instantly trusted. He expected to be pumped for information about his journey. Jonty noticed the look on his face was compassionate rather than inquisition, which surprised him.

The man's first words were not what Jonty expected. "I'm sorry, Mr Evans, but I have some sad news for you; I am about to leave and hope you will accompany me. I had received word you were coming in this morning, or I would have left already." The man had a pleasant, well-modulated, comforting voice, but Jonty had no idea what he was talking about.

Jonty shuffled in his seat. "Accompany you where, sir? And may I ask, who are you?" It sounded quite rude, but he had no idea who this man was. "I have been out of the country and out of communication for over eighteen months. Although the aide gave me your name, he did not give any title or position. Are you the Governor's representative? Or has Beauchamp left?"

The nice man smiled. "Ahh, I'm sorry I should explain; firstly, we currently don't have a Governor, the previous one, Beauchamp, retired in April. Secondly, I'm the first Prime Minister; Edmond Barton is the name. But your uncles all call me Toby."

Jonty smiled but just said, "Oh!"

Tom had told him about the first Parliament opening, but he had not thought about who the Prime Minister was or that there would be no other place for him to live but here.

"Mr Evans, Jonty, I'm sad to tell you that we're just heading to your uncle's funeral." He heard Jonty give a gasp but continued with his explanation. "Lord Charles, your Uncle Charlie, died two days ago, and his funeral is on this afternoon. I've included you in our party to go out there if that is suitable?" He saw the shattered look on Jonty's face and was moved by compassion. He knew this would have been a huge shock.

Jonty teared up, "Uncle Charlie is gone? He's really dead?" Tom had warned him, but the shock he felt was gut-wrenching. Uncle Charlie had died while Jonty was *en route* to Sydney. He was too late to see him. Jonty was pleased he was sitting down. The Prime Minster gave him a few minutes to regather himself. "So, that's where everyone was and why the knocker is swathed; they will all be in Parramatta." He said to himself but voiced his comments aloud. He supposed he should offer the man congratulations, but that moment had passed.

"Yes, they have all been there for a few days. Charlie's passing was expected, so all the family were with him. I summoned all the family from England about three months ago and Emu Plains a week ago. I believe Ed was with him at the end. He would not leave his brother's side. When your wire came through, I had it sent here. Luke had told me you were expected, so I had the Post Master redirect your mail. The family have been out there for some weeks, so they don't know you're coming."

Jonty nodded; he was struck dumb. This is not the welcome he expected. He knew that it was his Aunt Gracie who was the one who needed care now.

The man continued, "Are you willing to come with me, and we can talk *en route*?" The Prime Minister rose and waited for Jonty to join him.

An idea suddenly struck Jonty, "Are my wife and children otherwise well?" He at least wanted to know if his family were safe.

"Yes, they are all fine. You'll see them all soon enough, now we must go, or we'll be late. We'll be travelling in the Government Carriage. There will be a bit of a convoy, but most of them will have left already. I'll drop you off at your father-in-law's house. But if you're happy, we can discuss your trip on the way. You can tell me what you've been doing for the last eighteen months. And Jonty, call me Toby; we're nearly the same age. I could use a friendly ear close by."

Jonty nodded; the lump in his throat stopped him from speaking. He followed the Prime Minister out of the room, still stunned at the request. He was just a jeweller.

For the next hour, they talked. Toby asked question after question, and Jonty answered them as factually as possible. There was little of importance to relate until Jonty got to Harry and Peter. Jonty's ire got the better of him.

Toby turned his full attention to this part of the conversation. The entire situation was news to the Prime Minister. "Jonty, I need to know exactly what was said. Word for word if you can remember. I have heard nothing about this situation. I should have been notified by both England and the officials in Pretoria. I will see what I can do." Toby gave Jonty some hope to get Harry and Peter home.

Jonty told him about every conversation he had had with Harry, especially the one where he'd told him of the order from Kitchener to Captain Percy Hunt to take no prisoners. Their conversation became quite animated. Jonty was upset as he knew Harry was only following orders.

By the time they were arriving in Parramatta, the Prime Minister was fully aware of the outline of the situation. He would send a message as soon as he could. He was more than annoyed that he had not been told.

Over the past year, the lines of political correctness had been blurred. Was England or Australia responsible for these men?

Jonty knew Toby would do everything possible to bring Harry Morant and Peter Handcock home, even if he had to incarcerate them here.

Now that Toby had heard the story from Jonty, he knew that whatever he would be told officially would be vastly different, even to the point of denying the order issued by Kitchener. "Leave this with me, Jonty; I shall do my darndest to bring them back. They are Australians, so we'll bring them home."

Chapter 21 Journey's End

$\mathcal{T}$he Prime Minister's carriage stopped at Luke's house and waited to see if the family was there.

Jonty's Aunt Moira opened the door. She was shrouded in black and had been weeping. "Jonty," she squealed with undignified excitement. "You're back. Oh, my darling Jon, you are so welcome." It was only then she looked up and saw the official carriage in the street. "Ooh, Jon, who have you brought?"

Luke heard the voices at the door. The knocker was swathed, so he wasn't expecting visitors. In his own sadness, he really didn't feel like entertaining, but he stuck his head around the door when he heard a familiar laugh. "Welcome home, Jon; you came with the Prime Minister? Bring him in," Luke said as he greeted his son-in-law. "I was not expecting you until tomorrow. I'm so glad you are here, though; you would be the only one who would have been missing."

"Hello, Uncle Luke; please accept my deepest condolences."

Luke nodded.

Jonty explained the obvious, "I came with the government convoy. May I ask Toby in? We're a bit early for the service; Toby said three o'clock?" Jonty turned back to the carriage, and a well-dressed gentleman followed him back to the house.

Luke waited for his young friend. He greeted him, "Hello Toby, come in and make yourself at home." Luke was about to usher him into the sitting room when Toby asked Luke to use the facilities.

While Luke was busy with his visitor, Jonty was about to bound upstairs to his usual room when Lottie appeared from the downstairs apartment.

"Jon Jon, oh my darling Jon, you are back." She was in his arms and in tears. She had heard his voice and was unbelieving that he had arrived back.

Jonty asked where they were sleeping and when he found they were in the apartment downstairs, they walked down the internal staircase hand in hand.

Soon he was surrounded by his children. Carol had a small child in her arms. One he had not seen before. Without removing Lottie from under his protection, Jonty greeted Sammo, Patty, Paul, and Carol, mussing up the boy's immaculately combed hair.

They each chuckled.

He tickled the small child under his chin. "And who might you be, young sir?"

Lottie moved from his side and put her arms out for the lad. The shy child reached for her and said questioningly, "Mama?"

Jonty looked stunned, then shifted his gaze from her face to the child's cherubic one. Jonty's eyes grew as big as saucers; he looked at his wife's smiling face again, then his older children. "He's ours?" He was stunned.

"Jonathon Charles, this is Papa. He's back from his travels." Lottie cuddled the young boy as he snuggled to her neck, thumb firmly in his mouth.

At first, the little boy hid his face, then greeted Jonty with a toothy grin and his blue eyes wide open. "Papa?"

"Yes, apparently, I'm your Papa, and I'm home." The small boy put out his trusting arms to Jonty, and he took his unexpected son in his arms.

"Why didn't you write, Lotts? Why didn't you tell me?" Jonty asked softly so as not to scare the child, now snuggled to his neck. Small arms locked possessively.

The child was breathing in his scent.

Lottie snuggled up to him again under his empty arm. "Remember I was feeling ill just before you left? It took some weeks after you had gone before I realised I was nearly five months gone with child. As Carol was twelve, it honestly never occurred to me. By the time I realised, you were already in Africa and telling you was impossible. Remember, I did not have an address, and we've only had two letters from you." Lottie looked at her husband adoringly. "Do you mind?"

"Two letters! I must have written fifty." He bent and kissed Lottie again. "But, mind? Why no, absolutely not; I'm just stunned, that's all. What's he named?"

"I'se Sharles!" he said with a cute lisp while still clinging tightly to his father.

"Sharles, eh? Or do you mean Charles?" Jonty teased his son.

The little boy nodded, then leaned back to look at his father. "Swot I says, I'se Sharles!" he said indignantly.

Jonty swung around with little Charles in his arms and made him giggle. Their bond sealed, the child clung like a limpet, laughing. Jonty felt his heart leap. What a welcome home!

He shooed out the children from their bedroom, reluctantly handing his new son to his youngest daughter again. His oldest boys had already fixed their hair. "I must change," he said as they left. They waited until the door closed behind the departing young one before Jonty took Lottie in his arms and kissed her as he wished. More would have to wait until later. He thankfully still had some decent clothes they kept at Parramatta. Lottie had pulled his suit from their wardrobe while talking to the children. He changed quickly and was soon ready for the funeral. There would be much catching up to be had later on, but now the service was about to start.

Jonty insisted on carrying his little boy as often as possible; little Charles was delighted.

Lottie was almost bounding beside him; she was thrilled he was home.

Luke had spent some time with Toby before he said farewell and departed for the church, telling Luke he'd meet them there. Now was family time. They would all be sitting near the front, and as he'd been invited to the tea on the lawn of Eddie's house, Bramblemere Close, he'd see them there.

Toby left in his carriage. His entourage had already gone.

The family filled more than a quarter of the church. All sat in pews reserved for them. Simon, an expectant Allie, a small child, and Elise were surprised when Jonty walked in with Lottie. Jonty gently squeezed Simon's shoulder as he walked down the aisle and heard Simon gasp.

Jonty smiled at many of the family he had not seen for nearly two years. They had come from all over the world. He knew the new Earl, Teddy, and Bella had arrived with all their seven children, their spouses and grandchildren, from England in time to spend some time with his father. They had come with Eddie's children, Kit and Tina, and their families. They had been able to spend some weeks with Charlie before he died. Each took turns reading to him or reminiscing about their wonderful times together. Wills and Cathy's children had arrived from all the different Emporiums, as had all the Harlows and Leslies from their farms.

All had known Charlie's time was short. He had been failing for some time; he held on as long as he could. Charlie and Gracie celebrated their fifty-ninth wedding anniversary with their children only weeks before his passing. Charlie had rallied and enjoyed his time seeing all his extended family.

Jonty had not seen Chip, the Duke of Gracemere, for some time and was amazed at just how much he now looked like his father. Jonty had stayed with them in Kent for some months, both before and after his training. He had only seen some of the cousins a few times since.

Now fifty-nine, the Duke and Duchess had grown into their exalted roles as Uncle Charlie had done as the Earl. Both men had reluctantly accepted their roles and titles.

As was typical of Chip and Tina, they had arrived at the church early so as not to draw attention to themselves rather than the grieving family, so they were sitting inside in Ed's pew with bowed heads before others entered. Jonty knew he'd have a chance to see them later at Uncle Eddie's, if not before. He knew they would stay here for some months.

The funeral started.

Jonty could not take his eyes off the coffin that sat in front of him. He hated death. He felt he had avoided it twice now.

The service and eulogies were moving. There was some laughter and many tears. So much about Charlie's life was finally revealed to the listening multitude. Jonty knew a lot about his uncle's adult life, but he had not known about the traumas of his early years. It was only hinted at, but Jonty read between the words. Not much was mentioned except that he'd battled the repercussions all his life. Jonty grasped some of his history, but Eddie had not revealed much, just enough for Jonty to know that only part of the story was being told. There were innuendos of abuse to his uncle, and the repercussions had lasted all his life. Jonty would ask Uncle Luke now that Charlie was gone; he was sure he would now reveal what he knew. It explained much about his uncle and his willingness to assist the vulnerable.

Jonty had been fourteen when the previous Earl, Lottie's Grandfather, also named Charles, had died. The town had stopped for his funeral, and the church had been packed to overflowing. Uncle Charlie's funeral was even bigger. So many had arrived from Sydney that all accommodation in town was fully booked. For a man who hated the limelight, Uncle Charlie had every dignitary and clergyman in the colony turn out for his funeral. Every bishop was there, as was the head of every other denomination, and many of them partook in the service. The Archbishop, The Most Reverend Saumarez Smith, led the proceedings. All the heads of the various churches were there; some did readings, and some prayed. In the congregation were reformed drunks and laze-abouts who had cleaned up their lives thanks to Uncle Charlie's influence. They had come under the Earl's Shadow. No one was ever turned away from his door. He'd helped so many that only the Lord knew the number. He had inherited not only the official title from his father but also the honorary one. *The Earl's Shadow* was a title that the previous Earl had been reluctant to own, but it was well earned. Charlie had followed in his footsteps and done justice to it. It covered all those who had come to the two men for assistance. Both Earl's had generously aided where they could.

When Charlie was born, his parents were convicts. So, he was just a convict's son for his first twenty years. He grew up in a lowly inn and worked hard all his life. Then thanks to Chip's father, Duke Ned, they all discovered that Charlie's parents were, in reality, the Earl and Countess of Coxheath, and none of them had ever known. One thing led to another, and their convictions were quashed. Both had always pleaded innocence, and once their cases were investigated, both accusers withdrew the charges. Charlie had kept up the unofficial charity work his parents had started, and it was how the term, *The Earl's Shadow,* had come about. Charlie followed his father's example. Many others had since come under his shadow over the decades. Now both men had gone. The shadow may well fragment, but it would continue and be passed down through the generations. John Lockley had already continued his work.

The service was soon over, the funeral cortège left the church, and the residents of Parramatta stood in silence with their hats off and heads bowed some fifteen deep along the entire route to the cemetery.

Gracie and the older family travelled in the Government carriage with Toby and two of Jim Leslie's big carriages. All were swathed in black and travelled at a walking pace. The sand-covered cobbled roadway muffled the carriage noises as they passed through the avenue of the silent mourning throng. All the younger family walked in silence behind the hearse, and hundreds, if not thousands, of the community, stood to attention as the flag-draped coffin passed. Many mourners threw flowers onto the flatbed wagon, and soon, the flowers surrounded the coffin and nearly hid the flag. Many townspeople fell in behind the cortège as it slowly plodded uphill. The only sound was the muffled clip-clop of the many horses' hoofs. There was not a shout or a jeer. As the procession reached the cemetery gates, the crowd finally erupted into applause of appreciation for what Charlie had done for them all.

Luke took little Charles with him in the carriage; he had fallen asleep in the church in Jonty's arms. He had not let go of his Papa since they left for the service. Jonty was still in awe that he had a son he didn't even know about. He reluctantly handed the sleeping child to his father-in-law and followed on foot.

Children usually didn't attend funerals, but that was not what Charlie had wanted. He had also mentioned no black, but Gracie overruled him in that. Even so, this was to be a time of family celebration, celebrating his life. Charlie had not been scared of dying. He knew Heaven awaited him, and he looked forward to going there. His father, Charles, had a near-death experience over thirty years before when a snake had bitten him. Eventually, he talked to all the family about this incident. It had taken Lord Charles some years to fully process what had happened, but he never feared death. From that day onwards, Charlie believed every word and went to his next life with a smile. His faith had stayed strong all his life; he had shared this with his family many times.

So this day was to be a family affair and one of joy. Charlie had been determined that everyone should hear his words, so they were repeated. "You may hear that I am dead, but I shall be more alive than ever. I shall be in Heaven with our Lord. Do not grieve for me; grieve only for your loss. We shall be reunited again. Celebrate with me, for I am now healed." The Archbishop had started the funeral with these words of Charlie's, and he now repeated them at the graveside.

The words stayed with Jonty all day. He liked them and realised just how true they were.

Jonty had once again taken his young son in his arms. Gracie alighted from their carriage, assisted by Luke and her sister, Ellen. Eddie and Jenna were close by, and the other older family members stood nearby. An occasional tear would escape, but her stoic forbearance and beatific smile gave others confidence that she was all right.

As Jonty had claimed little Charles from the carriage, Gracie had stroked Jonty's cheek and welcomed him home. Her strength nearly made Jonty weep. He had forgotten just how strong her faith was. Of all the family, Aunt Gracie had always been the quiet achiever, yet she was the strength behind Uncle Charlie. Jonty had seen the many times that Charlie had turned to her for her contribution on some topic. He would always take her counsel, for he trusted her.

Now, holding the sleeping child in his arms, Jonty bent and kissed her before she walked to the open graveside. He looked down at the child in his arms; little Charles was his great uncle's namesake and his son's great-grandfather.

Lottie stood behind her grandparents' gravestones, resting a hand on their headstone. Jonty walked to her side. Jonty's best friend and cousin, Rick, his wife, Mary Louise, his sister, Bette and her husband, Edward, all stood next to Jack Princhester's headstone. Other family members stood behind them.

Jack was the benefactor of Princhester Court, the house now occupied by Teddy and Bella, as the principal seat of the Earls of Coxheath. Jack had died twenty-one years before, in 1880, as an unknown swagman who had befriended Rick. Before his funeral, a letter revealed him to be Sir John Princhester, Baron, and he bequeathed everything he owned to Rick and Mary Louise, who had taken him in and loved him for whom they thought him to be, just an unknown swagman, nothing more, nothing less.

Uncle Charlie was to be laid in a deep grave next to Jack. Gracie knew that one day she would join him. Other sites in the row were reserved but vacant, and he knew they had been saved for family. Jonty thought that he might one day lie there with Lottie. With that thought, he drew her close.

The Archbishop hushed the multitude spread amongst the graveyard and said the committal prayers. The coffin was lowered into the hole. Eddie's and Charlie's sons were the pallbearers. As he finished, Gracie bent and grabbed a handful of dirt and threw it in, followed by a single wild daisy; then she turned and walked away. The crowd parted as she walked through without pausing. Only then did she weep. She stopped beside her parent's grave a few rows back and sank onto the stone covering. Ellen and her two brothers, Tim and Sam, joined her, and they wept for time passed.

Bill and Molly Miller had died within weeks of each other, neither wishing to go on without the other. They had lived with Luke and Ellen since soon after their wedding when Ellen had fallen with child and had triplets. All hands were needed, and Molly had been delighted. Jenna, Vicky and Cathy's parents, Jack and Martha Turner, had done much the same, dying only months apart some fifteen years before. They were buried at Emu Plains in the cemetery adjoining St Paul's church.

Gracie's brother, Tim, had married Anna Lockley, the youngest sister. Bert Ellis had married the elder sister, Liza Lockley, so the three families were tightly enmeshed. Sam Miller, Gracie's younger brother, had married Bert's sister Isabelle.

Wills, Luke and Eddie watched from a short distance in case needed, but the ladies required time to process the loss. They all did.

Eddie had protected Charlie where he could. He'd done it all his life. Even at eighty, he looked after him. With only eleven months between the two boys, they had been close. Everything in life they did together where possible; now Charlie was gone. Ed now stood with his back to the crowd. Jenna saw his shoulders shake and knew he was intensely feeling his oldest brother's loss. She quietly walked to him and slipped her hand into his. It was not enough; he enfolded her and sobbed. Not caring who saw them. "He's gone, Jen!" His heart felt like it was breaking. "He's always been there for me, and now he's gone."

She knew his pain. She'd lost both parents too, and her oldest brothers, Marc and Alex. Ed had been her rock back then, as he always was. She said the words but knew they could not remove his pain. "And he is at peace, Ed, out of pain, and it is only our loss we need to deal with, our loneliness and our sadness. Do you remember what your mother told us? We grieve because we love; there is no grief without love. Your grandmother said that to your mother shortly before she died. She had just lost Grandfather Richard. They were some of the last words your grandmother said before she passed. I've never forgotten them, Ed." Releasing him a little, she snuggled under his arm and looked up at her husband of sixty years. "Ed, look around us; all these hundreds of family members love Christ because of the example your parents set. I have loved being part of this family, my darling man. Let's now go to Gracie; we have to be her support at this time too."

He nodded, sniffed and blew his nose.

Jenna had rarely seen him so broken, not even when his parents died.

They rejoined Gracie, and the three walked back to the carriages with Luke and Ellen following, Wills and Cathy a short distance behind. When they all left, everyone else would follow. The carriages hid them from the gathered crowd.

The afternoon was spent in respectful remembrance of Charlie's life. The laughs of the children brought happiness to all. But the joy was already beginning to return to the sombre gathering.

Jonty was never far from little Charles. Although he could both walk and run, the lad was content to cling tightly to his newfound Papa.

It took some time before Jonty was able to see his own parents. They had hung back, allowing him time to meet with others. When he was finally enfolded in his mother's arms, he greeted them with complete attention. While little Charles was being fed, his mother welcomed him home with a bear hug and a caress of his cheek. His father shook his hand and then also drew him into a loving bear hug.

Within a short time, he was the centre of attention relating the happenings of the past months. He told of the passage over, the trek and the eternal waiting; he left out any reference to the gems or the main meeting but did relate the two incidents with Chimbu. He had forgotten that most did not know of his adopted pet. Once that was revealed, he was pumped for information about the great golden lion. The unusual story caught the attention of many.

While telling this story, young Charles was back in his arms and Lottie by his side. She had known about the cub and Jonty's attachment to it. To hear that the beast had returned and remembered Jonty was a delight. She had not realised lions lived that long.

Toby was sitting, listening to the stories from a distance. He so wished his wife Jeanie and his children could meet this amazing family. Hopefully, at least, they could get to know Jonty and Lottie as friends. Jonty had not mentioned the lion to him but had told him more important things than he was relating to the family.

The Prime Minister caught Jonty's eye across the crowd and smiled. He knew now why this man had been summonsed to Africa; he knew how to keep his mouth shut. "Yes, this man can be trusted," he thought to himself. This jeweller was a rare man, one of great faith and absolutely trustworthy. Charlie had recommended that he was a man Toby should befriend. Any conversation would remain between them only. He released a sigh. He, too, gave thanks for the return of this young man. Well, not very young, as Charlie had told him Jonty was a mere seven years younger than he was. Yes, he would encourage friendship.

Once Jonty felt he'd satisfied the curiosity of the majority of the family, he suggested they disperse and talk to the rest of the assembled group. Time was short, and he had others he needed to see. Jim Leslie was one of those people, and he also wished to see Aunt Vicky and offer his condolences. He found her first sitting off to one side, with some of her children around her. Her twin grandsons, Jack and Timmy, were sitting on either side of her. She was in deep discussion with them, and Jonty caught the words 'marriage and commitment.' At thirty-three, the twin boys were both unmarried.

Jonty watched on as two obviously expectant ladies walked to the small group. Lottie's cousins, Sarah and Vicks, were the younger sisters to the twins; they had grown up and married in his absence. He smiled as he acknowledged them.

Lottie, still beside him, spoke softly, explaining what he was watching. "Aunt Vicky is giving both boys a good roasting, Jon. They are courting and have been for years, but neither will commit. The poor girls are sisters, Felicity and Phillipa Albert. Their great-grandfather James ran the Woolpack Inn. Do you remember the stories of Perry and Katy White?" She saw Jonty's confusion.

"Eh? White, any relation to Annie and Sam?" Jonty asked.

"Yes, they are cousins. Perry's father, Percival, inherited the Dukedom from Lady Mari's father, the bad Duke Julian when he died."

"Thought so! But that was generations ago. Hey, that makes them related to Uncle Edward and Jax." Jonty grinned, proud that he had worked out that. He knew that Sam's wife, Annie was Lady Mari's daughter.

"Yes, anyway, Katy was assigned to James Albert in 1814. Perry and Katy were friends with Uncle Ned before he came, and Grandfather Charles was assigned to him in 1820. Anyway, now they wish to marry the twins, of course. I think with Uncle Charlie now gone, they may settle down. At least, they will if Aunt Vicky has anything to do with it." Lottie had noticed his gaze and filled him in. "Sarah and Vicks married in a double service earlier this year. Sarah married Uncle Nick Turner's son John, and Vicky married Uncle Fergus Macdonald's son Lachlan; he's twelve years older than her but a real love match. Look!"

John and Lachlan walked up to their respective wives and stood behind them. Each placed a protective hand on the small of their backs. Both wives leaned into the loving embraces, and the men slid their arms around them, drawing them close.

Jonty smiled. His eyes flicked over various family members, and Lottie filled him in on each one. "Jon Jon, you heard about Uncle Harry's passing?" she asked gently.

"Yes, Toby told me. How's Aunt Vicky coping? I'm waiting to speak to her." Jonty saw others drawing near.

"She's doing amazingly well. Somehow, I think she knew his end was coming, but it was still a shock for us all. Not that she knew about the snake, of course, but she said he was getting very vague. At least this way, he didn't suffer the disease of the very elderly. He always said he wanted to die with his boots on; well, he did. She said he was getting very forgetful, not remembering that they lived in Australia and not England. Jim and Conny have been a godsend, knowing she's not totally alone out there. Jim's getting too old now for the horses, and the demand is slowing anyway, so he's not taken more in. Once this last lot is gone, Jim will concentrate on his carriage repairs. These new-fangled vehicles will become the way of transport soon. Have you seen one yet?" Lottie enquired.

"Seen what, Lotts?" Jonty asked, puzzled.

She explained. "A motor vehicle, they don't use horses and make a lot of noise. There is one in Sydney that they call a horseless carriage. Father even came to town and had a look, then insisted Jim see it too. It's something called a De Dion Bouton, and it's noisy and smelly. Now Jim says that soon everyone will have them." Lottie gave a resigned sigh.

Jonty shook his head. "Neither seen nor heard of them, Lotts." His eyes then wandered over to Jenna and Eddie. "Look at them; they have all ten children around them for the first time in a long time, and how many grandchildren and great-grandchildren are here now?"

Lottie chuckled. "Aunt Jenna worked out that they have over eighty children and grandchildren, including in-laws, and that they are all here together today. She's arranged that they even get a photograph. They have four more great-grandchildren on the way and have heaps of those already. Thea and Jax are expecting again. They, by the way, are delightfully happy. Thea loves living in *Rockley* as they renamed *Rock Cottage*. Look at the smiles on their faces. Sadly, Uncle Ed and Aunt Jenna have had so little chance to be with Kit and Tina's children; it's nice that one now lives back here. It's been great for Thea too. Ed and Jenna are frequently there babysitting."

They stood watching their Aunt and Uncle surrounded by almost a hundred blonde or light brown heads. Lottie continued, "They even have great, great, grandchildren now too. Uncle Charlie's grandson, Teddy's son, Charles Edward, oh, he's known as Chad, by the way; married Uncle Harry's great-niece Rosemarie, but she's called Rose, so they are keeping it in the family. They own the small baby. He was born shortly before they left England. If he'd come on time, they probably wouldn't have been able to come. He was a twin, but the little girl, Alexandrine Sarah, named after Aunt Vicky and Uncle Harry's daughter, never breathed. I wonder if Uncle Ed and Aunt Jenna will return with them, I wouldn't put it past them, you know. It's only a six-week trip now." Lottie snuggled closer. "One day, that will be us, Jon Jon. Only we have five angels, not ten."

Jonty turned to look down at her; he gently lifted her chin with a cocked finger and kissed her lovingly. "Gosh, Lotts," he said. She was his heart, his reason to breathe; she was his everything. He caressed her cheek with his thumb. "You have no idea how much I love you, you know. To be home and have you beside me makes my life complete. I know what Aunt

Gracie is going through is yet to come to us but hopefully not for many years. However, I have no desire even to contemplate that. I can't breathe even when I think of it." He kissed her gently again, not caring who saw. They were nearly all family.

"Enough of that, you two!" Carlo arrived with a lady whom Jonty did not recognise. "Hey, Jon, you have not met my wife, have you? Ruby love, this is your brother-in-law, Jonathon Evans, commonly known as Jonty. Jon, Ruby finally hooked me with the net, line, sinker, and entire boat. I fell for her hard, just like you two." Carlo had often teased Jon over the years about his affection for his sister.

"You're kidding, aren't you? Congratulations, Carlo, but I commiserate with you, Ruby." Jonty chuckled at her smiling face. "Welcome to the 'hanger-oners' club, Ruby. Have you worked out who everyone is yet?"

She chuckled at the family term for in-laws. "No, Jonty, I'm still a little overwhelmed. Just when I think I know who someone is, someone calls them by a different name to what someone else had introduced them as. Someone pointed out the Duke to me, then I heard the Prime Minister call him Charles, and then Aunt Jenna called him Chip. It's no wonder I'm a little confused."

Jonty knew precisely what she meant, "I was born to it quite literally, as I was born in this house, Ruby. I'm getting to the point of not knowing who everyone is, either. Including this young man." Little Charles was asleep in his arms again. He had woken for some food and gone straight back to sleep, quite content and secure. Jonty smiled. "He was a shock to my system, I can tell you, a delightful one, though. I knew Lottie had been unwell for months before I left, but we never expected another child at nearly forty." He looked down at the sleeping munchkin in his arms. "An absolute delight. I'm so sad I not only missed his first year but his first birthday too. Lottie tells me he's nearly eighteen months old." He stroked the child's head.

Across the garden, Jonty saw that Jim and Conny were finally accessible.

Ruby was obviously with child, and Carlo ushered her to a seat in the shade.

Jonty took the opportunity to go to Jim. "Lotts, I have to talk to Jim; I have some messages for him. Would you take our little sleeping angel, please?"

Lottie retrieved her son. "I'll go and sit with Conny for a while."

The two made their way over to Jim and Conny Leslie.

Jonty motioned that he wished to speak with Jim and didn't want others to overhear.

Toby waited for Jonty to head to Jim and made his excuses to join them. The three men stood to one side, talking about Harry Morant and Peter Handcock.

Jonty related Harry Morant's tale.

Jim was stunned. "Tell me everything, Jon, right from the beginning." He knew both men well and was surprised at what Jonty was relating to him. He was glad young Horace was not involved.

Jonty led them off to the side to a few bags of grain to sit on and prepared to relate the entire story again from the beginning.

Eddie had noted the three sitting away from the family groups; he wandered over soon after they sat down. Jonty motioned for Ed to sit, and he did and listened.

Toby pulled out a notepad and took notes this time. He noted conversations and dates as he had been unable to do so in the carriage.

Jonty added more information, this time relating the story to Jim and Eddie, "Jim, Horace Colless was with them; I'm guessing he's the son from Castlereagh. He's fine but knows the two men well. Horace wasn't involved, but he'll need someone to download to on his return. Horace is one of the Bushveldt Carbineers' trumpeters. He worked with Harry Morant's group. I'll tell Uncle Wills as he will know him, as will Theo and Will English, as they own the farm next door, but I wanted to let you know. Toby, Jim, and Uncle Ed, I don't think they will get off. Harry's already admitted he did it but is determined that he was only following orders. I know it's what he told me. But Kitchener has already denied he said that. Captain Hunt could have cleared it up in an instant, but of course, he's dead. I didn't hear Kitchener, but I know what Harry said only moments after receiving his orders from his Captain." Jonty fell silent for a bit. "There were a few more Lieutenants, Witton and Picton, but I didn't hear if they were charged. I only met them a few times. Gentlemen, I had it from Paul Kruger's own mouth that they didn't kill the minister; some rogue Boers did. A few more Boers tortured Hunt, but he was alive when they left him. When Harry's men found him, he'd been stomped on and cut open in various places. They buried him at the mission before Harry was even told. So Harry never even saw him. The minister was dead by then. I'm not saying Harry is an angel, he has a temper and can be a good-time lad, but I know what he told me, that they were to 'take no prisoners. He didn't want to kill. He joined up because things didn't go too well for him with a lady when he returned to England earlier that year. He told me he fell in love, but it didn't work out for him. His Captain, Percy Hunt, was dating the girl's sister, so they became close in those last few months. I was given letters from him and also from Peter. I'm to post them if I hear they are dead and not before. Harry wrote to his ex-wife Daisy and two poet friends." Jonty's story spellbound the listeners. Jonty waited until he dropped the names. "They are Banjo Patterson and Henry Lawson."

He heard a gasp from all except Toby.

Toby quietly said to Jonty, "I'll introduce you to them when they are in town next. Banjo is my cousin, Jonty, although we call him Barty. He's just returned from China." The look on Jonty's face was a joy to behold in the middle of a sad conversation. "He is coming for dinner next week; bring Lottie. You can hand him Harry's letter personally."

Stunned, Jonty nodded and stammered, "I'm honoured, Toby, but the letter must wait until I hear the trial's outcome."

Ed turned and called Chip and Teddy over, then outlined the basics. They both said they would meet with Toby later and draft a letter stating the demand that the two men be sent home for trial. Surely, something would be achieved with a Duke, an Earl and the Prime Minister on their side.

Teddy had already accepted the mantle of being the Earl. He'd lived in England since he was fifteen, being groomed for his future role. He had Chip's help and before him, Duke Ned, with whom he'd lived, so he had been taught well.

The funeral gave everyone time to reconnect; many of the extended family stayed to spend more time.

Jonty's family also stayed for two more days before returning to Sydney. He said he'd see his parents when they returned. Jonty relished the peace of being with his extended family.

Simon returned to Sydney with his expectant wife and son to reopen the shop.

Jonty eventually returned to work with Simon to find Sammo was now working there too. His design skills were as good as Simon's. Jonty decided to hand over more responsibility to them both as he discovered that Simon had taught Sammo to facet in the time he'd been away. Sammo had yet to cleave and cut diamonds. With the bag Jonty had brought home, that would no longer be a problem.

Toby asked to meet Jonty on his return. That meeting occurred at a dinner that included Banjo.

Jonty would not deliver Harry's letter but told him of the sad situation.

Their single meeting turned into a regular afternoon permanent booking. Each Wednesday, they met after Jonty finished work. Only then, finally, Toby could relax. Their talk was not about politics, but faith, family and just fellowship. Their friendship grew strong.

~

Jonty had spent hours meditating in the few weeks since returning from Parramatta and Uncle Charlie's funeral. The funeral coming right on the heels of his return made him think of the many blessings of his life. Over the past months, Jonty had worked through his priorities and realised that his faith and family were the only things he would fight for. This was not really a surprise for him, but that work and money didn't even rate on the *worthwhile* scale did shock him and brought clarity to his life. Jonty had thought long and hard over the previous months; he'd had little else to do and realised he wanted to spend more time with Lottie. Jonty spent his days cutting some diamonds; the boys could handle everything else. Business was brisk, but Simon and Sammo could handle most of it. The arrival of the new stones brought much interest.

Jonty eventually cleaved, then cut the red diamond from Nandi's brother Adem into two unique stones. They cut into one stone of three carats and one just a shade under five carats.

Simon set the first smaller stone in a simple tie pin for Jonty. He wore it every day and was often seen fingering it. Its flash caught the attention of many an eye. The second stone Simon set into the most exquisite gold and diamond brooch.

When the brooch was finished, Jonty contacted Tad English and asked him to write an article about Nandi, Adem, and the blood-red diamond. The story caught the imagination and heart of the community. Tad also had a photograph taken of the superb gemstone, which Simon hand coloured in brochures and placed in the shop window, with a short story of how it had come into Jonty's hands.

Tad's newspaper ran a feature front-page story and a bit about Jonty's summons to Africa. People could talk of little else and came to hear more.

Before the auction, Jonty took centre stage. "Dear listeners, we are called to sometimes walk down a path we do not wish to go. But we must trust that God will get the glory. Yet our Lord does not promise us happiness, only joy. He does not promise us health but does promise us Eternal Life. It took me a long time to work that out. I tried to change how I coped with things myself, but when I handed things over to God, he dealt with my issues. He kept the path I was to walk well-shrouded, so I only had my faith in Him to rely on. I first went to Africa to buy diamonds, as you know. I found those, of course, but I found not only simple beauty in the gems God made but the purity and innocence of a small girl who had not learned to distrust humanity. She gave me some of the most amazing things. A diamond was the least of these, for she trusted me. That, in itself, is a huge gift, but what she brought me next was amazing. A short time after her first visit, she brought me the most unique gift, an injured lion cub. I named him Chimbu. He was a light tawny colour and had three white stripes on his head."

The amazement on the listener's faces at hearing of the golden lion was incredulous.

Jonty continued the story, and for the next half hour, he was pumped for information about Chimbu. It seemed they could not get enough of this story. After some time, Jonty continued his saga, "When I was called to return, I never expected to find my friendly cub still alive, for nearly twenty years had passed. They rarely live that long even in captivity, but he was strong and fit." Jonty again filled them in on Chimbu's current interaction with him. "Friends, little did I realise that the gift of this cub so long ago would be something that would make such a profound change in my life. He had become the protector of quite a few villages in my absence. One of these was Nandi's village. He chased away the rogue lions, and the villagers left out food and goat's milk, his favourite treat, as a reward. Lions are called the king of the jungle, but the King of the earth sent this cub to protect many. On one of the various treks I had to go on, I heard of village after village where he had saved one or another's life, a child at one, a farmer at another." Jonty's passion was evident to the journalists as well as to everyone else listening as Jonty was unapologetic when he wiped away tears telling of Nandi's death. He was graphic enough to impart the knowledge of the squalor they lived in and the lack of facilities. The money from the sale of the brooch would assist the needs of these poor villagers and others. Jonty was staring at the back wall while he was talking, trying hard not to meet the eyes of the listeners. He did not see how they received the story, but the rapturous applause as he left the stage gave him some hint of what was to follow.

When the brooch finally went to auction, it achieved an incredible amount. Twice as much as Jonty had hoped. Jonty told of Nandi and her death, of the conditions of the locals and villagers and the primitive situation they lived under. Jonty's story of Nandi and the golden lion cub had melted hearts and opened purses. The next day, the newspaper reported an amount of over £5000 raised as a result of the auction.

Tad had even found an exquisite drawing of a gentle-looking tawny lion that looked amazingly like Chimbu, but it didn't show the stripes on his head.

After that, the auction and Jonty became the talk of the town. He thought back to why he had named the lion cub. He had once heard a friend speak about a trip to British New Guinea and about the Chimbu people and how easygoing they were. The cub was easy to look after, and the name sounded a bit like the Swahili name *Simba,* so Chimbu he became. He had not corrected Paul when he said it was Hindi. Jonty had certainly felt like this small king of the jungle had been sent by the King of the earth. The lion cub had opened doors that would never have opened otherwise. Through Chimbu's story and Nandi's trust in Jonty, the villagers' needs were being supplied from halfway across the world.

Jonty knew of the protection he'd felt when the unusual couple were together. They had absolute trust in each other. Never once had Chimbu scratched Jonty except when the baboon had attacked, and he had only been tiny. Nandi's gift of Chimbu was now paying off for her village.

~

Weeks passed.

Sadly the letter Toby sent urgently to Africa the day after the funeral was useless. By the time it reached Pretoria, Jonty's two friends had already been shot; though others had been arrested, the letter accomplished their return to Australia. Three weeks after Christmas, Jerome Bentley delivered a telegram to the shop. It was from Jurgen. He had wired Jonty with the sad news of his friend's demise.

Jurgen's telegram read. "Harry, Peter shot yesterday; Witton commuted." There was no mention of Picton or Bob Lenehan.

The telegram fell to the desk. "No! Oh no!" he yelled, and then he wept. He felt gutted; he collapsed into his chair and ran his fingers through his hair, distraught. Then realised he needed to report the news to Toby. Jonty knew Toby had not been informed or he would have sent word.

Simon and Sammo had raced in when they heard the yell. He lifted his glassy eyes to Simon and said, "Si, can you please mind the shop and hail me a cab for Government House."

Simon knew in an instant what had occurred. They had not long been talking about Jonty's friendship with Breaker Morant.

Jonty hoped Toby would still be there; he could hardly breathe. He bent over, with his hands on his knees, trying to draw in air. The shock and grief were almost overwhelming him. For some reason, he had brought Breaker's letter to work with him that morning and had it in his pocket.

On arrival at Government House, he was shown straight into the office. Jonty had grown up knowing the Lockley family had almost instant access to the hierarchy of the government. Now he was on first-name terms with the Prime Minister. He was amazed at how his life had turned out. It was different from the path he had expected as a simple jeweller. At only forty-five, Jonty hoped he had much living yet to come. Since his trip as a liaison, he was now included in society's inner circle. Yet this meeting was not a position he had wished to occur.

Jonty knew Toby had not been informed as soon as he saw him. Unable to say more than "Toby," he held out the telegram to the Prime Minister. Jonty's glassy eyes were filled with unshed tears; he bit his lip, trying hard not to weep.

Toby jumped up and asked him if he was all right.

Jonty shook his head and put his hand out as if to keep Toby away. The lump in his throat made it impossible to speak. He saw Toby's concerned scrutiny; he just dropped the letter for Banjo on Toby's desk, then departed. Jonty could do no more; he also left the telegram with Toby. He never wanted to see it again. He left the office in silence, knowing that Toby would do what he could for the others. Jonty knew that Banjo was expected for dinner that night. Toby would have to break the news to him and give him the letter. He could not bring himself to do that final act. Giving it to Toby was as good as delivering it, which is all he promised to do.

Jonty had said virtually nothing. Thank goodness Jurgen had sent him word. He would return and talk to Toby some other time; now, he just needed to get outside. He needed to walk and pray.

Jonty walked home. He was in no mood to return to work; he'd just lost two incredible friends. He wanted to have a strong cup of tea; be with Lottie, hold her and then pray with her. He had refused a lift from Government House with just a curt shake of his head. He needed time alone. He was finding it hard not to break down as he walked. There was little more he could do other than pray. He now knew that he had to post the other letters from Harry and Peter. They were sitting at home in his safe. He would put them in the afternoon mail. Hopefully, they would arrive before the official notifications reached the families and friends. They were all letters of farewell.

~

Jonty took the next day off. He wanted to be alone with Lottie. He asked his mother to take little Charles, and they went out.

They had packed some sandwiches, some boiled eggs, a bottle of water and some fruit. He didn't want anything fancy; he just wanted to be outdoors, away from people, work, and be alone with Lottie. They caught a cab out to Watsons Bay and asked to be collected mid-afternoon.

Jonty carried the picnic basket and a blanket. Lottie had a large parasol as she knew there was little shade on the headland. Just being alone with Lotts was something he had missed dreadfully. They just wanted to escape from the hurtful maddening world.

Jonty and Lottie settled down on their picnic blanket and relaxed. They would eat later. They chatted about the happenings of the past few years. He talked much about Chimbu, telling Lottie of the safety he felt when he was vulnerable. He no longer had nightmares, hadn't for years, but sometimes he'd have flashbacks of specific incidents, particularly about Nandi. When he did, he would touch the tie pin in his cravat and pray for her family. The blood-red diamond pin he now wore at every opportunity. He made sure most of the money from the sale of the other half was sent to Nandi's village via Jurgen. The red diamond brooch he had made brought in over £5000 at the auction. £4000 he sent to Africa and £1000 he used for the orphans and needy in Sydney, most through the Benevolent Society. The brooch had raised twice as much as he'd hoped. For Adem, that would mean the entire village could be rebuilt, new wells dug, and even the clinic and school could now be planned. Yes, it would make a huge difference. Jurgen had told him Nandi's brother's name. It was Adem, and Jonty discovered it meant *red earth*. He thought how appropriate. Jonty referred to this red stone as a blood diamond. It was, as Nandi gave her life for such gems.

Jonty's idea for the day's picnic was to spend quality time with his wife. "I just wanted to get away, Lotts. I needed you and you alone. No staff, no children, no gems, no nothing. Do you realise that come December this year, we will have been married twenty years? I have decided that it is time Simon took over more responsibility with the store. Sammo shows great promise, but Paul is more interested in his art. I'm happy with what either wish to do, as long as they are content. I have discovered that nothing is more important than faith and family, and I mean in that order too. Your family taught me that, Lotts; Mother and Father know about it too, but your family live it every moment of the day."

Lottie smiled lovingly at him. "Jon Jon, as you know, our family bond is strong because of those two things, faith and family. Grandfather sowed the seeds for that, with Grandmother firmly at his side. Uncle Ned had originally taught them about faith, and we were all taught at their knees. Jon Jon, we saw it in action daily. You only had to look at Uncle Charlie's funeral last year to know that, on the whole, most of us continue to follow that path. We pray together often and encourage others to join us. We all came under Grandfather's shadow."

Jonty was caressing her cheek with his thumb. "Lotts, as much as I adore my own family when things got tough for me, I turned to your father. Uncle Luke has always been there for me. He is the only one I fully unloaded to. Uncle Harry and Will English too, but even with Will, there were things I held back. I knew your father could guide me in faith and give me direction with that in mind. I knew I could not walk that path alone."

Lottie was lying back against his chest, relishing the closeness of her beloved husband. Her blonde curls blew in the breeze as they watched the harbour activities. For over an hour, they sat and watched the various movements of the ships. She didn't know what to say. She'd grown up seeing how all her uncles and aunts would drop what they were doing to assist someone in need.

Jonty felt he needed to say something more. "Lotts, when I was returning from that first trip, I didn't just want to be with you, but I needed to be with your family. When I was with them, I felt safe and surrounded by their love and acceptance. I didn't know the difference for years until something Will said sank in. It was a sense of belonging, not to each other but to God's extended family. Yes, there are religious bigots, but even Jesus had to deal with them. Your family put Jesus's words into being. It's part of the reason I wanted to come early on that first Christmas together." Jonty yawned.

Lottie smiled; she knew just what he meant. "I know, Jonty. My grandparents started us all with their example of walking in God's path. It wasn't that hard to follow them. I'm sure you have heard the term 'The Earl's Shadow?' Well, that was what my grandfather did. He followed the Lord so closely that the shadow he cast was one we all aimed to follow. He was horrified about the term because he said he just followed his Master, Jesus."

Jonty smiled. He remembered her grandfather well. "You know what I mean, then?"

She nodded.

Jonty yawned again. He had hardly slept last night as he'd been so upset about the shooting of his two friends in Pretoria. He had walked and wept and prayed most of the night.

Lottie suggested he lie down and put his head in her lap.

He did, just to be close to her. Lottie held the parasol over them both. His mind had emptied, his soul at peace; he had his wife and family content to accept him for what he was, a humble jeweller who'd been used as a liaison for enemies. Yet all he wanted was to be that simple jeweller again. He only ever had wanted to be a family man, the husband to Lottie and father to his five adorable children. As he lay listening to the sounds around him, Jonty drifted off into a deep and peaceful healing sleep.

Lottie lovingly stroked his hair. She kept playing with that errant lock of hair that never stayed in place. She was at peace now too. He was home, and with the gems he had brought with him, their family would never need for anything ever again. Their children would be set for life. Yes, the money was nice, but they could be happy without it. They had been before. She cared for nothing but him and their faith. Jonty had always been the love of her life. She, too, was content.

Their journey was not over, but from now on, they would walk forward together, gaining strength from each other and their faith.

She sat watching the ships sailing down the stunning harbour. A magnificent pair of white-breasted sea eagles soared overhead. Then the plaintive cries of the seagulls drew her attention towards the port. She was lost in the beauty surrounding her.

After some time, the breeze blew the wayward lock of hair across his forehead and into his eyes. Gazing down at the love of her life, still asleep in her lap, the corners of her rosebud lips curled upwards as she felt a wave of adoration sweep through her. She gently brushed the curl away.

He opened his eyes and caught the look of adulation on her face.

When she realised he had awoken, she broke into a beaming smile as their gazes met, but no words were spoken. Both knew their journey would continue with her by his side. However, it would no longer be just Jonty's journey but their journey. From now on, she would refuse to be left behind.

Jonty was now fully awake. He sat up, turned and said, "Lottie, have I told you just how much I love you?"

She nodded, grinning, then leaned in to kiss him.

The clouds were now behind him. He had found his peace in the arms of his beloved. He had finally handed over his burdens to God, and the ache in his heart had gone.

The end?
I don't think so…

Although Jonty's Journey is just a story,
Over the centuries, many have been caught up in the turmoil of war.
Most will never talk about it, and it eats them from the inside.
Their families suffer, as do they.

The description of DEEP PRAYER *is now a well-known 'thing'*
and many call it Meditation. But it's slightly different.
Releasing your burdens to God brings Peace, but it's oh-so-hard to do.
Casting all your care upon him is mentioned at least twice in the Bible.

First, in the Old Testament, in Psalm 55:22,
and then in the New Testament, in 1 Peter 5:7.

Cast thy burden upon the Lord, and he shall sustain thee: he shall
never suffer the righteous to be moved.
Psalm 55:22

Turn to the one who is always at our side.
Jesus will listen; He always does. Just ask Him…

Jonty followed His path, and his life found meaning

The eternal God is thy refuge,
and underneath are the (*God's*) everlasting arms:
Deuteronomy 33 verse 27a

(He will always be there to catch you!)

About Harry Harbord Morant
aka "The Breaker."

On the night before his execution, Morant wrote this short poem to the priest who would attend him:

To the Rev Canon Fisher
Pretoria

The night before we're shot.
We shot the Boers who killed and mutilated
our friend (the best mate on Earth)
Harry Harbord Morant
Peter Joseph Handcock

Lieutenant Harry Morant died at the hands of an Army firing squad on the morning of 27th February 1902, aged 37. He was defiant at the end, entreating the squad members to "shoot straight and not mess it up." The poem included in the story was his second last poem. He apparently sent it to Banjo Patterson.

Read more of Harry Harbord Morant, aka "The Breaker"
https://mypoeticside.com/poets/harry-morant-poems

Dame Daisy Bates was Harry's wife.
https://www.southaustralianhistory.com.au/bates.htm

Bibliography

<u>Bingara diamonds</u> - over 500,000 carats of gemstones have been mined from there since 1872 official discovery.
https://www.bingara.com.au/gwydir-shire-diamonds/

<u>1st Boer War</u>
https://en.wikipedia.org/wiki/First_Boer_War
https://en.wikipedia.org/wiki/94th_Regiment_of_Foot
https://en.wikipedia.org/wiki/Lydenburg#Colonial_history

<u>Kimberly diamonds</u>
https://en.wikipedia.org/wiki/Kimberley,_Northern_Cape#Discovery_of_diamonds

<u>Newspaper articles</u>
https://trove.nla.gov.au/newspaper/article/241329546?searchTerm=transvaal
https://trove.nla.gov.au/newspaper/article/78994642?searchTerm=transvaal

<u>Chapter 7 image</u>
The Idle and the Industrious Painter Sir John Everett Millais Bt PRA (1829-96)

<u>PTSD - from web MD</u>
https://www.webmd.com/mental-health/what-are-treatments-for-posttraumatic-stress-disorder

<u>Diamonds in Africa</u>
https://trove.nla.gov.au/newspaper/article/8545376?searchTerm=sapphires

<u>Jewellery Auction in Melbourne</u>
https://trove.nla.gov.au/newspaper/article/8502130?searchTerm=jewellery

<u>Harry Breaker Morant poems</u>
https://mypoeticside.com/poets/harry-morant-poems

<u>Chapter 15 photo - Artists Camp</u> - Edwards Beach Balmoral Beach Sydney
This photo is in public Domain
COLLECTION: Mosman (Sydney) Local Studies Collection
FILE: CC0\CC0041 TITLE: Camp at Balmoral, c.1890. NOTE: CC No. A22 SERIES: Carroll Collection. This camp, probably Lotus Camp at Edwards Beach, was one of several camps established in Mosman in the late 1800s as a semi-permanent retreat from urban living. The best known were the Artists' Camp, established by the cartoonist Livingston Hopkins ("Hop" of the Bulletin) at the northern end of Edwards Beach and Curlew Camp at Sirius Cove, home to the artists Arthur Streeton and Tom Roberts.
https://commons.wikimedia.org/wiki/
File:Sydney_artists%27_camp_at_Edwards_Beach,_Balmoral,_NSW_c._1890.jpg

<u>Arrival of 224 Camels on SS Abergeldie</u>
https://trove.nla.gov.au/newspaper/article/196753050?searchTerm=Abergeldie%201887

NB Simon Marshall is a fictitious character.

Fred McCubbin's **'Lost'** painting (painted over with **"On the Wallaby Track"**)
https://7news.com.au/sunrise/on-the-show/long-lost-frederick-mccubbin-artwork-found-hidden-inside-another-painting-at-national-gallery-of-victoria-c-1632829

The Golden Fleece, 1894 at Newstead, near Inverell by Tom Roberts

Bailed Up by Tom Roberts 1895 with handmade frame.

The Big Picture by Tom Roberts, completed in 1903
Opening of Parliament 1901
The Painting took two years to paint
with all 250 main guests individually identifiable.

Author Bio

Sheila Hunter and Sara Powter were a passionate mother-and-daughter team of amateur genealogists. While working together on their family tree, Sheila and Sara made a captivating discovery. Four convicts, with four very different perspectives, were sent to Australia during Convict times. Before her passing in 2002, Sheila adapted some of these histories into enchanting stories, the Australian Colonial Trilogy. A fourth she left unfinished. Sara later had these published. It inspired her to write more. The Lockleys of Parramatta were created.

Vividly living through the Colonial Era, this series delves further into the theme of overcoming adversity in Colonial Parramatta and how it developed, the demise of the Convict system and the discovery of gold.

Sara intricately weaves real archival data and a charming narrative to create a series of tales of faith, love, loss, and redemption. Sara has now completed Sheila Hunter's last unfinished manuscript. Watch for *'Dancing to her own tune'*. A prequel for all of their colonial novels, and it now has its own sequels, *'Amelia's Tears'* and *'A Lady in Irons'*.

Travelling the East coast in their retirement, Sara and her husband Stephen enjoyed the deep sense of belonging gained by uncovering a familial connection to a new area.

And so, two hundred years after her family's arrival in Australia, Sara continues the Australian Colonial stories with the *'Lockleys of Parramatta'* as well as the *'Unlikely Convict Ladies'* Trilogy and now a selection of stand-alone stories.

See her web page to keep up to date with more stories.
With an online store available for a signed copy of Sara's books.
www.sarapowter.com.au
(Australian Postage only)

Amazon QR

To be added to my mailing list
please email me at
saragpowter@gmail.com

Follow me on **BOOK BUB**
https://partners.bookbub.com/authors/6273615/edit

If you loved this book, these are similar
By Sheila Hunter
Co-Winner of 1999 NSW Senior Citizen of the Year, In the Year of the Senior Citizen
Australian Colonial Trilogy

Mattie
Coming of Age in Convict Australia
By Sheila Hunter
Woodslane/Hand in Hand Publications ISBN 9780994578204

Twelve-year-old London street urchin **Mattie Paul** is convicted of petty theft and sentenced to seven years of transportation to the penal colony of Port Jackson, NSW. Peg, another female convict, takes Mattie under her wing and gives her a chance to make something of her life by teaching her to read. Mattie seizes every opportunity that comes her way. Though life is not particularly kind to her, she battles through earning her freedom, marrying and becoming a mother in her homeland. On this amazing journey, she gets entangled with bushrangers, is widowed, and becomes an entrepreneur in the Bathurst goldfields. She mixes with escaped convicts, but her spirit is indomitable, and she becomes a pillar and much-loved treasure of her adopted community. Mattie may be a fictional character, but her experiences are only too real and invest us in immersing ourselves in the lives of those remarkable women who helped to make Australia what it is today.

ISBN 9781503252370 & ebook AISN BOOTTEDBTO
(The Story continues in The Earl's Shadow)
Released 2015
https://amazon.com/dp/150325237X   https://amazon.com/dp/B00TTEDBT0

Ricky
A boy in Colonial Australia

Ricky English and his mother immigrate from England to join his father in the new Colony of Sydney. On arrival, there is no sign of his father. Ricky's mum uses the tiny amount of money they brought to get lodgings in a run-down building. Things go from bad to worse when his mother dies, he is thrown out of the rooms, and the caretakers confiscate all their possessions.

Ricky lives on the streets of Sydney Town as a street waif. Ricky finds safe places to sleep and befriends freed convicts who can help him survive. One day he finds another lost child, and he helps reunite her with her family. These people try to help him, but because of his stubbornness, he insists on doing things his way, but he has found a mentor and confidante. The story follows him through his life. He survives and turns his life around, helping others along the way.

Paperback ISBN 9780994578211   Kindle ASIN: B00MLYN6IG
(The Story continues in Jonty's Journey)
Released 2014
https://amazon.com/dp/1500770574 https://amazon.com/dp/B00MLYN6IG

The Heather to The Hawkesbury
Scottish migrants in a harsh land

Mary Macdonald and her family; her brother **Fergus** MacKenzie; sister-in-law **Caro** MacLeod; cousin **Alex** Fraser and all their families who have had to emigrate from the Isle of Skye during the "Clearances." The story follows the four families from Scotland on the ship out to the NSW colony in the 1850s. Mary does not cope with the changes and losses that occur in the first months in the colony. The other women in the family rely on her, and she nearly crumbles. The families struggle together through accidents, losses, trials, floods, and hard work and forge a strong bond with their new country. Trials, tribulations and triumphs see the four families make a firm mark in their new homeland. The immigrants from Scotland helped make Australia what it is today.

ISBN 978994578228   ebook AISN B01A21JYWQ   Large Print ISBN1533473641
Available on Amazon/Kindle & Large Print
Released 2016
https://amazon.com/dp/1503251438   https://amazon.com/dp/B01A21JYWQ

Unlikely Convict Ladies - Trilogy

Dancing to her Own Tune

Co-authored by Sheila Hunter and Sara Powter

Sydney 1790s to England 1830s

Annie White is released after serving seven years as a convict in Sydney. She gets a visitor who, with his help, she can start a baking business. She is then asked to assist another sick man, **Sam** Corbett. Annie nurses him back to health, and a relationship develops. They settle into a life together, barely making ends meet; she realises she's expecting a child. Sam has his past laid bare and must adjust to the revelations. They both must face their accusers and find that the answers to their questions are not what they thought. Their life experiences seem to cling to them, and unable to shake it they finally, they end up back in England, facing their ghosts and discovering they are not who they think they are. How can they turn their anger and spite into love and forgiveness? The Dance of Life goes on.

ISBN 9780645110715   AISN B09JC378YV

Long-listed in the Historical Fiction Company Competition 2022

October2021

https://amazon.com/dp/064511071X   https://amazon.com/dp/B09JC378YV

Amelia's Tears

Parramatta 1828 – England 1840s

In the convict Female Factory, **Amelia** awaits her assignment. Forced to leave the relative safety of gaol, she must face her worst nightmare. The man's foul breath and black teeth reflect his soul's darkness. From the outset, he is violent and abusive. Things get even worse over the next few months, and then Amelia realises she is expecting a child. A glimmer of hope arises when she hears from her brother, Jim, who has enlisted a friend to help her. She writes to Jim, pouring out her heart and telling him of the horrors of her new life. He encourages her to stay firm in her faith. All she can do is pray. When Major **Ned** Grace, her brother's friend, enters her life in Parramatta, he starts to ease her path. Things have changed, as now she has a child in tow. How can Amelia forge a new life for herself? What man could want her with her background and a child at her side? Who is the gentleman who turns her tears of sadness into tears of great joy?

ISBN: 9780645110739   eISBN: 978-0-6451107-4-6   Hard Cover ISBN 979-842061-7953

April 2022

https://amazon.com/dp/0645110736   https://amazon.com/dp/B09SS855BR

A Lady in Irons

England 1800s - Parramatta 1808+

Katy is mourning the death of her husband after he dies in a shooting accident. Barely coping, she awaits the birth of their child. If it's a girl, she must hand the family home to her husband's brother. The day after giving birth to a daughter, she and her daughter are left on the side of a road. She collapses and is found by someone she thought had died in a fire ten years before. **Perry**, badly scarred himself, nurses her back to health. They marry and move in with her widowed friend, Mary.

After some years, she discovers her husband and friend in each other's arms. Now living in a love triangle, she flees. Grasping the only straw available, she intentionally gets arrested and is sent to a colony far away. By doing this, her marriage can be annulled. What happens in the Colony is not what she expects. Governor Macquarie comes to her rescue.

But what of Perry and her children?

ISBN: 9780645110784   eISBN:978-0645-4415-05

November 2022

https://amazon.com/dp/0645110787   https://amazon.com/dp/B0BCWSXB9Z

No More, My Love
Hunter Valley, NSW 1820s

Jess Elkin is distraught when tragedy ravages her family. She becomes the victim of a carriage accident and is nursed back to health by the driver, **Marcus Ryan**. Marcus was not expecting to fall in love. Yet, when Jess's fortunes take a sudden turn for the worse, Marcus must decide how far he will go to pursue her. As time passes in Newcastle, Australia, Marcus must take a business trip and is taken by pirates. Jess is left wondering if her will keep his promise to return to her... *Will she ever see him alive again?*

ISBN: 9780645441536   eISBN 9780645441581 e AISN B0BSBH143Q
April 2023
https://amazon.com/dp/0645441538   https://amazon.com/dp/B0BSBH143Q

The Vine Weaver
Hawkesbury River area 1820s+

Joel and Hetty Walker live on a secluded farm on the Hawkesbury River that the Walkers have turned into a healing haven.

Fran Rea has survived the abuse she received; she leaves the Female Factory in Parramatta by being carried to the hospital. Hetty rescues Fran and takes her to the farm, where Fran recovers and teaches Hetty to weave. This success spurns an entire cottage industry for the small farm.

The farmhand, **Hector Macdougal,** shows compassion to all, yet it is his words that change their lives, giving them a future beyond their dreams. It is to Hector that Fran turns when threatened.

The vines now must draw them close to survive the revelations of the future.

ISBN: 9780645441512   eISBN: 9780645441529
Coming June 2023

The story continues in Scotch at The Rocks...

Waiting at the Sliprails
The Bathurst Road 1830s

Bea Dawes's term of conviction nears an end, and she has few options other than marriage to a stranger or going on the street.

Jack Barnes, the hired drover, wants a wife. Bea accepts his offer; then she discovers that he could be gone for months at a time, leaving her alone with **Billy and Netty**, part of the tribe of aborigines who live on his secluded farm. Bea learns to love her husband and also this wonderful aboriginal couple.

Drought ravages the farm, and Jack must hit the long paddock with the flock. In his absence, a visitor arrives, and she destroys the peace and security of the farm. Can Bea cope? Will the drought ever end? When will Jack return?

ISBN: 9780645441543   eISBN: ISBN: 9780645441529
Coming August 2023

SCOTCH AT THE ROCKS
Glasgow, Scotland, early 1800s to The Rocks, Sydney 1830s

Orphaned children Brodie Stewart and Heather Anderson live on Glasgow's streets. Although hungry, somehow they survive and keep out of trouble. Heather finds a job and looks to be settled; things go pear-shaped for them both. Eventually, they marry by declaration, yet even that gets messed up, and they are both arrested soon after they make their vow. In 1838, they get transported to Sydney as convicts. Heather arrives within weeks of Brodie, and they are assigned close to each other. They are now living on the docklands in Sydney, called The Rocks. They now have to forge a new life halfway across the world from their home.

Adventures abound, and Brodie gets press-ganged. While he's away, Heather's life changes and soon, she's officially selling Scotch Whisky at a shop in The Rocks. You can take a Scot out of Scotland, but where did the Scotch come from?

ISBN 9780645441550 ISBN ebook

October/November 2023

In Defence of Her Honour
London 1800s to Parramatta 1819

William Miller had been raised and educated with the sons of the family. The youngest, Bert, had been his best friend. However, jealousy intervenes when Bill's excellent schoolwork curtails their friendship. He wins a scholarship and enters Oxford University. When Bill's father, the old butler, dies unexpectedly, Bert insists that Bill take over the position, but it's more to oppress him. Bert's jealousy grows and festers. Now looking for a way to rid themselves of the new butler, a ruckus ensues, and Bill is arrested for assaulting Bert. The housekeeper and her daughter **Molly** vouch for him, but it's too late; Bill has been arrested and sentenced to be transported. With Bill gone, Molly now needs to defend herself from Bert. After hitting him with a pan, she is arrested and sent to Sydney. Bill and Molly arrive with letters of introduction and compensation from Bert's father. Soon they are running the best Inn in Parramatta with an endorsement from the Governor.

ISBN 9780645441567 ISBN ebook

Coming 2024

Gentle Annie Soames
A 1788 First Fleet Convict Story

Annie Soames is shattered by the cancellation of her debut into society, so when she hears of a position as a carer for the Marchioness who lives nearby, she grabs it.

Oliver Quilpie, the recently married Marquess, discovers his arranged union is not to his taste; he is drawn to his wife's companion. Unfortunately, he is unable to keep his hands off her. For revenge, Annie decides to mimic his every move when out riding but is dressed as a highwayman. However, she had now fallen in love with him. This action finally leads to her arrest and transportation to a faraway land.

After some years, Oliver's wife dies, and his thoughts turn to Annie. He seeks to find her, but she has vanished. He is horrified to learn that she was transported to New South Wales as a convict on the Lady Penrhyn. He follows with a shipload of supplies. Will Annie want to see him?

ISBN 9780645441574 ISBN ebook

Coming 2024

Convict Shadows of the Past
Two Jennifers, two hundred years apart

When aged eight, **Jenny** Kellow learns of her convict family history and discovers that she was named after a convict from nearly two hundred years ago. Her grandfather's stories inspire her to dig deeper into her ancestors' convict past. From her grandfather, she hears stories of bushrangers, convicts, and life in the infant colony of Parramatta. She sets about retracing the footsteps of her convict great-great-great-grandmother to honour her. Jenny's search starts with microfiche back in the 60s, and she learns about the small tin mining town in Cornwall and the production of a cheese that sets London afire. Then she discovers her ancestor has brought these cheese-making skills to Parramatta, where she taught others her craft. Echoes of the past can still be heard if you know where to listen. But who was the first **Jennifer**? Why is she so elusive?

ISBN: 9798366251372   ISBN ebook

A NaNoWriMo 2022 book winner
Coming 2024

I can't stop Tomorrow

Irish Famine 1840s to Avoca Beach, Australia

Escaping bigotry and prejudice in Ireland, the O'Shane family live on a secluded farm on the west coast. Their farm is soon decimated by the potato blight. The two oldest girls, Clare and Kerry, head to their cousin, Sal Lockley, in Parramatta, Australia.
Shéamus is the annoying teenage boy who reluctantly draws Clare's affection. However, living in a convict town means ruffians abound.
John Moore is an Irishman, content to live alone on another secluded farm until he discovers Clare and two other lads need rescuing.
Can John protect her from the pain inflicted by an evil world?
Can Shéamus find his lost love?

ISBN: ISBN ebook
Coming 2024

Jonty's Journey

An Australian Colonial series
Lockleys of Parramatta

Hands upon the Anvil
A blacksmith's life and love is more than just work
Parramatta 1830s.

His parents were transported for their crimes. In a land of opportunity, can a steadfast lad rise above his origins and guide others to success?
Ten-year-old **Eddie Lockley** longs to help his mum and dad. Living in a convict town with his family, the keen youngster has already been working with the local blacksmith since his sixth birthday. But when a lieutenant won't stop abusing his older brother, the young boy yearns for the day when he can stand up and end the torment. Though he's thrilled when his mentor offers to send him off to learn his letters, Eddie fears he won't be around to watch his sibling's back. But as he takes on the biggest adventure of his life, the brave believer soon discovers God is looking out for everyone he loves. Does this young man in the making have what it takes to change everything for the better?

ISBN 9780994578235   Ebook ISBN 978-0-9945782-5-9   Hardcover 9798496177368
Released 2021
https://amazon.com/dp/0994578237   https://amazon.com/dp/B08TB51L19

Out Where The Brolgas Dance
Gold is found, and so is love
Parramatta 1840s
How can a question change so many people?

It's the 1840s, and discoveries across the Blue Mountains continue. Major Mitchell's new road is complete, and towns are planned and being built. Abundant land is available for those who want it.
William **"Wills"** Lockley, 18, has laid a solid foundation for a respectable career as a blacksmith, but the Lockley lust for adventure flows deeply within his veins. He dreads the monotony of work at the blacksmith's forge and yearns for adventure in a new frontier. Wills meets six Englishmen who have the means to make his dreams come true. What they discover changes the Colony and their lives forever. Gold fever ensues. Now on the road West, Wills has to deal with an uncertain romance. Does she even want him?

ISBN 9780994578242   Ebook ISBN 978-0-9945782-6-6   Hardcover ISBN 9798755445504
Released 2021
https://amazon.com/dp/0994578245   https://amazon.com/dp/B08T6NS3XX

Diamonds in the Dirt
Diamonds, love and money… but there is much more to life.
Parramatta 1850s

Luke, the youngest Lockley son, has completed University, and his life has no direction. No job, no money, and no love. Desperately alone, he prays for guidance. How can Luke trust that God has a plan for him if he can't even work out how to get a job? He does the only thing he can … he prays. Within a week, life has changed … oh, how it has changed as his brother Wills turns up with a suggestion. Would Luke be interested in joining the expedition with John Evans? Reverend William Clarke needs assistance on a Government Mineral Survey. The challenge, adventure and finds are life-changing for many. However, it gives Luke meaning, purpose and direction. The condition of his heart problems also takes a turn. Can he walk away?

ISBN:9780994578273 Ebook ISBN: 978-0-9945782-8-0 Hard cover ISBN 979-8788011141
Released 2022
https://amazon.com/dp/099457827X   https://amazon.com/dp/B09NH1MLXZ

The Earl's Shadow
Who or what is the 'shadow'? How does it affect so many?
<u>*Parramatta 1860s*</u>

Charles is the Earl of Coxheath and spends his youth as a convict in Parramatta, only to discover he was an Earl and didn't know. He had little education and few social skills. His eldest son **Charlie** is no different.

Now faced with his own mortality, Charles has to work out how to live the remainder of his life after a near-death experience. He is called to step way out of his comfort zone in London. His action will change the world for many. The echoes from the past still haunt Charlie. London is calling the family, and they can't postpone the trip. How does **Jim**, the Cobb and Co coach driver, fit in? And precisely what is *'The Earl's Shadow'* that he speaks about? What happens if the 'Shadow' is gone?

<u>ISBN</u>: 9780645110708 Ebook <u>ISBN</u> 978-0-9945782-9-7
Released June 2022
https://amazon.com/dp/0645110701   https://amazon.com/dp/B0B158SKSK

Once a Jolly Swagman
An old black Billy Can contain the secrets of an incredible life
An Australian Historical Novel
Set in 1870s Parramatta and Kent UK

Rick Lockley, battling his families expectations, runs away to become a swagman.

Jack, a jolly swagman takes him under his care. Even after years together, Rick knows little about the old man.

On his death, Jack leaves Rick his precious Billy Can; the contents reveal Jack's identity. Stunned, Rick finds he must travel to England to finalise Jack's wishes. There he uncovers Jack's life of love, betrayal and a link to his own family. Rick discovers there is much more to learn about this enigmatic man.

ISBN 9780645110753   Ebook ISBN 978-0-6451107-6-0
Released Sept 2022
https://amazon.com/dp/0645110752   https://amazon.com/dp/B0B5JN1WCV

Jonty's Journey
Gems, Love, Artists and a Golden Lion
<u>*Australia and South Africa 1880-1902*</u>

Sydney Jeweller, **Jonty** Evans' passion for gems takes him to Africa at a volatile time. He finds the diamonds he's looking for and gets given a lion cub. Jonty gets all but kidnapped. His experiences in the Transvaal plunge him into questioning everything he knows of life. Soon nightmares haunt him.

On return home, he nearly messes up his love life with **Lottie** before it even starts, and he struggles to settle. Lottie's father, **Luke** Lockley from Parramatta, takes him in hand and points him to someone who can help.

Jonty is then recalled to Africa as a liaison and reconnects with his lion, Chimbu when he saves the life of his security detail. His life journey introduces him to the most amazing Heidelberg artists, politicians, poets, rebels, and the scapegoat soldier Harry Breaker Morant. Can Jonty bury the past and regain the peace he's lost?

ISBN 9780645110777   Ebook ISBN: 978-0-6451107-9-1
Released Feb 2023
https://amazon.com/dp/0645110779   https://amazon.com/dp/B0BLJ7ND1Q

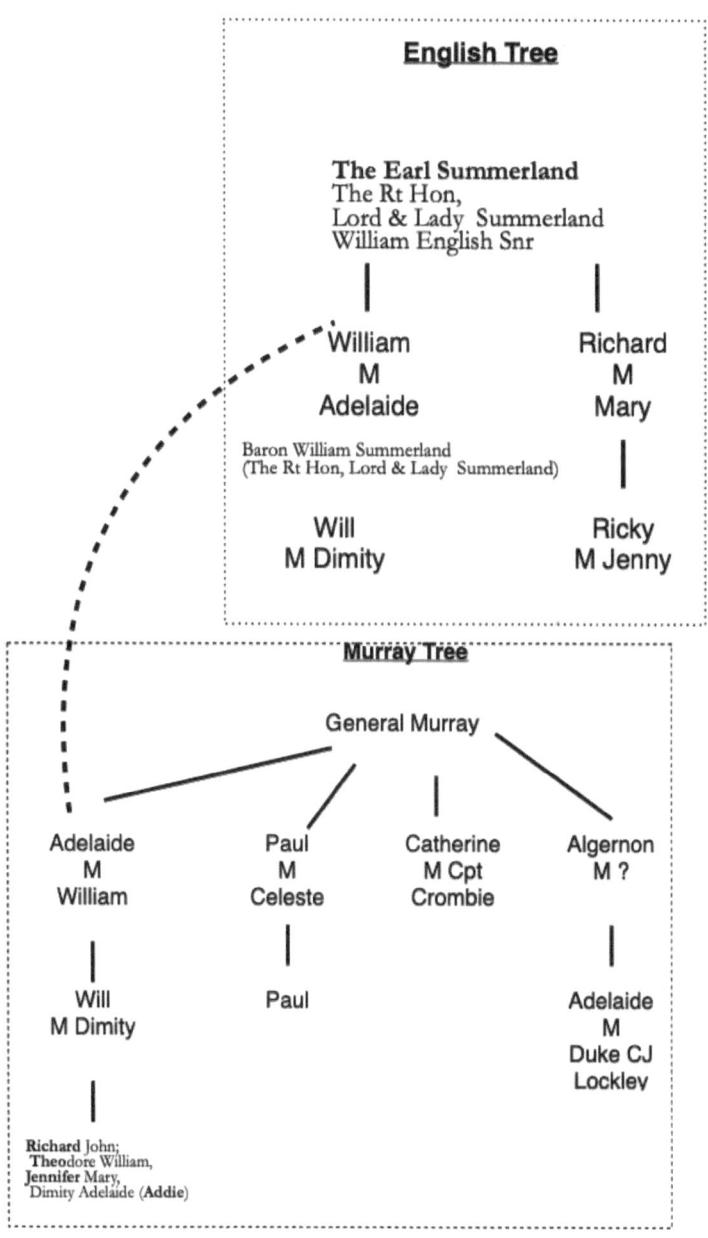

English Tree

The Earl Summerland
The Rt Hon,
Lord & Lady Summerland
William English Snr

William
M
Adelaide

Richard
M
Mary

Baron William Summerland
(The Rt Hon, Lord & Lady Summerland)

Will
M Dimity

Ricky
M Jenny

Murray Tree

General Murray

Adelaide
M
William

Paul
M
Celeste

Catherine
M Cpt
Crombie

Algernon
M ?

Will
M Dimity

Paul

Adelaide
M
Duke CJ
Lockley

Richard John;
Theodore William,
Jennifer Mary,
Dimity Adelaide (**Addie**)

Characters

Mr **Richard Lamb**, the Jeweller
Jonty Evans *(John & Colleen Evans - his parents)*
Mrs Caroline (**Caro**) **Evans** - Mr Tindale's sister
Captain **Douglas** Evans- supply ship captain Pitt Street
Philip b 1819 Phil; Law   m   Alice 4 children
Stephen b 1821 Stevie; Law   m   May 5 children
John b 1822   m 5/10/55 **Colleen** Murphy;
         #1 b 2/8/56 Jonathon (**Jonty**) Finn Douglas Evans
            m Dec 23, 1882, Charlotte (**Lottie**) Lockley - dang of Luke and Ellen Lockley
              1 Samuel Nicholas (**Sammo**) b 17th August 1883
              2 Patricia Marie (**Patty**) b 17th August 1883
              3 **Paul** William b May 1887
              4 Charlotte Caroline (**Carol**) Oct 22 1888
              5 Jonathon **Charles** b Oct 1900
         #2 **Maureen** Caroline Evans **Reenie** b 8 Aug 1858
         #3 William Luke John (**Billy**) b June 1860
         #4 Harriet (**Hettie**) Oct 63   *(more Lockley family below)*
Mr **Field** - the owner of Tiffany's jewellers in Antwerp
Paul Kruger - leader of the Boers

Will English- married **Dimity** Roger - Baron William Summerland (The Rt Hon, Lord & Lady
Summerland) 4 kids, 9 Grandfather Earl Summerland (William English Snr)
4 kids
         #1 **Richard John** (The Honourable Richard) m **Dominique**; -Summerland Hall
         #2 **Theodore** William,
         #3 **Jennifer** Mary,
         #4 Dimity Adelaide (**Addie**)

Ricky English - married **Jenny** (the Honourable Richard)
         Children 1+
Theodore (**Tad**) Falconer-Mead - AKA - Tad English m **Amabel** Landon
         Children 1, Henry John 2 Richard Joshua 3 Sarah Mary
John and Sadie (Sarah) Landon and daughter Amabel - m Tad.

Paul Murray on The SS *Abergeldie* Captain Cromby's nephew
         parents **Celeste** and **Paul** Murray
         looking for older Aunt, **Adelaide** Murray m **William** English
         It turns out to be Will's parents.
Catherine Murray m **Captain Cromby**
Algernon Murray - m? 1+ child **Adelaide** m **CJ Lockley** future Duke

DUKE of Gracemere family - family name also Lockley

Major Edward 'Ned' Grace b 1798 (47)- Parramatta (His Grace the 10th Duke of
Gracemere. Edward John Charles Lockley of Gracemere) at Maidstone m Dec 25, 1841,
Christina Meadows 'Pop and Lally'
- Gracemere House, London
Mrs Christina '**Tina' Meadows** Lady Christina Catherine Meadows, née Hunt b 1808 *(daughter
of Edmund d 1865 & Catherine; Earl of Riverdell)*
#1 Charles (**Chip**) Edward John, b 1 Sept 1842
M Dec 5th 1861 Christina (**Tina**) Lockley b 15 Aug 1842 (Eddie's daughter)
         #1 Charles John Edward (**CJ**) Dec 5, 1862 twin
         m 1882 **Adelaide** Murray
         #2 Christina Susanna (**Christie**) Dec 5, 1862 twin
         m 1882 Stephen (**Steve**) William Hunt b 51(Edmund's 2nd son)
         #3 **Gerald** Albert James b Nov 1863
         #4 Elizabeth (**Liza**) Sarah b Oct 1866
         #5 **James** Charles March 1868 twin
         #6 Constance (**Coco**) Marie March 1868 twin
     #2 **Sarah** Christina, The Lady Sarah Lockley (Sarah Joy) b 1 Sept 1842
m Anthony Winchester Dec 5th 1861 (Earl Winchester) (Harry Harlow's nephew)
         #1 **Henry** Anthony 3/3 1862 (Future Earl)
         #2 **Edward** Charles 4/3/ 1862 m
         #3 Adelaide (**Addie**) Sarah 5th July 64

#4 **Rose**marie Christina Rachel 1st August 1865 m
    m Charles Edward (**Chad**) 16 Sept 65 twin (Teddy's son- future Earl)
        #1 Charles Edward b 1901 Sept
        #2 Alexandrine twin sister stillborn
    #5 Sarah **Joy** Maud b May 1868
#3 The Lord William Edmund (**Liam**) April 1845
m 15/8/64 **Lily** Lockley (Eddie's daughter)
        #1 William (**Gil**) John Lockley May 65
        #2 Charles Edward James (**EJ**) Dec 12th, 68
#4 Lady Charlotte (**Charl**) Jennifer Victoria Jan 26/1/47 in Parramatta - twin
m 15/8/64 **Kit** Lockley (Eddie's son)
        #1 Robert (**Bobbie**) Christopher Charles Edward. Quad 20/4/65
        #2 **Luc**as Fynn Edmund John Quad. 20/4/65
        #3 Eleanor (**Nell**)Elizabeth Dawn Sarah Quad 20/4/65
        #4 **Clare** Christina Ellen Isabella Quad. 20/4/65
        #5 **Hugo** Kiran William Aug 1st 1867
        #6 Rebecca (**Becca**) Grace 26/12/69
        #7 **Thea** Louise Edwina b Aug 1880 when parents were 33
        M 1899 John **Jax** Styles - lived in Rock Cottage, Glebe
            #1 Edward b 1900
            #2 Angelina b 1902
#5 Lady Isabella (**Izzy**) Catherine Grace. 26/1/47 twin
15/8/64 **Neddie** Winslow-Smythe, Earl of Winslow.
        #1 George (**Georgie**) Edward Gerald b 7/2/67
        #2 Victoria (**Vicky**) Isabella b 7/12/69
Lockley Family in Parramatta
Charles John Lockley b March 1800 and d 27 April, Easter 1870 *Dad John Lockley m*
        Mum, Elle Staverly d 2/9/1855 m2 Richard Childs d 1855
M Feb 1820 **Sal McCarthy** d early 11/1/96 aged nearly 96 (Dar and Mama) 'Jolly Sailor'
#1 **Charlie** John b **Nov 1820** died Nov 1901
m Nov 1841 **Gracie Miller** b 1823
    #1 Edward (**Teddie**) William b 26/9/44 twin m 15/8/64 **Bella** Winslow-Smythe (in UK)
    7 children - move into 'Princhester Close' (2 sets twins)
        #1 Charles Edward (**Chad**) 16 Sept 65 twin
        m **Rose**marie Christina Rachel 1/8/65
        #1 Charles Edward b 1901 Sept
            #2 Alexandrine twin sister stillborn
        #2 John Gerald   16 Sept 1865
    #2 **John** Charles 26/9/44;   m **Sarah Joy Harlow** b 7/1/47 m 1867 (Harry & Vicky)
        #1 John Henry James (**Jack**) b 1 Jan 1968 twin
        #2 Timothy Charles Edward (**Timmy**) b 1 Jan 1968 twin
        #3 **Sarah** Grace b 1871   m Feb 1901 **John** Turner (Nick) b 66
        #4 Victoria (**Vicks**) Sally b 1873 m Feb 1901 **Lachlan** Macdonald 61
    #3 Emily (**Emma**) b 20 Dec 46   m Dec 1869 **George** Ellison b1844
    #4 **Molly** Grace b 1850   m Oct 69 **Henry** William Harlow b Oct 16, 48
#2 **Eddie** (Edward John) **b 16.10.1821** m Jennifer (**Jenna**) Turner m Dec 4 1841
(10 children)

#3 Elizabeth (**Liza**) Shannon b **1823** m 1841 **Bertie** Ellis
    4 children
#4 Susanna (**Anna**) Grace b 1824 m 1842 **Tim** Miller. (Lawyer with Phil Evans)
    4 children
#5 William (**Wills**) Lockley b 20/4 /**1826** (Wills) m 14/2/1845 **Cathy Turner**
        #1 Luke (**Lukie**)Henry William, b14 Jan 47
        #2 Philip (**Pip**)Charles; Sept 48,
        #3 Catherine Victoria Matilda (**Tilda**) 3/3/50   m 1874 **William** Miller b 50
        #4 Aurelia Lucy (**Goldie**) b 6th July 51   m 1872 **Alfred** Evans b 46 (Phil's son)
        #1 Catherine Alice (**Allie**) b 10/ 73 m 18 Apr 1899 **Simon** Mitchell b 73
        3 more children
        #5 Richard(**Rick**) b 26/10/55 twin m 25/12 75 **Mary Louise** Evans (Phil's)
        5 children
        #6 Elizabeth (**Bette**) b 26/10/55 twin m 2/81 **Edward** Styles b 14/10/42 m
            #1 **John** (**Jax**) **Christian** Styles b 13 Nov 1881 at sea
            M 1899 **Thea** Lockley b 1880 - lived in Rockley, Glebe (Ed's g daug.)
#6 **Luke** John b 3/ **1828**   m 2/8/1856 - **Ellen** Miller, b 4/10/1830;

#1 William (**Willy**)26/4/57 triplets m 78 Elizabeth Susanna (**Sanna) Harlow** 5/52
    #1 Henry Lucas (**Hal**) b Jan 80
#2 **Mary May**   26/4/57 triplets   m 76 **Marcus** Edward **Harlow** b 2/2/50
    #1 b late 1878
#3 Sarah (**Sally**) Elizabeth triplets 26/4/57 m 77 **Jimmy Ant** Harlow b 56
    #1 b late 78
#4 Charles Luke (**Carlo**) 20 Nov 60 twins m 1890 **Ruby** Morgan b 1870
#5 Charlotte (**Lottie**) 20/11/60 twins m 12/82 **Jonty** Evans b 2/8/56
    Five children

Sister **Vera** Abell - a nurse who looked after baby Will English.
   M **Ernest** Whitherton

Jonty's staff
Julia Green, Teenage nanny
Mary Henderson - Cook

Fictitious artist **Simon Mitchell** b 1873, aged 10 in 1883
Parents Simeon and Elise Mitchell née Beamish
Aunt May Beamish

Will English's Castlereagh overseer -
Andrew Rohan in Castlereagh.
Son Theo Takes over.

Paddy and Cara Connor (Maryanne's parents), Irish convicts
    Maryanne   m **Robert** Ellis - 3 children
    Moira 16 b 1828   m **Connor** Murphy 6 children (Luke &Ellen)
    Shauna 14 b 1830   m **Brodie** Murphy 4 children (Wills & Cathy)
Other children were not mentioned.

Finn & Maureen Murphy - Potato farmers at Emu Plains - 16 children
Eion, b 23 **Colleen b 25 m 55 John Evans 22,** **Deidre** b 26 (W&C), **Connor** b 28 (L&E) m
Moira Connor, **Brodie**, b 30 m Shauna Connor(W& C Parra); **Brennan**, b 32 **Shamus** b 34,
Imogen b 36(W&C), **Kerry** b 38 (L&E), **Eamon** b 40 **Fiona** b 43 **Siobhan**(L&E)b45, **Liam**
b 47 **Aidan**, b 50, **Declan** b 52, **Mary** b 54 (Jim & Conny)

REAL PEOPLE
Heidelburg Artists
Frederick McCubbin,
Tom Roberts and
Arthur Streeton
    And others as named *EXCEPT* Simon, Will, and Jonty
Paul Kruger - leader of the Boers
De Beer- a diamond merchant
Rt. Hon. William, Earl Beauchamp - the last Governor of NSW before Federation

Prime Minister- Sir Edmund Barton (Toby)
m Jane (Jeanie)
        6 Children

Scapegoats of the Empire - Boer War soldiers.
    - *Harry and Peter were shot* from the Bushveldt Carbineers
Harry "Breaker" Harbord Morant (shot)
Peter Handcock (shot)
George Witton
Henry Picton,
Captain Alfred Taylor
and Major Robert Lenehan
&
Horace Colless returned and lived in Chatswood until 1965. - He was my father's cousin. He
was the alternate bugler for the Bushveldt Carbineers. On his return, he brought his silver
natural trumpet, purchased in London in 1901. It is now in the Australian War Memorial.

NB
Harry Morant's ex-wife - Dame **Daisy Bates.** (On 13th March 1884, Morant married Daisy May O'Dwyer (Daisy Bates), *who became famous as an anthropologist. Morant declared his age to be twenty-one, but he was actually nineteen, which made their marriage illegal. The Morants separated soon afterwards and never formally divorced. Daisy threw Harry out after he first failed to pay for their wedding and then stole a saddle and several pigs. At a Court of Enquiry in South Africa, Morant claimed to have become engaged to one of two sisters in England, with Captain Percy Hunt being engaged to the other.*
https://en.wikipedia.org/wiki/Breaker_Morant

Banjo Patterson m 1903 Alice Walker in Tenterfield. He was related to Sir Edmund Barton.

Henry Lawson's ex- fiancé - later known as Dame **Mary Gilmore**

Silver Boer War Natural Trumpet
now in Australian War Memorial, Canberra

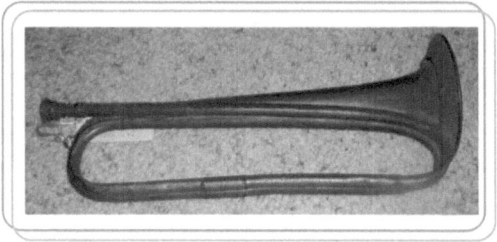

Engraved with a crown and

Henry Keats & Sons
105-103
Matthias Rd
London
N